THE BE

BOVA

VOLUME I

BAEN BOOKS
by Ben Bova

✷ ✷ ✷

Mars, Inc.
Laugh Lines
The Watchmen
The Exiles Trilogy
The Best of Bova: Volume I

With Les Johnson
Rescue Mode

THE BEST OF
BOVA
VOLUME I

BEN BOVA

BEST OF BEN BOVA: VOLUME ONE

This is a work of fiction. All the characters and events portrayed in this book
are fictional, and any resemblance to real people or incidents is purely coincidental.

Introduction © 2016 by Ben Bova; "A Long Way Back" first published in Amazing Stories
© February 1960; "Inspiration" first published in The Magazine of Fantasy & Science
Fiction © April 1994; "Vince's Dragon" first published in Dragons of Darkness © Oct
1981; "The Last Decision" first published in Stellar #4: Science Fiction Stories © May
1978; "Fitting Suits" first published in Analog Science Fiction and Fact © May 1990; "A
Small Kindness" first published in Analog Science Fiction/ Science Fact © April 1983;
"Born Again" first published in Analog Science Fiction/ Science Fact © May 1984;
"Blood of Tyrants" first published in Amazing Science Fiction © May 1970; "Bushido"
first published in Analog Science Fiction and Fact © July 1992; "Sam Gunn" first pub-
lished in The Magazine of Fantasy & Science Fiction © October 1983; "Amorality Tale"
first published in The Astral Mirror © October 1985; "A Country for Old Men" first published in Going Interstellar © June 2012; "Priorities" first published in Analog Science
Fiction/ Science Fact © December 1971; "To Be or Not" first published in Maxwell's
Demons © September 1978; "To Touch a Star" The Universe © November 1987; "Risk
Assessment" first published in The Williamson Effect © May 1996; "Men of Good Will"
first published in Galaxy Magazine © June 1964; "Foeman, Where Do You Flee?" first
published in Galaxy Magazine © January 1969; "Old Timer's Game" first published in
Carbide Tipped Pens: Seventeen Tales of Hard Science Fiction © December 2014; "The
Man Who Hated Gravity" first published in Analog Science Fiction and Fact © July 1989;
"Zero Gee" first published in Again, Dangerous Visions © March 1972; "A Slight
Miscalculation" first published in The Magazine of Fantasy and Science Fiction ©August
1971

A Baen Books Original

Baen Publishing Enterprises
P.O. Box 1403
Riverdale, NY 10471
www.baen.com

ISBN: 978-1-4767-8121-1

Cover art by Bob Eggleton

First Baen printing February 2016

Distributed by Simon & Schuster
1230 Avenue of the Americas
New York, NY 10020

Printed in the United States of America

10 9 8 7 6 5 4 3 2 1

To Toni and Tony and the radiant,
resplendent, romantic Rashida.

And to Lloyd McDaniel,
without whose unstinting help this book
would never have seen the light of day.

CONTENTS

The reasonable man adapts himself to the world; the unreasonable one persists in trying to adapt the world to himself. Therefore all progress depends on the unreasonable man.

—George Bernard Shaw

THE BEST OF
BOVA
VOLUME I

INTRODUCTION

Here it is, a lifetime's work in three volumes containing eighty stories published over fifty-four years, from 1960 to 2014. They range from the Baghdad of *The Thousand Nights and a Night* to the eventual end of the entire universe, from the green hills of Earth to the fiery surface of a dying star, from corporate board rooms to a baseball field in heaven. With plenty of stops in between.

Re-reading these stories—some of them for the first time in decades—I am struck with a bitter-sweet sadness, recalling friends who have died along the way, passions and problems that drove the invention of the various tales. It's as if I'm a ghost visiting departed scenes, people whom I have loved, all gone now.

Yet they live on, in these stories, and perhaps that is the real reason why human beings create works of fiction: they are monuments to days gone by, memories of men and women who have been dear to us—or visions of what tomorrow may bring.

Every human society has had its storytellers. There is a fundamental need in the human psyche to produce tales that try to show who we truly are, and why we do the things we do.

Most of the stories in this collection are science fiction: that is, the stories involve some aspect of future science or technology that is so basic to the tale that if that element were removed, the story would collapse.

To me, science fiction is the literature of our modern society.

Humankind depends on science and technology for its survival, and has been doing so since our earliest ancestors faced saber-toothed cats. We do not grow fangs or wings, we create tools. Tool-making—technology—is the way we deal with the often-hostile world in which we live.

Over the past few centuries, scientific studies of our world have led to vastly improved technologies, better tools with which to make ourselves healthier, richer and more free. Science fiction is the literature that speaks to this.

Every organism on Earth is struggling to stay alive, to have offspring, to enlarge its ecological niche as widely as possible. We humans have succeeded so well at that quest that there are more than seven billion of us on this planet, and we are driving many, many of our fellow creatures into extinction.

The stories in this collection examine various aspects of humankind's current and future predicaments. Some of the tales are somewhat dated: written half a century ago, they deal with problems that we have already solved, or bypassed. Many of the stories tell of the human race's drive to expand its habitat—its ecological niche—beyond the limits of planet Earth. Many deal with our interactions with our machines, which are becoming more intelligent with every generation.

The people in these stories include heroes and heels, lovers and loners, visionaries and the smugly blind.

I hope you enjoy their struggles.

—**Ben Bova**
Naples, Florida
November 2016

THE LONG WAY BACK

My first short story to be published in a national magazine, this tale appeared as the lead story in the February 1960 issue of Amazing *magazine.*

Looking back on it, I am somewhat surprised and terribly pleased to see how prophetic this story is. Not that we have had a nuclear war, of course. But the idea of energy shortages as central to the continued development of civilization, and the idea that is now known as the Solar Power Satellite, are both embedded in this tale, together with a few other goodies.

Notice that I carefully referred to this as "my first published science fiction short story." It is not the first short story of mine ever published, nor is it the first science fiction short story of mine to be bought by a magazine. My earliest short fiction was written while I was on the staff of the nation's first teen-age magazine, Campus Town, *which a few friends and I created right after we graduated from high school, in 1949. We sold every copy of the magazine we printed, but somehow after three issues we had gone broke.*

During that glorious time, however, I cranked out a couple of short stories that my colleagues deemed worthy of publication—my first fiction in print.

Shortly after we had all headed for college, I sold a science fiction short story to a local Philadelphia magazine. A check for the princely sum of five dollars arrived in the mail one morning. Babbling with excitement, I cashed the check at the nearest bank and hopped a trolley car for the offices of the magazine; I wanted to meet the geniuses who recognized my literary talent, and offer them new prodigies of prose.

Alas, their office was padlocked; the magazine had gone bankrupt. My five dollars was probably the last check of theirs to be cashed.

The disappointment taught me an important lesson: cash all checks immediately! Don't wait for the publisher to go into receivership.

I've lost track of that particular story. I doubt that it was very good, or I would have held on to it. So, herewith, is my first published science fiction short story.

TOM WOKE SLOWLY, his mind groping back through the hypnosis. He found himself looking toward the observation port, staring at stars and blackness.

The first man in space, he thought bitterly.

He unstrapped himself from the acceleration seat, feeling a little wobbly in free fall.

The hypnotic trance idea worked, all right.

The last thing Tom remembered was Arnoldsson putting him under, here in the rocket's compartment, the old man's sad soft eyes and quiet voice. Now 22,300 miles out, Tom was alone except for what Arnoldsson had planted in his mind for post-hypnotic suggestion to recall. The hypnosis had helped him pull through the blastoff unhurt and even protected him against the vertigo of weightlessness.

Yeah, it's a wonderful world, Tom muttered acidly. He got up from the seat cautiously, testing his coordination against zero gravity. His magnetic boots held to the deck satisfactorily.

He was lean and wiry, in his early forties, with a sharp angular face and dark, somber eyes. His hair had gone dead white years ago. He was encased up to his neck in a semi-flexible space suit they had squirmed him into Earthside because there was no room in the cramped cabin to put it on.

Tom glanced at the tiers of instrument consoles surrounding his seat—no blinking red lights, everything operating normally. *As if I could do anything about it if they went wrong.* Then he leaned toward the observation port, straining for a glimpse of the satellite.

The satellite.

Five sealed packages floating within a three-hundred foot radius of emptiness, circling the Earth like a cluster of moonlets. Five pieces sent up in five robot rockets and placed in the same orbit, to wait for a human intelligence to assemble them into a power-beaming satellite.

Five pieces orbiting Earth for almost eighteen years; waiting for nearly eighteen years while down below men blasted themselves and their cities and their machines into atoms and forgot the satellite endlessly circling, waiting for its creators to breathe life into it.

The hope of the world, Tom thought. *And little Tommy Morris is supposed to make it work . . . and then fly home again.* He pushed himself back into the seat. *Jason picked the wrong man.*

"Tom! Tom, can you hear me?"

He turned away from the port and flicked a switch on the radio console.

"Hello, Ruth. I can hear you."

A hubbub of excitement crackled through the radio receiver, then the woman's voice: "Are you all right? Is everything—"

"Everything's fine," Tom said flatly. He could picture the scene back at the station—dozens of people clustered around the jury-rigged radio, Ruth working the controls, trying hard to stay calm when it was impossible to, brushing back that permanently displaced wisp of brown hair that stubbornly fell over her forehead.

"Jason will be here in a minute," she said. "He's in the tracking shack, helping to calculate your orbit."

Of course Jason will be here, Tom thought. Aloud he said, "He needn't bother. I can see the satellite packages; they're only a couple of hundred yards from the ship."

Even through the radio he could sense the stir that went through them.

Don't get your hopes up, he warned silently. *Remember, I'm no engineer. Engineers are too valuable to risk on this job. I'm just a tool, a mindless screwdriver sent here to assemble this glorified tinkertoy. I'm the muscle, Arnoldsson is the nerve link, and Jason is the brain.*

Abruptly, Jason's voice surged through the radio speaker, "We did it, Tom! We did it!"

No, Tom thought, *you did it, Jason. This is all your show.*

"You should be able to see the satellite components," Jason said. His voice was excited yet controlled, and his comment had a ring of command in it.

"I've already looked," Tom answered. "I can see them."

"Are they damaged?"

"Not as far as I can see. Of course, from this distance—"

"Yes, of course," Jason said. "You'd better get right outside and start working on them. You've only got forty-eight hours' worth of oxygen."

"Don't worry about me," Tom said into the radio. "Just remember your end of the bargain."

"You'd better forget that until you get back here."

"I'm not forgetting anything."

"I mean you must concentrate on what you're doing up there if you expect to get back alive."

"When 1 get back we're going to explore the bombed-out cities. You promised that. It's the only reason I agreed to this."

Jason's voice stiffened. "My memory is quite as good as yours. We'll discuss the expedition after you return. Now you're using up valuable time. And oxygen."

"Okay. I'm going outside."

Ruth's voice came back on: "Tom, remember to keep the ship's radio open, or else your suit radio won't be able to reach us. And we're all here . . . Dr. Arnoldsson, Jason, the engineers . . . if anything comes up, we'll be right here to help you."

Tom grinned mirthlessly. *Right here: 22,300 miles away.*

"Tom?"

"Yes, Ruth."

"Good luck," she said. "From all of us."

Even Jason? he wanted to ask, but instead said merely, "Thanks."

He fitted the cumbersome helmet over his head and sealed it to the joints on his suit. A touch of a button on the control panel pumped the compartment's air into storage cylinders. Then Tom stood up and unlocked the hatch directly over his seat.

Reaching for the handholds just outside the hatch, he pulled himself through, and after a weightless comic ballet managed to plant his magnetized boots on the outer skin of the ship. Then, standing, he looked out at the universe.

Oddly, he felt none of the overpowering emotion he had once expected of this moment. Grandeur, terror, awe—no, he was strangely calm. The stars were only points of light on a dead-black background; the Earth was a fat crescent patched with colors; the sun, through his heavily-tinted visor, was like the pictures he had seen at planetarium shows, years ago.

As he secured a lifeline to the grip beside the hatch, Tom thought that he felt as though someone had stuck a reverse hypodermic into him and drained away all his emotions.

Only then did he realize what had happened. Jason, the engineer, the leader, the man who thought of everything, had made Arnoldsson condition his mind for this. No gaping at the universe for the first man in space, too much of a chance to take! There's a job to be done and no time for human frailty or sentiment.

Not even that, Tom said to himself. *He wouldn't even allow me one moment of human emotion.*

But as he pushed away from the ship and floated ghostlike toward the largest of the satellite packages, Tom twisted around for another look at Earth.

I wonder if she looked that way before the war?

Slowly, painfully, men had attempted to rebuild their civilization after the war had exhausted itself. But of all the things destroyed by the bombs and plagues, the most agonizing loss was man's sources of energy.

The coal mines, the oil refineries, the electricity-generating plants, the nuclear power piles . . . all shattered into radioactive rubble. There could be no return to any kind of organized society while men had to scavenge for wood to warm themselves and to run their primitive machines.

Then someone had remembered the satellite.

It had been designed, before the war, to collect solar energy and beam it to a receiving station on Earth. The satellite packages had been fired into a 24-hour orbit, circling the Earth over a fixed point on the Equator. The receiving station, built on the southeastern coast of the United States, saw the five units as a single second-magnitude star, low on the horizon all year, every year.

Of course the packages wavered slightly in their orbits, but not enough in eighteen years to spread very far apart. A man could still put them together into a power-beaming satellite.

If he could get there.

And if they were not damaged.

And if he knew how to put them together.

Through months that stretched into years, over miles of radioactive wilderness, on horseback, on carts, on foot, those who knew about the satellite spread the word, carefully, secretly, to what was left of North America's scientists and engineers. Gradually they trickled into the once-abandoned settlement.

They elected a leader: Jason, the engineer, one of the few men who knew anything about rockets to survive the war and the lunatic bands that hunted down anyone suspected of being connected with prewar science.

Jason's first act was to post guards around the settlement. Then he organized the work of rebuilding the power-receiving station and a man-carrying rocket.

They pieced together parts of a rocket and equipment that had been damaged by the war. What they did not know, they learned. What they did not have, they built or cannibalized from ruined equipment.

Jason sent armed foragers out for gasoline, charcoal and wood. They built a ramshackle electricity generator. They planted crops and hunted the small game in the local underbrush. A major celebration occurred whenever a forager came back towing a stray cow or horse or goat.

They erected fences around the settlement, because more than once they had to fight off the small armies of looters and anti-scientists that still roved the countryside.

But finally they completed the rocket . . . after exhausting almost every scrap of material and every ounce of willpower.

Then they picked a pilot: Thomas H. Morris, age 41, former historian and teacher. He had arrived a year before the completion of the rocket after walking 1,300 miles to find the settlement; his purpose was to organize some of the scientists and explore the bombed-out cities to see what could be salvaged out of man's shattered heritage.

But Tom was ideal for the satellite job: the right size—five-six and one-hundred thirty pounds; no dependents—wife and two sons dead of radiation sickness. True, he had no technical background whatsoever; but with Arnoldsson's hypnotic conditioning he could be taught all that was necessary for him to know . . . maybe.

Best of all, though, he was thoroughly expendable.

So Jason made a deal with him. There could be no expeditions into the cities until the satellite was finished, because every man was needed at the settlement. And the satellite could not be finished until someone volunteered to go up in the rocket and assemble it.

It was like holding a candy bar in front of a small child. He accepted Jason's terms.

The Earth turned, and with it the tiny spark of life alone in the emptiness around the satellite. Tom worked unmindful of time, his eyes and hands following Jason's engineering commands through Arnoldsson's post-hypnotic directions, with occasional radio conferences.

But his conscious mind sought refuge from the strangeness of space, and he talked almost constantly into his radio while he worked, talked about anything, everything, to the woman on the other end of the invisible link.

". . . and once the settlement is getting the power beamed from this contraption, we're going to explore the cities. Guess we won't be able to get very far inland, but we can still tackle Washington, Philadelphia and New York . . . plenty for us there."

Ruth asked, "What were they like before the war?"

"The cities? That's right, you're too young to remember. They were big, Ruth, with buildings so tall people called them skyscrapers." He pulled a wrench from its magnetic holder in the satellite's self-contained tool bin. "And filled with life, millions of people lived in each one . . all the people we have at the settlement could have lived on one floor of a good-sized hotel."

"What's a hotel?"

Tom grinned as he tugged at a pipe fitting. "You'll find out when you come with us . . . you'll see things you could never imagine."

"I don't know if I'll come with you."

He looked up from his work and stared Earthward. "Why?"

"Well . . . Jason . . . he says there isn't much left to see. And it's all radioactive and diseased."

"Nonsense."

"But Jason says . . ."

Tom snorted. "Jason hasn't been out of the settlement for six years.

I walked from Chicago to the settlement a year ago. I went through a dozen cities . . . they're wrecked, and the radioactivity count was higher than it is at the settlement, but it's not high enough to be dangerous."

"And you want to explore those cities; why?"

"Let's just say I'm a historian," Tom answered while his hands manipulated complex wiring unconsciously, as though they belonged not to him but to some unseen puppeteer.

"I don't understand," Ruth said.

"Look—those cities hold mankind's *memory*. I want to gather up the fragments of civilization before the last book is used for kindling and the last machine turns to rust. We need the knowledge in the cities if we expect to rebuild a civilization."

"But Jason and Dr. Arnoldsson and the engineers—they know all about—"

"Jason and the engineers," Tom snapped. "They had to stretch themselves to the breaking point to put together this rocket from parts that were already manufactured, waiting for them. Do you think they'd know how to build a city? Dr. Arnoldsson is a psychiatrist, his efforts at surgery are pathetic. Have you ever seen him try to set a broken leg? And what about agriculture? What about tool making or mining or digging wells, even . . . what about education? How many kids your own age can read or write?"

"But the satellite . . ."

"The satellite won't be of any use to people who can't work the machines. The satellite is no substitute for knowledge. Unless something is done, your grandchildren will be worshipping the machines, but they won't know how to repair them."

"No . . ."

"Yes, Ruth," he insisted.

"No," she whispered, her voice barely audible over the static-streaked hum in his earphones. "You're wrong, Tom. You're wrong. The satellite will send us the power we need. Then we'll build our machines and teach our children."

How can *you teach what you don't know?* Tom wanted to ask, but didn't. He worked without talking, hauling the weightless tons of satellite packages into position, electronically welding them together, splicing wiring systems too intricate for his conscious mind to understand.

Twice he pulled himself back along the lifeline into the ship for capsule meals and stimulants.

Finally he found himself staring at his gloved hands moving industriously within the bowels of one of the satellite packages. He stopped, suddenly aware that it was piercingly cold and totally dark except for the lamp on his helmet.

He pushed away from the unfinished satellite. Two of the packages were assembled now. The big parabolic mirror and two other uncrated units hung nearby, waiting impassively.

Tom groped his way back into the ship. After taking off his helmet and swallowing a couple of energy pills he said to the ship's radio:

"What time is it?" The abrupt sound of his own voice half-startled him.

"Nearly four a.m." It was Jason.

"Earth's blotted out the sun," Tom muttered. "Getting damned cold in here."

"You're in the ship?"

"Yes, it got too cold for the suit."

"Turn up the ship's heaters," Jason said. "What's the temperature in there?"

Tom glanced at the thermometer as he twisted the thermostat dial as far as it would go. "Forty-nine," he answered.

He could sense Jason nod. "The heaters are on minimum power automatically unless you turn them up. It'll warm you up in a few seconds. How's the satellite?"

Tom told him what remained to be done.

"You're not even half through yet." Jason's voice grew fainter and Tom knew that he was doing some mental arithmetic as he thought out loud. "You've been up about twenty hours; at the rate you're going you'll need another twenty-four to finish the job. That will bring you very close to your oxygen limit."

Tom sat impassively and stared at the gray metal and colored knobs of the radio.

"Is everything going all right?" Jason asked.

"How should I know? Ask Arnoldsson. "

"He's asleep. They all are."

"Except you."

"That's right," Jason said, "except me."

"How long did Ruth stay on the radio?"

"About sixteen hours. I ordered her to sleep a few hours ago."

"You're pretty good at giving orders," Tom said.

"Someone has to."

"Yeah." Tom ran a hand across his mouth. *Boy, could I use a cigarette. Funny, I haven't even thought about them in years.*

"Look," he said to the radio, "we might as well settle something right now. How many men are you going to let me have?"

"Don't you think you'd better save that for now and get back to work?"

"It's too damned cold out there. My fingers are still numb. You could have done a better job on insulating this suit."

"There are a lot of things we could have done," Jason said, "if we had the material."

"How about the expedition? How many men can 1 have?"

"As many as you can get," the radio voice answered. "I promised I won't stand in your way once the satellite is finished and operating."

"Won't stand in my way," Tom repeated. "That means you won't encourage anyone, either."

Jason's voice rose a trifle. "I can't encourage my people to go out and risk their lives just because you want to poke around some radioactive slag heaps!"

"You promised that if I put the satellite together and got back alive, I could investigate the cities. That was our deal."

"That's right. You can. And anyone foolish enough to accompany you can follow along."

"Jason, you know I need at least twenty-five armed men to venture out of the settlement . . ."

"Then you admit it's dangerous!" the radio voice crackled.

"Sure, if we meet a robber band. You've sent out enough foraging groups to know that. And we'll be travelling hundreds of miles. But it's not dangerous for the reasons you've been circulating . . . radioactivity and disease germs and that nonsense. There's no danger that one of your own foraging groups couldn't handle. I came through the cities last year alone, and I made it."

Tom waited for a reply from the radio, but only the hissing and crackling of electrical disturbances answered him.

"Jason, those cities hold what's left of a worldwide civilization. We can't begin to rebuild unless we reopen that knowledge. We need it, we need it desperately!"

"It's either destroyed or radioactive, and to think anything else is self-delusion. Besides, we have enough intelligence right here at the settlement to build a new civilization, better than the old one, once the satellite is ready."

"But you don't!" Tom shouted. "You poor damned fool, you don't even realize how much you don't know."

"This is a waste of time," Jason snapped. "Get outside and finish your work."

"I'm still cold, dammit," Tom said. He glanced at the thermometer on the control console. "Jason! *It's below freezing in here!*"

"What?"

"The heating unit isn't working at all!"

"Impossible. You must have turned it off instead of on."

"I can read, dammit! It's turned as high as it'll go. "

"What's the internal thermometer reading?"

Tom looked. "Barely thirty . . . and it's still going down."

"Hold on, I'll wake Arnoldsson and the electrical engineers."

Silence. Tom stared at the inanimate radio, which gave off only the whines and scratches of lightning and sun and stars, all far distant from him. For all his senses could tell him, he was the last living thing in the universe.

Sure, call a conference, Tom thought. *How much more work is there to be done? About twenty-four hours, he said. Another day. And another full night. Another night, this time with no heat. And maybe no oxygen, either. The heaters must have been working tonight until I pushed them up to full power. Something must have blown out. Maybe it's just a broken wire. I could fix that if they tell me how. But if it's not . . . no heat tomorrow night, no heat at all.*

Then Arnoldsson's voice floated up through the radio speaker: soft, friendly, calm, soothing.

The next thing Tom knew he was putting on his helmet. Sunlight was lancing through the tinted observation port and the ship was noticeably warmer.

"What happened?" he mumbled through the dissolving haze of hypnosis.

"It's all right, Tom." Ruth's voice. "Dr. Arnoldsson put you under and had you check the ship's wiring. Now he and Jason and the engineers are figuring out what to do. They said it's nothing to worry about . . . they'll have everything figured out in a couple of hours."

"And I'm to work on the satellite until they're ready?"

"Yes."

"Don't call us, we'll call you."

"What?"

"Nothing."

"It's all right, Tom. Don't worry."

"Sure, Ruth, I'm not worried." *That makes us both liars.*

He worked mechanically, handling the unfamiliar machinery with the engineers' knowledge through Arnoldsson's hypnotic communication.

Just like the pictures they used to show of nuclear engineers handling radioactive materials with remotely-controlled mechanical hands from behind a concrete wall. I'm only a pair of hands, a couple of opposed thumbs, a fortunate mutation of a self-conscious simian . . . but, God, why don't they call? She said it wasn't anything big. Just the wiring, probably. Then why don't they call?

He tried to work without thinking about anything, but he couldn't force his mind into stillness.

Even if I can fix the heaters, even f 1 don't freeze to death, I might run out of oxygen. And how am I going to land the ship? The takeoff was automatic, but even Jason and Arnoldsson can't make a pilot out of me.

"Tom?" Jason's voice.

"Yes!" He jerked to attention and floated free of the satellite.

"We've . . . eh, checked what you told us about the ship's electrical system while Arnoldsson had you under the hypnotic trance."

"And?"

"Well . . . it, eh, looks as though one of the batteries gave out. The batteries feed all the ship's lights, heat, and electrical power . . . with one of them out, you don't have enough power to run the heaters."

"There's no way to fix it?"

"Not unless you cut out something else. And you need everything else . . . the radio, the controls, the oxygen pumps . . ."

"What about the lights? I don't need them, I've got the lamp on my suit helmet."

"They don't take as much power as the heaters do. It wouldn't help at all."

Tom twisted weightlessly and stared back at Earth. "Well, just what the hell am I supposed to *do?*"

"Don't get excited," Jason's voice grated in his earphones. "We've calculated it all out. According to our figures, your suit will store enough heat during the day to last the night . . ."

"I nearly froze to death last night and the ship was heated most of the time!"

"It will get cold," Jason's voice answered calmly, "but you should be able to make it. Your own body warmth will be stored by the suit's insulation, and that will help somewhat. But you must not open the suit all night, not even to take off your helmet."

"And the oxygen?"

"You can take all the replacement cylinders from the ship and keep them at the satellite. The time you save by not having to go back and forth to the ship for fresh oxygen will give you about an hour's extra margin. You should be able to make it."

Tom nodded. "And of course I'm expected to work on the satellite right through the night."

"It will help you keep your mind off the cold. If we see that you're not going to make it—either because of the cold or the oxygen—we'll warn you and you can return to the settlement."

'Suppose I have enough oxygen to just finish the satellite, but if I do, I won't have enough to fly home. Will you warn me then?"

"Don't be dramatic."

"Go to hell."

"Dr. Arnoldsson said he could put you under," Jason continued unemotionally, "but he thinks you might freeze once your conscious mind went asleep."

"You've figured out all the details," Tom muttered. "All I have to do is put your damned satellite together without freezing to death and then fly 22,300 miles back home before my air runs out. Simple."

He glanced at the sun, still glaring bright even through his tinted visor. It was nearly on the edge of the Earth-disk.

"All right," Tom said, "I'm going into the ship now for some pills; it's nearly sunset."

Cold. Dark and so cold that numbers lost their meaning. Paralyzing cold, seeping in through the suit while you worked, crawling up your limbs until you could hardly move. The whole universe hung up in the sky and looked down on the small cold figure of a man struggling blindly with machinery he could not understand.

Dark. Dark and cold.

Ruth stayed on the radio as long as Jason would allow her, talking to Tom, keeping the link with life and warmth. But finally Jason took over, and the radio went silent.

So don't talk, Tom growled silently, *I can keep warm just by hating you, Jason.*

He worked through the frigid night, struggling ant-like with huge pieces of equipment. Slowly he assembled the big parabolic mirror, the sighting mechanism and the atomic convertor. With dreamy motions he started connecting the intricate wiring systems.

And all the while he raged at himself: *Why? Why did it have to be this way? Why me? Why did I agree to do this? I knew I'd never live through it. Why did I do it?*

He retraced the days of his life: the preparations for the flight, the arguments with Jason over exploring the cities, his trek from Chicago to the settlement, the aimless years after the radiation death of his two boys and Marjorie, his wife.

Marjorie and the boys, lying sick month after month, dying one after the other in a cancerous agony while he stood by helplessly in the ruins of what had been their home.

No! His mind warned him. *Don't think of that. Not that. Think of Jason, Jason who prevents you from doing the one thing you want, who is taking your life from you; Jason, the peerless leader; Jason, who's afraid of the cities. Why? Why is he afraid of the cities? That's the hub of everything down there. Why does Jason fear the cities?*

It wasn't until he finished connecting the satellite's last unit—the sighting mechanism—that Tom realized the answer.

One answer. And everything fell into place.

Everything . . . except what Tom Morris was going to do about it.

Tom squinted through the twin telescopes of the sighting mechanism again, then pushed away and floated free, staring at the Earth bathed in pale moonlight.

What do I do now? For an instant he was close to panic, but he forced it down. *Think,* he said to himself. *You're supposed to be a* Homo Sapiens . . . *use that brain. Think!*

The long night ended. The sun swung around from behind the bulk of Earth. Tom looked at it as he felt its warmth penetrating the insulated suit, and he knew it was the last time he would see the sun. He felt no more anger—even his hatred of Jason was drained out of him now. In its place was a sense of—finality.

He spoke into his helmet mike. "Jason."

"He is in conference with the astronomers." Dr. Arnoldsson's voice.

"Get him for me, please."

A few minutes of silence, broken only by the star-whisperings in his earphones.

Jason's voice was carefully modulated. "Tom, you made it."

"I made it. And the satellite's finished."

"It's finished? Good! Now, what we have to do—"

"Wait," Tom interrupted. "It's finished but it's useless."

"What?"

Tom twisted around to look at the completed satellite, its oddly-angled framework and bulbous machinery glinting fiercely in the newly-risen sun. "After I finished it I looked through the sighting mechanism to make certain the satellite's transmitters were correctly aimed at the settlement. Nobody told me to, but nobody said not to, either, so I looked. It's a simple mechanism. . . . The transmitters are pointed smack in the middle of Hudson's Bay."

"You're sure?"

"Certainly."

"You can rotate the antennas. "

"I know. I tried it. I can turn them as far south as the Great Lakes."

A long pause.

"I was afraid of this," Jason's voice said evenly. *I'll bet you were,* Tom answered to himself.

"You must have moved the satellite out of position while assembling its components."

"So my work here comes to nothing because the satellite's power beam can't reach the settlement's receivers."

"Not . . . not unless you use the ship . . . to tow the satellite into the proper orbital position," Jason stammered.

You actually went through with it, Tom thought. Aloud, he said,

"But if I use the ship's engine to tow the satellite, I won't have enough fuel left to get back to Earth, will I?" *Not to mention oxygen.*

A longer pause. "No."

"I have two questions, Jason. I think I know the answers to them both but I'll ask you anyway. One. You knew this would happen, didn't you?"

"What do you mean?"

"You've calculated this insane business down to the last drop of sweat," Tom growled. "You knew that I'd knock the satellite out of position while I was working on it, and the only way to get it back in the right orbit would be for me to tow it back and strand myself up here. This is a suicide mission, isn't it, Jason?"

"That's not true. . . ."

"Don't bother defending yourself. I don't hate you anymore, Jason, I understand you, dammit. You made our deal as much to get rid of me as to get your precious satellite put together."

"No one can force you to tow the satellite . . ."

"Sure, I can leave it where it is and come back home. If I can fly this ship, which I doubt. And what would I come back to? I left a world without power. I'd return to a world without hope. And some dark night one of your disappointed young goons would catch up with me . . . and no one would blame him, would they?"

Jason's voice was brittle. "You'll tow it into position?"

"After you answer my second question," Tom countered. "Why are you afraid of the cities?"

"Afraid? I'm not afraid."

"Yes, you are. Oh, you could use the hope of exploring the cities to lure me up here on this suicide-job, but you knew I'd never be back to claim my half of the bargain. You're afraid of the cities, and I think I know why. You're afraid of the unknown quantity they represent, distrustful of your own leadership when new problems arise . . ."

"We've worked for more than ten years to make this settlement what it is," Jason fumed. "We fought and died to keep those marauding lunatics from wrecking us. We are mankind's last hope! We can't afford to let others in . . . they're not scientists, they wouldn't understand, they'd ruin everything."

"Mankind's last hope, terrified of men." Tom was suddenly tired, weary of the whole struggle. But there was something he had to tell them.

"Listen, Jason," he said. "The walls you've built around the settlement weren't meant to keep you from going outside. You're not a self-sufficient little community. You're cut off from mankind's memory, from his dreams, from his ambitions. You can't even start to rebuild a civilization—and if you do try, don't you think the people outside will learn about it? Don't you think they've got a right to share in whatever progress the settlement makes? And if you don't let them, don't you realize that they'll destroy the settlement?"

Silence.

"I'm a historian," Tom continued, "and I know that a civilization can't exist in a vacuum. If outsiders don't conquer **it,** it'll rot from within. It's happened to Babylonia, Greece, Rome, China even. Over and ove again. The Soviets built an Iron Curtain around themselves, and wiped themselves out because of it. Don't you see, Jason? There are only two types of animals on this planet: the gamblers and the extinct. It won't be easy to live with the outsiders, there'll be problems of every type. But the alternative is decay and destruction. *You've got to take the chance, if you don't, you're dead."*

A long silence. Finally Jason said, "You've only got about a half-hour's worth of oxygen left. Will you tow the satellite into the proper position?"

Tom stared at the planet unseeingly. "Yes," he mumbled. "I'll have to check some calculations with the astronomers."

Jason's voice buzzed flatly in his earphones. A background murmur, scarcely audible over the crackling static.

Then Ruth's voice broke through, "Tom, Tom, you can't do this! You won't be able to get back!"

"I know," he said, as he started pulling his way along the lifeline back to the ship.

"No! Come back, Tom, please. Come back. Forget the satellite. Come back and explore the cities. I'll go with you. Please. Don't die, Tom, please don't die . . ."

"Ruth, Ruth, you're too young to cry over me. I'll be all right, don't worry."

"No, it isn't fair."

"It never is," Tom said. "Listen, Ruth. I've been dead a long time. Since the bombs fell, I guess. My world died then and I died with it. When I came to the settlement, when I agreed to make this flight, I think we all knew I'd never return, even if we wouldn't admit it to ourselves. But I'm just one man, Ruth, one small part of the story. The story goes on, with or without me. There's tomorrow . . . your tomorrow. I've got no place in it, but it belongs to you. So don't waste your time crying over a man who died eighteen years ago."

He snapped off his suit radio and went the rest of the way to the ship in silence. After locking the hatch and pumping air back into the cabin, he took off his helmet.

Good clean canned air, Tom said to himself. *Too bad **it** won't last longer.*

He sat down and flicked a switch on the radio console. "All right, do you have those calculations ready?"

"In a few moments." Arnoldsson's voice. Ten minutes later Tom reemerged from the ship and made his ghostlike way back to the satellite's sighting mechanism. He checked the artificial moon's position, then went back to the ship.

"On course," he said to the radio. "The transmitters are pointing a little northwest of Philadelphia."

"Good," Amoldsson's voice answered. "Now, your next blast should be three seconds' duration in the same direction . . ."

"No," Tom said, "I've gone as far as I'm going to."

"What?"

"I'm not moving the satellite any farther."

"But you still have not enough fuel to return to Earth. Why are you stopping here?"

"I'm not coming back," Tom answered. "But I'm not going to beam the satellite's power to the settlement, either."

"What are you trying to pull?" Jason's voice. Furious. Panicky.

"It's simple, Jason. If you want the satellite's power, you can dismantle the settlement and carry it to Pennsylvania. The transmitters are aimed at some good farming country, and within miles of a city that's still half-intact."

"You're insane!"

"Not at all. We're keeping our deal, Jason. I'm giving you the satellite's power, and you're going to allow exploration of the cities. You won't be able to prevent your people from rummaging through the cities now; and you won't be able to keep the outsiders from joining you, not once you get out from behind your own fences."

"You can't do this! You . . ."

Tom snapped off the radio. He looked at it for a second or two, then smashed a heavy-booted foot against the console. Glass and metal crashed satisfactorily.

Okay, Tom thought, *it's done. Maybe Jason's right and I'm crazy, but we'll never know now. In a year or so they'll be set up outside Philadelphia, and a lot better for it. I'm forcing them to take the long way back, but it's a better way. The only way, maybe.*

He leaned back in the seat and stared out the observation port at the completed satellite. Already it was taking in solar energy and beaming it Earthward.

In ten years they'll send another ship up here to check the gadget and make sure everything's okay. Maybe they'll be able to do it in five years. Makes no difference. I'll still be here.

INSPIRATION

Many academic papers have been written about the influence of scientific research on science fiction, and vice versa. Whole books have been written about the interplay between science and science fiction. It struck me that it might be interesting to try a story that explores that theme.

I did a bit of historical research. When H. G. Wells first published "The Time Machine," Albert Einstein was sixteen. William Thomson, newly made Lord Kelvin, was the grand old man of physics, and a stern guardian of the orthodox Newtonian view of the universe. Wells' idea of considering time as a fourth dimension would have been anathema to Kelvin; but it would have lit up young Albert's imagination.

Who knows? Perhaps Einstein was actually inspired by Wells.

At any rate, there was the kernel of a story. But how could I get Wells, Einstein, and Kelvin together? And why? To be an effective story, there must be a fuse burning somewhere that will cause an explosion unless the protagonist acts to prevent it.

My protagonist turned out to be a time traveler, sent on a desperate mission to the year 1896, where he finds Wells, Einstein, and Kelvin and brings them together.

And one other person, as well.

HE WAS AS CLOSE to despair as only a lad of seventeen can be.

"But you heard what the professor said," he moaned. "It is all finished. There is nothing left to do."

The lad spoke in German, of course. I had to translate it for Mr. Wells.

Wells shook his head. "I fail to see why such splendid news should upset the boy so."

I said to the youngster, "Our British friend says you should not lose hope. Perhaps the professor is mistaken."

"Mistaken? How could that be? He is famous. A nobleman! A baron!"

I had to smile. The lad's stubborn disdain for authority figures would become world-famous one day. But it was not in evidence this summer afternoon in AD 1896.

We were sitting in a sidewalk café with a magnificent view of the Danube and the city of Linz. Delicious odors of cooking sausages and bakery pastries wafted from the kitchen inside. Despite the splendid warm sunshine, though, I felt chilled and weak, drained of what little strength I had remaining.

"Where is that blasted waitress?" Wells grumbled. "We've been here half an hour, at the least."

"Why not just lean back and enjoy the afternoon, sir?" I suggested tiredly. "This is the best view in all the area."

Herbert George Wells was not a patient man. He had just scored a minor success in Britain with his first novel and had decided to treat himself to a vacation in Austria. He came to that decision under my influence, of course, but he did not yet realize that. At age twenty-nine, he had a lean, hungry look to him that would mellow only gradually with the coming years of prestige and prosperity.

Albert was round-faced and plumpish; still had his baby fat on him, although he had started a moustache as most teenaged boys did in those days. It was a thin, scraggly black wisp, nowhere near the full white brush it would become. If all went well with my mission.

It had taken me an enormous amount of maneuvering to get Wells and this teenager to the same place at the same time. The effort had nearly exhausted all my energies. Young Albert had come to see Professor Thomson with his own eyes, of course. Wells had been more difficult; he had wanted to see Salzburg, the birthplace of Mozart. I had taken him instead to Linz, with a thousand assurances that he would find the trip worthwhile.

He complained endlessly about Linz, the city's lack of beauty, the sour smell of its narrow streets, the discomfort of our hotel, the dearth of restaurants where one could get decent food—by which he meant burnt mutton. Not even the city's justly famous Linzertorte pleased him.

"Not as good as a decent trifle," he groused. "Not as good by half."

I, of course, knew several versions of Linz that were even less pleasing, including one in which the city was nothing more than charred radioactive rubble and the Danube so contaminated that it glowed at night all the way down to the Black Sea. I shuddered at that vision and tried to concentrate on the task at hand.

It had almost required physical force to get Wells to take a walk across the Danube on the ancient stone bridge and up the Postlingberg to this little sidewalk café. He had huffed with anger when we had started out from our hotel at the city's central square, then soon was puffing with exertion as we toiled up the steep hill. I was breathless from the climb also. In later years a tram would make the ascent, but on this particular afternoon we had been obliged to walk.

He had been mildly surprised to see the teenager trudging up the precipitous street just a few steps ahead of us. Recognizing that unruly crop of dark hair from the audience at Thomson's lecture that morning, Wells had graciously invited Albert to join us for a drink.

"We deserve a beer or two after this blasted climb," he said, eying me unhappily.

Panting from the climb, I translated to Albert, "Mr. Wells . . . invites you . . . to have a refreshment with us."

The youngster was pitifully grateful, although he would order nothing stronger than tea. It was obvious that Thomson's lecture had shattered him badly. So now we sat on uncomfortable cast-iron chairs and waited—they for the drinks they had ordered, me for the inevitable. I let the warm sunshine soak into me and hoped it would rebuild at least some of my strength.

The view was little short of breathtaking: the brooding castle across the river, the Danube itself streaming smoothly and actually blue as it glittered in the sunlight, the lakes beyond the city and the blue-white snow peaks of the Austrian Alps hovering in the distance like ghostly petals of some immense unworldly flower.

But Wells complained, "That has to be the ugliest castle I have ever seen."

"What did the gentleman say?" Albert asked.

"He is stricken by the sight of the Emperor Friedrich's castle," I answered sweetly.

"Ah. Yes, it has a certain grandeur to it, doesn't it?"

Wells had all the impatience of a frustrated journalist. "Where is that damnable waitress? Where is our beer?"

"I'll find the waitress," I said, rising uncertainly from my iron-hard chair. As his ostensible tour guide, I had to remain in character for a while longer, no matter how tired I felt. But then I saw what I had been waiting for.

"Look!" I pointed down the steep street. "Here comes the professor himself!"

William Thomson, First Baron Kelvin of Largs, was striding up the pavement with much more bounce and energy than any of us had shown. He was seventy-one, his silver-gray hair thinner than his impressive gray beard, lean almost to the point of looking frail. Yet he climbed the ascent that had made my heart thunder in my ears as if he were strolling amiably across some campus quadrangle.

Wells shot to his feet and leaned across the iron rail of the café. "Good afternoon, Your Lordship." For a moment I thought he was going to tug at his forelock.

Kelvin squinted at him. "You were in my audience this morning, were you not?"

"Yes, m'lud. Permit me to introduce myself: I am H. G. Wells."

"Ah. You're a physicist?"

"A writer, sir."

"Journalist?"

"Formerly. Now I am a novelist."

"Really? How keen."

Young Albert and I had also risen to our feet. Wells introduced us properly and invited Kelvin to join us.

"Although I must say," Wells murmured as Kelvin came 'round the railing and took the empty chair at our table, "that the service here leaves quite a bit to be desired."

"Oh, you have to know how to deal with the Teutonic temperament," said Kelvin jovially as we all sat down. He banged the flat of his hand on the table so hard it made us all jump. "Service!" he bellowed. "Service here!"

Miraculously, the waitress appeared from the doorway and trod stubbornly to our table. She looked very unhappy; sullen, in fact. Sallow pouting face with brooding brown eyes and downturned mouth. She pushed back a lock of hair that had strayed across her forehead.

"We've been waiting for our beer," Wells said to her. "And now this gentleman has joined us—"

"Permit me, sir," I said. It was my job, after all. In German I asked her to bring us three beers and the tea that Albert had ordered and to do it quickly.

She looked the four of us over as if we were smugglers or criminals of some sort, her eyes lingering briefly on Albert, then turned without a word or even a nod and went back inside the café.

I stole a glance at Albert. His eyes were riveted on Kelvin, his lips parted as if he wanted to speak but could not work up the nerve. He ran a hand nervously through his thick mop of hair. Kelvin seemed perfectly at ease, smiling affably, his hands laced across his stomach just below his beard; he was the man of authority, acknowledged by the world as the leading scientific figure of his generation.

"Can it be really true?" Albert blurted at last. "Have we learned everything of physics that can be learned?"

He spoke in German, of course, the only language he knew. I immediately translated for him, exactly as he asked his question.

Once he understood what Albert was asking, Kelvin nodded his gray old head sagely. "Yes, yes. The young men in the laboratories today are putting the final dots over the i's, the final crossings of the t's. We've just about finished physics; we know at last all there is to be known."

Albert looked crushed.

Kelvin did not need a translator to understand the youngster's emotion. "If you are thinking of a career in physics, young man, then I heartily advise you to think again. By the time you complete your education there will be nothing left for you to do."

"Nothing?" Wells asked as I translated. "Nothing at all?"

"Oh, add a few decimal places here and there, I suppose. Tidy up a bit, that sort of thing."

Albert had failed his admission test to the Federal Polytechnic in Zurich. He had never been a particularly good student. My goal was to get him to apply again to the Polytechnic and pass the exams.

Visibly screwing up his courage, Albert asked, "But what about the work of Roentgen?"

Once I had translated, Kelvin knit his brows. "Roentgen? Oh, you mean that report about mysterious rays that go through solid walls? X rays, is it?"

Albert nodded eagerly.

"Stuff and nonsense!" snapped the old man. "Absolute bosh. He may impress a few medical men who know little of science, but his X rays do not exist. Impossible! German daydreaming."

Albert looked at me with his whole life trembling in his piteous eyes. I interpreted:

"The professor fears that X rays may be illusory, although he does not as yet have enough evidence to decide, one way or the other."

Albert's face lit up. "Then there is hope! We have not discovered everything as yet!"

I was thinking about how to translate that for Kelvin when Wells ran out of patience. "Where is that blasted waitress?"

I was grateful for the interruption. "I will find her, sir."

Dragging myself up from the table, I left the three of them, Wells and Kelvin chatting amiably while Albert swiveled his head back and forth, understanding not a word. Every joint in my body ached, and I knew that there was nothing anyone in this world could do to help me. The café was dark inside, and smelled of stale beer. The waitress was standing at the bar, speaking rapidly, angrily, to the stout barkeep in a low venomous tone. The barkeep was polishing glasses with the end of his apron; he looked grim and, once he noticed me, embarrassed.

Three seidels of beer stood on a round tray next to her, with a single glass of tea. The beers were getting warm and flat, the tea cooling, while she blistered the bartender's ears.

I interrupted her vicious monologue. "The gentlemen want their drinks," I said in German.

She whirled on me, her eyes furious. "The gentlemen may have their beers when they get rid of that infernal Jew!"

Taken aback somewhat, I glanced at the barkeep. He turned away from me.

"No use asking him to do it," the waitress hissed. "We do not serve Jews here. I do not serve Jews and neither will he!"

The café was almost empty this late in the afternoon. In the dim shadows I could make out only a pair of elderly gentlemen quietly smoking their pipes and a foursome, apparently two married couples, drinking beer. A six-year-old boy knelt at the far end of the bar, laboriously scrubbing the wooden floor.

"If it's too much trouble for you," I said, and started to reach for the tray.

She clutched at my outstretched arm. "No! No Jews will be served here! Never!"

I could have brushed her off. If my strength had not been drained away I could have broken every bone in her body and the barkeep's, too. But I was nearing the end of my tether and I knew it.

"Very well," I said softly. "I will take only the beers."

She glowered at me for a moment, then let her hand drop away. I removed the glass of tea from the tray and left it on the bar. Then I carried the beers out into the warm afternoon sunshine.

As I set the tray on our table, Wells asked, "They have no tea?"

Albert knew better. "They refuse to serve Jews," he guessed. His voice was flat, unemotional, neither surprised nor saddened.

I nodded as I said in English, "Yes, they refuse to serve Jews."

"You're Jewish?" Kelvin asked, reaching for his beer.

The teenager did not need a translation. He replied, "I was born in Germany. I am now a citizen of Switzerland. I have no religion. But, yes, I am a Jew."

Sitting next to him, I offered him my beer. "No, no," he said with a sorrowful little smile. "It would merely upset them further. I think perhaps I should leave."

"Not quite yet," I said. "I have something that I want to show you." I reached into the inner pocket of my jacket and pulled out the thick sheaf of paper I had been carrying with me since I had started out on this mission. I noticed that my hand trembled slightly.

"What is it?" Albert asked.

I made a little bow of my head in Wells' direction. "This is my translation of Mr. Wells' excellent story, 'The Time Machine.'"

Wells looked surprised, Albert curious. Kelvin smacked his lips and put his half-drained seidel down.

"Time machine?" asked young Albert.

"What's he talking about?" Kelvin asked.

I explained, "I have taken the liberty of translating Mr. Wells' story about a time machine, in the hope of attracting a German publisher."

Wells said, "You never told me—"

But Kelvin asked, "Time machine? What on earth would a time machine be?"

Wells forced an embarrassed, self-deprecating little smile. "It is merely the subject of a tale I have written, m'lud: a machine that can travel through time. Into the past, you know. Or the, uh, future."

Kelvin fixed him with a beady gaze. "Travel into the past or the future?"

"It is fiction, of course," Wells said apologetically.

"Of course."

Albert seemed fascinated. "But how could a machine travel through time? How do you explain it?"

Looking thoroughly uncomfortable under Kelvin's wilting eye, Wells said hesitantly, "Well, if you consider time as a dimension—"

"A dimension?" asked Kelvin.

"Rather like the three dimensions of space."

"Time as a fourth dimension?"

"Yes. Rather."

Albert nodded eagerly as I translated. "Time as a dimension, yes! Whenever we move through space we move through time as well, do we not? Space and time! Four dimensions, all bound together!"

Kelvin mumbled something indecipherable and reached for his half-finished beer.

"And one could travel through this dimension?" Albert asked. "Into the past or the future?"

"Utter bilge," Kelvin muttered, slamming his emptied seidel on the table. "Quite impossible."

"It is merely fiction," said Wells, almost whining. "Only an idea I toyed with in order to—"

"Fiction. Of course," said Kelvin, with great finality. Quite abruptly, he pushed himself to his feet. "I'm afraid I must be going. Thank you for the beer."

He left us sitting there and started back down the street, his face flushed. From the way his beard moved I could see that he was muttering to himself.

"I'm afraid we've offended him," said Wells.

"But how could he become angry over an idea?" Albert wondered. The thought seemed to stun him. "Why should a new idea infuriate a man of science?"

The waitress bustled across the patio to our table. "When is this Jew leaving?" she hissed at me, eyes blazing with fury. "I won't have him stinking up our café any longer!"

Obviously shaken, but with as much dignity as a seventeen-year-old could muster, Albert rose to his feet. "I will leave, Madame. I have imposed on your so-gracious hospitality long enough."

"Wait," I said, grabbing at his jacket sleeve. "Take this with you. Read it. I think you will enjoy it."

He smiled at me, but I could see the sadness that would haunt his eyes forever. "Thank you, sir. You have been most kind to me."

He took the manuscript and left us. I saw him already reading it as he walked slowly down the street toward the bridge back to Linz proper. I hoped he would not trip and break his neck as he ambled down the steep street, his nose stuck in the manuscript.

The waitress watched him too. "Filthy Jew. They're everywhere! They get themselves into everything."

"That will be quite enough from you," I said as sternly as I could manage.

She glared at me and headed back for the bar.

Wells looked more puzzled than annoyed, even after I explained what had happened.

"It's their country, after all," he said, with a shrug of his narrow shoulders. "If they don't want to mingle with Jews, there's not much we can do about it, is there?"

I took a sip of my warm flat beer, not trusting myself to come up with a properly polite response. There was only one time line in which Albert lived long enough to have an effect on the world. There were dozens where he languished in obscurity or was gassed in one of the death camps.

Wells' expression turned curious. "I didn't know you had translated my story."

"To see if perhaps a German publisher would be interested in it," I lied.

"But you gave the manuscript to that Jewish fellow."

"I have another copy of the translation."

"You do? Why would you—"

My time was almost up, I knew. I had a powerful urge to end the charade. "That young Jewish fellow might change the world, you know."

Wells laughed.

"I mean it," I said. "You think that your story is merely a piece of fiction. Let me tell you, it is much more than that."

"Really?"

"Time travel will become possible one day."

"Don't be ridiculous!" But I could see the sudden astonishment in his eyes. And the memory. It was I who had suggested the idea of time travel to him. We had discussed it for months back when he had been working for the newspapers. I had kept the idea in the forefront of his imagination until he finally sat down and dashed off his novel.

I hunched closer to him, leaned my elbows wearily on the table. "Suppose Kelvin is wrong? Suppose there is much more to physics than he suspects?"

"How could that be?" Wells asked.

"That lad is reading your story. It will open his eyes to new vistas, new possibilities."

Wells cast a suspicious glance at me. "You're pulling my leg."

I forced a smile. "Not altogether. You would do well to pay attention to what the scientists discover over the coming years. You could build a career writing about it. You could become known as a prophet if you play your cards properly."

His face took on the strangest expression I had ever seen: he did not want to believe me, and yet he did; he was suspicious, curious, doubtful and yearning—all at the same time. Above everything else he was ambitious; thirsting for fame. Like every writer, he wanted to have the world acknowledge his genius.

I told him as much as I dared. As the afternoon drifted on and the shadows lengthened, as the sun sank behind the distant mountains and the warmth of day slowly gave way to an uneasy deepening chill,

I gave him carefully veiled hints of the future. A future. The one I wanted him to promote.

Wells could have no conception of the realities of time travel, of course. There was no frame of reference in his tidy nineteenth-century English mind of the infinite branchings of the future. He was incapable of imagining the horrors that lay in store. How could he be? Time branches endlessly and only a few, a precious handful of those branches, manage to avoid utter disaster.

Could I show him his beloved London obliterated by fusion bombs? Or the entire northern hemisphere of Earth depopulated by man-made plagues? Or a devastated world turned to a savagery that made his Morlocks seem compassionate?

Could I explain to him the energies involved in time travel or the damage they did to the human body? The fact that time travelers were volunteers sent on suicide missions, desperately trying to preserve a time line that saved at least a portion of the human race? The best future I could offer him was a twentieth century tortured by world wars and genocide. That was the best I could do.

So all I did was hint, as gently and subtly as I could, trying to guide him toward that best of all possible futures, horrible though it would seem to him. I could neither control nor coerce anyone; all I could do was to offer a bit of guidance. Until the radiation dose from my trip through time finally killed me.

Wells was happily oblivious to my pain. He did not even notice the perspiration that beaded my brow despite the chilling breeze that heralded nightfall.

"You appear to be telling me," he said at last, "that my writings will have some sort of positive effect on the world."

"They already have," I replied, with a genuine smile.

His brows rose.

"That teenaged lad is reading your story. Your concept of time as a dimension has already started his fertile mind working."

"That young student?"

"Will change the world," I said. "For the better."

"Really?"

"Really," I said, trying to sound confident. I knew there were still a thousand pitfalls in young Albert's path. And I would not live long enough to help him past them. Perhaps others would, but there were no guarantees.

I knew that if Albert did not reach his full potential, if he were turned away by the university again or murdered in the coming holocaust, the future I was attempting to preserve would disappear in a global catastrophe that could end the human race forever. My task was to save as much of humanity as I could.

I had accomplished a feeble first step in saving some of humankind, but only a first step. Albert was reading the time-machine tale and starting to think that Kelvin was blind to the real world. But there was so much more to do. So very much more.

We sat there in the deepening shadows of the approaching twilight, Wells and I, each of us wrapped in our own thoughts about the future. Despite his best English self-control, Wells was smiling contentedly. He saw a future in which he would be hailed as a prophet. I hoped it would work out that way. It was an immense task that I had undertaken. I felt tired, gloomy, daunted by the immensity of it all. Worst of all, I would never know if I succeeded or not.

Then the waitress bustled over to our table. "Well, have you finished? Or are you going to stay here all night?"

Even without a translation Wells understood her tone. "Let's go," he said, scraping his chair across the flagstones.

I pushed myself to my feet and threw a few coins on the table. The waitress scooped them up immediately and called into the café, "Come here and scrub down this table! At once!"

The six-year-old boy came trudging across the patio, lugging the heavy wooden pail of water. He stumbled and almost dropped it; water sloshed onto his mother's legs. She grabbed him by the ear and lifted him nearly off his feet. A faint tortured squeak issued from the boy's gritted teeth.

"Be quiet and your do work properly," she told her son, her voice murderously low. "If I let your father know how lazy you are . . ."

The six-year-old's eyes went wide with terror as his mother let her threat dangle in the air between them.

"Scrub that table good, Adolph," his mother told him. "Get rid of that damned Jew's stink."

I looked down at the boy. His eyes were burning with shame and rage and hatred. Save as much of the human race as you can, I told myself. But it was already too late to save him.

"Are you coming?" Wells called to me.

"Yes," I said, tears in my eyes. "It's getting dark, isn't it?"

VINCE'S DRAGON

One of the little burdens I bear as gracefully as I can manage is the fact that of the six Hugo Awards decorating my office, none of them are for writing. My work as an editor, first at Analog and then at Omni, has greatly overshadowed my work as a writer. Like Orson Welles, who has always maintained that he is an amateur actor and a professional director, I have always considered editing a temporary part of my life. Writing is my life.

I was very flattered, then, to have one of the writers I "discovered" while editing Analog—Orson Scott Card—ask me to contribute an original story to an anthology he was creating. It was a pleasure to publish Scott's first short stories and novelettes in Analog. But when he asked me to contribute to his planned anthology about dragons I was nonplussed. Dragons? In science fiction? No matter what my dear friend Anne McCaffrey might have said, dragons are the stuff of fantasy, not science fiction. They are aerodynamically impossible and biochemically illogical. A giant flying reptilian that breathes flame? Not science fiction of the kind I write! No sir!

On the other hand, there is more to the world than hard-and-fast literary categories, and I got this niggling idea of how a dragon might be useful to certain kinds of people I used to know when I was growing up in the narrow streets of South Philadelphia.

Writers are always told to write about what they know, so I invented the world's first—and probably last—Mafia dragon.

THE THING THAT WORRIED VINCE about the dragon, of course, was that he was scared that it was out to capture his soul.

Vince was a typical young Family man. He had dropped out of South Philadelphia High School to start his career with the Family. He boosted cars, pilfered suits from local stores, even spent grueling and terrifying hours learning how to drive a big trailer rig so he could help out on hijackings.

But they wouldn't let him in on the big stuff.

"You can run numbers for me, kid," said Louie Bananas, the one-armed policy king of South Philly.

"I wanna do somethin' big," Vince said, with ill-disguised impatience. "1 wanna make somethin' outta myself."

Louie shook his bald, bullet-shaped head. "1 dunno, kid. You don't look like you got th' guts."

"Try me! Lemme in on th' sharks."

So Louie let Vince follow Big Balls Falcone, the loan sharks' enforcer, for one day. After watching Big Balls systematically break a guy's fingers, one by one, because he was ten days late with his payment, Vince agreed that loan sharking was not the business for him.

Armed robbery? Vince had never held a gun, much less fired one. Besides, armed robbery was for the heads and zanies, the stupids and desperate ones. *Organized* crime didn't go in for armed robbery. There was no need to. And a guy could get hurt.

After months of wheedling and groveling around Louie Bananas' favorite restaurant, Vince finally got the break he wanted.

"Okay, kid, okay," Louie said one evening as Vince stood in a corner of the restaurant watching him devour linguine with clams and white sauce. "I got an openin' for you. Come here."

Vince could scarcely believe his ears.

"What is it, *Padrone?* What? I'll do anything!"

Burping politely into his checkered napkin, Louie leaned back in his chair and grabbed a handful of Vince's curly dark hair, pulling Vince's ear close to his mouth.

Vince, who had an unfortunate allergy to garlic, fought hard to suppress a sneeze as he listened to Louie whisper, "You know that ol' B&O warehouse down aroun' Front an' Washington?"

"Yeah." Vince nodded as vigorously as he could, considering his hair was still in Louie's iron grip.

"Torch it."

"Burn it down?" Vince squeaked.

"Not so loud, *chidrool!*"

"Burn it down?" Vince whispered.

"Yeah."

"But that's arson."

Louie laughed. "It's a growth industry nowadays. Good opportunity for a kid who ain't afraid t' play with fire."

Vince sneezed.

It wasn't so much of a trick to burn down the rickety old warehouse, Vince knew. The place was ripe for the torch. But to burn it down without getting caught, that was different.

The Fire Department and Police and, worst of all, the insurance companies all had special arson squads who would be sniffing over the charred remains of the warehouse even before the smoke had cleared.

Vince didn't know anything at all about arson. But, desperate for his big chance, he was willing to learn.

He tried to get in touch with Johnnie the Torch, the leading local expert. But Johnnie was too busy to see him, and besides Johnnie worked for a rival Family, 'way up in Manayunk. Two other guys that Vince knew, who had something of a reputation in the field, had mysteriously disappeared within the past two nights.

Vince didn't think the library would have any books on the subject that would help him. Besides, he didn't read too good.

So, feeling very shaky about the whole business, very late the next night he drove a stolen station wagon filled with jerry cans of gasoline and big drums of industrial paint thinner out to Front Street.

He pushed his way through the loosely-nailed boards that covered the old warehouse's main entrance, feeling little and scared in the darkness. The warehouse was empty and dusty, but as far as the insurance company knew, Louie's fruit and vegetable firm had stocked the place up to the ceiling just a week ago.

Vince felt his hands shaking. *If I don't do a good job, Louie'll send Big Balls Falcone after me.*

Then he heard a snuffling sound.

He froze, trying to make himself invisible in the shadows.

Somebody was breathing. And it wasn't Vince.

Kee-rist, they didn't tell me there was a night watchman here!

"I am not a night watchman."

Vince nearly jumped out of his jockey shorts.

"And I'm not a policeman, either, so relax."

"Who—" His voice cracked. He swallowed and said again, deeper, "Who are you?"

"I am trying to get some sleep, but this place is getting to be a regular Stonehenge. People coming and going all the time!"

A bum, Vince thought. *A bum who's using this warehouse to flop.*

"And I am not a bum!" the voice said, sternly.

"I didn't say you was!" Vince answered. Then he shuddered, because he realized he had only thought it.

A glow appeared, across the vast darkness of the empty warehouse. Vince stared at it, then realized it was an eye. A single glowing, baleful eye with a slit of a pupil, just like a cat's. But this eye was the size of a bowling ball!

"Wh . . . wha . . ."

Another eye opened beside it. In the light from their twin smolderings, Vince could just make out a scaly head with a huge jaw full of fangs.

He did what any man would do. He fainted.

When he opened his eyes he wanted to faint again. In the eerie moonlight that was now filtering through the old warehouse's broken windowpanes, he saw a dragon standing over him.

It had a long, sinuous body covered with glittering green and bluish scales, four big paws with talons on them the size of lumberjacks' saws. Its tail coiled around and around, the end twitching slightly all the way over on the other side of the warehouse.

And right over him, grinning down toothily at him, was this huge fanged head with the giant glowing cat's eyes.

"You're cute," the dragon said.

"Huh?"

"Not at all like those other bozos Louie sent over here the past couple of nights. They were older. Fat, blubbery men."

"Other guys . . . ?"

The dragon flicked a forked tongue out between its glistening white fangs. "Do you think you're the first arsonist Louie's sent here? I mean, they've been clumping around here for the past several nights."

Still flat on his back, Vince asked, "Wh . . . wh . . . what happened to them?"

The dragon hunkered down on its belly and seemed, incredibly, to *smile at* him. "Oh, don't worry about them. They won't bother us." The tongue flicked out again and brushed Vince's face. "Yes, you are *cute!*"

Little by little, Vince's scant supply of courage returned to him. He kept speaking with the dragon, still not believing this was really happening, and slowly got up to a sitting position.

"I can read your mind," the dragon was saying. "So you might as well forget about trying to run away."

"I . . . uh, I'm supposed to torch this place," Vince confessed.

"I know," said the dragon. Somehow, it sounded like a female dragon.

"Yes, you're right," she admitted. "I am a female dragon. As a matter of fact, all the dragons that you humans have ever had trouble with have been females."

"You mean like St. George?" Vince blurted.

"That pansy! Him and his silly armor. Aunt Ssrishha could have broiled him alive inside that pressure cooker he was wearing. As it was, she got to laughing so hard at him that her flame went out."

"And he killed her."

"He did not!" She sounded really incensed, and a little wisp of smoke trickled out of her left nostril. "Aunt Ssrishha just made herself invisible and flew away. She was laughing so hard she got the hiccups."

"But the legend . . ."

"A human legend. More like a human public relations story. Kill a dragon. The human who can kill a dragon hasn't been born yet!"

"Hey, don't get sore. I didn't do nuthin."

"No. Of course not." Her voice softened. "You're cute, Vince." His mind was racing. Either he was crazy or he was talking with a real, fire-breathing dragon.

"Uh, what's your name?"

"Ssrzzha," she said. "I'm from the Polish branch of the dragon family."

"Shh . . . **Zz**," Vince tried to pronounce.

"You may call me 'Sizzle,'" the dragon said, grandly.

"Sizzle. Hey, that's a cute name."

"I knew you'd like it."

If I'm crazy, they'll come and wake me up sooner or later, Vince thought, and decided to at least keep the conversation going.

"You say all the dragons my people have ever fought were broads . . . I mean, females?"

"That's right, Vince. So you can see how silly it is, all those human lies about our eating young virgins."

"Uh, yeah. I guess so."

"And the bigger lies they tell about slaying dragons. Utter falsehoods."

"Really?"

"Have you ever seen a stuffed dragon in a museum? Or dragon bones? Or a dragon's head mounted on a wall?"

"Well . . . I don't go to museums much."

"Whereas I could show you some very fascinating exhibits in certain caves, if you want to see bones and heads and—"

"Ah, no, thanks. I don't think I really wanna see that," Vince said hurriedly.

"No, you probably wouldn't."

"Where's all the male dragons? They must be *really* big."

Sizzle huffed haughtily and a double set of smoke rings wafted past Vince's ear.

"The males of our species are tiny! Hardly bigger than you are. They all live out on some islands in the Indian Ocean. We have to fly there every hundred years or so for mating, or else our race would die out."

"Every hundred years! You only get laid once a century?"

"Sex is not much fun for us, I'm afraid. Not as much as it is for you, but then you're descended from monkeys, of course. Disgusting little things. Always chattering and making messes."

"Uh, look . . . Sizzle. This's been fun an' it was great meetin' you an' all, but it's gettin' late and I gotta go now, and besides—"

"But aren't you forgetting why you came here?"

Truth to tell, Vince had forgotten. But now he recalled, "I'm supposed t' torch this warehouse."

"That's right. And from what 1 can see bubbling inside your cute little head, if you don't burn this place down tonight, Louie's going to be very upset with you."

"Yeah, well, that's my problem, right? I mean, you wanna stay here an' get back t' sleep, right? I don't wanna bother you like them other guys did, ya know? I mean, like, I can come back when you go off to th' Indian Ocean or something."

"Don't be silly, Vince," Sizzle said, lifting herself ponderously to her four paws. "I can sleep anywhere. And I'm not due for another mating for several decades, thank the gods. As for those other fellows . . . well, they annoyed me. But you're cute!"

Vince slowly got to his feet, surprised that his quaking knees held him upright. But Sizzle coiled her long, glittering body around him, and with a grin that looked like a forest made of sharp butcher knives, she said:

"I'm getting kind of tired of this old place, anyway. What do you say we belt it out?"

"Huh?"

"I can do a much better job of torching this firetrap than you can, Vince, cutie," said Sizzle. "And *I* won't leave any telltale gasoline fumes behind me."

"But . . ."

"You'll be completely in the clear. Anytime the police come near, I can always make myself invisible."

"Invisible?"

"Sure. See?" And Sizzle disappeared.

"Hey, where are ya?"

"Right here, Vince." The dragon reappeared in all its glittering hugeness.

Vince stared, his mind churning underneath his curly dark hair.

Sizzle smiled at him. "What do you say, cutie? A life of crime together? You and I could do wonderful things together, Vince. I could get you to the top of the Family in no time."

A terrible thought oozed up to the surface of Vince's slowly-simmering mind. "Uh, wait a minute. This is like I seen on TV, ain't it? You help me, but you want me to sell my soul to you, right?"

"Your *soul*? What would I do with your soul?"

"You're workin' for th' devil, an' you gimme three wishes or somethin' but in return I gotta let you take my soul down t' hell when I die."

Sizzle shook her ponderous head and managed to look slightly affronted. "Vince—I admit that dragons and humans haven't been the best of friends over the millennia, but we do *not* work for the devil. I'm not even sure that he exists. I've never seen a devil, have you?"

"No, but—"

"And I'm not after your soul, silly boy."

"You don' want me ta sign nuthin?"

"Of course not."

"An' you'll help me torch this dump for free?"

"More than that, Vince. I'll help you climb right up to the top of the Family. We'll be partners in crime! It'll be the most fun I've had since Aunt Hsspss started the Chicago Fire."

"Hey, I just wanna torch this one warehouse!"

"Yes, of course."

"No Chicago Fires or nuthin like that."

"I promise."

It took several minutes for Vince to finally make up his mind and say, "Okay, let's do it."

Sizzle cocked her head slightly to one side. "Shouldn't you get out of the warehouse first, Vince?"

"Huh? Oh yeah, sure."

"And maybe drive back to your house, or—better yet—over to that restaurant where your friends are."

"Whaddaya mean? We gotta torch this place first."

"I'll take care of that, Vince deary. But wouldn't it look better if you had plenty of witnesses around to tell the police they were with you when the warehouse went up?"

"Yeah . . ." he said, feeling a little suspicious.

"All right, then," said Sizzle. "You just get your cute little body over to the restaurant and once you're safely there I'll light this place up like an Inquisition pyre."

"How'll you know . . . ?"

"When you get to the restaurant? I'm telepathic, Vince."

"But how'll I know . . . ?"

"When this claptrap gets belted out? Don't worry, you'll see the flames in the sky!" Sizzle sounded genuinely excited by the prospect.

Vince couldn't think of any other objections. Slowly, reluctantly, he headed for the warehouse door. He had to step over one of Sizzle's saber-long talons on the way.

At the doorway, he turned and asked plaintively, "You sure you ain't after my soul?"

Sizzle smiled at him. "I'm not after your soul, Vince, you can depend on that."

The warehouse fire was the most spectacular anyone had seen in a long time, and the police were totally stymied about its cause. They questioned Vince at length, especially since he had forgotten to get rid of the gasoline and paint thinner in the back of the stolen station wagon. But they couldn't pin a thing on him, not even car theft, once Louie had Big Balls Falcone explain the situation to the unhappy wagon's owner.

Vince's position in the Family started to rise. Spectacularly.

Arson became his specialty. Louie gave him tougher and tougher assignments and Vince would wander off a night later and the job would be done. Perfectly.

He met Sizzle regularly, sometimes in abandoned buildings, sometimes in empty lots. The dragon remained invisible then, of course, and the occasional passerby got the impression that a young, sharply-dressed man was standing in the middle of a weed-choked, bottle-strewn empty lot, talking to thin air.

More than once they could have heard him asking, "You really ain't interested in my soul?"

But only Vince could hear Sizzle's amused reply, "No, Vince. I have no use for souls, yours or anyone else's."

As the months went by, Vince's rapid rise to Family stardom naturally attracted some antagonism from other young men attempting to get ahead in the organization. Antagonism sometimes led to animosity, threats, even attempts at violence.

But strangely, wondrously, anyone who got angry at Vince disappeared. Without a trace, except once when a single charred shoe of Fats Lombardi's was found in the middle of Tasker Street, between Twelfth and Thirteenth.

Louie and the other elders of the Family nodded knowingly. Vince was not only ambitious and talented. He was smart. No bodies could be laid at his doorstep.

From arson, Vince branched into loan-sharking, which was still the heart of the Family's operation. But he didn't need Big Balls Falcone to terrify his customers into paying on time. Customers who didn't pay found their cars turned into smoking wrecks. Right before their eyes, an automobile parked at the curb would burst into flame.

"Gee, too bad," Vince would say. "Next time it might be your house," he'd hint darkly, seeming to wink at somebody who wasn't there. At least, somebody no one else could see. Somebody very tall, from the angle of his head when he winked.

The day came when Big Balls Falcone himself, understandably put out by the decline in his business, let it be known that he was coming after Vince. Big Balls disappeared in a cloud of smoke, literally.

The years rolled by. Vince became quite prosperous. He was no longer the skinny, scared kid he had been when he had first met Sizzle. Now he dressed conservatively, with a carefully-tailored vest buttoned neatly over his growing paunch, and lunched on steak and lobster tails with bankers and brokers.

Although he moved out of the old neighborhood row house into a palatial ranch-style single near Cherry Hill, over in Jersey, Vince still came back to the Epiphany Church every Sunday morning for Mass. He sponsored the church's Little League baseball team and donated a free Toyota every year for the church's annual raffle.

He looked upon these charities, he often told his colleagues, as a form of insurance. He would lift his eyes at such moments. Those around him thought he was looking toward heaven. But Vince was really searching for Sizzle, who was usually not far away.

"Really, Vince," the dragon told him, chuckling, "you still don't trust me. After all these years. I don't want your soul. Honestly I don't."

Vince still attended church and poured money into charities.

Finally Louie himself, old and frail, bequeathed the Family fortunes to Vince and then died peacefully in his sleep, unassisted by members of his own or any other Family. Somewhat of a rarity in Family annals.

Vince was now *Capo* of the Family. He was not yet forty, sleek, hair still dark, heavier than he wanted to be, but in possession of his own personal tailor, his own barber, and more women than he had ever dreamed of having.

His ascension to *Capo* was challenged, of course, by some of Louie's other lieutenants. But after the first few of them disappeared without a trace, the others quickly made their peace with Vince.

He never married. But he enjoyed life to the full.

"You're getting awfully overweight, Vince," Sizzle warned him one night, as they strolled together along the dark and empty waterfront where they had first met. "Shouldn't you be worrying about the possibility of a heart attack?"

"Naw," said Vince. "I don't get heart attacks, I give 'em!" He laughed uproariously at his own joke.

"You're getting older, Vince. You're not as cute as you once were, you know."

"I don't hafta be *cute*, Sizzle. 1 got the power now. I can look and act any way I wanna act. Who's gonna get in my way?"

Sizzle nodded, a bit ruefully. But Vince paid no attention to her mood.

"I can do anything I want!" he shouted to the watching heavens. "I got th' power and the rest of those dummies are scared to death of me. Scared to death!" He laughed and laughed.

"But Vince," Sizzle said, "I helped you to get that power."

"Sure, sure. But I got it now, an' I don't really need your help anymore. I can get anybody in th' Family to do whatever I want!"

Dragons don't cry, of course, but the expression on Sizzle's face would have melted the heart of anyone who saw it.

"Listen," Vince went on, in a slightly less bombastic tone, "I know you done a lot to help me, an' I ain't gonna forget that. You'll still be part of my organization, Sizzle old girl. Don't worry about that."

But the months spun along and lengthened into years, and Vince saw Sizzle less and less. He didn't need to. And secretly, down inside him, he was glad that he didn't have to.

I don't need her no more, and I never signed nuthin about givin' away my soul or nuthin. I'm free and clear!

Dragons, of course, are telepathic.

Vince's big mistake came when he noticed that a gorgeous young redhead he was interested in seemed to have eyes only for a certain slick-looking young punk. Vince thought about the problem mightily, and then decided to solve two problems with one stroke.

He called the young punk to his presence, at the very same restaurant where Louie had given Vince his first big break.

The punk looked scared. He had heard that Vince was after the redhead.

"Listen kid," Vince said gruffly, laying a heavily be-ringed hand on the kid's thin shoulder. "You know the old clothing factory up on Twenty-Eighth and Arch?"

"Yessir," said the punk, in a whisper that Vince could barely hear.

"It's a very flammable building, dontcha think?"

The punk blinked, gulped, then nodded. "Yeah. It is. But . . ."

"But what?"

His voice trembling, the kid said, "I heard that two, three different guys tried beltin' out that place. An' they . . . they never came back!"

"The place is still standin', ain't it?" Vince asked severely.

"Yeah."

"Well, by tomorrow morning, either *it* ain't standin' or *you* ain't standin.' *Capisce?*"

The kid nodded and fairly raced out of the restaurant. Vince grinned. One way or the other, he had solved a problem, he thought.

The old factory burned cheerfully for a day and a half before the Fire Department could get the blaze under control. Vince laughed and phoned his insurance broker.

But that night, as he stepped from his limousine onto the driveway of his Cherry Hill home, he saw long coils of glittering scales wrapped halfway around the house.

Looking up, he saw Sizzle smiling at him.

"Hello, Vince. Long time no see."

"Oh, hi Sizzle ol' girl. What's new?" With his left hand, Vince impatiently waved his driver off. The man backed the limousine down the driveway and headed for the garage back in the city, goggle-eyed that The Boss was talking to himself.

"That was a real cute fellow you sent to knock off the factory two nights ago," Sizzle said, her voice almost purring.

"Him? He's a punk."

"I thought he was really cute."

"So you were there, huh? I figured you was, after those other guys never came back."

"Oh Vince, you're not cute anymore. You're just soft and fat and ugly."

"You ain't gonna win no beauty contests yourself, Sizzle."

He started for the front door, but Sizzle planted a huge taloned paw in his path. Vince had just enough time to look up, see the expression on her face, and scream.

Sizzle's forked tongue licked her lips as the smoke cleared.

"Delicious," she said. "Just the right amount of fat on him. And the poor boy thought I was after his *soul!*"

THE LAST DECISION

One of the things that makes science fiction such a vital and vivid field is the synergy that manifests itself among the writers. Whereas in most other areas of contemporary letters the writers appear to feel themselves in competition with each other (for headlines, if nothing else) the writers of science fiction have long seen themselves as members of a big family. They share ideas, they often work together, and they help each other whenever they can.

A large part of this synergy stems from the old, original Milford Science Fiction Writers Conference, which used to be held annually in Milford, Pennsylvania. Everlasting thanks are due to Damon Knight, James Blish, and Judith Merrill, who first organized the conferences. For eight days out of each June, a small and dedicated group of professional writers—about evenly mixed between old hands and newcomers—ate, slept, breathed, and talked about writing. Lifelong friendships began at Milford, together with the synergy that makes two such friends more effective working together than the simple one-plus-one equation would lead you to think.

I met Gordon R. Dickson at the first Milford I attended, back in the early Sixties, and we became firm friends until the day he died. We collaborated on a children's fantasy, Gremlins, Go Home! some years later, and even though Gordy lived in Minneapolis and I on the East Coast, it was a rare six months when we did not see each other.

"The Last Decision" is an example of the synergy between writers.

51

Gordy wrote a marvelous story, "Call Him Lord," which stuck in my mind for years. In particular, I was haunted by the character of the Emperor of the Hundred Worlds, as powerful a characterization as I have found anywhere, even though he is actually a minor player in Gordy's story. I wanted to see more of the Emperor, and finally asked Gordy if he would allow me to "use" the character in a story of my own. He graciously gave his permission, and the result is "The Last Decision."

THE EMPEROR OF THE HUNDRED WORLDS stood at the head of the conference chamber, tall, gray, grim-faced. Although there were forty other men and women seated in the chamber, the Emperor knew he was alone.

"Then it is certain?" he asked, his voice grave but strong despite the news they had given him. "Earth's Sun will explode?"

The scientists had come from all ends of the Empire to reveal their findings to the Emperor. They shifted uneasily in their sculptured couches under his steady gaze. A few of them, the oldest and best-trusted, were actually on the Imperial Planet itself, only an ocean away from the palace. Most of the others had been brought to the Imperial planetary system from their homeworlds, and were housed on the three other planets of the system.

Although the holographic projections made them look as solid and real as the Emperor himself, there was always a slight lag in their responses to him. The delay was an indication of their rank within the scientific order, and they had even arranged their seating in the conference chamber the same way: the farther away from the Emperor, the lower in the hierarchy.

Some things cannot be conquered, the Emperor thought to himself as one of the men in the third rank of couches, a roundish, bald, slightly pompous little man, got to his feet. *Time still reigns supreme. Distance we can conquer, but not time. Not death.*

"Properly speaking, Sire, the Sun will not explode, it will not become a nova. Its mass is too low for that. But the eruptions that it will suffer will be of sufficient severity to heat Earth's atmosphere to incandescence. It will destroy all life on the surface. And, of course, the oceans will be drastically damaged; the food chain of the oceans will be totally disrupted."

Goodbye to Earth, then, thought the Emperor.

But aloud he asked, "The power satellites, and the shielding we have provided the planet—they will not protect it?"

The scientist stood dumb, patiently waiting for his Emperor's response to span the light-minutes between them. *How drab he looks,* the Emperor noted. *And how soft.* He pulled his own white robe closer around his iron-hard body. He was older than most of them in the conference chamber, but they were accustomed to sitting at desks and lecturing to students. He was accustomed to standing before multitudes and commanding.

"The shielding," the bald man said at last, "will not be sufficient. There is nothing we can do. Sometime over the next three to five hundred years, the Sun will erupt and destroy all life on Earth and the inner planets of its system. The data are conclusive."

The Emperor inclined his head to the man, curtly, a gesture that meant both "thank you" and "be seated." The scientist waited mutely for the gesture to reach him.

The data are conclusive. The integrator woven into the molecules of his cerebral cortex linked the Emperor's mind with the continent-spanning computer complex that was the Imperial memory.

Within milliseconds he reviewed the equations and found no flaw in them. Even as he did so, the other hemisphere of his brain was picturing Earth's daystar seething, writhing in a fury of pent-up nuclear agony, then erupting into giant flares. The Sun calmed afterward and smiled benignly once again on a blackened, barren, smoking rock called Earth.

A younger man was on his feet, back in the last row of couches. The Emperor realized that he had already asked for permission to speak. Now they both waited for the photons to complete the journey between them. From his position in the chamber and the distance between them, he was either an upstart or a very junior researcher.

"Sire," he said at last, his face suddenly flushed in embarrassed self-consciousness or, perhaps, the heat of conviction, "the data may be conclusive, true enough. But it is *not* true that we must accept this catastrophe with folded hands."

The Emperor began to say, "Explain yourself," but the intense young man never hesitated to wait for an Imperial response. He was taking no chances of being commanded into silence before he had finished.

"Earth's Sun will erupt only if we do nothing to prevent it. A colleague of mine believes that we have the means to prevent the eruptions. I would like to present her ideas on the subject. She could not attend this meeting herself." The young man's face grew taut, angry. "Her application to attend was rejected by the Coordinating Committee."

The Emperor smiled inwardly as the young man's words reached the other scientists around him. He could see a shock wave of disbelief and indignation spread through the assembly. The hoary old men in the front row, who chose the members of the Coordinating Committee, went stiff with anger.

Even Prince Javas, the Emperor's last remaining son, roused from his idle daydreaming where he sat at the Emperor's side and seemed to take an interest in the meeting for the first time.

"You may present your colleague's proposal," the Emperor said. *That is what an Emperor is for,* he said silently, looking at his youngest son, seeking some understanding on his handsome untroubled face. *To be magnanimous in the face of **disaster.***

The young man took a fingertip-sized cube from his sleeve pocket and inserted it into the computer input slot in the arm of his couch. The scientists in the front ranks of the chamber glowered and muttered to each other.

The Emperor stood lean and straight, waiting for the information to reach him. When it did, he saw in his mind a young dark-haired woman whose face would have been seductive if she were not so intensely serious about her subject. She was speaking, trying to keep her voice dispassionate, but almost literally quivering with excitement. Equations appeared, charts, graphs, lists of materials and costs; yet her intent, dark-eyed face dominated it all.

Beyond her, the Emperor saw a vague, star-shimmering image of vast ships ferrying megatons of equipment and thousands upon thousands of technical specialists from all parts of the Hundred Worlds toward Earth and its troubled Sun.

Then, as the equations faded and the starry picture went dim and even the woman's face began to pale, the Emperor saw the Earth, green and safe, smelt the grass and heard birds singing, saw the Sun shining gently over a range of softly rolling, ancient wooded hills. He closed his eyes. *You go too far, woman.* But how was she to know that his eldest son had died in hills exactly like these, killed on Earth, killed *by* Earth, so many years ago?

✳ **II** ✳

HE SAT NOW. The Emperor of the Hundred Worlds spent little time on his feet anymore. *One by one the vanities are surrendered.* He sat in a powered chair that held him in a soft yet firm embrace. It was mobile and almost alive: part personal vehicle, part medical monitor, part communications system that could link him with any place in the Empire.

His son stood. Prince Javas stood by the marble balustrade that girdled the high terrace where his father had received him. He wore the gray-blue uniform of a fleet commander, although he had never bothered to accept command of even one ship. His wife, the Princess Rihana, stood at her husband's side.

They were a well-matched pair, physically. Gold and fire. The Prince had his father's lean sinewy grace, golden hair and star-flecked eyes. Rihana was fiery, with the beauty and ruthlessness of a tigress in her face. Her hair was a cascade of molten copper tumbling past her shoulders, her gown a metallic glitter.

"It was a wasted trip," Javas said to his father, with his usual sardonic smile. "Earth is . . . well," he shrugged, "nothing but Earth. It hasn't changed in the slightest."

"Ten wasted years," Rihana said.

The Emperor looked past them, beyond the terrace to the lovingly landscaped forest that his engineers could never make quite the right shade of terrestrial green.

"Not entirely wasted, daughter-in-law," he said at last. "You only aged eighteen months."

"We are ten years out of date with the affairs of the Empire," she answered. The smoldering expression on her face made it clear that she believed her father-in-law deliberately plotted to keep her as far from the throne as possible.

"You can easily catch up," the Emperor said, ignoring her anger. "In the meantime, you have kept your youthful appearance."

"I shall always keep it! *You* are the one who denies himself rejuvenation treatments, not me."

"And so will Javas, when he becomes Emperor."

"Will he?" Her eyes were suddenly mocking.

"He will," said the Emperor, with the weight of a hundred worlds behind his voice.

Rihana looked away from him. "Well even so, I shan't. I see no reason why I should age and wither when even the foulest shopkeeper can live for centuries."

"Your husband will age."

She said nothing. *And as he ages,* the Emperor knew, *you will find younger lovers. But of course, you have already done that, haven't you?*

He turned toward his son, who was still standing by the balustrade.

"Kyle Arman is dead." Javas blurted.

For a moment, the Emperor failed to comprehend. "Dead?" he asked, his voice sounding old and weak even to himself.

Javas nodded. "In his sleep. A heart seizure."

"But he is too young—"

"He was your age, Father."

"And he refused rejuvenation treatments," Rihana said, sounding positively happy. "As if he were royalty! The pretentious fool. A servant . . . a menial."

"He was a friend of this house," the Emperor said.

"He killed my brother," said Javas.

"Your brother failed the test. He was a coward. Unfit to rule." *But Kyle passed you,* the Emperor thought. *You were found fit to rule . . . or was Kyle still ashamed of what he had done to my firstborn?*

"And you accepted his story." For once, Javas' bemused smile was gone. There was iron in his voice. "The word of a backwoods Earthman."

"A pretentious fool," Rihana gloated.

"A proud and faithful man," the Emperor corrected. "A man who put honor and duty above personal safety or comfort."

His eyes locked with Javas'. After a long moment in silence, the Prince shrugged and turned away.

"Regardless," Rihana said, "we surveyed the situation on Earth, as you requested us to."

Commanded, the Emperor thought. *Not requested.*

"The people there are all primitives. Hardly a city on the entire planet! It's all trees and huge oceans."

"I know. I have been there."

Javas said, "There are only a few millions living on Earth. They can be evacuated easily and resettled on a few of the frontier planets. After all, they *are* primitives."

"Those 'primitives' are the baseline for our race. They are the pool of original genetic material, against which our scientists constantly measure the rest of humanity throughout the Hundred Worlds."

Rihana said, "Well, they're going to have to find another primitive world to live on."

"Unless we prevent their Sun from exploding."

Javas looked amused, "You're not seriously considering that?"

"I am . . . considering it. Perhaps not very seriously."

"It makes no difference," Rihana said. "The plan to save the Sun— to save your precious Earth—will take hundreds of years to implement. You will be dead long before the first steps can be brought to a conclusion. The next Emperor can cancel the entire plan the day he takes the throne."

The Emperor turned his chair slightly to face his son, but Javas looked away, out toward the darkening forest.

"I know," the Emperor whispered, more to himself than to her. I know that full well."

✳ III ✳

HE COULD NOT SLEEP. The Emperor lay on the wide expanse of warmth, floating a single molecular layer above the gently soothing waters. Always before, when sleep would not come readily, a woman had solved the problem for him. But lately not even lovemaking helped.

The body grows weary but the mind refuses sleep. Is this what old age brings?

Now he lay alone, the ceiling of his tower bedroom depolarized so that he could see the blazing glory of the Imperial Planet's night sky.

Not the pale tranquil sky of Earth, with its bloated Moon smiling inanely at *you,* he thought. This was truly an Imperial sky, brazen with blue giant stars that studded the heavens like brilliant sapphires. No moon rode that sky; none was needed. There was never true darkness on the Imperial Planet.

And yet Earth's sky seemed so much friendlier. You could pick out old companions there; the two Bears, the Lion, the Twins, the Hunter, the Winged Horse.

Already I think of Earth in the past tense. Like Kyle. Like my *son.*

He thought of the Earth's warming Sun. How could it turn traitor? How could it . . . begin to die? In his mind's eye he hovered above the Sun, bathed in its fiery glow, watching its bubbling, seething surface. He plunged deeper into the roiling plasma, saw filaments and streamers arching a thousand Earthspans into space, heard the pulsing throb of the star's energy, the roar of its power, blinding bright, overpowering, ceaseless merciless heat, throbbing, roaring, pounding . . .

He was gasping for breath and the pounding he heard was his own heartbeat throbbing in his ears. Soaked with sweat, he tried to sit up. The bed enfolded him protectively, supporting his body.

"Hear me," he commanded the computer. His voice cracked.

"Sire?" answered a softly female voice in his mind.

He forced himself to relax. Forced the pain from his body. The dryness in his throat eased. His breathing slowed. The pounding of his heart diminished.

"Get me the woman scientist who reported at the conference on the Sun's explosion, ten years ago. She was not present at the conference, her report was presented by a colleague."

The computer needed more than a second to reply, "Sire, there were four such reports by female scientists at that conference."

"This was the only one to deal with a plan to save the Earth's Sun."

✳ **IV** ✳

MEDICAL MONITORS were implanted in his body now. Although the Imperial physicians insisted that it was impossible, the Emperor could feel the microscopic implants on the wall of his heart, in his aorta, alongside his carotid artery. The Imperial psychotechs called it a psychosomatic reaction. But since his mind was linked to the computers that handled all the information on the planet, the Emperor knew what his monitors were reporting before the doctors did.

They had reduced the gravity in his working and living sections of the palace to one-third normal, and forbade him from leaving these areas, except for the rare occasions of state when he was needed in the Great Assembly Hall or another public area. He acquiesced in this: the lighter gravity felt better and allowed him to be on his feet once again, free of the power chair's clutches.

This day he was walking slowly, calmly, through a green forest of Earth. He strolled along a parklike path, admiring the lofty maples and birches, listening to the birds and small forest animals' songs of life. He inhaled scents of pine and grass and sweet clean air. He felt the warm sun on his face and the faintest cool breeze. For a moment he considered how the trees would look in their autumnal reds and golds. But he shook his head.

No. There is enough autumn in my life. I'd rather be in springtime.

In the rooms next to the corridor he walked through, tense knots of technicians worked at the holographic systems that produced the illusion of the forest, while other groups of white-suited meditechs studied the readouts from the Emperor's implants.

Two men joined the Emperor on the forest path: Academician Bomeer, head of the Imperial Academy of Sciences, and Supreme Commander Fain, chief of staff of the Imperial Military Forces. Both were old friends and advisors, close enough to the Emperor to be housed within the palace itself when they were allowed to visit their master.

Bomeer looked young, almost sprightly, in a stylish robe of green and tan. He was slightly built, had a lean, almost ascetic face that was spoiled by a large mop of unruly brown hair.

Commander Fain was iron gray, square-faced, a perfect picture of a military leader. His black and silver uniform fit his muscular frame like a second skin. His gray eyes seemed eternally troubled.

The Emperor greeted them and allowed Bomeer to spend a few minutes admiring the forest simulation. The scientist called out the correct names for each type of tree they walked past and identified several species of birds and squirrel. Finally the Emperor asked him about the young woman who had arrived on the Imperial Planet the previous month.

"I have discussed her plan thoroughly with her," Bomeer said, his face going serious. "I must say that she is dedicated, energetic, close to brilliant. But rather naive and overly sanguine about her own ideas."

"Could her plan work?" asked the Emperor.

"Could it work?" the scientist echoed. He had tenaciously held onto his post at the top of the scientific hierarchy for nearly a century. His body had been rejuvenated more than once, the Emperor knew. But not his mind.

"Sire, there is no way to tell if it could work! Such an operation has never been done before. There are no valid data. Mathematics, yes. But even so, there is no more than theory. And the costs! The time it would take! The technical manpower! Staggering."

The Emperor stopped walking. Fifty meters away, behind the hologram screens, a dozen meditechs suddenly hunched over their readout screens intently.

But the Emperor had stopped merely to repeat to Bomeer, "Could her plan work?"

Bomeer ran a hand through his boyish mop, glanced at Commander Fain for support and found none, then faced his Emperor again. "I . . . there is no firm answer, Sire. Statistically, I would say that the chances are vanishingly small."

"Statistics!" The Emperor made a disgusted gesture. "A refuge for scoundrels and sociotechs. Is there anything scientifically impossible in what she proposes?"

"Nnn . . . not *theoretically* impossible, Sire," Bomeer said slowly. "But in the practical world of reality it . . . it is the *magnitude* of the project. The costs. Why, it would take half of Commander Fain's fleet to transport the equipment and material."

Fain seized his opportunity to speak. "And the Imperial Fleet, Sire, is spread much too thin for safety as it is."

"We are at peace, Commander," said the Emperor.

"For how long, Sire? The frontier worlds grow more restless every day. And the aliens beyond our borders—"

"Are weaker than we are. I have reviewed the intelligence assessments, Commander."

"Sire, the relevant factor in those reports is that the aliens are growing stronger and we are not."

With a nod, the Emperor resumed walking. The scientist and the commander followed him, arguing their points unceasingly.

Finally they reached the end of the long corridor, where the holographic simulation showed them Earth's Sun setting beyond the edge of an ocean, turning the restless sea into an impossible glitter of opalescence.

"Your recommendations, then, gentlemen?" he asked wearily. Even in the one-third gravity his legs felt tired, his back ached.

Bomeer spoke first, his voice hard and sure. "This naive dream of saving the Earth's Sun is doomed to fail. The plan must be rejected."

Fain added, "The Fleet can detach enough squadrons from its noncombat units to initiate the evacuation of Earth whenever you order it, Sire."

"Evacuate them to an unsettled planet?" the Emperor asked.

"Or resettle them on the existing frontier worlds. The Earth residents are rather frontier-like themselves; they have purposely been kept primitive. They would get along well with some of the frontier populations. They might even serve to calm down some of the unrest on the frontier worlds."

The Emperor looked at Fain and almost smiled. "Or they might fan that unrest into outright rebellion. They are a cantankerous lot, you know."

"We can deal with rebellion," said Fain.

"Can you?" the Emperor asked. "You can kill people, of course. You can level cities and even render whole planets uninhabitable. But does that end it? Or do the neighboring worlds become fearful and turn against us?"

Fain stood as unmoved as a statue. His lips barely parted as he asked. "Sire, if I may speak frankly?"

"Certainly, Commander."

Like a soldier standing at attention as he delivers an unpleasant report to his superior officer, Fain drew himself up and monotoned, "Sire, the main reason for unrest among the frontier worlds is the lack of Imperial firmness in dealing with them. In my opinion, a strong hand is desperately needed. The neighboring worlds will respect their

Emperor if—and only if—he acts decisively. The people value strength, Sire, not meekness."

The Emperor reached out and put a hand on the Commander's shoulder. Fain was still iron-hard under his uniform.

"You have sworn an oath to protect and defend this Realm," the Emperor said. "If necessary, to die for it."

"And to protect and defend you, Sire." The man stood straighter and firmer than the trees around them.

"But this Empire, my dear Commander, is more than blood and steel, It is more than any one man. It is an *idea*."

Fain looked back at him steadily, but with no real understanding in his eyes. Bomeer stood uncertainly off to one side.

Impatiently, the Emperor turned his face toward the ceiling hologram and called, "Map!"

Instantly the forest scene disappeared and they were in limitless space. Stars glowed around them, overhead, on all sides, underfoot. The pale gleam of the galaxy's spiral arms wafted off and away into unutterable distance.

Bomeer's knees buckled. Even the Commander's rigid self-discipline was shaken.

The Emperor smiled. He was accustomed to walking godlike on the face of the Deep.

"This is the Empire, gentlemen," he lectured in the darkness. "A handful of stars, a pitiful scattering of worlds set apart by distances that take years to traverse. All populated by human beings, the descendants of Earth."

He could hear Bomeer breathing heavily. Fain was a ramrod outline against the glow of the Milky Way, but his hands were outstretched, as if seeking balance.

"What links these scattered dust motes? What preserves their ancient heritage, guards their civilization, protects their hard-won knowledge and arts and sciences? The Empire. Gentlemen. We are the mind of the Hundred Worlds, their memory, the yardstick against which they can measure their own humanity. We are their friend, their father, their teacher and helper."

The Emperor searched the black starry void for the tiny yellowish speck of Earth's Sun, while saying:

"But if the Hundred Worlds decide that the Empire is no longer their friend, if they want to leave their father, if they feel that their teacher and helper has become an oppressor . . . what then happens to the human race? It will shatter into a hundred fragments, and all the civilization that we have built and nurtured and protected over all these centuries will be destroyed."

Bomeer's whispered voice floated through the darkness. "They would never . . ."

"Yes. They would never turn against the Empire because they know that they have more to gain by remaining with us than by leaving us."

"But the frontier worlds," Fain said.

"The frontier worlds are restless, as frontier communities always are. If we use military might to force them to bow to our will, then other worlds will begin to wonder where their own best interests lie."

"But they could never hope to fight against the Empire!"

The Emperor snapped his fingers and instantly the three of them were standing again in the forest at sunset.

"They could never hope to *win* against the Empire," the Emperor corrected. "But they could destroy the Empire and themselves. I have played out the scenarios with the computers. Widespread rebellion is possible, once the majority of the Hundred Worlds becomes convinced that the Empire is interfering with their freedoms."

"But the rebels could never win," the Commander said. "I have run the same wargames myself, many times."

"Civil war," said the Emperor. "Who wins a civil war? And once we begin to slaughter ourselves, what will your aliens do, my dear Fain? Eh?"

His two advisors fell silent. The forest simulation was now deep in twilight shadow. The three men began to walk back along the path, which was softly illuminated by bioluminescent flowers.

Bomeer clasped his hands behind his back as he walked. "Now that I have seen some of your other problems, Sire, I must take a stronger stand and insist—yes, Sire, *insist*—that this young woman's plan to save the Earth is even more foolhardy than I had at first thought it to be. The cost is too high, and the chance of success is much too slim. The frontier worlds would react violently against such an extravagance. And," with a nod to Fain, "it would hamstring the Fleet."

For several moments the Emperor walked down the simulated

forest path without saying a word. Then, slowly, "I suppose you are right. It is an old man's sentimental dream."

"I'm afraid that's the truth of it, Sire," said Fain.

Bomeer nodded sagaciously.

"I will tell her. She will be disappointed. Bitterly."

Bomeer gasped. "She's here?"

The Emperor said, "Yes, I had her brought here to the palace. She has crossed the Empire, given up more than two years of her life to make the trip, lost a dozen years of her career over this wild scheme of hers . . . just to hear that I will refuse her."

"In the palace?" Fain echoed. "Sire, you're not going to see her in person? The security . . ."

"Yes, in person. I owe her that much." The Emperor could see the shock on their faces. Bomeer, who had never stood in the same building with the Emperor until he had become Chairman of the Academy, was trying to suppress his fury with poor success. Fain, sworn to guard the Emperor as well as the Empire, looked worried.

"But Sire," the Commander said, "no one has personally seen the Emperor, privately, outside of his family and closest advisors," Bomeer bristled visibly, "in years . . . decades!"

The Emperor nodded but insisted, "She is going to see me. I owe her that much. An ancient ruler on Earth once said, 'When you are going to kill a man, it costs nothing to be polite about it.' She is not a man, of course, but I fear that our decision will kill her soul."

They looked unconvinced.

Very well then, the Emperor said to them silently. *Put it down as the whim of an old man . . . a man who is feeling all his years . . . a man who will never recapture his youth.*

SHE IS ONLY A CHILD.

The Emperor studied Adela de Montgarde as the young astrophysicist made her way through the guards and secretaries and halls and antechambers toward his own private chambers. He had prepared to meet her in his reception room, changed his mind and moved the meeting to his office, then changed it again and now waited for her in his study. She knew nothing of his indecision, she merely followed the directions given her by the computer-informed staff of the palace.

The study was a warm old room, lined with shelves of private tapes that the Emperor had collected over the years. A stone fireplace big enough to walk into spanned one wall; its flames soaked the Emperor in lifegiving warmth. The opposite wall was a single broad window that looked out on the real forest beyond the palace walls. The window could also serve as a hologram frame; the Emperor could have any scene he wanted projected from it.

Best to have reality this evening, he told himself. *There is too little reality in my life these days.* So he eased back in his powerchair and watched his approaching visitor on the viewscreen above the fireplace of the richly carpeted, comfortably paneled old room.

He had carefully absorbed all the computer's information about Adela de Montgarde: born of a noble family on Gris, a frontier world whose settlers were slowly, painfully transforming it from a ball of rock into a viable habitat for human life. He knew her face, her life history, her scientific accomplishments and rank. But now, as he watched her approaching on the viewscreen built into the stone fireplace, he realized how little knowledge had accompanied the computer's detailed information.

The door to the study swung open automatically, and she stood uncertainly, framed in the doorway.

The Emperor swiveled his powerchair around to face her. The view screen immediately faded and became indistinguishable from the other stones.

"Come in, come in, Dr. Montgarde."

She was tiny, the smallest woman the Emperor remembered seeing. Her face was almost elfin, with large curious eyes that looked as if they had known laughter. She wore a metallic tunic buttoned to the throat, and a brief skirt. Her figure was childlike.

The Emperor smiled to himself. *She certainly won't tempt me with her body.*

As she stepped hesitantly into the study, her eyes darting all around the room, he said:

"I am sure that my aides have filled your head with all sorts of nonsense about protocol—when to stand, when to bow, what forms of address to use. Forget all of it. This is an informal meeting, common politeness will suffice. If you need a form of address for me, call me Sire. I shall call you Adela, if you don't mind."

With a slow nod of her head she answered, "Thank you, Sire. That will be fine." Her voice was so soft that he could barely hear it. He thought he detected a slight waver in it.

She's not going to make this easy for me, he said to himself. Then he noticed the stone that she wore on a slim silver chain about her neck.

"Agate," he said.

She fingered the stone reflexively. "Yes. It's from my homeworld . . . Gris. Our planet is rich in minerals."

"And poor in cultivable land."

"Yes. But we are converting more land every year."

"Please sit down." the Emperor said. "I'm afraid it's been so long since my old legs have tried to stand in a full gravity that I'm forced to remain in this power chair or lower the gravitational field in this room. But the computer files said that you are not accustomed to low-g fields."

She glanced around the warm, richly furnished room.

"Any seat you like. My chair rides like a magic carpet."

Adela picked the biggest couch in the room and tucked herself into a corner of it. The Emperor glided his chair over to her.

"It's very kind of you to keep the gravity up for me," she said.

He shrugged. "It costs nothing to be polite. But tell me, of all the minerals that Gris is famous for, why did you choose to wear agate?"

She blushed.

The Emperor laughed. "Come, come, my dear. There's nothing to be ashamed of. It's well known that agate is a magical stone that protects the wearer from scorpions and snakes. An ancient superstition, of course, but it could possibly be significant, eh?"

"No . . . it's not that!"

"Then what is it?"

"It . . . agate also makes the wearer eloquent in speech."

"And a favorite of princes," added the Emperor.

Her blush had gone. She sat straighter and almost smiled. "And it gives one victory over her enemies."

"You perceive me as your enemy?"

"Oh no!" She reached out toward him, her small, childlike hand almost touching his.

"Who then?"

"The hierarchy . . . the old men who pretend to be young and refuse to admit any new ideas into the scientific community."

"I am an old man." the Emperor said.

"Yes." She stared frankly at his aged face. "I was surprised when I saw you a few moments ago. I have seen holographic pictures, of course . . . but you . . . you've *aged*."

"Indeed."

"Why can't you be rejuvenated? It seems like a useless old superstition to keep the Emperor from using modern biomedical techniques."

"No, no, my child, it is a very wise tradition. You complain of the inflexible old men at the top of the scientific hierarchy. Suppose you had an inflexible old man in the Emperor's throne? A man who would live not merely six or seven score of years, but many centuries? What would happen to the Empire then?"

"Ohh. I see." And there was real understanding and sympathy in her eyes.

"So the king must die, to make room for new blood, new ideas, new vigor."

"It's sad," she said. "You are known everywhere as a good Emperor. The people love you."

He felt his eyebrows rise. "Even on the frontier worlds?"

"Yes. They know that Fain and his troops would be standing on our necks if it weren't for the Emperor. We are not without our sources of information."

He smiled. "Interesting."

"But that is not why you called me here to see you," Adela said.

She grows bolder. "True. You want to save Earth's Sun. Bomeer and all my advisors tell me that it is either impossible or foolish. I fear that they have powerful arguments on their side."

"Perhaps," she said. "But I have the facts."

"I have seen your presentation. I understand the scientific basis of your plan."

"We can do it!" Adela said, her hands suddenly animated. "We can! The critical mass is really minuscule compared to—"

"Megatons are miniscule?"

"Compared to the effect it will produce. Yes."

And then she was on her feet, pacing the room, ticking off points on her fingers, lecturing, pleading, cajoling. The Emperor's powerchair nodded back and forth, following her intense, wiry form as she paced.

"Of course it will take vast resources! And time—more than a century before we know to a first-order approximation that the initial steps are working. I'll have to give myself up to cryosleep for decades at a time. But we *have* the resources! And we have the time . . . just barely. We can do it. if we want to."

The Emperor said, "How can you expect me to divert half the resources of the Empire to save Earth's Sun?"

"Because Earth is *important,*" she argued back, a tiny fighter standing alone in the middle of the Emperor's study. "It's the baseline for all the other worlds of the Empire. On Gris we send biogenetic teams to Earth every five years to check our own mutation rate. The cost is enormous for us, but we do it. We have to."

"We can move Earth's population to another G-type star. There are plenty of them."

"It won't be the same."

"Adela, my dear, believe me, I would like to help. I know how important Earth is. But we simply cannot afford to try your scheme now. Perhaps in another hundred years or so."

"That will be too late."

"But new scientific advances . . ."

"Under Bomeer and his ilk? Hah!"

The Emperor wanted to frown at her, but somehow his face would not compose itself properly. "You are a fierce, uncompromising woman," he said.

She came to him and dropped to her knees at his feet. "No, Sire. I'm not. I'm foolish and vain and utterly self-centered. I want to save Earth because I know I can do it. I can't stand the thought of living the rest of my life knowing that I could have done it, but never having had the chance to try."

Now we're getting at the truth, the Emperor thought.

"And someday, maybe a million years from now, maybe a billion, Gris' sun will become unstable. I want to be able to save Gris, too. And any other world whose star threatens it. I want all the Empire to know that Adela de Montgarde discovered the way to do it!"

The Emperor felt his breath rush out of him.

"Sire," she went on, "I'm sorry if I'm speaking impolitely or stupidly. It's just that I know we can do this thing, do it successfully, and you're the only one who can make it happen."

But he was barely listening. "Come with me," he said, reaching out to grasp her slim wrists and raising her to her feet. "It's time for the evening meal. I want you to meet my son."

✳ VI ✳

Javas put on his usual amused smile when the Emperor introduced Adela. *Will nothing ever reach under his everlasting facade of polite boredom?* Rihana, at least, was properly furious. He could see the anger in her face: A virtual barbarian from some frontier planet. Daughter of a petty noble. Practically a commoner. Dining with them!

"Such a young child to have such grandiose schemes," the Princess said when she realized who Adela was.

"Surely," said the Emperor, "you had grandiose schemes of your own when you were young, Rihana. Of course, they involved lineages and marriages rather than astrophysics, didn't they?"

None of them smiled.

The Emperor had ordered dinner out on the terrace, under the glowing night sky of the Imperial Planet. Rihana, who was responsible for household affairs, always had sumptuous meals spread for them: the best meats and fowl and fruits of a dozen prime worlds. Adela looked bewildered by the array placed in front of her by the human servants. Such riches were obviously new to her. The Emperor ate sparingly and watched them all.

Inevitably the conversation returned to Adela's plan to save Earth's Sun. And Adela, subdued and timid at first, slowly turned tigress once again. She met Rihana's scorn with coldly furious logic. She countered Javas' skepticism with: "Of course, since it will take more than a century before the outcome of the project is proven, you will probably be the Emperor who is remembered by all the human race as the one who saved the Earth."

Javas' eyes widened slightly. *That hit home,* the Emperor noticed. *For once something affected the boy. This girl should be kept at the palace.*

But Rihana snapped, "Why should the Crown Prince care about saving Earth? His brother was murdered by an Earthman."

The Emperor felt his blood turn to ice.

Adela looked panic-stricken. She turned to the Emperor, wide-eyed, open-mouthed.

"My eldest son died on Earth. My second son was killed putting down a rebellion on a frontier world, many years ago. My third son died of a viral infection that *some* tell me," he stared at Rihana, "was assassination. Death is a constant companion in every royal house."

"Three sons." Adela seemed ready to burst into tears.

"I have not punished Earth, nor that frontier world, nor sought to find a possible assassin," the Emperor went on, icily. "My only hope is that my last remaining son will make a good Emperor, despite his . . . handicaps."

Javas turned very deliberately in his chair to stare out at the dark forest. He seemed bored by the antagonism between his wife and his father. Rihana glowered like molten steel.

The dinner ended in dismal, bitter silence. The Emperor sent them all away to their rooms while he remained on the terrace and stared hard at the stars strewn across the sky so thickly that there could be no darkness.

He closed his eyes and summoned a computer-assisted image of Earth's Sun. He saw it coalesce from a hazy cloud of cold gas and dust, saw it turn into a star and spawn planets. Saw it beaming out energy that allowed life to grow and flourish on one of those planets. And then saw it age, blemish, erupt, swell, and finally collapse into a dark cinder.

Just as I will, thought the Emperor. *The Sun and I have both reached the age where a bit of rejuvenation is needed. Otherwise . . . death.*

He opened his eyes and looked down at his veined, fleshless, knobby hands. *How different from hers! How young and vital she is.*

With a touch on one of the control studs set into the arm of his powerchair, he headed for his bedroom.

I cannot be rejuvenated. It is wrong even to desire it. But the Sun? Would it be wrong to try? Is it proper for puny men to tamper with the destinies of the stars themselves?

Once in his tower-top bedroom he called for her. Adela came to him quickly, without delay or question. She wore a simple knee-length gown tied loosely at the waist. It hung limply over her boyish figure.

"You sent for me, Sire." It was not a question but a statement. The Emperor knew her meaning: *I will do what you ask, but in return I expect you to give me what I desire.*

He was already reclining in the soft embrace of his bed. The texture of the monolayer surface felt soft and protective. The warmth of the water beneath it eased his tired body.

"Come here, child. Come and talk to me. I hardly ever sleep anymore; it gives my doctors something to worry about. Come and sit beside me and tell me all about yourself . . . the parts of your life story that are not on file in the computers."

She sat on the edge of the huge bed, and its nearly-living surface barely dimpled under her spare body.

"What would you like to know?" she asked.

"I have never had a daughter," the Emperor said. "What was your childhood like? How did you become the woman you are?"

She began to tell him. Living underground in the mining settlements on Gris. Seeing sunlight only when the planet was far enough from its too-bright star to let humans walk the surface safely. Playing in the tunnels. Sent by her parents to other worlds for schooling. The realization that her beauty was not physical. The few lovers she had known. The astronomer who had championed her cause to the Emperor at that meeting nearly fifteen years ago. Their brief marriage. Its breakup when he realized that being married to her kept him from advancing in the hierarchy.

"You have known pain too," the Emperor said.

"It's not an Imperial prerogative," she answered softly. "Everyone who lives knows pain."

By now the sky was milky white with the approach of dawn. The Emperor smiled at her.

"Before breakfast everyone in the palace will know that you spent the night with me. I'm afraid I have ruined your reputation."

She smiled back. "Or perhaps *made* my reputation."

He reached out and took her by the shoulders. Holding her at arm's length, he searched her face with a long, sad, almost fatherly look.

"It would not be a kindness to grant your request. If I allow you to pursue this dream of yours, have you any idea of the enemies it would make for you? Your life would be so cruel, so filled with envy and hatred."

"I know that," Adela said evenly. "I've known that from the beginning."

"And you are not afraid?"

"Of course I'm afraid! But I won't turn away from what I must do. Not because of fear. Not because of envy or hatred or any other reason."

"Not even for love?"

He felt her body stiffen. "No," she said. "Not even for love."

The Emperor let his hands drop away from her and called out to the computer, "Connect me with Prince Javas, Acadamician Bomeer, and Commander Fain."

"At once, Sire."

Their holographic images quickly appeared on separate segments of the farthest wall of the bedroom. Bomeer, halfway across the planet in late afternoon, was at his ornate desk. Fain appeared to be on the bridge of a warship, in orbit around the planet. Javas, of course, was still in bed. It was not Rihana who lay next to him.

The Emperor's first impulse was disapproval, but then he wondered where Rihana was sleeping.

"I am sorry to intrude on you so abruptly," he said to all three of the men, while they were still staring at the slight young woman sitting on the bed with their Emperor. "I have made my decision on the question of trying to save the Earth's Sun."

Bomeer folded his hands on the desktop. Fain, on his feet, shifted uneasily. Javas arched an eyebrow and looked more curious than anything else.

"I have listened to all your arguments and find that there is much merit in them. I have also listened carefully to Dr. Montgarde's arguments, and find much merit in them, as well."

Adela sat rigidly beside him. The expression on her face was frozen: she feared nothing and expected nothing. She neither hoped nor despaired. She waited.

"We will move the Imperial throne and all its trappings to Earth's only Moon," said the Emperor.

They gasped. All of them.

"Since this project to save the Sun will take many human

generations, we will want the seat of the Empire close enough to the project so that the Emperor may take a direct view of the progress."

"But you can't move the entire Capital," Fain protested. "And to Earth! It's a backwater—"

"Commander Fain," the Emperor said sternly. "Yesterday you were prepared to move Earth's millions. I ask now that the Fleet move the Court's thousands. And Earth will no longer be a backwater once the Empire is centered once again at the original home of the human race."

Bomeer sputtered, "But . . . but what if her plan fails? The sun will explode . . . and . . . and . . ."

"That is a decision to be made in the future."

He glanced at Adela. Her expression had not changed, but she was breathing rapidly now. The excitement had hit her body, it hadn't yet penetrated her emotional defenses.

"Father," Javas said, "may I point out that it takes *five years* in realtime to reach the Earth from here? The Empire cannot be governed without an Emperor for five years."

"Quite true, my son. You will go to Earth before me. Once there, you will become acting Emperor while I make the trip."

Javas' mouth dropped open. "The acting Emperor? For five years?"

"With luck," the Emperor said, grinning slightly, "old age will catch up with me before I reach Earth, and you will be the full-fledged Emperor for the rest of your life."

"But I don't want . . ."

"I know, Javas. But you will be Emperor some day. It is a responsibility you cannot avoid. Five years of training will stand you in good stead."

The Prince sat up straighter in his bed, his face serious, his eyes meeting his father's steadily.

"And son," the Emperor went on, "to be an Emperor—even for five years—you must be master of your own house."

Javas nodded. "I know, Father. I understand. And I will be."

"Good."

Then the Prince's impish smile flitted across his face once again. "But tell me . . . suppose, while you are in transit toward Earth, I decide to move the Imperial Capital elsewhere? What then?"

His father smiled back at him. "I believe I will just have to trust you not to do that."

"You would trust me?" Javas asked.

"I always have."

Javas' smile took on a new pleasure. "Thank you, Father. I will be waiting for you on Earth's Moon. And for the lovely Dr. Montgarde, as well."

Borneer was still livid. "All this uprooting of everything . . . the costs . . . the manpower . . . over an unproven theory!"

"Why is the theory unproven, my friend?" the Emperor asked.

Bomeer's mouth opened and closed like a fish's, but no words came out.

"It is unproven," said the Emperor, "because our scientists have never gone so far before. In fact, the sciences of the Hundred Worlds have not made much progress at all in several generations. Isn't that true, Bomeer?"

"We . . . Sire, we have reached a natural plateau in our understanding of the physical universe. It has happened before. Our era is one of consolidation and practical application of already-acquired knowledge, not new basic breakthroughs."

"Well, this project will force some new thinking and new breakthroughs, I warrant. Certainly we will be forced to recruit new scientists and engineers by the shipload. Perhaps that will be impetus enough to start the climb upward again, eh, Bomeer? I never did like plateaus."

The academician lapsed into silence.

"And I see you, Fain," the Emperor said, "trying to calculate in your head how much of your Fleet strength is going to be wasted on this old man's dream."

"Sire, I had no—"

The Emperor waved him into silence. "No matter. Moving the Capital won't put much of a strain on the Fleet, will it?"

"No, Sire. But this project to save Earth . . ."

"We will have to construct new ships for that, Fain. And we will have to turn to the frontier worlds for those ships." He glanced at Adela. "I believe that the frontier worlds will gladly join the effort to save Earth's Sun. And their treasuries will be enriched by our purchase of thousands of new ships."

"While the Imperial treasury is depleted."

"It's a rich Empire, Fain, it's time we shared some of our wealth with the frontier worlds. A large shipbuilding program will do more to reconcile them with the Empire than anything else we can imagine."

"Sire," said Fain bluntly, "I still think it's madness."

"Yes, I know. Perhaps it is. I only hope that I live long enough to find out, one way or the other."

"Sire," Adela said breathlessly, "you will be reuniting all the worlds of the Empire into a closely knit human community such as we haven't seen in centuries!"

"Perhaps. It would be pleasant to believe so. But for the moment, all I have done is to implement a decision to *try* to save Earth's Sun. It may succeed; it may fail. But we are sons and daughters of planet Earth, and we will not allow our original homeworld to be destroyed without struggling to our uttermost to save it."

He looked at their faces again. They were all waiting for him to continue. *You grow pompous, old man.*

"Very well. You each have several lifetimes of work to accomplish. Get busy, all of you."

Bomeer's and Fain's images winked off immediately. Javas' remained.

"Yes, my son? What is it?"

Javas' ever-present smile was gone. He looked serious, even troubled. "Father . . . I am not going to bring Rihana with me to Earth. She wouldn't want to come, I know—at least, not until all the comforts of the court were established there for her."

The Emperor nodded.

"If I'm to be master of my own house," Javas went on, "it's time we ended this farce of a marriage."

"Very well, son. That is your decision to make. But, for what it's worth, I agree with you."

"Thank you, Father." Javas' image disappeared. For a long moment the Emperor sat gazing thoughtfully at the wall where the holographic images had appeared.

"I believe that I will send you to Earth on Javas' ship. I think he likes you, and it is important that the two of you get along well together."

Adela looked almost shocked. "What do you mean by 'get along well together'?"

The Emperor grinned at her. "That's for the two of you to decide."

"You're scandalous!" she said, but she was smiling too.

He shrugged. "Call it part of the price of victory. You'll like Javas; he's a good man. And I doubt that he's ever met a woman quite like you."

"I don't know what to say."

"You'll need Javas' protection and support, you know. You have defeated all my closest advisors, and that means that they will become your enemies. Powerful enemies. That is also part of the price of your triumph."

"Triumph? I don't feel very triumphant."

"I know," the Emperor said. "Perhaps that's what triumph really is: Not so much glorying in the defeat of your enemies as weariness that they couldn't see what seemed so obvious to you."

Abruptly, Adela moved to him and put her lips to his cheek. "Thank you, Sire."

"Why, thank you, child."

For a moment she stood there, holding his old hands in her tiny young ones.

Then, "I . . . have lots of work to do."

"Of course. We will probably never see each other again. Go and do your work. Do it well."

"I will," she said. "And you?"

He leaned back into the bed. "I've finished my work. I believe that now I can go to sleep, at last." And with a smile he closed his eyes.

FITTING SUITS

Science fiction is a marvelous vehicle for social commentary. Trouble is, most of the decision-makers in our society don't read science fiction. We are constantly falling into predicaments and facing crises that could have been avoided if people paid attention to science-fiction stories written decades earlier.

In a sense, science fiction—at its best—serves as a kind of simulations laboratory for society. Like a scientist setting up a controlled experiment, a writer can set up a social situation, stress one particular facet of that society, and see where the extrapolation leads. The classic example of this is Cyril M. Kornbluth's 1951 novelette "The Marching Morons." Based on the simple notion that ignoramuses have more children than geniuses, Kornbluth's tale chillingly foretold the global population problems that the rest of the world began to notice only a generation later.

"Fitting Suits" is a short-short story that was triggered by a news story I read: A civil servant resigned her government post because a citizen sued her personally for allegedly not performing her job properly. That led me to thinking. Which led me to writing.

Always think before you write.

HISTORY, AS WE KNOW, is sometimes made by the unlikeliest of persons. Take Carter C. Carter, for example. All he wanted was immortality. Instead he created paradise.

All of you are too young to remember the America of the early twenty-first century, a democracy of the lawyers, by the lawyers, for the lawyers. It was impossible to sneeze in the privacy of your own home without someone suing you as a health menace. Inevitably the lawyers would also sue the home builder for failure to make the structure virus-proof. And the corporations that manufactured your air-conditioning system, wallpaper, carpeting, and facial tissues. To say nothing of the people who sold you your pet dog, cat, and/or goldfish.

It got so bad that eventually a public servant resigned her sinecure because of a lawsuit. A social worker employed by a moderate-sized midwestern city was slapped with a personal liability suit for alleged failure to do her job properly. She had advised an unemployed teenaged mother to try to find a job to support herself, since her welfare benefits were running out. Instead, the teenager went to a lawyer and sued the social worker for failure to find her more money.

Rather than face a lawsuit that would have ruined her financially, whether she lost or won, the social worker resigned her position, left the state, and took up a new career. She entered law school. The teenager lived for years off the generous verdict awarded her by a jury of equally unemployed men and women.

This was the America in which Carter C. Carter lived. We have much to thank him for.

He was, of course, totally unaware that he would change the course of history. He had no interest even in the juridical malaise of his time. All he wanted to do was to avoid dying.

Carter C. Carter had an inoperable case of cancer. "The Big C," it was called in those days. So he turned to another "C," cryonics, as a way to avoid permanent death. When declared clinically dead by a complaisant doctor (a close friend since childhood), Carter C. Carter had himself immersed in a canister of liquid nitrogen to await the happy day when medical science could revive him, cure him, and set him out in society once more, healthily alive.

He left his life savings, a meager $100,000 (it was worth more in those days) in a trust fund to provide for his maintenance while frozen. It would also provide a nest egg once he was awakened. He was banking heavily on compound interest.

His insurance company, however, refused to pay off on his policy, on the grounds that Carter was not finally dead. Mrs. Carter, whose sole inheritance from her husband was his $500,000 life insurance policy, promptly sued the insurance company. The insurance company's lawyers, in turn, sued the Carter estate on the grounds that he was trying to cheat, not death, but the insurance company.

After several years of legal maneuvering the suit came to court. It was decided in favor of the insurance company. Mrs. Carter promptly sued the judge and each individual member of the jury for personal liability on the grounds that they had "willfully and deliberately denied her her legal rights." And caused her intense pain and suffering while doing so.

The judge, near retirement age, had a vision of his pension being eaten up by legal proceedings. He quit the bench and signed a public apology to Mrs. Carter in return for her dropping the suit against him. The jurors, none of them wealthy, quickly settled out of court. The insurance company did likewise, in advance of having its entire board of directors sued.

Mrs. Carter's lawyers, unsatisfied with their share of the loot, looked for bigger game. Fueled by Carter's modest nest egg (Mrs. C. would not let them touch her own money), they began suing members of the National Institutes of Health and the Justice Department, on the grounds that they had failed to provide proper medical and legal grounds for judging the rights of the cryonically undead.

A new fad erupted. Suddenly taxpayers were suing local bureaucrats for personal liability over failure to fill potholes in their streets. In one state the governor and entire legislature were sued for raising taxes to cover a budget imbalance. In another, the state environmental protection agency was sued for failing to regulate the pollution emissions of diesel trucks. The Secretary of Defense was sued simultaneously for invading Mexico and for failing to conquer Mexico. Politicians everywhere were sued for not fulfilling their campaign promises.

Bureaucrats resigned or retired rather than spend the rest of their lives and fortunes in court. Politicians thought twice, thrice, and even more about promises they had no intention of keeping.

A crisis struck the civil service at local, state, and federal levels. Faced with the threat of personal liability suits over alleged failures to perform their jobs, government employees were quitting those jobs faster than they could be replaced. It did not really matter if they won or lost their suits, the time and cost of defending themselves were more than they could bear.

Several states tried to pass laws exempting civil servants from personal liability suits. Each legislator proposing or supporting such a law was sued black and blue. The idea died long before it reached the Supreme Court—which was down to five members at the time, since four justices had hastily retired.

Faced with empty desks and unfilled job openings, government departments reluctantly turned to computers to fill the roles that human bureaucrats had abandoned.

"At least they can't sue a computer," said one department head, wise in the ways of bureaucracies.

To everyone's surprise, the computers worked better than the humans they replaced. Thanks to their programming, they were industrious, unfailingly polite, and blindingly fast. And much cheaper than people. They worked all hours of the night and day, even weekends. They never took coffee breaks or asked for raises. They transferred information with electrical alacrity, and eventually with the speed of light, when photonics began to replace electronics.

Computers' programs could easily be changed to accommodate new facts, something that had been impossible with human bureaucrats.

Taxpayers *liked* the computers. The usual gloom and oppressive atmosphere of government offices was replaced by bright humming efficiency. Citizens could even handle most problems from their homes, with their personal computers talking to the government's computers to settle problems swiftly and neatly.

In the meantime, with fewer and fewer liability suits to sustain them, lawyers began to sue one another in a frenzy that eventually came to be called "the time of great dying." Within a century the last lawyer in the U.S. was replaced by a computer and sent into a richly deserved retirement in Death Valley.

By the time Carter C. Carter was finally revived from his cryonic sleep, decision-making computers had replaced humans at all levels of government except the very top posts, where policy was decided by elected officials. All permanent government "employees" had electrons and/or photons flowing through them instead of blood.

Carter, however, was dismayed to learn that his modest nest egg had long since been devoured by rapacious lawyers, and that—thanks to compound interest—he *owed* the estates of his erstwhile legal representatives a total of some six million dollars.

The shock stopped his heart. Since he had not had time to make out a new will, he was declared finally dead and cremated.

But his memory lives on. The happy and efficient society in which we live, unthreatened by the personal liability suits that ruined many an earlier life, is directly attributable to that unlikely hero of heroes, Carter C. Carter.

A SMALL KINDNESS

To this day, I'm not quite certain of how this story originated. I've been to Athens, and found it a big, noisy, dirty city fouled with terrible automobile pollution—and centered on the awe-inspiring Acropolis.

The world's most beautiful building, the Parthenon, is truly a symbol of what is best and what is worst in us. Of its beauty, its grace, its simple grandeur I can add nothing to the paeans that have been sung by so many others. But over the millennia, the dark forces of human nature have almost destroyed the Parthenon. It has been blasted by cannon fire, defaced by conquerors and tourists, and now is being eaten away by the acidic outpourings of automobile exhausts.

A pessimist would say, with justice, that this is a case where human technology is obviously working against the human spirit. An optimist would say that since we recognize the problem, we ought to take steps to solve it.

In a way, that's what "A Small Kindness" is about—I think.

JEREMY KEATING HATED THE RAIN. Athens was a dismal enough assignment, but in the windswept rainy night it was cold and black and dangerous.

Everyone pictures Athens in the sunshine, he thought. The

Acropolis, the gleaming ancient temples. They don't see the filthy modern city with its endless streams of automobiles spewing out so much pollution that the marble statues are being eaten away and the ancient monuments are in danger of crumbling.

Huddled inside his trenchcoat, Keating stood in the shadows of a deep doorway across the street from the taverna where his target was eating a relaxed and leisurely dinner—his last, if things went the way Keating planned.

He stood as far back in the doorway as he could, pressed against the cold stones of the building, both to remain unseen in the shadows and to keep the cold rain off himself. Rain or no, the automobile traffic still clogged Filellinon Boulevard, cars inching by bumper to bumper, honking their horns, squealing on the slickened paving. The worst traffic in the world, night and day. A million and a half Greeks, all in cars, all the time. They drove the way they lived— argumentatively.

The man dining across the boulevard in the warm, brightly-lit taverna was Kabete Rungawa, of the Tanzanian delegation to the World Government conference. "The Black Saint of the Third World," he was called. The most revered man since Gandhi. Keating smiled grimly to himself. According to his acquaintances in the Vatican, a man had to be dead before he could be proclaimed a saint.

Keating was a tall man, an inch over six feet. He had the lean, graceful body of a trained athlete, and it had taken him years of constant painful work to acquire it. The earlier part of his adult life he had spent behind a desk or at embassy parties, like so many other Foreign Service career officers. But that had been a lifetime ago, when he was a minor cog in the Department of State's global machine. When he was a husband and father.

His wife had been killed in the rioting in Tunis, part of the carefully-orchestrated Third World upheaval that had forced the new World Government down the throats of the white, industrialized nations. His son had died of typhus in the besieged embassy, when they were unable to get medical supplies because the U. S. government could not decide whether it should negotiate with the radicals or send in the Marines.

In the end, they negotiated. But by then it was too late. So now Keating served as a roving attaché to U.S. embassies or consulates, serving where his special talents were needed. He had found those talents in the depths of his agony, his despair, his hatred.

Outwardly he was still a minor diplomatic functionary, an interesting dinner companion, a quietly handsome man with brooding eyes who seemed both unattached and unavailable. That made him a magnetic lure for a certain type of woman, a challenge they could not resist. A few of them had gotten close enough to him to trace the hairline scar across his abdomen, all that remained of the surgery he had needed after his first assignment, in Indonesia. After that particular horror, he had never been surprised or injured again.

With an adamant shake of his head, Keating forced himself to concentrate on the job at hand. The damp cold was seeping into him. His feet were already soaked. The cars still crawled along the rainy boulevard, honking impatiently. The noise was making him irritable, jumpy.

"Terminate with extreme prejudice," his boss had told him, that sunny afternoon in Virginia. "Do you understand what that means?"

Sitting in the deep leather chair in front of the section chief's broad walnut desk, Keating nodded. "I may be new to this part of the department, but I've been around. It means to do to Rungawa what the Indonesians tried to do to me."

No one ever used the words *kill* or *assassinate* in these cheerfully lit offices. The men behind the desks, in their pinstripe suits, dealt with computer printouts and satellite photographs and euphemisms. Messy, frightening things like blood were never mentioned here.

The section chief steepled his fingers and gave Keating a long, thoughtful stare. He was a distinguished-looking man with silver hair and smoothly tanned skin. He might be the board chairman you meet at the country club, or the type of well-bred gentry who spends the summer racing yachts.

"Any questions, Jeremy?"

Keating shifted slightly in his chair. "Why Rungawa?"

The section chief made a little smile. "Do you like having the World Government order us around, demand that we disband our armed forces, tax us until we're as poor as the Third World?"

Keating felt emotions burst into flame inside his guts. All the pain of his wife's death, of his son's lingering agony, of his hatred for the gloating ignorant sadistic petty tyrants who had killed them—all erupted in a volcanic tide of lava within him. But he clamped down on his bodily responses, used every ounce of training and willpower at his command to force his voice to remain calm. One thing he had learned about this organization, and about this section chief in particular: never let anyone know where you are vulnerable.

"I've got no great admiration for the World Government," he said.

The section chief's basilisk smile vanished. There was no need to appear friendly to this man. He was an employee, a tool. Despite his attempt to hide his emotions, it was obvious that all Keating lived for was to avenge his wife and child; it would get him killed, eventually, but for now his thirst for vengeance was a valuable handle for manipulating the man.

"Rungawa is the key to everything," the section chief said, leaning back in his tall swivel chair and rocking slightly.

Keating knew that the World Government, still less than five years old, was meeting in Athens to plan a global economic program. Rungawa would head the Tanzanian delegation.

"The World Government is taking special pains to destroy the United States," the section chief said, as calmly as he might announce a tennis score. "Washington was forced to accept the World Government, and the people went along with the idea because they thought it would put an end to the threat of nuclear war. Well, it's done that—at the cost of taxing our economy for every unemployed black, brown, and yellow man, woman, and child in the entire world."

"And Rungawa?" Keating repeated.

The section chief leaned forward, pressed his palms on his desktop and lowered his voice. "We can't back out of the World Government, for any number of reasons. But we can—with the aid of certain other Western nations—we can take control of it, if we're able to break up the solid voting bloc of the Third World nations."

"Would the Russians—"

"We can make an accommodation with the Russians," the section chief said impatiently, waving one hand in the air. "Nobody wants to go back to the old cold-war confrontations. It's the Third World that's got to be brought to terms."

"By eliminating Rungawa."

"Exactly! He's the glue that holds their bloc together. 'The Black Saint.' They practically worship him. Eliminate him and they'll fall back into their old tangle of bickering selfish politicians, just as OPEC broke up once the oil glut started."

It had all seemed so simple back there in that comfortable sunny office. Terminate Rungawa and then set about taking the leadership of the World Government. Fix up the damage done by the Third World's jealous greed. Get the world's economy back on the right track again.

But here in the rainy black night of Athens, Keating knew it was not that simple at all. His left hand gripped the dart gun in his trench coat pocket. There was enough poison in each dart to kill a man instantly and leave no trace for a coroner to find. The darts themselves dissolved on contact with the air within three minutes. The perfect murder weapon.

Squinting through the rain, Keating saw through the taverna's big plate-glass window that Rungawa was getting up from his table, preparing to leave the restaurant.

Terminate Rungawa. That was his mission. Kill him and make it look as if he'd had a heart attack. It should be easy enough. One old man, walking alone down the boulevard to his hotel. "The Black Saint" never used bodyguards. He was old enough for a heart attack to be beyond suspicion.

But it was not going to be that easy, Keating saw. Rungawa came out of the tavema accompanied by three younger men. And he did not turn toward his hotel. Instead, he started walking down the boulevard in the opposite direction, toward the narrow tangled streets of the most ancient part of the city, walking toward the Acropolis. In the rain. Walking.

Frowning with puzzled aggravation, Keating stepped out of the doorway and into the pelting rain. It was icy cold. He pulled up his collar and tugged his hat down lower. He hated the rain. Maybe the old bastard will catch pneumonia and die naturally, he thought angrily.

As he started across the boulevard a car splashed by, horn bleating, soaking his trousers. Keating jumped back just in time to avoid being hit. The driver's furious face, framed by the rain-streaked car window, glared at him as the auto swept past. Swearing methodically under his breath, Keating found another break in the traffic and sprinted across the boulevard, trying to avoid the puddles even though his feet were already wet through.

He stayed well behind Rungawa and his three companions, glad that they were walking instead of driving, miserable to be out in the chilling rain. As far as he could tell, all three of Rungawa's companions were black, young enough and big enough to be bodyguards. That complicated matters. Had someone warned Rungawa? Was there a leak in the department's operation?

With Keating trailing behind, the old man threaded the ancient winding streets that huddled around the jutting rock of the Acropolis. The four blacks walked around the ancient citadel, striding purposefully, as if they had to be at an exact place at a precise time. Keating had to stay well behind them because the traffic along Theonas Avenue was much thinner, and pedestrians, in this rain, were nowhere in sight except for his quarry. It was quieter here, along the shoulder of the great cliff. The usual nightly *son et lumière* show had been cancelled because of the rain; even the floodlights around the Parthenon and the other temples had been turned off.

For a few minutes Keating wondered if Rungawa was going to the Agora instead, but no, the old man and his friends turned in at the gate to the Acropolis, the Sacred Way of the ancient Athenians.

It was difficult to see through the rain, especially at this distance. Crouching low behind shrubbery, Keating fumbled in his trench coat pocket until he found the miniature "camera" he had brought with him. Among other things, it was an infrared snooperscope. Even in the darkness and rain, he could see the four men as they stopped at the main gate. Their figures looked ghostly gray and eerie against a flickering dark background.

They stopped for a few moments while one of them opened the gate that was usually locked and guarded. Keating was more impressed than surprised. They had access to everything they wanted. But why do they want to go up to the Parthenon on a rainy wintry night? And how can I make Rungawa's death look natural if I have to fight my way past three bodyguards?

The second question resolved itself almost as soon as Keating asked it. Rungawa left his companions at the gate and started up the steep, rain-slickened marble stairs by himself.

"A man that age, in this weather, could have a heart attack just from climbing those stairs," Keating whispered to himself. But he knew that he could not rely on chance.

He had never liked climbing. Although he felt completely safe and comfortable in a jet plane and had even made parachute jumps calmly, climbing up the slippery rock face of the cliff was something that Keating dreaded. But he did it, nevertheless. It was not as difficult as he had feared. Others had scaled the Acropolis, over the thirty-some centuries since the Greeks had first arrived at it. Keating clambered and scrambled over the rocks, crawling at first on all fours while the cold rain spattered in his face. Then he found a narrow trail. It was steep and slippery, but his soft-soled shoes, required for stealth, gripped the rock well enough.

He reached the top of the flat-surfaced cliff in a broad open area. To his right was the Propylaea and the little temple of Athene Nike. To his left, the Erechtheum, with its Caryatids patiently holding up the roof as they had for twenty-five hundred years. The marble maidens stared blindly at Keating. He glanced at them, then looked across the width of the clifftop to the half-ruined Parthenon, the most beautiful building on Earth, a monument both to man's creative genius and his destructive folly.

The rain had slackened, but the night was still as dark as the deepest pit of hell. Keating brought the snooperscope up to his eyes again and scanned from left to right.

And there stood Rungawa! Directly in front of the Parthenon, standing there with his arms upraised, as if praying.

Too far away for the dart gun, Keating knew. For some reason, his hands started to shake. Slowly, struggling for absolute self-control, Keating put the "camera" back into his trench coat and took out the pistol. He rose to his feet and began walking toward Rungawa with swift but unhurried, measured strides.

The old man's back was to him. All you have to do, Keating told himself, is to get within a few feet, pop the dart into his neck, and then wait a couple of minutes to make certain the dart dissolves. Then go down the way you came and back to the *pensione* for a hot bath and a bracer of cognac.

As he came to within ten feet of Rungawa he raised the dart gun. It worked on air pressure, practically noiseless. No need to cock it. Five feet. He could see the nails on Rungawa's upraised hands, the pinkish palms contrasting with the black skin of the fingers and the backs of his hands. Three feet. Rungawa's suit was perfectly fitted to him, the sleeves creased carefully. Dry. He was wearing only a business suit, and it was untouched by the rain, as well-creased and unwrinkled as if it had just come out of the store.

"Not yet, Mr. Keating," said the old man, without turning to look at Jeremy. "We have a few things to talk about before you kill me."

Keating froze. He could not move his arm. It stood ramrod straight from his left shoulder, the tiny dart gun in his fist a mere two feet from Rungawa's bare neck. But he could not pull the trigger. His fingers would not obey the commands of his mind.

Rungawa turned toward him, smiling, and stroked his chin thoughtfully for a moment.

"You may put the gun down now, Mr. Keating."

Jeremy's arm dropped to his side. His mouth sagged open; his heart thundered in his ears. He wanted to run away, but his legs were like the marble of the statues that watched them.

"Forgive me," said Rungawa. "I should not leave you out in the rain like that."

The rain stopped pelting Jeremy. He felt a gentle warmth enveloping him, as if he were standing next to a welcoming fireplace. The two men stood under a cone of invisible protection. Jeremy could see the raindrops spattering on the stony ground not more than a foot away.

"A small trick. Please don't be alarmed." Rungawa's voice was a deep rumbling bass, like the voice a lion would have if it could speak in human tongue.

Jeremy stared into the black man's eyes and saw no danger in them, no hatred or violence; only a patient amusement at his own consternation. No, more: a tolerance of human failings, a hope for human achievement, an *understanding* born of centuries of toil and pain and striving.

"Who are you?" Jeremy asked in a frightened whisper.

Rungawa smiled, and it was like sunlight breaking through he storm clouds. "Ah, Mr. Keating, you are as intelligent as we had hoped. You cut straight to the heart of the matter."

"You knew I was following you. You set up this meeting."

"Yes. Yes, quite true. Melodramatic of me, I admit. But would you have joined me at dinner if I had sent one of my aides across the street to invite you? I think not."

It's all crazy, Jeremy thought. I must be dreaming this.

"No, Mr. Keating. It is not a dream."

An electric jolt flamed through Jeremy. Jesus Christ. he can read my mind!

"Of course I can," Rungawa said gently, smiling, the way doctor tells a child that the needle will hurt only for an instant. "How else would I know that you were stalking me?"

Jeremy's mouth went utterly dry. His voice cracked and failed him. If he had been able to move his legs he would have fled like a chimpanzee confronted by a leopard.

"Please, do not be afraid, Mr. Keating. Fear is an impediment to understanding. If we had wanted to kill you, it would have been most convenient to let you slip while you were climbing up here."

"What . . ." Jeremy had to swallow and lick his lips before he could ask, "Just who are you?"

"I am a messenger, Mr. Keating. Like you, I am merely a tool of my superiors. When I was assigned to this task, I thought it appropriate to make my home base in Tanzania." The old man's smile returned, and a hint of self-satisfaction glowed in his eyes. "After all, Tanzania is where the earliest human tribes once lived. What more appropriate place for me to—um, shall we say, *associate* myself with the human race?"

"Associate . . . with the human race." Jeremy felt breathless, weak. His voice was hollow.

"I am not a human being, Mr. Keating. I come from a far-distant world, a world that is nothing like this one."

"No . . . that can't . . ."

Rungawa's smile slowly faded. "Some of your people call me a saint. Actually, compared to your species, I am a god."

Jeremy stared at him, stared into his deep black eyes, and saw eternity in them, whirlpools of galaxies spinning majestically in infinite depths of space, stars exploding and evolving, worlds created out of dust.

He heard his voice, weak and childlike, say, "But you look human."

"Of course! Completely human. Even to your X-ray machines."

An alien. Jeremy's mind reeled. An extraterrestrial. With a sense of humor.

"Why not? Is not humor part of the human psyche? The

intelligences who created me made me much more than human, but I have every human attribute—except one. I have no need for vengeance, Mr. Keating."

"Vengeance," Jeremy echoed.

"Yes. A destructive trait. It clouds the perceptions. It is an obstacle in the path of survival."

Jeremy took a deep breath, tried to pull himself together. "You expect me to believe all this?"

"I can see that you do, Mr. Keating. I can see that you now realize that not *all* the UFO stories have been hoaxes. We have never harmed any of your people, but we did require specimens for careful analysis."

"Why?"

"To help you find the correct path to survival. Your species is on the edge of a precipice. It is our duty to help you avoid extinction, if we—"

"Your duty?"

"Of course. Do not your best people feel an obligation to save other species from extinction? Have not these human beings risked their fortunes and their very lives to protect creatures such as the whale and the seal from slaughter?"

Jeremy almost laughed. "You mean you're from some interstellar Greenpeace project?"

"It is much more complex than that," Rungawa said. "We are not merely trying to protect you from a predator, or from an ecological danger. You human beings are your own worst enemy. We must protect you from yourselves—without your knowing it."

Before Jeremy could reply, Rungawa went on, "It would be easy for us to create a million creatures like myself and to land on your planet in great, shining ships and give you all the answers you need for survival. Fusion energy? A toy. World peace? Easily accomplished. Quadruple your global food production? Double your intelligence? Make you immune to every disease? All this we can do."

"Then why . . . ?" Jeremy hesitated, thinking. "If you did all that for us, it would ruin us, wouldn't it?"

Rungawa beamed at him. "Ah, you truly understand the problem! Yes, it would destroy your species, just as your Europeans destroyed the cultures of the Americas and Polynesia. Your anthropologists are wrong. There *are* superior cultures and inferior ones. A superior culture always crushes an inferior, even if it has no intention of doing so."

In the back of his mind, Jeremy realized that he had control of his legs again. He flexed the fingers of his left hand slightly, even the index finger that still curled around the trigger of the dart gun. He could move them at will once more.

"What you're saying," he made conversation, "is that if you landed here and gave us everything we want, our culture would be destroyed."

"Yes," Rungawa agreed. "Just as surely as you whites destroyed the black and brown cultures of the world. We have no desire to do that to you."

"So you're trying to lead us to the point where we can solve our own problems."

"Precisely so, Mr. Keating."

"That's why you've started this World Government," Keating said, his hand tightening on the gun.

"You started the World Government yourselves," Rungawa corrected. "We merely encouraged you, here and there."

"Like the riots in Tunis and a hundred other places."

"We did not encourage that."

"But you didn't prevent them, either, did you?"

"No. We did not."

Shifting his weight slightly to the balls of his feet, Keating said, "Without you the World Government will collapse."

The old man shook his head. "No, that is not true. Despite what your superiors believe, the World Government will endure even the death of 'the Black Saint.'"

"Are you sure?" Keating raised the gun to the black man's eye level. "Are you absolutely certain?"

Rungawa did not blink. His voice became sad as he answered, "Would I have relaxed my control of your limbs if I were not certain?"

Keating hesitated, but held the gun rock-steady.

"You are the test, Mr. Keating. You are the key to your species' future. We know how your wife and son died. Even though we were not directly responsible, we regret their deaths. And the deaths of all the others. They were unavoidable losses."

"Statistics," Keating spat. "Numbers on a list."

"Never! Each of them was an individual whom *we* knew much

better than you could, and we regretted each loss of life as much as you do yourself. Perhaps more, because we understand what each of those individuals could have accomplished, had they lived."

"But you let them die."

"It was unavoidable, I say. Now the question is, Can you rise above your own personal tragedy, for the good of your fellow humans? Or will you take vengeance upon me and see your species destroy itself?"

"You just said the World Government will survive your death."

"And it will. But it will change. It will become a world dictatorship, in time. It will smother your progress. Your species will die out in an agony of overpopulation, starvation, disease and terrorism. You do not need nuclear bombs to kill yourselves. You can manage it quite well enough merely by producing too many babies."

"Our alternative is to let your people direct us, to become sheep without even knowing it, to jump to your tune."

"No!" Rungawa's deep voice boomed. "The alternative is to become adults. You are adolescents now. We offer you the chance to grow up and stand on your own feet."

"How can I believe that?" Keating demanded.

The old man's smile showed warmth. "The adolescent always distrusts the parent. That is the painful truth, is it not?"

"You have an answer for everything, don't you?"

"Everything, perhaps, except you. You are the key to your species' future, Mr. Keating. If you can accept what I have told you, and allow us to work with you despite all your inner thirst for vengeance, then the human species will have a chance to survive."

Keating moved his hand a bare centimeter to the left and squeezed the gun's trigger. The dart shot out with a hardly audible puff of compressed air and whizzed past Rungawa's ear. The old man did not flinch.

"You can kill me if you want to," he said to Keating. "That is your decision to make."

"I don't believe you," Jeremy said. "I can't believe you! It's too much, it's too incredible. You can't expect a man to accept everything you've just told me—not all at once!"

"We do expect it," Rungawa said softly. "We expect that and more. We want you working with us, not against us."

Jeremy felt as if his guts were being torn apart. "Work with you?" he screamed. "With the people who murdered my wife and son?"

"There are other children in the world. Do not deny them their birthright. Do not foreclose their future."

"You bastard!" Jeremy seethed. "You don't miss a trick, do you?"

"It all depends on you, Mr. Keating. You are our test case. What you do now will decide the future of the human species."

A thousand emotions raged through Jeremy. He saw Joanna being torn apart by the mob and Jerry in his cot screaming with fever, flames and death everywhere, the filth and poverty of Jakarta and the vicious smile of the interrogator as he sharpened his razor.

He's lying, Jeremy's mind shouted at him. He's got to be lying. All this is some clever set of tricks. It can't be true. It can't be!

In a sudden paroxysm of rage and terror and frustration Jeremy hurled the gun high into the rain-filled night, turned abruptly and walked away from Rungawa. He did not look back, but he knew the old man was smiling at him.

It's a trick, he kept telling himself. A goddamned trick. He knew damned well I couldn't kill him in cold blood, with him standing there looking at me with those damned sad eyes of his. Shoot an old man in the face. I just couldn't do it. All he had to do was keep me talking long enough to lose my nerve. Goddamned clever black man. Must be how he lived to get so old.

Keating stamped down the marble steps of the Sacred Way, pushed past the three raincoated guards who had accompanied Rungawa, and walked alone and miserable back to the *pensione*.

How the hell am I going to explain this back at headquarters? I'll have to resign, tell them that I'm not cut out to be an assassin.

They'll never believe that. Maybe I could get a transfer, get back into the political section, join the Peace Corps, anything!

He was still furious with himself when he reached the *pensione*. Still shaking his head, angry that he had let the old man talk him out of his assigned mission. Some form of hypnosis, Keating thought. He must have been a medicine man or a voodoo priest when he was younger.

He pushed through the glassed front door of the *pensione*, muttering to himself. "You let him trick you. You let that old black man hoodwink you."

The room clerk roused himself from his slumber and got up to reach Jeremy's room key from the rack behind the desk. He was a short, sturdily-built Greek, the kind who would have faced the Persians at Marathon.

"You must have run very fast," he said to Keating in heavily accented English.

"Huh? What? Why do you say that?"

The clerk grinned, revealing tobacco-stained teeth. "You did not get wet."

Keating looked at the sleeve of his trench coat. It was perfectly dry. The whole coat was as clean and dry as if it had just come from a pressing. His feet were dry; his shoes and trousers and hat were dry.

He turned and looked out the front window. The rain was coming down harder than ever, a torrent of water.

"You run so fast you go between raindrops, eh?" The clerk laughed at his own joke.

Jeremy's knees nearly buckled. He leaned against the desk. "Yeah. Something like that."

The clerk, still grinning, handed him his room key. Jeremy gathered his strength and headed for the stairs, his head spinning.

As he went up the first flight, he heard a voice, even though he was quite alone on the carpeted stairs.

"A small kindness, Mr. Keating," said Rungawa, inside his mind. "I thought it would have been a shame to make you get wet all over again. A small kindness. There will be more to come."

Keating could hear Rungawa chuckling as he walked alone up the stairs. By the time he reached his room, he was grinning himself.

BORN AGAIN

Assuming the UFO believers are right, and we are being infiltrated by a generally benign race of intelligent extraterrestrials, why have they come to Earth and what do they want of us?

In "A Small Kindness," we saw the first meeting between Jeremy Keating and the alien Black Saint of the Third World, Kabete Rungawa.

Now we see the result of that meeting, and how it changes Keating's life. Changes it? In a literal sense, it ends his life.

Which leads to the title of the story.

THE RESTAURANT'S SIGN, out on the roadside, said *Gracious Country Dining.* There was no indication that just across the Leesburg Pike the gray unmarked headquarters of the Central Intelligence Agency lay screened behind the beautifully wooded Virginia hills.

Jeremy Keating sat by force of old habit with his back to the wall. The restaurant was almost empty, and even if it had been bursting with customers, they would all have been agency people—almost. It was the *almost* that would have worried him in the old days.

Keating looked tense, expectant, a trimly built six-footer in his late thirties, hair still dark, stomach still flat, wearing the same kind of conservative bluish-gray three-piece suit that served almost as a uniform for agency men when they were safely home.

Only someone who had known him over the past five years would realize that the pain and the sullen, smoldering anger that had once lit his eyes were gone now. In their place was something else, equally intense but lacking the hate that had once fueled the flames within him. Keating himself did not fully understand what was happening to him. Part of what he felt now was excitement, a fluttering, almost giddy anticipation. But there was fear inside him, too, churning in his guts.

It had been easy to get into the agency; it would not be so easy getting out.

He was halfway finished with his fruit juice when Jason Lyle entered the quiet dining room and threaded his way through the empty tables toward Keating. Although he had never been a field agent, Lyle moved cautiously, walking on the balls of his feet, almost on tiptoe. Watching him, Keating thought that there must be just as many booby traps in the corridors of bureaucratic power as there are in the field. You don't get to be section chief by bulling blindly into trouble.

Keating rose as Lyle came to his table and extended his hand. They exchanged meaningless greetings, smiling at each other and commenting on the unbelievably warm weather, predicted an early spring and lots of sunshine, a good sailing season.

When their waitress came, Lyle ordered a vodka martini; Keating asked for another glass of grapefruit juice. The last time Keating had seen Jason Lyle, the section chief had ordered him to commit a murder. *Terminate with extreme prejudice* was the term used. Keating had received such orders, and obeyed them willingly, half a dozen times over the previous four years. Until this last one, a few weeks ago.

Now Lyle sat across the small restaurant table, in this ersatz rustic dining room with its phony log walls and gingham tablecloths, and gave Keating the same measured smile he had used all those other times. But Lyle's eyes were wary, probing, trying to see what had changed in Keating.

Lyle was handsome in a country-club, old-money way: thick silver hair impeccably coiffed, his chiseled features tanned and taut from years of tennis and sailing. He was vain enough to wear contact lenses instead of bifocals, and tough enough to order death for his own agents, once he thought they were dangerous to the organization—or to himself.

Keating listened to the banalities and let his gaze slide from Lyle to the nearby windows where the bright Virginia sunshine was pouring in. He knew that Lyle had carefully reviewed all the medical reports, all the debriefing sessions and psychiatric examinations that he had undergone in the past three weeks.

They had wrung his brain dry with their armory of drugs and electronics. But there was one fact Keating had kept from them, simply because they had never in their deepest probes thought to ask the question. One simple fact that had turned Keating's life upside down: the man that he had been ordered to assassinate was not a human being. He had not been born on Earth.

Keating nodded at the right places in Lyle's monologue and volunteered nothing. The waitress took their lunch order, went away, and came back eventually with their food.

Finally, as he picked up his fork and stared down at what the menu had promised as sliced Virginia ham, Lyle asked as casually as a snake gliding across a meadow:

"So tell me, Jeremy, just what happened out there in Athens?"

Keating knew that the answers he gave over this luncheon would determine whether he lived or died.

"I got a vision of a different world, Jason," he answered honestly. "I'm through with killing. I want out."

Lyle's eyes flashed, whether at Keating's use of his first name or his intended resignation or his mention of a vision, it was impossible to tell.

"It's not that simple, you know," he said.

"I know." And Keating did. Lyle had to satisfy himself that this highly trained agent had not been turned around by the Russians. Or, worse still, by the fledgling World Government.

"Why?" Lyle asked mildly. "Why do you want to quit?"

Keating closed his eyes for a moment, trying to decide on the words he must use. Each syllable must be chosen with scrupulous care. His life hung in the balance.

But in that momentary darkness, alone with only his own inner vision, Keating saw the man he had been, the life he had led. The years as an ordinary Foreign Service officer, a very minor cog in the giant bureaucratic machinery of the Department of State, moving from one embassy to another every two years. He saw

Joanna, young and loving and alive, laughing with him on the bank of the Seine, dancing with him on the roof garden of the hotel that steaming-hot Fourth of July in Delhi, smiling at him through her exhaustion as she lay in the hospital bed with their newborn son at her breast.

And he saw her being torn apart by the raging mob attacking the embassy at Tunis. While Qaddafi's soldiers stood aside and watched, grinning. Saw his infant son screaming his life away as typhus swept the besieged embassy. Saw himself giving his own life, his body and mind and soul—gladly—to avenge their deaths. The training, where his anger and hatred had been honed to a cutting edge. The missions to track and kill the kind of men whom he blamed for the murder of his wife and child. Missions that always began in Lyle's office, in the calm, climate-controlled sanctuary of the section chief, and his measured reptilian smile.

Keating opened his eyes. "You let them take me, that first mission, didn't you?"

The admission was clear on Lyle's surprised face. "What are you talking about?"

"My first mission for you, the job in Jakarta. You allowed them to find me, didn't you? You tipped them off. Those interrogation sessions, that slimy little colonel of theirs with his razor—he was the final edge on my training, wasn't he?"

"That's crazy," Lyle snapped. "We shot our way in there and saved your butt, didn't we?"

Keating nodded. "At the proper moment."

"That was years ago."

But I still carry the scars, Keating replied silently. *They still burn.*

Lyle fluttered a hand in the air, as if waving away the past. Leaning forward across the table slightly, he said in a lowered voice, "I need to know, Jeremy. What happened to you in Athens? Why do you suddenly want to quit?"

Keating did not close his eyes again. He had seen enough of the past, and the shame of it seethed inside him. "Let's just say that I experienced a religious conversion."

"A *what?*"

"I've been reborn." Keating smiled, realizing the aptness of it. "I have renounced my old life."

For the first time in the years Keating had known the man, Lyle made no attempt to mask his feelings.

"Born again? Fat chance! I've heard a lot of strange stories in my time, but this one—"

"Is the truth."

"Just tell me what happened to you in Athens," Lyle insisted. "I've got to know. It's important to both of us."

"So that you can decide whether to terminate me?"

"We don't do that," Lyle snapped.

"No, of course not. But I just might happen to have a car accident, or take an overdose of something."

Lyle glowered at him. "You hold a lot of very sensitive information inside your skull, Jeremy. We have to protect you."

"And yourself. It wouldn't look good on your record to have a trained assassin going over to the other side."

The section chief actually smiled with relief, and Keating could see that Lyle was grateful that the subject had finally been brought out into the open.

"Have you, Jeremy?" he asked in a whisper. "Gone over?"

"Which side would I go to? The Russians? But we're working under the table with them these days, aren't we? Neither the Russians nor the Americans want the World Government running things. We're both trying to bring the World Government down before it gets a firm control over us."

"The World Government," Lyle said slowly, testingly.

Keating shook his head. "If I admit to that, I'm a dead man, and we both know it. I'm not that foolish, Jason."

Lyle said nothing, but looked unconvinced.

"There's the Third World," Keating went on. "They love the World Government, with its one-nation, one-vote system. They're using the World Government to bleed the rich nations white; you told me that yourself. But then, the rich nations are almost all white to begin with, aren't they?"

"This is no time for jokes!"

"A sense of humor helps, Jason. Believe me. But you can't picture me working for a bunch of blacks and browns and yellows, can you? That's so completely against your inner convictions that you can't imagine a fellow WASP going over to the Third World."

"Perhaps I can imagine it, at that," Lyle said, with dawning apprehension lighting his eyes. "Your assignment was to terminate Rungawa."

"Ah, yes," Keating said. "Kabete Rungawa. The Black Saint of the Third World. The spiritual leader of the poor nations."

Lyle almost spat. "That old bastard is as spiritual as . . ."

"As Gandhi," Keating said, sudden steel in his voice. "And as powerful politically. That's why you want him terminated."

Lyle stared at Keating for long, silent moments before saying, "Rungawa. *He* turned you around! Jesus Christ, you fell for that black bastard's mealy-mouthed propaganda line."

"Yes, I did," said Keating. "Not in the way you're thinking, though. Rungawa is quite a person. He made me see that murdering him would be a horrible mistake. He opened my eyes."

"You admit it?"

"Why not? It's already in the debriefing reports, isn't it?"

The glitter in Lyle's cold blue eyes told Keating that it was.

"But here's something that isn't in the reports, Jason. Something so utterly fantastic that you won't believe it."

The section chief leaned forward in anticipation. Hearing secrets was his trade.

"Kabete Rungawa is an extraterrestrial."

"What?"

"He looks human, but he's actually from another world."

Lyle's mouth hung open for a second, then clicked shut. "Are you joking, Jeremy, or what?" he asked angrily.

"That's what he told me," Keating said.

"And you believed him?"

Keating felt a smile cross his lips as he recalled that cold, rainy night in front of the Parthenon. His mission had been to terminate Rungawa, and he had finally tracked the Black Saint to the Acropolis.

"He was very convincing," Keating said softly. "Very convincing."

Lyle looked down at his untouched lunch, then back into Keating's eyes. "Jeremy, either you're lying through your teeth or you've gone around the bend."

"It's the truth, Jason."

"You want me to believe that you *think* it's the truth."

"Would I tell such a crazy story if it weren't the truth?"

The section chief seemed to suddenly realize that he held a knife and fork in his hands. He attacked the Virginia ham vigorously as he said, "Yes, I think you might. A completely wild story might make us believe that you've flipped out, might convince us that you ought to be retired."

"To a mental institution?"

"This isn't Russia," Lyle snapped. But then, looking up from his platter at Keating again, he added, "A good long rest might be what you need, though. You wouldn't be the first field agent to suffer from burnout."

"A permanent rest?" Keating asked.

Lyle turned his attention back to his food. "Just relax and eat your lunch. We'll take care of you, Jeremy. The agency takes care of its own."

Keating took the afternoon off and drove far out into the wooded Virginia hills, without any conscious destination, merely drove through the late March sunshine in his agency-furnished inconspicuous gray Ford. He did not have to be told that it was bugged; that anything said inside the car would be faithfully recorded back at headquarters. And there were tracking transmitters built into the car, naturally. Even if he drove it to Patagonia, satellite sensors would spot him as plainly as they count missile silos in Siberia.

And he knew, just as surely, that he expected a contact, a message, a set of instructions or some sort of help from the entity he had refrained from killing that rainy night atop the Acropolis.

How can I be so certain that he'll help me? Keating asked himself as he drove. There's no doubt in my mind that he is what he said he is: an extraterrestrial, a creature from another world, sent here to keep us from blowing ourselves to kingdom come with our nuclear toys. But will he help *me*? Am I important enough to his plans to be rescued? Does he know what Lyle is going to do to me? Does he give a damn?

No answers came out of the sky as Keating drove blindly toward Charlottesville. It was not until he turned onto Interstate 64 and saw the signs for Monticello that he realized where he was heading.

He joined a group of five Japanese tourists and followed the guides through Thomas Jefferson's home, half listening to the guides' patter, half looking at the furnishings and gadgets of the brightest man ever to live in the White House. In the back of his mind Keating realized that he had slept in hotel rooms far more luxurious than Jefferson's bedroom. Was *he* one of them? he wondered. Were they tinkering with our world's politics that far back?

Keating kept pace with the other tourists, but his attention was actually focused on a message that never came. He felt certain that they—whoever they were—would contact him. But by the time his group had been ushered back to the main entrance of the house, at the end of the tour, there had been no contact. He was out in the cold, completely alone.

He drove back in darkness to the apartment in Arlington that the agency had provided for him. It was a pleasant-enough set of rooms, with a view of the Washington Monument and the Capitol dome. Keating could sense the bugs that infested the walls, the phone, most likely the entire building. A fancy jailhouse, he knew.

His apartment was on the top floor of the six-story building. Death row? Very likely. Lyle could not risk letting him go loose. And there were no close relatives or friends to raise a fuss about him.

He knew that he had to make a break for it, and it had to be tonight. If Rungawa and his people would not help him, then he would have to do it alone. Have dinner, then take the car and drive out to the nearest shopping mall. *Use the crowds to lose whatever tails they've put on me. Then get to Rungawa, one way or another. He owes me a favor.*

Keating took a frozen dinner from the refrigerator, microwaved it into a semblance of food, and sat in front of the living room TV set to eat what might be his last meal. But after a few bites of the lukewarm Salisbury steak, he felt himself nodding off. For a moment he felt panic surge through him like an electric current, but long years of practice damped it down. A short nap won't hurt, he told himself. Forty winks. He drowsed off in the comfortable reclining chair, while the TV screen played out a drama about corporate power and sexual passion in the cosmetics business.

"Mr. Keating."

He awoke with a start, looked around the living room. No one.

"Here, Mr. Keating. Here."

The TV screen showed the kindly looking face of an elderly black man: Kabete Rungawa.

"You!"

Rungawa smiled and lowered his eyes briefly, almost as if embarrassed.

"Forgive this unorthodox way of communicating with you. Your erstwhile colleagues have listening devices on the telephone . . ."

"And in the walls," Keating said.

Rungawa replied, "They will not hear this conversation. As far as their devices are concerned, you are still asleep and the eleven o'clock news is on the air."

Hunching forward in his chair, Keating asked, "How do I know that I'm *not* asleep, and that this isn't just a dream?"

"That is a question of faith, Mr. Keating," said the black man gravely. "Can you trust your own senses? Only your own inner faith can give you the answer."

"They're going to kill me," Keating said.

"You told them about us." Rungawa's face became somber.

"I told them about *you*."

"That was not wise."

"Don't worry about it," Keating said. "Lyle thinks that either I'm a colossal liar or a crackpot."

The black man almost smiled. "Still, we would prefer that no one knew of our presence. I told you only because my life was at stake."

"Well, it's my life that's at stake now. Lyle's going to terminate me."

"Yes, we know. It will happen tonight."

"How can I—"

"You can't. You mustn't. The game must be played to its conclusion."

"Game? It's my *life* we're talking about!"

"It is your faith we are talking about," the black man said solemnly, in his rumbling bass voice. "You believed what I told you that night in front of the Parthenon. You spared my life."

"But you're not going to spare mine," Keating said.

"Have faith, Mr. Keating. Haven't your own prophets told you that faith can carry you beyond death? Christ, Mohammed, Buddha—haven't they all tried to tell you the same thing?"

"Don't talk philosophy to me! I need help!"

"I know you do, Mr. Keating. It will come. Have faith."

Keating started to reply, but found that he could not open his mouth, could not even move his tongue. He no longer had control of his limbs. He sat frozen in the recliner chair, unable to move his legs, his arms. He could not even lift a finger from the padded armrest.

His throat was dry with sudden fear, his innards trembled with a fear that was fast approaching panic. *I don't want to die!* his mind screamed silently, over and again. *I don't want to die!*

"I know the terror you feel, Mr. Keating," Rungawa's deep voice said gravely. "It pains me to put you through this. But it must be done. They will never rest until you are dead and can no longer harm or embarrass them. I am truly sorry, but you will not be the first casualty we suffer."

Don't let them kill me! Keating shrieked inside his head.

But Rungawa said only, "Good night, Mr. Keating."

Jeremy's eyes slowly closed, like the curtain going down on the last act of a tragic play. Locked inside his paralyzed body, imprisoned within his own unresponding flesh, Keating saw nothing but darkness as he awaited inevitable death.

Slowly, slowly, the thundering of his heart eased. In the background he could hear the television set's sound again. The eleven o'clock news chattered away, to be followed by a talk show. Still Keating sat, unable to move a voluntary muscle, unable even to open his eyes. He tried to picture Joanna and little Jerry, Jr., tried to tell himself that he would be with them at last, but a cold voice in his mind laughed mockingly and told him that he had never believed in life after death. *Get accustomed to the darkness, Jeremy,* he told himself. *This is all there will ever be.*

He wanted to cry, but even that was denied him. *You're already as good as dead,* the ice-hard voice said. *What did you have to live for, anyway?*

Time became meaningless. The voices from the television set changed, but Keating paid scant attention to them. They were nothing more than background sound effects; like the muted organ music played in a cathedral before the funeral service begins.

The click of the lock sounded like a pistol shot to him. He heard the front door open and then softly close. They had the key to the apartment, of course. The jailers always have the keys. The floor was carpeted, but Keating clearly heard the soft footfalls approaching him. Like a man who had been blind from birth, Keating's sense of hearing seemed magnified, hypersensitive. He could hear the man's breathing from halfway across the living room.

He knew it was not Lyle himself. The section chief would never dirty his own hands. With something of a shock Keating realized that he hardly knew anyone else at the agency. Four years of service and he had barely made an acquaintance. The voice inside his head laughed scornfully again. *You've been dead for years, old boy. You just didn't realize it.*

"Wake up, man. Come on, wake up!"

Jeremy's eyes snapped open.

A swarthy, pinch-faced, dapper little man with a neatly trimmed black mustache was leaning over him.

"Wha . . . who . . . ?" Jeremy's tongue felt thick, his eyes gummy. But he could speak. He could move again.

"Never mind who," the man said. "We gotta get you outta here! Fast!"

Feeling almost dizzy with surprise, Jeremy sat up straight in the recliner and planted his feet on the floor. "What's going on?"

"I don't got time to explain, man. We only got a couple minutes before they get here! Come on!"

He looked Hispanic, or maybe Italian. He wore a white suit with a double-breasted jacket; strange outfit for an undercover agent. Or an extraterrestrial. Confused, Jeremy struggled to his feet. Out of the corner of his eye, he saw that the television set was playing an old black-and-white movie now.

"Splash some water on your face, wake yourself up. We gotta move fast."

Jeremy tried to shake the cobwebs out of his head. He lumbered to the bathroom and ran the cold water. The little man watched from the doorway. His suit was rumpled, baggy; it looked as if he had been wearing it for a long time. He pulled a small silver flask from his inside pocket, opened it, and took a long pull from it.

"Take a swig of this; it'll open your eyes for you." Jeremy took the pint-sized flask and sniffed at its open mouth. Spanish brandy. He took a small, testing sip.

"Where are we . . ."

He never finished the sentence. A searing explosion of pain blasted through him. The flask fell from his spasming fingers, and the last thing he saw was the little man deftly catching it before it hit the floor.

Jeremy lurched to the sink, then collapsed across it and slid to the tile flooring. The pain faded away into darkness. He could feel nothing. He could not hear his heart beating, could not draw a breath.

Vaguely, far off in the darkly vast distance, he heard the electronic bleep of a pocket radio and the little man's voice saying, "Okay, he's had his heart attack. Looks very natural."

He opened his eyes and saw a featureless expanse of white. For what seemed like a measureless eternity he stared blankly at it. Then, at last, realizing that he was breathing slowly, rhythmically, he deliberately blinked his eyes and tried to turn his head.

The expanse of white was nothing more than the ceiling of the room he was in. He was lying in a bed, covered with a sheet and a thin white blanket. It looked like a hospital room, or perhaps a private room in an expensive rest home. Modern furniture, all in white: dresser, desk and chair, night table beside the bed, comfortable-looking upholstered chair beside the window. Sunshine streaming in, but the window blinds were angled so that he could not see outside. And he noticed that there were no mirrors in the room; not one, even over the dresser. Three doors. One of them was slightly ajar and showed the corner of a bathroom sink. The second must be a closet, Keating reasoned. The third door opened just then and Kabete Rungawa stepped in.

"You have awakened," he said, smiling. Somehow, even when he smiled, his face had the sadness of the ages etched into it.

Keating said nothing.

"You have returned from the dead, Mr. Keating. Welcome back to life."

"I was really dead?"

"Oh, yes. Quite. Your agency is very thorough."

"Then how . . . ?"

Rungawa asked permission to sit on the edge of the bed by making a slight gesture and raising his snowy eyebrows. Keating nodded and the old man sat beside him. The bed sagged disturbingly under him, even though he looked small and almost frail.

"Your own medical science can bring a man back from clinical death, in certain cases," the Black Saint said gently. "Our science is somewhat more advanced than that."

"And the agency . . . Lyle . . ."

"Mr. Lyle was present at your cremation. He was given your ashes, since you had no next of kin listed in your personnel file."

Keating thought swiftly. "You switched bodies at the crematorium."

"Something like that," said Rungawa.

"Then you really are . . . what you said you were."

Rungawa's smile broadened. "Did you doubt it? Even when you risked your life on it?"

"There's a difference between knowing here," Jeremy tapped his temple, "and believing, here in the guts, where . . ."

He stopped in midsentence and stared at the hand that had moved from his head to his midriff. *It was not his hand.*

"What have you done to me?" Jeremy's voice sounded high, shrill, frightened as a little child's.

"It was necessary," Rungawa's deep voice purred softly, "to give you a new body, Mr. Keating."

"A new . . ."

"Your former body was destroyed. We salvaged your mind—your soul, if you want to use that term."

"Where . . . whose body . . . is this?"

Rungawa blinked slowly once, then replied. "Why, it is your own body, Mr. Keating."

"But you said . . ."

"Ahh, I understand. We did not steal it from anyone." The black man smiled slightly. "We created it for you especially, just as this body of mine was created for me. You would not expect a being from another world, thousands of light-years from your Earth, to look like a human being, would you?"

Jeremy swallowed once, twice, then managed to say, "No, I guess not."

"It is a very good body, Mr. Keating. A bit younger than your former shell, quite a bit stronger, and with a few special sensitivities added to it."

Jeremy threw back the bedclothes and saw that he was naked. Good strong legs, flat ridged midsection. His hands looked heavier, fingers shorter and somewhat blunter. His skin was pink, like a baby's, new and scrubbed-looking.

Wordlessly, he swung his legs to the floor and stood up. No dizziness, no feeling of weakness at all. He padded to the bathroom, Rungawa a few steps behind him, and confronted himself in the mirror.

The face he saw was squarish, with curly red-blond hair and a light sprinkling of faint freckles across its snub nose and broad cheeks. The eyes were pale blue.

"Christ, I look like a teenager!"

"It is a fully adult body," Rungawa said gravely.

Jeremy turned to the black man, a nervous giggle bubbling from his throat. "When you say born again, you really mean it!"

"You spared my life, Mr. Keating," said Rungawa. "Now we have spared yours."

"So we're even."

Rungawa nodded solemnly.

"What happens now?" Jeremy asked.

The black man turned away and strode slowly back toward the hospital bed. "What do you mean, Mr. Keating?"

Following him, Jeremy said, "As far as the rest of the world is concerned, Jeremy Keating is dead. But here I am! Where do I go from here?"

Rungawa turned to face him. "Where do you wish to go, Mr. Keating?"

Jeremy felt uncertain, but only for a moment. He was slightly shorter than he had been before, and the Black Saint looked disconcertingly taller.

"I think you know what I want," he said. "I think you've known it all along."

"Really?"

"Yes. This has all been an elaborate form of recruitment, hasn't it?"

Rungawa really smiled now, a dazzling show of pleasure. "You are just as perceptive as we thought, Mr. Keating."

"So it has been a game, all along."

"A game that you played with great skill," Rungawa said. "You began by sparing the life of a man whom you had been instructed to assassinate. Then you quite conspicuously tried to get your employers to murder you."

"I wouldn't put it that way."

"But that is what you did, Mr. Keating. You were *testing* us! You set up a situation in which we would have to save your life."

"Or let me die."

Rungawa shook his head. "You accepted what I had told you in Athens. You believed that we would be morally bound to save your life. Your faith saved you, Mr. Keating."

"And you, on your part, have been testing me to see if I could accept the fact that there's a group of extraterrestrial creatures here on Earth, masquerading as human beings, trying to guide us away from a nuclear holocaust."

Nodding agreement, Rungawa said, "We have been testing each other."

"And we both passed."

"Indeed."

"But why me? Out of seven billion human beings, why recruit me?"

Rungawa leaned back and half sat on the edge of the empty hospital bed. "As I told you in Athens, Mr. Keating, you are a test case. If *you* could accept the fact that extraterrestrials were trying to help your race to avoid its own destruction, then we felt sure that our work would meet with eventual success."

Keating stood naked in the middle of the antiseptic white room, feeling strong, vibrant, very much alive.

"So I've been born again," he said. "A new life."

The Black Saint beamed at him. "And a new family, of sorts. Welcome to the ranks of the world saviors, Mr. Keating. There are very few of us, and so many of your fellow humans who seem intent on destroying themselves."

"But we'll save the world despite them."

"That is our task," Rungawa said.

Keating grinned at him. "Then give me some clothes and let's get to work."

BLOOD OF TYRANTS

*This story was something of an experiment. Two experiments, really:
one in style, the other in marketing.*

*It was at one of the Milford Conferences in the early Sixties that
Harlan Ellison conceived of the anthology he would eventually call
Dangerous Visions. In those days, the major market for science fiction
short stories was among the magazines such as Analog, Fantasy &
Science Fiction, Galaxy, and Amazing. Harlan and many other writers
were dissatisfied with the limitations imposed by the magazine
publishers. Dangerous Visions was Harlan's attempt to break out of the
taboos and shibboleths of the magazine market, a gigantic anthology of
stories that would not be bound by the conventions of newsstand
morality.*

*Dangerous Visions was a huge success, and Harlan immediately set
to work on a second such volume, Again, Dangerous Visions. Much to
my surprise, he asked me to contribute a story to the new project. I was
surprised because, even though Harlan and I were friends, I did not write
the kind of story that I considered a "Dangerous Vision:" a story that
went beyond the constraints of taste and subject matter published in the
science fiction magazines.*

*So I tried an experiment in style, an attempt to write a short story as
if it were the shooting script for a film. The subject matter was something
that I had been mulling over for years, the idea that our society is
breeding barbarians in the decaying ghettos of our major cities, and*

113

sooner or later these barbarians are going to declare war against the civilization that produced them. Much the same train of thought eventually led to a full-blown novel, City of Darkness.

I finished the short story and presented it to Harlan. He hated it. He found every fault in it that it is possible to find in Western literature, and then some. Chagrined, I told him that the only other story I had on hand that had not yet been published was one that I had just finished writing, "Zero Gee." *Harlan loved that one, and published it in* Again, Dangerous Visions. *Perhaps what he really wanted was not so much a "Dangerous Vision," but a technologically solid science fiction story, because that's what* "Zero Gee" *is.*

Harlan and I remained friends, of course. We went on to collaborate on a short story called "Brillo," *which led to a lawsuit against the ABC television network, Paramount Pictures, and a certain Hollywood producer. But that's another story. For now, take a look at* "Blood of Tyrants."

STILL PHOTO.

Danny Romano, switchblade in hand, doubling over as the bullet hits slightly above his groin. His face going from rage to shock. In the background other gang members battling: tire chains, pipes, knives. Behind them a grimy wall bearing a tattered political poster of some WASP promising "EQUAL OPPORTUNITY FOR ALL."

Fast montage of scenes, quick cutting from one to the next.

Background music: Gene Kelly singing, "You Are My Lucky Star."

Long shot of the street. Kids stil fighting. Danny crawling painfully on all fours. CUT TO tight shot of Danny, eyes fixed on the skinny kid who shot him, switchblade still in hand. The kid, goggle-eyed, tries to shoot again, gun jams, he runs. CUT TO long shot again, police cruisers wailing into view, lights flashing. CUT TO Danny being picked up off the street by a pair of angry-faced cops. He struggles, feebly. Nightstick fractures skull, ends his struggling. CUT TO Danny being slid out of an ambulance at hospital emergency entrance. CUT TO green-gowned surgeons (backs visible only), working with cool indifference under the glaring overhead lights. CUT TO Danny lying unconscious in hospital bed. Head bandaged. IV stuck in arm. Private room. Uniformed cop opens door from hallway, admits two men. One is obviously a plainclothes policeman: stocky, hard-faced, tired-eyed. The other looks softer, unembittered, even smiles. He peers at Danny through rimless glasses, turns to the plainclothesman and nods.

Establishing shots.

Washington, D.C.: Washington Monument, Capitol building (seen from foreground of Northeast district slums), pickets milling around White House fence.

An office interior.

Two men are present. Brockhurst, sitting behind the desk, is paunchy, bald, hooked on cigarettes, frowning with professional skepticism. The other man, Hansen, is the rimless-glasses man from the hospital scene.

"I still don't like it; it's risky," says Brockhurst from behind his desk.

"What's the risk?" Hansen has a high, thin voice. "If we can rehabilitate these gang leaders, and then use them to rehabilitate their fellow delinquents, what's the risk?" "It might not work."

"Then all we've lost is time and money."

Brockhurst glowers, but says nothing.

Another montage of fast-cut scenes. Background music: Mahalia Jackson singing, "He's Got the Whole World in His Hands."

Danny, between two cops, walks out of the hospital side door and into a police van. Bandages gone now. CUT TO Danny being unloaded from van, still escorted, at airport. He is walked to a twin-engine plane. CUT TO interior of plane. Five youths are already aboard: two blacks, two Puerto Ricans, one white. Each is sitting, flanked by a white guard. A sixth guard takes Danny's arm at the entry-hatch and sits him in the only remaining pair of seats. Danny tries to look cool, but he's really delighted to be next to the window.

Interior of a "classroom."

A large room. No windows, cream-colored walls, perfectly blank. About fifty boys are fidgeting in metal folding-chairs. Danny is sitting toward the rear. All the boys are now dressed in identical gray coveralls. Two uniformed guards stand by the room's only exit, a pair of large double doors.

The boys are mostly quiet; they don't know each other, they're trying to size up the situation. Hansen comes through the double doors (which a guard quickly closes behind him) and strides to the two-steps-up platform in the front of the room. He has a small microphone in his hand. He smiles and tries to look confident as he speaks.

"I'm not going to say much. I'd like to introduce myself. I'm Dr. Hansen. I'm not a medical doctor, I'm a specialist in education . . ."

A loud collective groan.

"No, no . . ." Hansen chuckles slightly. "No, it's not what you think. I work with teaching machines. You know, computers? Have you heard of them? Well, never mind."

One of the kids stands up and starts for the door. A guard points a cattle prod toward the kid's chair. He gets the idea, goes back sullenly and sits down.

"You're here whether you like it or not," Hansen continues, minus the smile. "I'm confident that you'll soon like it. We're going to change you. We're going to make your lives worth living. And it doesn't matter in the slightest whether you like it or not. You'll learn to like it soon enough. No one's going to hurt you, unless you try to get rough. But we *are* going to change you."

Interior of the "reading room."

A much smaller room. Danny and Hansen are alone in it. Same featureless plastic walls. No furniture except an odd-looking chair in the middle of the floor. It somewhat resembles an electric chair. Danny is trying to look contemptuous to cover up his fear.

"You ain't gettin' me in that!"

"It's perfectly all right; there's nothing here to hurt you. I'm merely going to determine how well you can read."

"I can read."

"Yes, of course." Doubtfully. "But how well? That's what I need to know."

"I don't see no books around."

"When you sit in the chair and the electrodes are attached to your scalp . . ."

"You gonna put those things on my head?"

"It's completely painless."

"No you ain't!"

Hansen speaks with great patience. "There's no use arguing about it. If I have to, I'll get the guards to strap you in. But it will be better if you cooperate. Mr. Carter—the one you call, uh, 'Spade,' I believe—he took the test without hesitating a moment. You wouldn't want him to know that we had to hold you down, would you?"

Danny glowers, but edges toward the chair. "Motherhumpin' sonofabitch."

Series of fadeins and fadeouts.

Danny in the "reading room," sitting in the chair, cranium covered by electrode network. The wall before him has become a projection screen, and he is reading the words on it. MUSIC UNDER is Marine Corps Band playing Cornell University *Alma Mater*: ("Far Above Cayuga's Waters . . .")

DANNY (hesitantly): "The car . . . hummed . . . cut quiet-ly to it-self . . ."

FADEOUT

FADEIN

DANNY (tense with concentration): "So my fellow Americans, ask not what your country can do for you . . ."

FADEOUT

FADEIN

DANNY: "'Surrender?'" he shouted. "'I have not yet begun to fight!'"

FADEOUT

FADEIN

DANNY (enjoying himself): "Robin pulled his bowstring back carefully, knowing that the Sheriff and all the townspeople were watching him."

FADEOUT

Interior of Brockhurst's office.

Hansen is pacing impatiently before the desk, an intense smile on his face.

"I tell you, it's succeeding beyond my fondest hopes!

Those boys are soaking it up like sponges. That Romano boy alone has absorbed more knowledge . . ."

Brockhurst is less than optimistic. "They're really learning?"

"Not only learning. They're beginning to change. The process is working. We're changing their attitudes, their value systems, everything. We're going to make useful citizens out of them."

"All of them?"

"No, of course not. Only the best of them: half a dozen, I'd say, out of the fifty here—Romano, 'Spade' Carter, three or four others. At least six out of fifty, better than one out of ten. And this is just the first batch! When we start processing larger numbers of them . . ."

Brockhurst cuts Hansen short with a gesture. "Do you actually think these—students—of yours will go back to their old neighborhoods and start to rehabilitate their fellow gang members?"

"Yes, of course they will. They'll have to! They're being programmed for it!"

Interior of library.

Danny is sitting at a reading table, absorbed in a book. Bookshelves line the walls. A lumpy-faced redhead sits one table away, also reading. Hansen enters quietly, walks to Danny.

"Hello, Danny. How's it going today?"

Danny looks up and smiles pleasantly. "Fine, Mr. Hansen."

"I just got the computer's scoring of your economics exam. You got the highest mark in the class."

"Did I? Great. I was worried about it. Economics is kind of hard to grasp. Those booster pills you gave me must have helped."

"You did extremely well What are you reading?"

"Biography, by Harold Lamb. It's about Genghis Khan."

Hansen nods. "I see, look, it's about time we started thinking about what you're going to do when you go back home. Why don't you drop over to my office tonight, after supper?"

"Okay."

"See you then."

"Right."

Hansen moves away, toward the other boy. Danny closes his book, stands up. He turns to the bookshelf directly behind him and reaches unhesitatingly for another volume. He puts the two books under his arm and starts for the door. The title of the second book is *Mein Kampf.*

Brockhurst's office.

Six boys are standing in front of Brockhurst's desk, the six Hansen spoke of. They are now dressed in casual slacks, shirts, sport coats. Hansen is sitting beside the desk, beaming at them. Brockhurst, despite himself, looks impressed.

"You boys understand how important your mission is." Brockhurst is lapsing into a military tone. "You can save your friends a lot of grief . . . perhaps save their lives."

Danny nods gravely. "It's not just our friends that we'll be saving, it'll be our cities, all the people in them, our whole country."

"Exactly."

Hansen turns to Brockhurst. "They've been well-trained. They're ready to begin their work."

"Very well. Good luck, boys. We're counting on you."

Exterior shot, a city street.

Mid-afternoon, a hot summer day. A taxi pulls to the curb of the dingy, sun-baked street. Danny steps out, ducks down to pay the cabbie. He drives away quickly. Danny stands alone, in front of a magazine/tobacco store. He is dressed as he was in Brockhurst's office. Taking off the jacket, he looks slowly up and down the street. Deserted, except for a few youngsters sitting, listlessly, in the shade. With a shrug, he steps to the store.

Interior, the store.

Magazine racks on one side of the narrow entrance; store counter featuring cigarettes and candy on the other. No one at the counter. Overhead, a battered fan drones ineffectually. Farther back, a grimy table surrounded by rickety chairs. Three boys, two girls, all Danny's age, sit there. The boys in jeans and tee shirts, girls in shorts and sleeveless tops. They turn as he shuts the door, gape at him.

"Nobody going to say hello?" He grins at them.

"Danny!"

They bounce out of the chairs, knocking one over.

"We thought you was dead!"

"Or in jail . . . nobody knew what happened to you."

"It's been almost a year!"

They cluster around him as he walks slowly back toward the table. But no one touches him.

"What happened to ya?"

"You look . . . different, sort of." The girl gestures vaguely.

"What'd they do to you? Where were you?"

Danny sits down. "It's a long story. Somebody get me a coke, huh? Who's been running things, Marco? Find him for me, I want to see him. And, Speed . . . get word to the Bloodhounds. I want to see their Prez . . . is it still Waslewski? And the one who shot me . . ."

"A war council?"

Danny smiles. "Sort of. Tell them that, if that's what it'll take to bring them here."

Interior, the back of the store.

It is night. Danny sits at the table, his shirt-sleeves rolled up, watching the front door. Two boys flank him: Marco, slim and dark, his thin face very serious; and Speed, bigger, lighter, obviously excited but managing to keep it contained. Both boys are trying to hide their nervousness with cigarettes. The door opens, and a trio of youths enter. Their leader, Waslewski, is stocky, blond, intense. His eyes cover the whole store with a flick. Behind him is the skinny kid who shot Danny, and a burlier boy who's trying to look cool and menacing.

"Come on in," Danny calls from his chair. "Nobody's going to hurt you."

Waslewski fixes his eyes on Danny and marches to the table. He takes a chair. His cohorts remain standing behind him. "So you ain't dead after all."

"Not yet."

"Guess you're pretty lucky."

Danny grins. "Luckier than you'll ever know." Nodding toward the boy who shot him, "What's his name?"

"O'Banion."

"All right, O'Banion. You put a bullet in me; I lived through it. You were doing your job for the Bloodhounds; I was doing my job for the Champions. Nothing personal and no hard feelings on my part."

Waslewski's eyes narrow. "What're you pullin'? I thought this was gonna be a war council."

"It is, but not the regular kind." Danny leans forward, spreads his hands on the table. "Know where I've been the past ten months? In Washington, in a special school the government set up, just to handle jay-dees. They pump knowledge into you with a computer . . . just like opening your head and sticking a hose in it."

The other boys, Bloodhounds and Champions alike, squirm a bit.

"You know what they taught me? They taught me we're nuts to fight each other. That's right . . . gangs fighting each other is strictly crazy. What's it get us? Lumps, is all. And dead."

Waslewski is obviously disgusted. "You gonna preach a sermon?"

"Damned right I am. You know why the gangs fight each other? Because *they* keep us up tight. They've got the money, they've got the power that runs this city, and they make sure we gangs stay down in the garbage. By fighting each other, we keep them sitting high and running the big show."

"They? Who the hell's they?"

"The people who run this city. The fat cats. The rich cats. The ones who've got limousines and broads with diamonds hanging from each tit. They *own* this city. They own the buildings and the people in the buildings. They own the cops. They own us."

"Nobody owns me!" says the burly kid behind Waslewski.

"Shuddup." Waslewski is frowning with thought now, trying to digest Danny's words.

"Look," Danny says. "This city is filled with money. It's filled with broads and good food and everything a guy could want for the rest of his life. What do we get out of it? Shit, that's what! And why? Because we let them run us, that's why. We fight each other over a crummy piece of turf, a couple of blocks of lousy street, while *they* sit back in plush restaurants and penthouses with forty-two-inch broads bending over them."

"So . . . whattaya expect us to do?"

"Stop fighting each other. Make the gangs work together to take over this city. We can do it! We can crack this city wide open, like a peanut. Instead of fighting each other, we can conquer this whole fucking city and run it for ourselves!"

Waslewski sags back in his seat. The other boys look at each other, amazed, unbelieving, yet obviously attracted by the idea.

"Great . . . real cool." Waslewski's voice and face exude sarcasm. "And what do the cops do? Sit back and let us take over? And what about the rest of the people? There's millions of 'em."

"Listen. We know how to fight. What we've got to do is get all the gangs together and fight together, like an army. It's just a matter of using the right strategy, the right tactics. We can do it. But we've got to work together. Not just the Bloodhounds and the Champions, but *all* the gangs! All of us, together, striking all at once. We can rack up the fuzz and take this town in a single night. They'll never know what hit them."

Marco objects, "But Danny, we can't . . ."

"Look, I know it'll take a lot of work. I figure we'll need two years, at least. We've got to get our guys spotted at key places all over the city: the power plants, all the radio and TV stations. We'll need guys inside the National Guard armories, inside the precinct stations, if we can do it. It'll mean a lot of guys will have to take jobs. Learn to work hard for a couple years. But in the end, we'll have this city for ourselves!"

"You got it all figured out?"

"To the last inch."

Waslewski unconsciously pushes his chair slightly back from the table, He glances at his two lieutenants; they are wide-eyed.

"I gotta think about this. I can't say yes or no just like that."

"Okay, you think about it. But don't spill it to anybody except your top boys. And remember, I'm going to be talking to all the gangs around here . . . and then to the gangs in the rest of the city. They'll go for it, I know. Don't get yourself left out."

Waslewski gets up slowly. "Okay. I'll get back to you right away. I think you can count us in." His aides nod agreement.

"Good. Now we're rolling." Danny gets up and sticks out his hand. Waslewski hesitates a beat, and then—acting rather stunned—shakes hands with Danny.

Montage of scenes. Background music: "The Army Caisson Song."

Danny escorting Waslewski and two other boys into a Job Corps training-center office. CUT TO half-a-dozen boys sitting in a personnel office waiting room. CUT TO a boy signing up in a National Guard armory.

Interior, Brockhurst's office.

Hansen is sitting on the front inch of the chair beside the desk, tense with excitement.

"It's a brilliant idea. Romano is working out better than any of his classmates, and this idea simply proves it!"

Brockhurst looks wary, probing for the weak point. "Why's he doing it? What's the sense of having gang members formed into a police auxiliary?"

"Sense? It makes perfect sense. The boys can work hand-in-hand with the police, clue them in on trouble before it erupts into violence. The police can get to know the boys and the boys will get to know the police. Mutual exposure will breed mutual trust and confidence. Instead of working against each other, they'll be working together. With violence between the gangs and the police dwindling, a major source of trouble will be eliminated."

"It just doesn't sound right to me. I can't picture those young punks turning into volunteer cops."

"But it's worth a try, isn't it? What do we have to lose?"

Brockhurst makes a sour face. "I suppose you're right. It's worth a try."

Interior, a one-room apartment.

The room is small but neat. The bed in the corner is made up in military style. The walls are covered with street maps of the city, over which are colored markings showing the territory of each gang. Danny sits at the only table, together with five other boys. One is a black, two others are Puerto Rican. The table is heaped high with papers.

"Okay," Danny says. "The Hellcats will handle the power station in their turf and the precinct house. And they've offered to put eight of their guys on our task force for the downtown area. What else?" He looks around at his aides.

The black says, "The Hawks have a beef. They claim the Jaguars have been cuttin' into their turf pretty regular for the past month. They've tried talkin' it out with 'em, but no dice. I tried talkin' to both sides, but they're up pretty tight about it."

Danny frowns. "Those damned Hawks have been screwing up for months."

"They're gonna rumble 'less you can stop 'em."

Thoughtfully, "There hasn't been a rumble all winter. Even the newspapers are starting to notice it. Maybe it'd be a good idea to let them fight it out . . . so long as nobody winds up spilling his guts about us to the squares."

"Somebody's gonna get hurt bad if they rumble. Lotta bad blood between them two gangs."

"I know." Danny thinks it over for a moment. "Look, tell them if they've got to rumble, do it without artillery. No guns, nothing that'll tip the squares to what we've got stashed away."

"Okay."

Interior, a Congressman's office.

The room is high-ceilinged, ornately decorated. The Congressman's broad desk is covered with mementos, framed photographs, neat piles of papers. The Congressman, himself, is in his mid-forties, just starting to turn fleshy. Sitting before him are Brockhurst, Hansen and—in a neat business suit—Danny.

"And so, with the annual appropriation coming up," Brockhurst is saying, "I thought you should have a personal report on the program."

The Congressman nods. "From all I've heard, it seems to be highly successful."

"It is." Brockhurst allows himself to smile. "Of course, this is only the beginning; only a half-dozen cities have been touched so far, although we have a hundred more boys in training at the moment. But I think you can judge the results for yourself."

Hansen interrupts. "And I hope you can realize the necessity for keeping the program secret, for the time being. Premature publicity—"

"Could ruin everything. I understand." Turning his gaze to Danny. "And this is your star pupil, eh?"

Danny smiles. "I . . . uh, Sir, I'd merely like to add my thanks for what this program has done for me and my friends. It's just like Dr. Hansen has been saying: all we boys need is some training and opportunity."

Interior, a firehouse.

A boy sits at a tiny desk in the deserted garage. Behind him are the powerful fire trucks. No one else is in sight. Through the window alongside the desk, snow is falling on a city street. The window has a holiday wreath on it.

The boy is thumbing through the big calendar on the desk. He flips past December and into the coming year. He stops on July, notes that the Fourth falls on a Sunday. Smiling, he puts a red circle around the date.

Interior, a Congressional hearing room.

The committee members, half of them chatting with each other, sit at a long table in the front of the room. Brockhurst is sitting at the witness's desk, reading from a prepared text. Hansen sits beside him. The visitors' pews are completely empty, and a uniformed guard stands impassively at the door.

"Mr. Chairman, since the inception of this program, juvenile gang violence has decreased dramatically in five of the six cities where we have placed rehabilitated subjects. In one city, gang violence has dwindled to truly miniscule proportions. The boys are being rehabilitated, using Job Corps and other OEO facilities to train themselves for useful work, and then taking on—and keeping—full-time jobs."

Brockhurst looks up from his text. "Mr. Chairman, if I may be allowed a new twist on an old saying, we're beating their switchblades into plowshares."

Interior, Danny's apartment.

Danny is pacing angrily across the room, back and forth. Three abject youths sit on the bed in the corner. At the table sit Marco and Speed.

"He nearly blew it!" Danny's voice is not loud, but clearly close to violence. "You stupid assholes can't keep your own people happy. He gets sore over a bitch and goes to the cops! If we didn't have a man in the precinct station last night, the whole plan would've been blown sky-high!"

One of the boys on the bed says, miserably, "But we didn't know . . ."

"That's even worse! You're supposed to know. You're the Prez of the Belters, you're supposed to know every breath your people take."

"Well . . . whadda we do now?"

"You do nothing! You go back to your hole and sit tight. Don't even go to the can unless you get the word from me. Understand? Let the cops tumble to us because you've got one half-wit who can't keep his mouth shut, every gang in the city is going to be after your blood. And they'll get it!"

Danny motions them to the door. They leave quickly. He turns to his lieutenants.

"Speed, you know anybody in the Belters who can do a good job as Prez?"

Speed hesitates only a beat before answering, "Yeah, kid named Molie. Sharp. He'd keep 'em in line okay."

"All right. Good. Get him here. Tonight. If I like him, we get that asshole who just left and his half-wit fink to kill each other. Then Molie becomes their President."

"Kill each other?"

"Right. Can't let the fink hang around. And we can't make the cops worry that he was killed because he knew something. And that asshole is no good for us. So we make it look like they had a fight over the bitch. And fast, before something else happens. We've only got a month to go."

Speed nods. "Okay, Danny. I'm movin.' He's already halfway to the door.

Exterior, night.

A park in the city. Holiday crowd is milling around. City skyline is visible over the trees. A band finishes the final few bars of "Stars and Stripes Forever." A hush. Then the small thud of a skyrocket being launched, and overhead, a red-white-and-blue firework blossoms against the night sky. The crowd gives its customary gasp of delight.

Danny stands at the edge of the crowd. In the flickering light of the fireworks, he looks at his wrist watch, then turns to Speed and Marco and nods solemnly. They hurry off into the darkness.

Exterior, tollbooth across a major bridge.

A car full of youths pulls up at one of the three open toll gates. The boys spill out, guns in hands, club down the nearest tollbooth collector. The next closest one quickly raises his hands. The third collector starts to run, but he's shot down.

Interior, National Guard armory.

One hugely grinning boy in Army fatigues is handing out automatic weapons to a line-up of other boys, from a rack that has an unlocked padlock hanging from its open door.

Interior, subway train.

Four adults—two old ladies, a middle-aged man and a younger man—ride along sleepily. The train stops, the doors open. A combat team of twenty boys steps in through the three open doors. Their dress is ragged. but each boy carries a newly-oiled automatic weapon. The adults gasp. One boy yanks open the motorman's cubicle door and drags out the portly motorman. Another boy steps into the cubicle and shuts the doors. The train starts up again with the boys wordlessly standing, guns ready, while the adults huddle in a corner of the car.

Interior, police precinct station.

The desk sergeant is yawning. The radio operator, in the back of the room, is thumbing through a magazine. A boy—one of the police auxiliary—sits quietly on a bench by the door. He gets up, stretches, opens the front door. In pour a dozen armed boys. The desk sergeant freezes in mid-yawn. Two boys sprint toward the radio operator. He starts to grab for his microphone, but a blast of fire cuts him down.

Interior, a city power station.

Over the rumbling, whining noise of the generators, a boy walks up to his supervisor, who's sitting in front of a board full of dials and switches, and pokes a pistol in his face. The man, startled, gets slowly out of his chair. Two other boys appear and take the man away. The first boy sits in the chair and reaches for the phone hanging on the instrument board.

Interior, newspaper office.

There is no sign of the usual news staff. All the desks are manned by boys, with Danny sitting at one of the desks in the center of the complex. Boys are answering phones, general hubbub of many simultaneous conversations. The mood is excited, almost jubilant. A few boys stand at the windows behind Danny, with carbines and automatic rifles in their hands. But they look relaxed.

Speed comes over to Danny from another desk, carrying a bundle of papers. "Here's the latest reports: every damned precinct station in town. We got 'em all! And the armories, the power stations, the TV studios. All the bridges and tunnels are closed down. Everything!"

Danny doesn't smile. "What about City Hall?"

"Took some fighting, but Shockie says we've got it nailed down. A few diehards in the cellblock, that's all. Our guys are usin' their own tear gas on 'em."

"The Mayor and the Councilmen?"

"The Mayor's outta town for the holidays, but we got most of the Councilmen, and the Police Chief, and the local FBI guys, too!"

Danny glances at his watch. "Okay, time for Phase Two. Round up every cop in town. On duty or off. Knock their doors down if you have to, pull them out of bed. But get them all into cells before dawn."

"Right!" Speed's grin is enormous.

Exterior, sun rising over city skyline.

From the air, the city appears normal. Nothing out of the ordinary. No fires, no milling crowds, not even much motor traffic on the streets. ZOOM TO the toll plaza at one of the city's main bridges. A lone sedan is stopped at an impromptu roadblock, made up of old cars and trucks strung lengthwise across the traffic lanes. A boy with an automatic rifle in the crook of one arm is standing atop a truck cab, waving the amazed automobile driver back into the city. On the other side of the tollbooth, an oil truck and moving van are similarly stopped before another roadblock.

Interior, a TV studio.

Danny is sitting at a desk, the hot lights on him. He is now wearing an Army shirt, open at the collar. A Colt automatic rests on the desk before him. Adults are manning the cameras, mike boom, lights, control booth; but armed boys stand behind each one.

"Good morning," Danny allows himself to smile pleasantly. "Don't bother trying to change channels. I'm on every station in town. Your city has been taken over. It's now our city. My name is Danny Romano; I'm your new Mayor. Also your Police Chief, Fire Chief, District Attorney, Judge, and whatever other jobs I want to take on. The kids you've been calling punks, jaydees . . . the kids from the

Street gangs . . . we've taken over your city. You'll do what we tell you from now on. If you cooperate, nobody's going to hurt you. If you don't, you'll be shot. Life is going to be a lot simpler for all of us from now on. Do as you're told and you'll be okay."

Interior, Brockhurt's office.

General uproar. Brockhurst is screaming into a telephone. A couple dozen people are shouting at each other, waving their arms. Hansen is prostrate on the couch.

"No, I don't know anything more about it than you do," Brockhurst's voice is near frenzy. His shirt is open at the neck, tie ripped off, jacket rumpled, face sweaty. "How the hell do I know? The FBI . . . the Army . . . somebody's got to do *something!*"

His secretary fights her way through the crowd. "Mr. Brockhurst . . . on line three . . . it's the *President!*"

Every voice hushes. Brockhurst slams the phone down, takes his hand off it, looks at it for a long moment. Then, shakily, he punches a button at the phone's base and lifts the receiver.

"Yessir, Yes, this is Brockhurst . . . No, sir, I have no idea of how this came about . . . it . . . it seems to be genuine, sir. Yes, we've tried to communicate with them . . . Yessir, Romano is one of our, eh, graduates. No, sir. No, I don't . . . but . . . I agree, we can't let them get away with it. The Army? Isn't there any other way? I'm afraid he's got several million people bottled up in that city, and he'll use them as hostages. If the Army attacks, he might start executing them wholesale."

Hansen props himself up on one elbow and speaks weakly, "Let me go to them. Let me talk to Danny. Something's gone wrong . . . something . . ."

Brockhurst waves him silent with a furious gesture. "Yes, Mr. President, I agree. If they won't surrender peacefully, then there's apparently no alternative. But if they fight the Army, a lot of innocent people are going to be hurt. . . . Yes, I know you can't just . . . but . . . no other way, yes, I see. Very well, sir, you are the Commander-in-Chief. Yessir. Of course, sir. Before the day is out. Yessir."

Exterior, city streets.

Tanks rumbling down the streets. Kids firing from windows,

throwing Molotov cocktails. One tank bursts into flames. The one behind it fires its cannon point blank into a building: the entire structure explodes and collapses. Soldiers crouching in doorways, behind burned-out automobiles, firing at kids running crouched-down a half-block away. Two boys go sprawling. A soldier kicks a door in and tosses in a grenade. A few feet up the street, a teenage girl lies dead. A tank rolls past a children's playground, while a dazed old man sits bloody-faced on the curbstone, watching. Flames and smoke and the constant pock-pock-pock sound of automatic rifles, punctuated by explosions.

No picture. Sound only.

The sounds of a phone being dialed, the tick of circuits, the buzz of a phone ringing, another click as it is picked up.

"Yeah."

"Hey, Spade, that you?"

"It's me."

"This is Midget."

"I know the voice, Midge."

"You see what Danny did?"

"I see what happened to him. How many dead, how many thousands? Or is it millions?"

"They ain't tellin'. Gotta be millions, though. Whole damned city's flattened. Army must've lost fifty thousand men all by itself."

"They killed Danny."

"They claim they killed him, but I ain't seen pictures of his body yet."

"It's a mess, all right."

"Yeah. Listen . . . they got Federal men lookin' for us now, you know?"

"I know. All Danny's 'classmates' are in for it."

"You gonna be okay?"

"They won't find me, don't worry. There's plenty of places to hide and plenty of people to hide me."

"Good. Now listen, this mess of Danny's oughtta teach us a lesson."

"Damned right."

"Yeah. We gotta work together now. When we make our move, it's gotta be in all the cities. Not just one. Every big city in the god damn country."

"Gonna take a long time to do it."

"I know, but we can make it. And when we do, they can't send the Army against every big city all at once."

"Specially if we take Washington and get *their* Prez."

"Right. Okay, gotta run now. Stay loose and keep in touch."

"Check. See you in Washington one of these days."

"You bet your sweet ass."

BUSHIDO

The challenge of "Bushido" was to make the reader feel sympathy for an enemy, a character who hates the United States. Who hates you. How well I succeeded is a question only you, the reader, can answer. But I can tell you how I went about making this "bad guy" as sympathetic as possible.

First I gave him a crippling terminal disease. Then I made him a brilliant scientist. And I showed enough of his background to make the reader understand why Saito Konda hates the U.S. and Americans.

Finally, I brought onto the scene a character out of history who stands in bold contrast to the protagonist: Isoruku Yamamoto, Grand Admiral of the Japanese Imperial Fleet at the outset of World War II. Whereas Konda is physically crippled, Yamamoto is a warrior, a man of action. Whereas Konda feels helpless and impotent, the admiral is a leader of men in war. But there is a flip side to their relationship, as well. Konda knows Yamamoto's fate and can save him from the death that he suffered in the war. Helpless and impotent to save himself, Konda can nonetheless save the man he most admires—and by doing so, he can gain revenge on the United States.

How can you feel sympathetic toward a man who wants to reverse the outcome of World War II and make Japan conquer the U.S.?

I have long felt that writers should erase the word "villain" from their vocabulary. Scrub the concept out of your mind, in fact. There are no villains in the world, only people doing what they feel they must do. I'm sure that Adolph Hitler felt he was doing what was best for the German people and the entire human race, no matter how horrible the actions he authorized.

Nobody sits in a dark corner cackling with glee over the evil they have unleashed. Not in good fiction. But every good story has not only a protagonist (the "good guy" or gal), but an antagonist, a character who is in conflict with the protagonist. As a thought experiment, try to visualize a story you admire told from the point of view of the ostensible villain . . . oops, excuse me—the ostensible antagonist. Imagine Hamlet being told from Claudius' point of view. (Frankly, Claudius seems to be the only sane person in the whole castle.)

Incidentally, there's a bit of science in this story that most other writers have conveniently ignored. Time travel requires faster-than-light travel. Which explains, perhaps, why no one has yet built a time machine.

So: Did I succeed in making Saito Konda a sympathetic character? Crippled in body, brilliant in mind, warped in spirit—yes, he is all that. But do you feel sorry for him?

KONDA GRIMACED AGAINST THE PAIN, hoping that his three friends could not see his suffering. He did not want their sympathy. He was far beyond such futile emotions. All that was left to him was hate—and the driving will to succeed.

He was sitting in his laboratory, his home, his hospital room, his isolation chamber. They were all the same place, the same metal-skinned module floating five hundred kilometers above the Earth.

The two men and one woman having tea with him had been his friends since undergraduate days at the University of Tokyo, although they had never met Konda in the flesh. That would be the equivalent of murdering him.

They were discussing their work.

"Do you actually believe you can succeed?" asked Miyoko Toguri, her almond eyes shining with admiration. Once Konda had thought she might have loved him; once he had in fact loved her. But that was long ago, when they had been foolish romantic students.

"I have solved the equations," Konda replied, hiding his pain. "As you know, if the mathematics have beauty, the experiment will eventually be successful."

"Eventually," snorted Raizo Yamashita. Like the others, he was sitting on the floor, in deference to Konda's antiquated sense of propriety. Raizo sat cross-legged, his burly body hunched slightly over the precisely placed low lacquered table, his big fists pressed against his thighs. *"Eventually* could be a thousand years from now."

"I think not," said Konda, his eyes still on lovely Miyoko. He wondered how she would look in a traditional kimono, with her hair done properly. As it was, she was wearing a Western-style blouse and skirt, yet she still looked beautiful to him.

The two men wore the latest-mode glitter slacks and brightly colored shirts. Konda's nostrils flared at their American ways. The weaker America becomes in real power, the more our people imitate her decadent styles. He himself was in a comfortable robe of deep burgundy, decorated with white flying cranes.

It happened that Konda reached for the teapot at the same moment that Miyoko did. Their hands met without touching. He poured tea for himself, she for herself. When they put the pots down again, her holographic image merged with the real teapot on Konda's table. Her hand merged with his. He could not feel the warmth of her living flesh, of course. If he did, it would undoubtedly kill him.

Tomoyuki Umezi smiled, somewhat ruefully. The window behind him showed the graceful snow-capped cone of Fujiyama. He raised his tiny cup.

"To the stars," he toasted.

The other three touched their cups to his. But they felt no physical contact. Only their eyes could register the holographic images.

"And to time," Konda added, as usual.

Back in their university days, Tomo had laughingly suggested that they form a rock group and call it the Four Dimensions, since three of them were trying to conquer space while Konda was pouring his soul and all the energy of his wasting body into mastering time.

They had never met physically. Konda had been in isolation chambers all his life, first in an incubator in the AIDS ward of the charity hospital, later in the observation sections of medical research facilities. He had been born with no effective immune system, the genetic gift of his mother, a whore, and whoever his father might have been. They had also gifted him with a chameleon virus that was slowly, inexorably, turning his normal body cells into cancerous tumors.

The slow and increasingly painful death he was suffering could be brought to a swift end merely by exposure to the real world and its teeming viruses and bacteria. But the medical specialists prevented that. From his unwanted birth, Konda had been their laboratory animal, their prized specimen, kept alive for them to study. Isolated from all the physical contamination that his body could never cope with, Konda learned as a child that his mind could roam the universe and all of history. He became an outstanding scholar, a perverse sort of celebrity within academic circles, and was granted a full scholarship to Tokyo University, where he "met" his three lifelong friends. Now he lived in a special module of a space station, five hundred kilometers above the Earth's surface, waited upon by gleaming antiseptic robots.

The four of them did their doctoral theses jointly, a theoretical study of faster-than-light propulsion. Their studies were handsomely supported by the corporations that funded the university. Japan drew much of its economic strength from space, beaming electrical energy to cities throughout Asia from huge power satellites. But always there was competition from others: the Europeans, the Chinese, the Arabs were all surging forward, eager to displace Japan and despoil its wealth.

The price of peaceful competition was a constant, frenetic search for some new way to stay ahead of the foreign devils. If any nation achieved a faster-than-light drive, the great shoguns of industry insisted that it must be Japan. The life of the nation depended on staying ahead of its competitors. There could be no rest as long as economic ruin lurked on the horizon.

For all the years since their university days, the three others continued to work on turning their theories into reality, on producing a workable interstellar propulsion system: a star drive. Miyoko accepted the chair of the physics department at the University of Rangoon, the first woman to be so honored. Dour Raizo became the doyen of the research laboratory at a major aerospace firm in Seattle, U.S.A., long since absorbed into the Mitsubishi Corporation. Tomo waited patiently for his turn at the mathematics chair in Tokyo.

From the beginning, Konda had been far more fascinated with the temporal aspects of spacetime than the spatial. Since childhood he had been intrigued by history, by the great men who had lived in bygone ages. While his friends labored over the star drive, Konda strove to produce a time machine.

In this he followed the intellectual path blazed by Hawking and Taylor and the AAPV group from the unlikely location of South Carolina, a backwater university in the backwater U.S.A.

He felt he was close to success. Alone, isolated from the rest of humanity except for the probing doctors and these occasional holographic meetings with his three distant friends, he had discovered that it should be possible to tap the temporal harmonics and project an object—or even a person—to a predetermined point in spacetime. It was not much different from achieving interstellar flight, in theory. Konda felt that his work would be of inestimable aid to his three friends.

His equations told him that to move an eighty-kilo human being from the crest of one spacetime wave to the harmonically similar crest of another would take all the energy generated by all of Japan's power satellites orbiting between the Earth and the Moon for a period of just over six hours. When he was ready for the experiment, the Greater Nippon Energy Consortium had assured him, the electrical power would be made available to him. For although the consortium had no interest in time travel, Konda had presented his work to them as an experiment that could verify certain aspects of faster-than-light propulsion.

Konda had to assemble the equipment for his experiments, using the robots who accompanied him in his isolation module of the space station. His friends helped all they could. Konda had to tell them what he was trying to do. But he never told them why. He never showed them the hatred that drove him onward.

They thought he was trying to help them in their quest for a star drive. They believed that if he could transport an object across time, it would help them learn how to transport objects across lightyears of space. But Konda had another goal in mind, something very different.

Konda dreamed of making contact with a specific person, longed with all his soul to reach across the years and summon one certain hero out of history: Isoruku Yamamoto, Grand Admiral of the Japanese Imperial Fleet in the year 1941 (old calendar). Admired by all, even his enemies, Yamamoto was known as "the sword of his emperor."

Konda remembered the day when he first told his friends of his yearning to reach the doughty old admiral. "There are no men like Yamamoto anymore," he had said. "He was a true samurai. A warrior in the ancient tradition of Bushido."

Raizo Yamashita had laughed openly. "A warrior who started a war that we lost. Badly."

Tomoyuki was too polite to laugh, but he asked curiously, "Didn't Yamamoto boast that he would defeat the Americans and dictate the terms of their surrender in the White House? He didn't even live long enough to see the war end in Japan's humiliation."

Miyoko rushed to Konda's defense before he could reply for himself. "Admiral Yamamoto was killed in the war. Isn't that true, Sai?"

"Yes," answered Konda, feeling weak with helpless rage at the thought. "He was assassinated by the cowardly Americans. They feared him so much that they deliberately set out to murder him."

"But to contact a man from the distant past," Tomo mused. "That could be dangerous."

Raizo bobbed his burly head up and down in agreement. "I read a story once where a man went back to the Age of Dinosaurs and killed a butterfly—accidentally, of course. But when he came back to his own time the human race didn't even exist!" He frowned, thinking hard. "Or something like that; I don't remember, exactly."

As usual, Miyoko stood up for Konda. "Sai won't tamper with history, will you?"

Konda forced himself to smile faintly and shake his head. But he could not answer, not in honesty. For his overwhelming desire was to do precisely that: to tamper with history. To change it completely, even if it did destroy his world.

So he hid his motives from even his dearest friends, because they would never understand what drove him. How could they? They could walk in the sunlight, feel wind on their faces, touch one another, and make love. He was alone in his orbital prison, always alone, waiting for death alone. But *before I die,* he told himself, *I will succeed in my quest.*

Once his equipment was functioning he plucked a series of test objects—a quartz wristwatch, a bowl of steaming rice, a running video camera—over times of a few minutes. Then a few hours. The first living thing he tried was a flower, a graceful chrysanthemum that was donated by one of the space station's crew members who grew the flowers as a hobby. Then a sealed beaker of water teeming with protozoa, specially sent to the station from the university's biology department. Then a laboratory mouse.

Often the power drain meant that large sections of Shanghai or Hong Kong or one of the other customer cities in Greater East Asia had to be blacked out temporarily. At the gentle insistence of the energy consortium, Konda always timed these experiments for the sleeping hours between midnight and dawn, locally. That way, transferring the solar power satellites' beams from the cities on Earth to Konda's laboratory made a minimum of inconvenience for the blacked-out customers.

Carefully he increased the range of his experiments—and his power requirements. He reached for a puppy that he remembered from his childhood, the pet of a nurse's daughter who had sent him digitized messages for a while, until she grew tired of speaking to the digital image of a friend she would never see in the flesh. The puppy appeared in the special isolation chamber in Konda's apparatus, a ball of wriggling fur with a dangling red tongue. Konda watched it for a few brief moments, then returned it to its natural spacetime, thirty years in the past. His eyes were blurred with tears as the puppy winked out of sight. Self-induced allergic reaction, he told himself as he wiped his eyes.

He spent the next several days meticulously examining his encapsulated world, looking for changes that might have been caused by his experiment with the puppy. The calendar was the same. The computer programs he had set up specifically to test for changes in the spacetime continuum appeared totally unaffected. Of course, he thought, if I changed history, if I moved the flow of the continuum, everything around me would be changed—including not only the computer's memory, but my own.

Still, he scanned the news media and the educational channels of hundreds of TV stations all around the world that he orbited. Nothing appeared out of place. All was normal. His experiment had not changed anything. He still had the wasting immunodeficiency disease that his mother had bequeathed him. His body was still rotting away.

He thought of bringing the puppy back and killing it with a painless gas, to see what effect the change would make on history. But he feared to tamper with the space-time continuum until he actually had

Yamamoto in his grasp. He wondered idly if he could kill the puppy, then told himself angrily that of course he could; the dog must be long dead by now, anyway.

He knew he was ready for the climax of his experiments: snatching Yamamoto from nearly a century in the past. *The time for hesitation is over*, Konda told himself sternly. *Set up the experiment and do it, even if it destroys this world and everything in it.*

So he did. Making arrangements for the necessary power from Greater Nippon Electric took longer than he had expected: blacking out most of Asia for several hours was not something the corporate executives agreed to lightly. But at last they did agree.

As a final step in his preparations he asked the commander of the space station to increase its spin so that his isolation area would be at almost a full Earthly gravity.

"Will that not be uncomfortable for you?" the station commander asked. She was new to her post, the first woman to command one of Japan's giant orbiting stations. She had been instructed to take special care of the guest in the isolation module.

"I am prepared for some inconvenience," Konda replied to her image in his comm screen. He was already seated in his powered wheelchair. The low-g of the station had allowed him to move about almost normally, despite the continued atrophy of his limbs. His body spent most of its energy continually trying to destroy the fast-mutating viruses that were, in their turn, doing their best to destroy him. The lifelong battle had left him pitifully weak and frail—in body. But he had the spirit of a true samurai. He followed the warrior's path as well as he was able.

In truth he dreaded the higher gravity. He even feared it might put such a strain on his heart that it would kill him. But it was a risk he was prepared to take. Yamamoto would find his sudden emergence into the twenty-first century startling enough; there was no need to embarrass him with a low-gravity environment that might make him physically ill or overwhelm his spirit with sudden fear.

The moment finally arrived. The great power satellites turned their emitting antennas to the huge receiver that had been built near the space station. Half of Asia, from Beijing to Bangkok, went dark.

Grand Admiral Isoruku Yamamoto, commander in chief of the Japanese Imperial Fleet, suddenly appeared in the middle of Konda's living quarters. He had been seated, apparently, when the wave harmonics had transported him. He plopped unceremoniously onto the floor, a look of pain and surprise widening his eyes. Konda wanted to laugh; thank the gods that the field included the admiral's flawlessly white uniform. A naked Yamamoto would have been too much to bear.

Konda had divided his living quarters in two with an impervious clear plastic wall. Both sides were as antiseptic as modern biotechnology could make them. Yamamoto, coming from nearly a hundred years in the past, was undoubtedly carrying a zoo of microbes that could slay Konda within days, if not hours.

For a frozen instant they stared at each other: the admiral in his white uniform sitting on the floor; the scientist in his powered wheelchair, his face gaunt with the ravages of the disease that was remorselessly killing him.

Then Yamamoto glanced around the chamber. He saw the banks of gauges and winking lights, the gleaming robots standing stiffly as if at attention, the glareless light panels overhead. He heard the hum of electrical equipment, smelled the mixed odors of laboratory and hospital.

Yamamoto climbed to his feet, brushing nonexistent dust from his jacket and sharply creased trousers. He was burly in build, thickset and powerful. His heavy jaw and shaved scalp made him look surly, obtuse. But his eyes gleamed with intelligence. Two fingers were missing from his left hand, the result of an accident during the battle of Tsushima, young ensign Yamamoto's first taste of war.

Konda bowed his head as deeply as he could in his wheelchair and hissed with respect.

Yamamoto granted him a curt nod. "I am dreaming," he said. "This is a dream."

"No, this is not a dream," said Konda, wheeling his chair to the clear partition that divided the room. "This is reality. You, most revered and honored admiral, are the first man to travel through time."

Yamamoto snorted with disdain. "A dream," he repeated. But then he added, "Yet it is the most unusual dream I have ever had."

For hours Konda tried to convince the admiral that he was not dreaming. At times Konda almost thought he was dreaming himself, so powerful was Yamamoto's resistance. Yet he persisted, for what Konda wanted to do depended on Yamamoto's acceptance of the truth.

Finally, after they had shared a meal served by the robots and downed many cups of sake, Yamamoto raised a hand. On the other side of the partition, Konda immediately fell silent. Even through the plastic wall he could feel the power of Yamamoto's personality, a power based on integrity, and strength, and limitless courage.

"Let us arrange a truce," Yamamoto suggested. "I am willing to accept your statements that you have created a time machine and have brought me here to the future. Whether I am dreaming or not is irrelevant, for the time being."

Konda drew in a breath. "I accept the truce," he said. It was the best that he would get from the utterly pragmatic man across the partition.

He felt terribly weary from trying to convince the admiral of the truth. He had deliberately wrapped his entire module in a stasis field, making it a small bubble of space-time hovering outside the normal flow of time. He wanted true isolation, with not even a chance of interference from the space station crew or the doctors. He and Yamamoto could live in the module outside the normal time stream for days or even years, if Konda chose. When he was ready to turn off the field and the bubble collapsed, no discernible time would have elapsed in the real world. He would return himself to the instant the experiment began, and Yamamoto would return to his writing desk in 1941. Not even his three friends would know if the experiment had worked or not.

If his friends still existed when Konda ended the experiment.

They slept. The robots had prepared a comfortable cot for Yamamoto, and suitable clothing. Konda slept in his chair, reclined in almost a horizontal position. His dreams were disturbing, bitter, but he suppressed their memory once he awoke once again.

Time within the windowless chamber was arbitrary; often Konda worked around the clock, although less and less as his body's weariness continued to erode his strength. When Yamamoto awoke, Konda began the admiral's history lessons. He had painstakingly assembled a vast library of microform books and videotapes about the events of the past century. Konda had been especially careful to get as many discs of boastful American films from the World War II years. This would be a delicate matter, he knew, for he intended to show Yamamoto his own death at the hands of the murderous Yankees.

Slowly, slowly Konda unreeled the future to his guest. Yamamoto sat in stolid silence as he watched the attack on Pearl Harbor, muttering now and then, "No aircraft carriers at anchor. That is bad." And later, "Nagumo should have sent in a third attack. The fool."

By the time the viewing screen at last went dark, Yamamoto looked through the partition toward Konda with a new look in his eyes. *He is beginning to believe me*, Konda told himself.

"This dream is very realistic," the admiral said, his voice dark with concern.

"There is more," Konda said. Sadly, he added, "Much more."

Konda lost track of time. The two men ate and slept and watched the ancient discs. Yamamoto put away his uniform, folding it carefully, almost reverently, and wore the comfortable loose kimono that Konda had provided for him. The admiral had far more energy and endurance than Konda. While the scientist slept, the admiral read from the microform books. When Konda awakened Yamamoto always had a thousand questions waiting for him.

He truly believes, Konda realized. *He sees that this is not a dream. He knows that I am showing him his own future.* The admiral watched the disastrous battle of Midway in stoic silence, his only discernible reaction the clenching of his heavy jaw whenever the screen showed a Japanese ship being sunk.

To his surprise, Konda felt enormous reluctance when it came time to show Yamamoto his death. For a whole day he showed no further videos and even cut off the power to the microform book reader.

"Why have you stopped?" Yamamoto asked.

From behind his impermeable plastic screen, Konda grimaced with pain. But he tried to hide it by asking the older man, "Do you still believe that all this is a dream?"

Yamamoto's eyes narrowed into an intense stare. "All of life is a dream, my young friend."

"Or a nightmare."

"You are ill," said the admiral.

"I am dying."

"So are we all." Yamamoto got to his feet, walked slowly around his half of the room. In his dark blue kimono he needed only a set of swords to look exactly like a samurai warrior of old.

Slowly, haltingly, Konda told him of his disease. The gift of his unknown parents. He had never spoken to anyone about this in such detail. He cursed his whore of a mother and damned the father that had undoubtedly spread his filth to many others. An American. He knew his father had to be an American. A tourist, probably. Or a miserable businessman come to Tokyo to ferret out the secrets of Japanese success.

He railed against the fate that kept him confined inside a diseased body and kept the dying body confined inside this chamber of complete exile. He raged and wept in front of the man he had plucked from the past. Not even to his three best friends had he dared to speak of the depth of his hatred and despair. But he could do it with Yamamoto, and once he started, his emotion was a torrent that he could not stop until he was totally exhausted.

The older man listened in silent patience, for many hours. Finally, when Konda had spent his inner fury and sat half dead in his powered chair, Yamamoto said, "It does no good to struggle against death. What a man should seek is to make his death meaningful. It cannot be avoided. But it can be glorious."

"Can it?" Koncla snapped. "You think so? Your own death was not glorious; it was a miserable assassination!"

Yamamoto's eyes flickered for an instant, then his iron self-control reasserted itself. "So that is what you have been hiding from me."

Almost snarling with searing rage, Konda spun his chair to the console that controlled the video screen.

"Here is your glorious death, old man! Here is how you met your fate!"

He had spent years collecting all the tapes from libraries in the United States and Japan. Most of the tapes were re-creations, dramatizations of the actual events. Yamamoto's decision to visit the front lines, in the Solomon Islands, to boost the sagging spirits of his men who were under attack by the Americans. The way the sneaking Americans broke the Japanese naval code and learned that Yamamoto would be within reach of their longest-range fighter planes for a scant few minutes. Their decision to try to kill the Japanese warrior, knowing that his death would be worth whole battle fleets and air armadas. The actual mission, where the American cowards shot down the plane that carried Grand Admiral Isoruku Yamamoto, killing him and all the others aboard.

The screen went dark.

"If your flight had been late by five minutes," Konda said, "the Americans would have had to turn back and you would not have been murdered."

The admiral was still staring at the blank screen. "I have always been a stickler for punctuality. A fatal flaw, I suppose."

Yamamoto sat silently for a few moments, while Konda wondered what thoughts were passing through his mind. Then he turned to face the younger man once more. "Show me the rest," he said. "Show me what happened after I died."

Still seething with anger, Konda unreeled the remaining history of the war. The Imperial Fleet destroyed. The home cities of Japan firebombed. The kamikaze suicide attacks where untrained youths threw away their lives to no avail. The ultimate horror of Hiroshima and Nagasaki.

The humiliating surrender signed aboard an American battleship in Tokyo harbor.

The robots offered meals at their preprogrammed times. Neither Konda nor Yamamoto ate as they watched the disastrous past unfold on the video screen, defeat and slaughter and the ultimate dishonor.

"Does Japan still exist?" the admiral asked when the screen finally went blank. "Is there an emperor still alive, living in exile, perhaps?"

Konda blinked. "The emperor lives in his palace in Tokyo. Japan not only exists, it is one of the richest nations on Earth."

For the first time Yamamoto looked confused. "How can that be?"

Reluctantly, grudgingly, Konda showed the old man more recent history tapes. The rise of Japan's industrial strength. Japan's move into space. Yamamoto saw the Rising Sun emblem on the Moon's empty wastes, on the red deserts of Mars, on the giant factory ships that plied among the asteroids, on the gleaming solar power satellites that beamed electrical power to the hungry cities of Earth.

At last the admiral rubbed his eyes and turned away from the darkened screen.

"We lost the war," he said. "But somehow Japan has become the leading nation of the world."

Konda burst into a harshly bitter laughter. "The leading nation of the world? Japan has become a whore! A nation of merchants and tradesmen. There is no greatness in this."

"There is wealth," Yamamoto replied drily.

"Yes, but at what price? We have lost our souls," Konda said. "Japan no longer follows the path of honor. Every day we become more like the Americans." He almost spat that last word.

Yamamoto heaved a heavy sigh. Konda tapped at the control console keypad again. The video screen brightened once more. This time it showed modern Japan: the riotous noise and flash of the Ginza, boys wearing Mohawk haircuts and girls flaunting themselves in shorts and halters; parents lost in a seductive wonderland of gadgetry while their children addicted themselves to electronic and chemical pleasures; foreigners flooding into Japan, blackening the slopes of Fujiyama, taking photographs of the emperor himself.

"My father was one of those American visitors," Konda said, surprised at how close to tears he was again. "A diseased, depraved foreigner."

Yamamoto said nothing.

"You see how Japan is being destroyed," Konda said. "What good is it to be the world's richest nation if our soul is eaten away?"

"What would you do?"

Konda wheeled his chair to the plastic partition so close that he almost pressed his face against it.

"Go back to your own time," he said, nearly breathless, "and win the war! You know enough now to avoid the mistakes that were made. You can concentrate your forces at Midway and overwhelm the Americans! You can invade the west coast of the U.S. before they are prepared! You can prevent your own assassination and lead Japan to victory!"

The admiral nodded gravely. "Yes, I could do all of those things. Then the government that launched the war against America would truly dictate surrender terms in the White House—and rule much of the world afterward."

"Yes! Exactly!"

Yamamoto regarded the younger man solemnly through the clear plastic partition. "But if I do that, would that not change the history that you know? Such a Japan would be very different from the one you have just shown me."

"Good!" Konda exulted. "Excellent!"

"Your parents would never meet in such a world. You would never be born."

Konda gave a fierce sigh of relief. "I know. My miserable existence would never come to be. For that I would be glad. Grateful!"

Yamamoto shook his head. "I have sent many warriors to their deaths, but never have I deliberately done anything that I knew would kill one certain individual."

"I can follow the warrior's path," Konda said, barely able to control the trembling that racked his body. "You are not the only one who can live by the code of Bushido."

The older man fell silent.

"I want to die!" Konda blurted. "I want to have never been born! Take my life. Take it in exchange for your own. For the greatness of Japan, you must live and I must never have come into existence."

"For the greatness of Japan," Yamamoto muttered.

They ate a meal together, each of them on his own side of the partition, and then slept. Konda dreamed of himself as one of the kamikaze pilots, a headband proclaiming his courage tied across his forehead, a ceremonial sword strapped to his waist, diving his plane into an American warship, exploding into a blossom of fire and glory.

He woke to find himself still alive, still dying slowly.

Yamamoto was back in his stiff white uniform. The old man knew that his time here was drawing to its conclusion.

With hardly a word between them, Konda directed the admiral to the spot in the room where the wave harmonics converged. Yamamoto stood ramrod straight, hands balled into fists at his side. The generators whined to life, spinning up beyond the range of human hearing. Konda felt their power, though; their vibrations rattled him in his chair.

Only seconds to go. Konda forced himself to his feet and brought his right hand to his brow in a shaky salute to Japan's greatest warrior. Yamamoto solemnly saluted back.

"Go back and win the war," Konda said, his voice shaking with emotion.

Yamamoto muttered something. Konda could not quite hear the words; he was too intent on watching the display screens of his equipment.

The admiral disappeared. As suddenly as a light blinking out, one instant he was there staring solemnly at Konda, the next he was gone back to his own time.

"Banzai," Konda whispered.

His finger hovered, trembling, over the key that would break the stasis and return him to the mainstream of spacetime. *If all has gone well, this will be the end of me. Saito Konda will no longer exist.* He pulled in a deep, final breath, almost savoring it, and then leaned savagely hard on the key.

And nothing happened. He blinked, looked around. His chamber was unchanged. His equipment hummed to itself. The display screens showed that everything was quite normal. The comm unit was blinking its red message light.

A terrible fear began to worm its way up Konda's spine. He called out to the comm unit, "Respond!"

The station commander's face took form on the screen. "When will you begin your experiment, sir?" she asked.

Konda saw the digital clock numbers on the screen: hardly ten seconds had passed since he had first put his chamber in stasis.

"It didn't work," he mumbled. "It's all over for now. You can return my module to the low-gravity mode."

The commander nodded once and the screen went dark. Konda felt a lurch in the pit of his stomach and then a sinking, falling sensation. He floated up out of his chair like a man in a dream.

Was I dreaming? he asked himself. *Did it actually happen? Why hasn't the world changed? Why am I still alive?*

Puzzled, almost dazed, he activated the rewind of the cameras that had recorded every instant of his experiment. When the recorder stopped, he pressed the PLAY button.

And there was Yamamoto in the chamber with him. Konda stared, put the tape in fast forward. Their voices chittered and jabbered like a pair of monkeys', they sped through their days together in a jerky burlesque of normal movement. But it was Yamamoto. It had really happened.

Konda sank onto his bed, suddenly so totally exhausted that he could not stand even in the low gravity. The experiment had worked. He had shown Yamamoto everything and sent him back to win his war against the Americans and save Japan's soul. Yet nothing seemed changed.

He wanted to sleep but he could not. Instead, in a growing frenzy he began to tune in to television broadcasts from Earth. One channel after another, from Japan, China, the Philippines, Australia, the United

States, Europe. Nothing had changed! The world was just the way it had been before he had snatched Yamamoto out of the past.

Konda beat his frail fists on his emaciated thighs in utter frustration. He tore at his hair. *Why? Why hasn't anything changed?*

Frantically he searched through his history discs. It was all the same. The war. Japan's defeat. The humiliation of achieving world economic power at the sacrifice of all that the Japanese soul had held dear in earlier generations.

I still live, Konda cried silently. *My mother was born and grew up and plied her filthy trade and gave birth to a diseased, unclean son.*

In desperation, he went back to the tapes of Yamamoto's assassination. It was all the same. Exactly, precisely the same. Either the experiment had not worked at all, and Konda had hallucinated his days with Yamamoto, or . . .

He saw one thing on one of the tapes that he did not recall being there before. The screen showed the twin-engine plane that would carry the admiral and his staff from the base at Rabaul to the island of Bougainville. The narrator pointed out Yamamoto's insistence on punctuality, " . . . as if the admiral knew that he had an appointment with death."

A moment or two later, while the screen showed American planes attacking the Japanese flight, the narrator quoted Yamamoto as saying, "I have killed many of the enemy . . . I believe the time has come for me to die, too."

"He did it deliberately!" Konda howled in the emptiness of his chamber. "He knew and yet he let them kill him!"

For hours Konda raved and tore through his quarters, pounding his fists against the walls and furniture until they bled, smashing the equipment that had fetched the greatest warrior of history to his presence, raging and screaming at the blankly immobile robots.

Finally, totally spent, bleeding, his chest heaving and burning as if with fever, he sat in the wreckage of his laboratory before the one display screen he had not smashed and called up the tape of Yamamoto's visit. For hours he watched himself and the doughty old admiral, seeking the answer he desperately needed to make sense out of his universe.

He should have gone back and changed everything, Konda's mind kept repeating. *He should have gone back and changed everything.*

For days he sat there, without eating, without sleeping, like a catatonic searching for the key that would release him.

He came to the very end of the tape, with Yamamoto standing at attention and gravely returning his own salute.

He heard himself say to the admiral, "Go back and win the war."

He saw Yamamoto's lips move, and then the old man disappeared.

Konda rewound the tape and replayed that last moment, with the sound volume turned up high enough to hear the admiral's final words.

"Go back and win the war," his own voice boomed.

Yamamoto replied, "We did win it."

Haggard, breathless, Konda stared at the screen as the old admiral disappeared and returned to his own time, his own death. Willingly.

Tears misted his eyes. He went to his powered chair and sank wearily into it. *Yamamoto did not understand anything. Not a thing!*

Or perhaps he did. Perhaps the old warrior saw and understood it all. Better than I have, thought Konda. *He sees more clearly than I do.*

In the warrior's code there is only one acceptable way for a man to deal with the shame of defeat. Konda leaned his head back and waited for death to take him, also. He did not have to wait very long.

SAM GUNN

Back when I was the Editor of Analog Science Fiction *magazine (1971-78), one of my tasks was to feed story ideas to writers.*

For years I tried to get one writer after another to write a story for the magazine around a certain idea. All I ever got for my efforts was a series of blank stares and muttered promises to "give it a shot."

When I finally stopped being an editor and began to write short fiction again, I tackled the idea myself. "Sam Gunn" is the result. Sam is inventive and irreverent, feisty and tough, good-hearted and crafty, a womanizer, a little guy who is constantly struggling against the "big guys" of huge corporations and government bureaucracies.

Ed Ferman, who was then the editor and publisher of The Magazine of Fantasy and Science Fiction, *not only bought the story, he published it in his magazine's 34th anniversary issue, which pleased me no end.*

Over the years since then I've written dozens of stories about Sam. Here's what he looked like when I first set my inner eye on him.

THE SPRING-WHEELED TRUCK rolled to a silent stop on the Sea of Clouds. The fine dust kicked up by its six wheels floated lazily back to the mare's soil. The hatch to the truck cab swung upward, and a space-suited figure climbed slowly down to the lunar surface, clumped a dozen ponderously careful steps, then turned back toward the truck.

"Yeah, this is the spot. The transponder's beeping away, all right."

Two more figures clambered down from the cab, bulbous and awkward-looking in the bulky space suits. One of them turned a full three hundred sixty degrees, scanning the scene through the gold-tinted visor of the suit's bubble helmet. There was nothing to be seen except the monotonous gray plain, pockmarked by craters like an ancient, savage battlefield that had been petrified into solid stone long eons ago.

"Christ, you can't even see the ringwall from here."

"That's what he wanted—to be out in the open, without a sign of civilization in sight. He picked this spot himself, you know."

"Helluva place to want to be buried."

"That's what he specified in his will. Come on, let's get to work. I want to get back to Selene City before the sun sets."

It was a local joke: the three space-suited workers had more than two hundred hours before sunset.

Grunting even in the general lunar gravity, they slid the coffin from the back of the truck and placed it gently on the roiled, dusty ground. Then they winched the four-meter-high crate from the truck and put it down softly next to the coffin. While one of them scoured a coffin-sized hole in the ground with the blue-white flame of a plasma torch, the other two uncrated the big package.

"Ready for the coffin," said the worker with the torch.

The leader of the trio inspected the grave. The hot plasma had polished the stony ground. The two workers heard him muttering over their helmet earphones as he used a hand laser to check the grave's dimensions. Satisfied, he helped them drag the gold-filigreed coffin to the hole and slide it in.

"A lot of work to do for a dead man."

"He wasn't just any ordinary man."

"It's still a lot of work. Why in hell couldn't he be recycled like everybody else?'

"Sam Gunn," said the leader, "never did things like everybody else. Not in his whole cursed long life. Why should he be like the rest of us in death?"

They chattered back and forth through their suit radios as they uncrated the big package. Once they had removed all the plastic and the bigger-than-life statue stood sparkling in the sunlight, they stepped back and gaped at it.

"It's glass!"

"Christ, I never saw anything so damned big."

"Must have cost a fortune to get it here. Two fortunes."

"He had it done at Island One, I hear. Brought the sculptor up from Earthside and paid enough to keep her at L-4 for two whole years. God knows how many times he tried to cast a statue this big and failed."

"I didn't know you could make a glass statue so big."

"In zero gee you can. It's hollow. If we were in air, I could ping it with my finger and should hear it ring."

"Crystal."

"That's right."

One of the workers, the young man, laughed softly.

"What's so funny'?" the leader asked.

"Who else but Sam Gunn would have the gall to erect a crystal statue to himself and then have it put out in the middle of this godforsaken emptiness, where nobody's ever going to see it? It's a monument to himself, for himself. What ego. What monumental ego."

The leader chuckled. too. "Yeah, Sam had an ego, all right. But he was a smart little guy, too."

"You knew him?" the young woman asked.

"Sure. Knew him well enough to tell you that he didn't pick this spot for his tomb just for the sake of his ego. He was smarter than that."

"What was he like?"

"When did you know him?"

"Come on, we've still got work to do. He wants the statue positioned exactly as he stated in his will, with its back toward Selene and the face looking up toward Earth."

"Yeah, okay, but when did you know him, huh?"

"Oh golly, years ago. Decades ago. When the two of us were just young pups. The first time either of us came here, back in—Lord, it's thirty years ago. More."

"Tell us about it. Was he really the rascal that the history tapes say he was? Did he really do all the things they say?" asked the young woman.

"He was a phony!" the young man snapped. "Everybody knows

that. A helluva showman, sure, but he never did half the stuff he took credit for. Nobody could have, not in one lifetime."

"He lived a pretty intense life," said the leader. "If it hadn't been for a faulty suit valve he'd still be running his show from here to Titan."

"A showman. That's what he was. No hero."

"What was he like?" the young woman repeated.

So, while the two youngsters struggled with the huge, fragile crystal statue, the older man sat himself on the lip of the truck's cab hatch and told them what he knew about the first time Sam Gunn came to the Moon.

The skipper used the time-honored cliché—he said—"Houston, we have a problem here."

There were eight of us, the whole crew of Artemis IV, huddled together in the command module. After six weeks of living on the Moon the module smelled like a pair of unwashed gym socks.

With a woman President the space agency figured it would be smart to name the second round of lunar explorations after a female: Artemis was Apollo's sister. Get it?

But it had just happened that the computer who picked the crew selections for Artemis IV picked all men. Six weeks without even the sight of a woman, and now our blessed-be-to-God return module refused to light up. We were stranded. No way to get back home.

As usual, capcom in Houston was the soul of tranquility. "Ah, A-IV, we read you and copy that the return module is no-go. The analysis team is checking the telemetry. We will get back to you soonest."

It didn't help that capcom, that shift, was Sandi Hemmings, the woman we all lusted after. Among the eight of us, we must have spent enough energy dreaming about cornering Sandi in zero gravity to propel each of us right back to Houston. Unfortunately, dreams have a very low specific impulse and we were still stuck on the Moon, a quarter-million miles from the nearest woman.

Sandi played her capcom duties strictly by the book, especially since all our transmissions were taped for later review.

She kept the traditional Houston poker face, but managed to say, "Don't worry, boys. We'll figure it out and get you home."

Praise God for small favors.

We had spent hours checking and rechecking the cursed return module. It was an engineer's hell: everything checked but nothing worked. The thing just sat there like a lump of dead metal. No electrical power. None. Zero. The control board just stared at us as cold and glassy-eyed as a banker listening to your request for an unsecured loan. We had pounded it. We had kicked it. In our desperation we had even gone through the instruction manual, page by page, line by line. Zip. Zilch. The bird was dead.

When Houston got back to us, six hours after the skipper's call, it was the stony, unsmiling image of the mission coordinator who glowered at us as if we had deliberately screwed up the return module. He told us:

"We have identified the problem, Artemis IV. The return module's main electrical power supply has malfunctioned."

That was like telling Othello that he was a Moor.

"We're checking out bypasses and other possible fixes," Old Stone Face went on. "Sit tight, we'll get back to you."

The skipper gave him a patient sigh. "Yes, sir."

"We're not going anywhere," said a whispered voice. Sam Gunn's, I was certain.

The problem, we finally discovered, was caused by a micrometeoroid, no less. A little grain of sand that just happened to roam through the solar system for four and a half billion years and then decided to crash-dive itself right into the main fuel cell of our return module's power supply. It was so tiny that it didn't do any visible damage to the fuel cell: just hurt it enough to let it discharge electrically for most of the six weeks we had been on the Moon. And the other two fuel cells, sensing the discharge through the module's idiot computer, tried to recharge their partner for six weeks. The result: all three of them were dead and gone by the time we needed them.

It was Sam who discovered the pinhole in the fuel cell, the eighteenth time we checked out the power supply. I can remember his exact words, once he realized what had happened:

"Shit!"

Sam was a feisty little guy who would have been too short for astronaut duty if the agency hadn't lowered the height requirements so that women could join the corps. He was a good man, a whiz with a computer and a born tinkerer who liked to rebuild old automobiles and then race them on the abandoned freeways whenever he could

scrounge up enough old-fashioned petrol to run them. The Terror of
Clear Lake, we used to call him. The Texas Highway Patrol had other
names for him. So did the agency administrators; they cussed near
threw him out of the astronaut corps at least half a dozen times.

But we all loved Sam, back in those days, as we went through
training and then blasted off for our first mission to the Moon. He was
funny, he kept us laughing. And he did the things and said the things
that none of us had the guts to do or say.

The skipper loved Sam a little less than the rest of us, especially
after six weeks of living in each other's dirty laundry. Sam had a way
of almost defying any order he received; he reacted very poorly to
authority figures. Our skipper, Lord love him, was as stiff-backed an
old-school authority figure as any of them. He was basically a good
Joe, and I'm cursed if I can remember his real name. But his big
problem was that he had memorized the rule book and tried never to
deviate from it.

Well, anyway, there we were, stranded on the lunar surface after six
weeks of hard work. Our task had been to make a semi-permanent
underground base out of the prefabricated modules that had been, as
the agency quaintly phrased it, "landed remotely on the lunar regolith
in a series of carefully-coordinated unmanned logistics missions." In
other words, they had dropped nine different module packages over
a fifty-square-kilometer area of Mare Nubium and we had to find
them all, drag them to the site that Houston had picked for Base
Gamma, set them up properly, scoop up enough of the top layers of
soil to cover each module and the connecting tunnels to a depth of
0.3048 meter (that's one foot, in English), and then link in the electric
power reactor and all the wiring, plumbing, heating and air
circulation units. Which we had done, adroitly and efficiently, and
now that our labors were finished and we were ready to leave—no go.
Too bad we couldn't have covered the return module with 0.3048
meter of lunar soil; that would have protected the fuel cells from that
sharpshooting micrometeoroid.

The skipper decided it would be bad procedure to let us mope
around and brood.

"I want each of you to run a thorough inventory of all your personal
supplies: the special foods you've brought with you, your spare
clothing, entertainment kits, the works."

"That'll take four minutes," Sam muttered, loud enough for us all to hear him. The eight of us were crammed into the command module, eight guys squeezed into a space built for three, at most. It was barely high enough to stand in, and the metal walls and ceiling always felt cold to the touch. Sam was pressed in with the guys behind me; I was practically touching noses with the skipper. The guys in back giggled at his wisecrack. The skipper scowled.

"Goddammit, Gunn, can't you behave seriously for even a minute? We've got a real problem here."

"Yessir," Sam replied. If he hadn't been squeezed in so tightly, I'm sure he would have saluted. "I'm merely attempting to keep morale high, sir."

The skipper made an unhappy snorting noise, and then told us that we would spend the rest of the shift checking out all the supplies that were left: not just our personal stuff, but the mission's supplies of food, the nuclear reactor, the water recirculation system, equipment of all sorts, air tanks, the works.

We knew it was busywork, but we had nothing else to do. So we wormed our way out of the command module and crawled through the tunnels toward the other modules that we had laid out and then covered with bulldozed soil. It was a neat little buried base we had set up, for later explorers to use. I got a sort of claustrophobic feeling, just then, that this buried base might turn into a mass grave for eight astronauts.

I was dutifully heading back for barracks module A, where four of us had our bunks and personal gear, to check out my supplies as the skipper had ordered. Sam snaked up beside me. Those tunnels, back in those days, were prefabricated Earthside to be laid out once we got to the construction site. I think they were designed by midgets. You couldn't stand up in them; they were too low. You had to really crawl along on hands and knees if you were my size. Sam was able to shuffle through them with bent knees, knuckle-walking like a miniature gorilla. He loved the tunnels.

"Hey, wait up," he hissed to me.

I stopped.

"Whattaya think will get us first, the air giving out or we starve to death?"

He was grinning cheerfully. I said, "I think we're going to poison our air with methane. We'll fart ourselves to death in another couple of days."

Sam's grin widened. "C'mon, I'm setting up a pool on the computer. I hadn't thought of air pollution. You wanna make a bet on that?" He started to King-Kong down the shaft to the right, toward the computer and life-support module. If I had had the space, I would have shrugged. Anyway, I followed him there.

Three of the other guys were in the computer module, huddled around the display screen like Boy Scouts around a campfire.

"Why aren't you checking out the base's supplies, like the skipper said?" I asked them.

"We are, Straight Arrow," replied Mickey Lee, our refugee from Chinatown. He tapped the computer screen. "Why go sorting through all that junk when the computer has it already listed in alphabetical order for us?"

That wasn't what the skipper wanted, and we all knew it, but Mickey was right. Why bother with busywork? We wrote down lists that would keep the skipper happy. By hand. If we had let the computer print out the lists, Skip would have gotten wise to us right away.

While we scribbled away, copying what was on the screen, we talked over our basic situation.

"Why the hell can't we use the nuke to recharge the fuel cells?" Julio Marx asked. He was our token Puerto Rican Jew, a tribute to the agency's Equal Opportunity policy. Julio was also a crackerjack structural engineer who had saved my life the day I had started to unfasten my helmet in the barracks module just when one of those blessed prefab tunnels had cracked its airlock seal. But that's another story.

Sam gave Julio a sorrowful stare. "The two systems are incompatible, Jules." Then, with a grin, Sam launched into the phoniest Latin accent you ever heard. "The nuclear theeng, man, it got too many volts for the fuel cells. Like, you plug the nukie to the fuel cells, man. you make a beeg boom and we all go to dat big San Juan in thee sky. You better steek to plucking chickens, man, an' leave the electricity alone."

Julio, who towered a good inch and a half over Sam, grinned back at him and answered, "Okay, Shorty, I dig."

"Shorty! Shorty!" Sam's face went all red. "All right, that's it. The hell with the betting pool. I'm gonna let you guys all die of boredom. Serve you right."

We made a big fuss and soothed his feathers and cajoled him into setting up the pool. With a great show of hurt feelings and reluctant but utterly selfless nobility, Sam pushed Mickey Lee out of the chair in front of the computer terminal and began playing the keyboard like a virtuoso pianist. Within a few minutes the screen was displaying a list of possible ways for us to die, with Sam's swiftly calculated odds next to each entry. At the touch of a button, the screen displayed a graph, showing how the odds for each mode of dying changed as time went on.

Suffocation, for example, started off as less than a one percent possibility. But within a month the chances began to rise fairly steeply. "The air scrubbers need replacement filters," Sam explained, "and we'll be out of them inside of two more weeks."

"They'll have us out of here in two weeks, for Christ's sake," Julio said.

"Or drop fresh supplies for us," said Ron Avery, the taciturn pilot whom we called Cowboy because of his lean, lanky build and his slow Western drawl.

"Those are the odds," Sam snapped. "The computer does not lie. Pick your poison and place your bets."

I put fifty bucks down on Air Contamination, not telling the other guys about my earlier conversation with Sam. Julio took Starvation. Mickey settled on Dehydration (Lack of Water), and Ron picked Murder—which made me shudder.

"What about you, Sam?" I asked.

"I'll wait. Let the other guys have a chance," he said.

"You gonna let the skipper in on this'?" Julio asked. Sam shook his head. "If I tell him . . ."

"I'll tell him," Ron volunteered, with a grim smile. "I'll even let him have Murder, if he wants it. I can always switch to Suicide."

"Droll fellow," said Sam.

Well, you probably read about the mission in your history tapes. Houston was supporting three separate operations on the Moon at the same time, and they were stretched to the limit down there. Old Stone Face promised us a rescue flight in a week. But they had a problem with the booster when they tried to rush things on the pad too much, and the blessed launch had to be pushed back a week, and then another week. They sent an unmanned supply craft to us, but the descent stage got gummed up, so our fresh food, air filters, water supply and other stuff just orbited over us about fifty miles up.

Sam calculated the odds of all these foul-ups and came to the conclusion that Houston was working overtime to kill us.

"Must be some sort of an experiment," he told me. "Maybe they need some martyrs to make people more aware of the space program."

We learned afterward that Houston was in deep trouble because of us. The White House was firing people left and right, Congressional committees were gearing up to investigate the fiasco, and the CIA was checking out somebody's crackbrained idea that the Russians were behind all our troubles.

Meanwhile, we were stranded on Mare Nubium with nothing much to do but let our beards grow and hope for sinus troubles that would cut off our ability to sense odors.

Old Stone Face was magnificent, in his unflinching way. He was on the line to us every day, despite the fact that his superiors in Houston and Washington were either being fired directly by the President himself or roasted over the simmering coals of media criticism. There must have been a zillion reporters at Mission Control by the second week of our marooning; we could feel the hubbub and tension whenever we talked with Stony.

"The countdown for your rescue flight is proceeding on an accelerated schedule," he told us. It would never occur to him to say, "We're hurrying as fast as we can."

"Liftoff is now scheduled for 0700 hours on the twenty-fifth."

None of us needed to look at a calendar to know that the twenty-fifth was seventeen days away. Sam's betting pool was looking more serious every hour. Even the skipper had finally taken a plunge: Suffocation.

If it weren't for Sandi Hemmings we might have all gone crazy. She took over as capcom during the night shift, when most of the reporters and the agency brass were asleep. She gave us courage and the desire to pull through, partly just by smiling at us and looking female enough to make us want to survive, but mainly by giving us the straight info with no nonsense.

"They're in deep trouble over at Canaveral," she would tell us.

"They've had to go to triple shifts and call up boosters that they didn't think they would need until next year. Some senator in Washington is yelling that we ought to ask the Russians or the Japanese to help out."

"As if either of them had upper stages that could make it to the Moon and back," one of our guys muttered.

"Well," Sandi said, with her brightest smile, "you'll all be heroes when you finally get back here. The girls will be standing in line to admire you."

"You won't have to stand in line, Sandi," Ron Avery answered, in a rare burst of words. "You'll always be first with us."

The others crowded into the command module added their heartfelt agreement.

Sandi laughed, undaunted by the prospect of the eight of us grabbing at her. "I hope you shave first," she said.

A night or two later she spent hours reading to us the suggestions made by the Houston medical team on how to stretch out our dwindling supplies of food, water and air. They boiled down to one basic rule: lie down and don't exert yourselves. Great advice, especially when you're beginning to really worry that you're not going to make it through this mess. Just what we needed to do, lie back in our bunks and do nothing but think.

I caught a gleam in Sam's eye, though, as Sandi waded through the medics' report. The skipper asked her to send the report through our computer printer. She did, and he spent the next day reading and digesting it. Sam spent that day—well, I couldn't figure out where he'd gotten to. I just didn't see him all day long, and Base Gamma really wasn't big enough to hide in, even for somebody as small as Sam.

After going through the medics' recommendations, the skipper ordered us to take tranquilizers. We had a scanty supply of downers in the base pharmaceutical stores, and Skip divided them equally among us. At the rate of three a day, they would last four days, with four pills left over. About as useful as a cigarette lighter in hell, but the skipper played it by the book and ordered us to start gobbling tranquilizers.

"They will ease our anxieties and help us to remain as quiet as possible while we wait for the rescue mission," he told us.

He didn't bother to add that the rescue mission, according to Sandi's unofficial word, was still twelve days off. We would be out of food in three more days, and the recycled water was starting to taste as if it hadn't been recycled, if you know what I mean. The air was getting foul, too, but that was probably just our imaginations.

Sam appeared blithely unconcerned, even happy. He whistled cheerfully as Skip rationed out the tranquilizers, then scuttled off down the tunnel that led toward our barracks module. By the time I got to my bunk, Sam was nowhere in sight. His whistling was gone. So was his pressure suit.

He had gone out on the surface? For what? To increase his radiation dose? To get away from the rest of us? That was probably it. Underneath his wiseguy shell, Sam was probably as worried and tense as any of us, and he just didn't want us to know it. He needed some solitude, and what better place to get it than the airless rocky expanse of Mare Nubium?

That's what I thought, so I didn't go out after him.

The same thing happened the next "morning" (by which I mean the time immediately after our sleep shift), and the next. The skipper would gather us together in the command module, we would each take our ceremonial tranquilizer pill and a sip of increasingly bad water, and then we would crawl back to our bunks and try to do nothing that would use up body energy or air. I found myself resenting it whenever I had to go to the toilet: I kept imagining my urine flowing straight into our water tank without reprocessing. I guess I was beginning to go crazy.

But Sam was as happy as could be: chipper, joking. laughing it up. He would disappear each morning for several hours, and then show up again with a lopsided grin on his face, telling jokes and making us all feel a little better.

Until Julio suddenly sat up in his bunk, the second or third morning after we had run out of tranquilizers, and shouted:

"Booze!"

Sam had been sitting on the edge of Julio's bunk, telling an outrageous story of what he planned to do with Sandi once we got back to Houston.

"Booze!" Julio repeated. "I smell booze! I'm cracking up. I'm losing my marbles."

For once in his life, Sam looked apologetic, almost ashamed.

"No you're not," he said to Julio, in as quiet a voice as I've ever heard Sam speak. "I was going to tell you about it tomorrow—the stuff is almost ready for human consumption."

You never saw three grown men so suddenly attentive.

With a self-deprecating little grin, Sam explained, "I've been tinkering with the propellants and other junk out in the return module. They're not doing us any good, just sitting out there. So I made a small still. Seems to be working okay. I tasted a couple sips today. It'll take the enamel off your teeth, but it's not all that bad. By tomorrow—"

He never got any further. We did a Keystone Kops routine, rushing for our space suits, jamming ourselves through the airlock and running out to the inert, idle, cussedly useless return module.

Sam was not kidding us. He had jury-rigged an honest-to-backwoods still inside the return module, fueling it with propellants from the module's tanks. The basic alcohol also came from the propellant, with water from the fuel cells, and a few other ingredients that Sam had scrounged from miscellaneous supplies.

We lost no time pressurizing the module, lifting our helmet visors, and sampling his concoction. It was terrible. We loved it.

By the time we had staggered back to our barracks module, laughing and belching, we had made up our minds to let the other three guys in barracks B share in Sam's juice. But the skipper was a problem. Once he found out about it, he'd have Sam up on charges and drummed out of the agency, even before the rescue mission reached us. Old Stone Face would vote to leave Sam behind, I knew, if he found out about it.

"Have no fear," Sam told us, with a giggle. "I will, myself, reveal my activities to our skipper."

And before we could stop him, he had tottered off toward the command module, whistling in a horribly sour off-key way.

An hour went by. Then two. We could hear Skip's voice yelling from the command module, although we couldn't make out the words. None of us had the guts to go down the tunnel and try to help Sam. After a while the tumult and the shouting died. Mickey Lee gave me a questioning glance. Silence; ominous silence.

"You think Skip's killed him?" he asked.

"More likely," said Julio, "that Sam's talked the skipper to death."

Timidly, we slunk down the tunnel to the command module. The other three guys were there with Sam and the skipper; they were all quaffing Sam's rocket juice and grinning at each other.

We were shocked, but we joined right in. Six days later, when the guys from Base Alpha landed their return module crammed with food and fresh water for us, we invited them to join the party. A week after that, when the rescue mission from Canaveral finally showed up, we had been under the influence for so long that we told them to go away.

I had never realized before then what a lawyer Sam was. He had convinced the skipper to read the medics' report carefully, especially the part where they recommended using tranquilizers to keep us calm and minimize our energy consumption. Sam had then gotten the skipper to punch up the medical definition of alcohol's effects on the body, out of Houston's medical files. Sure enough, if you squinted the right way, you could claim that alcohol was a sort of tranquilizer. That was enough justification for the skipper, and we just about pickled ourselves until we got rescued.

The crystal statue glittered under the harsh rays of the unfiltered sun. The work leader, still sitting on the lip of the truck's hatch, said, "It looks beautiful. You guys did a good job. Is the epoxy set?"

"Needs another few minutes," said the young man, tapping the toe of his boot against the base that they had poured on the lunar plain.

"What happened when you got back to Houston?" the young woman asked. "Didn't they get angry at you for being drunk?"

"Sure," said the leader. "But what could they do? Sam's booze pulled us through, and we could show that we were merely following the recommendations of the medics. Old Stone Face hushed it all up and we became heroes, just like Sandi told us we would be—for about a week."

"And Sam?"

"He left the astronaut corps for a while and started his own business. The rest you know about from the history books. Hero, showman, scoundrel, patriot, it's all true. He was all those things."

"Did he and Sandi ever, uh . . . get together?" the young man asked.

"She was too smart to let him corner her. She used one of the other guys to protect her; married him, finally. Cowboy, I think it was. They eloped and spent their honeymoon in orbit. Zero gee and all that. Sam pretended to be very upset about it, but by that time he was surrounded by women, all of them taller than he was."

The three of them walked slowly around the gleaming statue.

"Look at the rainbows it makes where the sun hits it," said the young woman. "It's marvelous."

"But if he was so smart," said the young man, "why'd he pick this spot 'way out here for his grave? It's miles from Selene City. You can't even see the statue from the city."

"Silly. This is the place where Base Gamma was," said the young woman. "Isn't that right?"

"No," the leader said. "Gamma was all the way over on the other side of Nubium. It's still there. Abandoned, but still there. Even the blasted return module is still sitting there, as dumb as ever."

"Then why put the statue here?"

The leader chuckled. "Sam was a pretty shrewd guy. He set up, in his will, a tourist agency that will guide people to the important sites on the Moon. They start at Selene City and go along the surface in those big cruisers that're being built back at the city. Sam's tomb is going to he a major tourist attraction, and he wanted it far enough out in the mare so that people wouldn't be able to see it from Selene; they have to buy tickets and take the bus."

Both the young people laughed tolerantly.

"I guess he was pretty smart, at that," the young man confessed.

"And he had a long memory, too," said the leader. "He left this tourist agency to me and the other guys from Artemis IV, in his will. We own it. I figure it'll keep me comfortable for the rest of my life."

"Why did he do that?"

The leader shrugged inside his cumbersome suit. "Why did he build that still? Sam always did what he darned well felt like doing. No matter what you think of him, he always remembered his friends."

The three of them gave the crystal statue a final admiring glance, then clumped back to the truck and started the hour long drive to Selene City.

AMORALITY TALE

This is, of course, an alternate history tale. How might the world have changed if the incidents in this story had actually happened in the 1970s? As more than one character has said in more than one story, "It just might work!"

To: The President of the United States
The White House
From: Rev. Joshua Folsom
Associate Director (pro tem.) National Security Agency

Dear Mr. President:

Although the immediate crisis seems to have passed, and our beloved Nation has apparently weathered the worst of the storm, I fear that we are and will continue to be in the gravest danger for some time to come. Frankly, sir, I do not see how we can avoid eventual retribution and disaster.

When you appointed me Associate Director (pro tem.) of the National Security Agency, it was with the understanding that once I had rooted out those responsible for the Collapse, I could quickly return to my pastoral duties in the verdant hills of our dearly beloved Kentucky. As this report will show, our objective is impossible to accomplish, even though we now know how the Collapse began and who started it. I therefore wish to return home as soon as possible.

What I have found, sir, is a conspiracy so widespread, so pervasive (and perverse) that I do not see how anyone, even you, sir, with all your God-given courage and intelligence, and all the mighty powers of your high Office, can possibly avert the disaster that surely awaits our Nation and the world.

I could wax wroth at the things I have seen, and the attitudes of the men and women (especially the women) I have interrogated. I struggle to remain calm, so that I can set the facts on paper for you to see and judge. Lord knows, Someone Else is also watching and judging us all.

The facts, as I have been able to piece them together, are these:

We are facing nothing less than a global conspiracy led by the daughters of the so-called "Hippie Generation:" that is, the daughters of the women who came of age in the late 1960s and early 1970s. The fact that this is a *global* conspiracy, and that the Soviets and even the Chinese have been affected by it, offers scant consolation to America. We are all on the road to perdition and the total destruction of civilization.

It began, as you might suspect, in Los Angeles, that hotbed of drugs and licentiousness. You may recall the peace demonstrations that followed your Declaration of Nuclear Mobilization. Instead of rallying around their President and showing the Soviets and the other Godless Communists around the world that we are fully prepared to do battle against Evil even though Armageddon may result, the libertine element in our society organized marches, rallies, speeches, teach-ins, and other demonstrations in favor of "peace" (by which they meant surrender to the Satanists in the Kremlin).

I'm sure I don't have to remind you of how the media displayed these misguided youths in their various rallies around the nation. They made it look as if everyone in America under the age of sixty was against you, sir, and your firm, manly stand against the Soviets.

We would have survived even that, however, if it had not been for a fateful coincidence and a certain Ms. Debbie Morganthaler, a student majoring in cinema history at UCLA.

As the attached documentation shows, I interrogated Ms. Morganthaler personally. She is twenty years old, blonde, preternaturally endowed, and a dedicated voluptuary. On a moral scale of one to ten, she would rate well below zero. She apparently has no moral sense whatever, no shame, and has steadfastly maintained ever since her arrest that, "What we did wasn't *wrong;* it was *beautiful.*"

She also has a way of blinking her large blue eyes and taking deep breaths that has a decidedly disturbing effect on young men. As you may have already been informed, sir, she escaped custody several weeks ago and we have been unable, as yet, to locate her. It seems clear that she is being hidden and protected by an army of accomplices.

Ms. Morganthaler, in my opinion, does not have the intelligence to have planned and executed the Collapse. Either we are the victims of an incredible natural coincidence (a theory favored by many of my Secular Humanist colleagues here at NSA) or we have been deliberately tested in the scales by our Creator—and found wanting. Others of my colleagues believe that we are the victims of a subtle, malicious Communist plot. But inasmuch as the Soviet and Chinese societies have also Collapsed, I cannot put credence into that theory.

The coincidence (if there is one) is this: Ms. Morganthaler attended a performance of an ancient Greek drama, *Lysistrata,* as part of UCLA's week-long peace demonstration. I was unfamiliar with the play, of course, since it is a filthy pagan Humanistic perversion. I assume that you, sir, are as innocent of its content as I was. I hereby quote the description of the play from the Fifteenth Edition of the *Encyclopedia Britannica.* Please excuse the lewd references; they are from the Encyclopedia, and they are necessary to an understanding of what has happened to us:

Lysistrata, ancient Greek comedy produced in 411 BC by Aristophanes, in which Lysistrata, an Athenian woman, ends the Second Peloponnesian War by having all the Greek women deny their husbands sexual relations while the fighting lasts. Before proclaiming her plans, she has the older women seize the Acropolis in order to control the treasury. The Spartan men, unable to endure prolonged celibacy, are the first to petition for peace, on any terms. Then Lysistrata, in order to hasten the war's end, has a nude girl exposed to the two armies. Thereupon the Athenians and Spartans both, goaded by frustration, make peace quickly and depart for home with their wives.

This is the kind of smut that Ms. Morganthaler and her ilk exposed themselves to routinely. When I interrogated her, she admitted quite freely that the play made a considerable impression on her young mind. I quote from the transcript of her interrogation:

"Y'know, I heard my mom tell me about the Peace Movement back in the Sixties, when all the kids were saying, 'Make love, not war.' Y'know? And I saw this play, y'know, and all of a sudden it hit me! She got it ass-backwards! [Excuse the profanity, sir; it is included for the sake of completeness.] Lysistrata, I mean. Instead of saying no to the guys, what if every woman in the whole world said *yes!* Y'know, anytime! All the time! With any guy!"

Even now, my hands shake to think of how this Devil's spawn of an idea swept the nation and the world.

Within a few days, Ms. Morganthaler and her debauched friends arranged a massive peace demonstration in front of the Los Angeles City Hail. Hundreds were arrested, most of them young women. They allowed themselves to be taken into custody overnight, but by dawn's early light the entire group of them were on the streets once again, accompanied by most of the arresting officers—who appeared to be, according to eyewitness accounts, very disheveled, somewhat stunned and exhausted, yet grinning like a pack of happy apes.

Thus began the so-called Piece Movement. The entire LAPD quickly fell prey to the fiendish plot, and from Los Angeles it spread the length of California like a brushfire. Military bases, police departments, even the state legislature was soon engulfed in the deviltry. From California the Movement invaded Oregon and Nevada, barely hesitating a moment as it spread eastward. It leapfrogged much of the Bible Belt (but not for long, alas) and sprang up on the East Coast, especially in cities such as New York and Boston—longtime centers of sin, perversion, and Liberals.

Mexico was traumatized by the Piece Movement. Five centuries of Catholic mind control were swept away almost overnight. The civil war in El Salvador ceased within a week, and both Nicaragua and Cuba stopped sending troops and arms to their neighbor. The troops were making love, not war, and their guns lay rusting in the jungles where the soldiers had discarded them.

You might expect that the bulwark of American righteousness, the American Mother, would have stood firm against the Satanists. As I

said, the Bible Belt did not fall immediately to the Piece Movement.
But (and my face reddens with shame to report it) even the stout-
souled wives and mothers of our once-Christian land succumbed to
the diabolical Movement. I quote from my personal interrogation of
Mrs. Nancy-Jean Wiggins, of Muncie, Indiana, a city that once prided
itself on being "the buckle on the Bible Belt."

Buckle, indeed!

Mrs. Wiggins is married to a deacon of the United Methodist
Church, is the mother of four teenaged children (two daughters, two
sons), and was selected by the FBI computer as a typically average
American midwestern wife and mother.

When asked why she did not resist the Piece Movement, Mrs.
Wiggins replied:

"Why, I certainly did resist it! Long as I could! But what's a body to
do, when every woman in the town is makin' cow eyes at all the fellas?
That hussy Rachel McCoy was rubbin' up against my hubby and I saw
that the only way to save my happy home was to rub him harder and
better. So I did. And then my Marylou came home early from school
with four boys taggin' after her and they all looked so *peaceful* and
happy and *contented*, and my hubby hadn't gone down to the bowling
alley in two whole weeks. [Mrs. Wiggins uses the term 'bowling alley'
as a euphemism for 'saloon.'] So I just said to myself, I said, 'Nancy-
Jean, this is God's mysterious will at work: He told us to love one
another, and I guess this is what He meant when He said that, and we
just hadn't been understanding Him rightly until now.'"

As you know, sir, the Devil can quote Scripture when it suits his
purposes.

In less than two months, the United States ceased to have a credible
military organization. Air Force officers were making love in missile
silos. Our troops both at home and overseas lost every shred of
discipline, and God alone knows what took place aboard our Navy's
far-flung ships. The moral Collapse engulfed our entire Nation,
reaching up even into the House of Representatives and the Senate. It
was unfortunate that a Fox News camera crew happened to be in the
Senate gallery the afternoon that the orgy broke out, but inasmuch as
the Fox crew and everyone else in the gallery soon joined in the
debauchery, the video footage was poorly focused and of minimal
quality. At any rate, by the time the Fox News executives decided to

show it on television, everyone was much too busy fornicating to watch others doing the same thing.

Only the fact that the Piece Movement spread with the speed of light through Europe, Asia, and Africa has saved our beloved United States from total annihilation at the hands of the Godless Communists. Western Europe fell into a frenzy of lust, especially Italy, where the Leaning Tower of Pisa finally toppled, but no one noticed or cared. The Pope ordered the Vatican sealed off from all outside contact. No one has heard a word from the Vatican for four months now, although there are rumors that certain of the younger Cardinals have been seen along the Via Venetto, dressed in mufti.

The Warsaw Pact nations quickly fell to the Piece Movement, Poland being the first to succumb. According to some journalists, the Movement averted an imminent Russian invasion and thus saved the Poles from further repression. Martial law collapsed overnight (literally) in Poland, and the Russian troops assigned to crush Polish resistance were soon grappling with other matters. Tanks became bordellos, heavy artillery pieces became symbols of the new Movement, and were soon decorated with flowers by smiling Polish women and laughing Russian soldiers.

Despite every precaution, Russia itself fell to the onslaught. Reliable intelligence reports confirm that the sudden deaths of eight Politburo members (average age, seventy-three) can be attributed to the Movement. The USSR is in chaos, but the Russians do not seem to care.

Even China, long a model of organized patience, has gone wild. Someone in Beijing found a maxim of Confucius which, roughly translated, means, "If you can't beat them, join them." Seismographs as far away as San Francisco have borne vivid testimony to the vigor with which a billion Chinese are copulating.

Australia was the lone holdout, and I must confess that for several weeks I was tempted to emigrate Down Under. Separated from the rest of the world by the purifying ocean, this huge island continent remained steadfastly immune to the Piece Movement, mainly (I am told) because the average Australian male is inordinately shy of women and prefers to drink beer in the company of his fellow men, talking about sports rather than sex.

Unfortunately, a female American tourist—no doubt an *agent provocateur*—found the chink in the Aussie armor. She put the proposition in sporting terms. She bet the captain of the Australian Americas Cup yacht crew that his team could not equal the endurance record set recently by the crew of the American yacht, *Pulsar*. The Aussies accepted her challenge, although no one seems to know if they won the bet or not. No one has seen any of them since that fateful day.

However, once the average Australian male understood that the national honor was at stake, they leaped into the action with typical Australian enthusiasm. Sales of Foster's Lager have fallen nearly to zero, and Australian women are raising funds to erect a monument to the Unknown American Tourist.

That is the whole sad story. A complete moral Collapse, everywhere in the world. True, there are no viable armies, navies, air forces, or nuclear strike units anywhere on the globe anymore. There is no threat of war. People everywhere are concentrating whatever energies they have left, after fornicating all night, to harvest record crops of food—although the food is merely to keep them nourished enough to continue their eternal lechery.

The world is at peace. Everyone seems deliriously happy. But what good is the world if we have lost our immortal souls? My own dear wife has disappeared into the suburban warrens of Alexandria. Her last words to me were, "Josh, you're a party-poop!"

I have sent out teams of investigators to locate her. None of them have returned. One was polite enough to send his badge and tape recorder back to the Agency, by mail. No return address.

The American economy, like most industrial economies, is flourishing; industrial production seems to have benefitted from the Collapse. Retail sales of almost everything except guns are up: especially flowers, candy, and birth control devices. The Moral Majority has simply disappeared from the land. Yet, strangely, church attendance is increasing. However, the last minister to preach a sermon about the Sins of the Flesh was laughed out of his pulpit.

I must add, sir, that the rumors you may have heard about your own wife are entirely false. After very careful investigation, I can happily assure you that she has remained steadfastly true to you and you alone. I know that she gave away the pistol that she formerly kept on her person, but there appears to be no need for weapons anymore. Alas, why protect our bodies when we have already sold our souls?

(Not that your wife has sold her soul, you understand. I merely meant that the incidence of violent crime has dropped to an undetectably low level. No one feels threatened anymore.)

The appropriate agencies are still searching for Ms. Morganthaler, but I do not hold out much hope for finding her. Most of the agents we have sent out have either disappeared or resigned.

I have no further desires now except to return to my ancestral home in the beloved green hills of Kentucky. A distant grand-niece of mine from back in Christian County has volunteered to drive me home this coming weekend. She is a comely young thing, and she has given me great comfort during the past few trying weeks.

She asked me if she could bring a few of her girl friends with her. There is plenty of room in the car. Therefore, I respectfully request to be relieved of my duties to you, sir, so that I can retire to my home, far from the turmoil of this modern world, to spend my remaining days in peace and contentment, as best I can.

A COUNTRY FOR OLD MEN

You know you're getting old when you start receiving Lifetime Achievement awards. That's been happening to me with increasing frequency lately, so I know something of how Alexander Alexandrovich Ignatiev feels.

Heading for a new frontier, six lightyears from Earth, Ignatiev is an old man in the midst of youngsters. "Old" and "young" are relative terms here, for in this tale biomedical advancements have lengthened the human lifespan considerably.

Still, Ignatiev feels old, useless, bitterly unhappy with his one-way trip to a distant star. He has a different frontier to explore, his own inner strength and determination, his own inner desire to feel useful, admired, even loved.

"IT'S OBVIOUS!" said Vartan Gregorian, standing imperiously before the two others seated on the couch. "I'm the best damned pilot in the history of the human race!"

Planting his fists on his hips, he struck a pose that was nothing less than preening.

Half buried in the lounge's plush curved couch, Alexander Ignatiev bit back an impulse to laugh in the Armenian's face. But Nikki Deneuve, sitting next to him, gazed up at Gregorian with shining eyes.

Breaking into a broad grin, Gregorian went on, "This bucket is moving faster than any ship ever built, no? We've flown farther from Earth than anybody ever has, true?"

Nikki nodded eagerly as she responded, "Twenty percent of lightspeed and approaching six lightyears."

"So, I'm the pilot of the fastest, highest-flying ship of all time!" Gregorian exclaimed. "That makes me the best flier in the history of the human race. QED!"

Ignatiev shook his head at the conceited oaf. But he saw that Nikki was captivated by his posturing. Then it struck him. *She loves him! And Gregorian is showing off for her.*

The ship's lounge was as relaxing and comfortable as human designers back on Earth could make it. It was arranged in a circular grouping of sumptuously appointed niches, each holding high curved banquettes that could seat up to half a dozen close friends in reasonable privacy.

Ignatiev had left his quarters after suffering still another defeat at the hands of the computerized chess program and snuck down to the lounge in mid-afternoon, hoping to find it empty. He needed a hideaway while the housekeeping robots cleaned his suite. Their busy, buzzing thoroughness drove him to distraction; it was impossible to concentrate on chess or anything else while the machines were dusting, laundering, straightening his rooms, restocking his autokitchen and his bar, making the bed with crisply fresh linens.

So he sought refuge in the lounge, only to find Gregorian and Denueve already there, in a niche beneath a display screen that showed the star fields outside. Once the sight of those stars scattered across the infinite void would have stirred Ignatiev's heart. But not any more, not since Sonya died.

Sipping at the vodka that the serving robot had poured for him the instant he had stepped into the lounge, thanks to its face recognition program, Ignatiev couldn't help grousing, "And who says you are the pilot, Vartan? I didn't see any designation for pilot in the mission's assignment roster."

Gregorian was moderately handsome and rather tall, quite slim, with thick dark hair and laugh crinkles at the corners of his dark brown eyes. Ignatiev tended to think of people in terms of chess pieces, and he counted Gregorian as a prancing horse, all style and little substance.

"I am flight systems engineer, no?" Gregorian countered. "My assignment is to monitor the flight control program. That makes me the pilot."

Nikki, still beaming at him, said, "If you're the pilot, Vartan, then I must be the navigator."

"Astrogator," Ignatiev corrected bluntly.

The daughter of a Quebecoise mother and French Moroccan father, Nicolette Denueve had unfortunately inherited her father's stocky physique and her mother's sharp nose. Ignatiev thought her unlovely— and yet there was a charm to her, a *gamin*-like wide-eyed innocence that beguiled Ignatiev's crusty old heart. She was a physicist, bright and conscientious, not an engineering monkey like the braggart Gregorian. Thus it was a tragedy that she had been selected for this star mission.

She finally turned away from Gregorian to say to Ignatiev, "It's good to see you, Dr. Ignatiev. You've become something of a hermit these past few months."

He coughed and muttered, "I've been busy on my research." The truth was he couldn't bear to be among these youngsters, couldn't stand the truth that they would one day return to Earth while he would be long dead.

Alexander Alexandrovich Ignatiev, by far the oldest man among the starship's crew, thought that Nikki could have been the daughter he'd never had. Daughter? he snapped at himself silently. Granddaughter, he corrected. Great-granddaughter, even. He was a dour astrophysicist approaching his hundred and fortieth birthday, his short-cropped hair iron gray but his mind and body still reasonably vigorous and active thanks to rejuvenation therapies. Yet he felt cheated by the way the world worked, bitter about being exiled to this one-way flight to a distant star.

Technically, he was the senior executive of this mission, an honor that he found almost entirely empty. To him, it was like being the principal of a school for very bright, totally wayward children. Each one of them must have been president of their school's student body, he thought: accustomed to getting their own way and total strangers to discipline. Besides, the actual commander of the ship was the artificial intelligence program run by the ship's central computer.

If Gregorian is a chessboard knight, Ignatiev mused to himself, then what is Nikki? Not the queen; she's too young, too uncertain of herself for that. Her assignment to monitor the navigation program was something of a joke: the ship followed a ballistic trajectory, like an arrow shot from Earth. Nothing for a navigator to do except check the ship's position each day.

Maybe she's a bishop, Ignatiev mused, if a woman can be a bishop: quiet, self-effacing, possessing hidden depths. And reliable, trustworthy, always staying to the color of the square she started on. She'll cling to Gregorian, unless he hurts her terribly. That possibility made Ignatiev's blood simmer.

And me? he asked himself. A pawn, nothing more. But then he thought, maybe I'm a rook, stuck off in a corner of the board, barely noticed by anybody.

"Dr. Ignatiev is correct," said Gregorian, trying to regain control of the conversation. "The proper term is astrogator."

"Whatever," said Nikki, her eyes returning to Gregorian's handsome young face.

"Young" was a relative term. Gregorian was approaching sixty, although he still had the vigor, the attitudes and demeanor of an obstreperous teenager. Ignatiev thought it would be appropriate if the Armenian's face were blotched with acne. Youth is wasted on the young, Ignatiev thought. Thanks to life-elongation therapies, average life expectancy among the starship crew was well above two hundred. It had to be.

The scoopship was named *Sagan*, after some minor twentieth-century astronomer. It was heading for Gliese 581, a red dwarf star slightly more than twenty lightyears from Earth. For Ignatiev, it was a one-way journey. Even with all the life-extension therapies, he would never survive the eighty-year round trip. Gregorian would, of course, and so would Nikki.

Ignatiev brooded over the unfairness of it. By the time the ship returned to Earth, the two of them would be grandparents and Ignatiev would be long dead.

Unfair, he thought as he pushed himself up from the plush banquette and left the lounge without a word to either one of them. The universe is unfair. I don't deserve this: to die alone, unloved, unrecognized, my life's work forgotten, all my hopes crushed to dust.

As he reached the lounge's hatch, he turned his head to see what the two of them were up to. Chatting, smiling, holding hands, all the subverbal signals that lovers send to each other. They had eyes only for one another, and paid absolutely no attention to him.

Just like the rest of the goddamned world, Ignatiev thought.

He had labored all his life in the groves of academe, and what had it gotten him? A membership in the International Academy of Sciences, along with seventeen thousand other anonymous workers. A pension that barely covered his living expenses. Three marriages: two wrecked by divorce and the third—the only one that really mattered—destroyed by that inevitable thief, death.

He hardly remembered how enthusiastic he had been as a young postdoc, all those years ago, his astrophysics degree in hand, burning with ambition. He was going to unlock the secrets of the universe! The pulsars, those enigmatic cinders, the remains of ancient supernova explosions: Ignatiev was going to discover what made them tick.

But the universe was far subtler than he had thought. Soon enough he learned that a career in science can be a study in anonymous drudgery. The pulsars kept their secrets, no matter how assiduously Ignatiev nibbled around the edges of their mystery.

And now the honor of being the senior executive on the human race's first interstellar mission. Some honor, Ignatiev thought sourly. They needed someone competent but expendable. Send old Ignatiev, let him go out in a fizzle of glory.

Shaking his head as he trudged along the thickly carpeted passageway to his quarters, Ignatiev muttered to himself, "If only there were something I could accomplish, something I could discover, something to put some *meaning* to my life."

He had lived long enough to realize that his life would be no more remembered than the life of a worker ant. He wanted more than that. He wanted to be remembered. He wanted his name to be revered. He wanted students in the far future to know that he had existed, that he had made a glowing contribution to humankind's store of knowledge and understanding. He wanted Nikki Deneuve to gaze at him with adoring eyes.

"It will never be," Ignatiev told himself as he slid open the door to his quarters. With a wry shrug, he reminded himself of a line from some old English poet: "Ah, that a man's reach should exceed his grasp, or what's a heaven for?"

Alexander Ignatiev did not believe in heaven. But he thought he knew what hell was like.

✳ ❚❚ ✳

AS HE ENTERED HIS QUARTERS he saw that at least the cleaning robots had finished and left; the sitting room looked almost tidy. And he was alone.

The expedition to Gliese 581 had left Earth with tremendous fanfare. The first human mission to another star! Gliese 581 was a very ordinary star in most respects: a dim red dwarf, barely one-third of the Sun's mass. The galaxy is studded with such stars. But Gliese 581 was unusual in one supremely interesting way: it possessed an entourage of half a dozen planets. Most of them were gas giants, bloated conglomerates of hydrogen and helium. But a couple of them were rocky worlds, somewhat like Earth. And one of those—Gliese 581g—orbited at just the right "Goldilocks" distance from its parent star to be able to have liquid water on its surface.

Liquid water meant life. In the solar system, wherever liquid water existed, life existed. In the permafrost beneath the frozen rust-red surface of Mars, in the ice-covered seas of the moons of Jupiter and Saturn, in massive Jupiter's planet-girdling ocean: wherever liquid water had been found, life was found with it.

Half a dozen robotic probes confirmed that liquid water actually did exist on the surface of Gliese 581g, but they found no evidence for life. Not an ameba, not even a bacterium. But that didn't deter the scientific hierarchy. Robots are terribly limited, they proclaimed. We must send human scientists to Gliese 581g to search for life there, scientists of all types, men and women who will sacrifice half their lives to the search for life beyond the solar system.

Ignatiev was picked to sacrifice the last half of his life. He knew he would never see Earth again, and he told himself that he didn't care. There was nothing on Earth that interested him anymore, not since Sonya's death. But he wanted to find something, to make an impact, to keep his name alive after he was gone.

Most of the two hundred scientists, engineers and technicians aboard *Sagan* were sleeping away the decades of the flight in cryonic suspension. They would be revived once the scoopship arrived at Gliese 581's vicinity. Only a dozen were awake during the flight, assigned to monitor the ship's systems, ready to make corrections or repairs if necessary.

The ship was highly automated, of course. The human crew was a backup, a concession to human vanity unwilling to hand the operation of the ship completely to electronic and mechanical devices. Human egos feared fully autonomous machines. Thus a dozen human lives were sacrificed to spend four decades waiting for the machines to fail.

They hadn't failed so far. From the fusion powerplant deep in the ship's core to the tenuous magnetic scoop stretching a thousand kilometers in front of the ship, all the systems worked perfectly well. When a minor malfunction arose, the ship's machines repaired themselves, under the watchful direction of the master AI program. Even the AI system's computer program ran flawlessly, to Ignatiev's utter frustration. It beat him at chess with depressing regularity.

In addition to the meaningless title of senior executive, Alexander Ignatiev had a specific technical task aboard the starship. His assignment was to monitor the electromagnetic funnel that scooped in hydrogen from the thin interstellar medium to feed the ship's nuclear fusion engine. Every day he faithfully checked the gauges and display screens in the ship's command center, reminding himself each time that the practice of physics always comes down to reading a goddamned dial.

The funnel operated flawlessly. A huge gossamer web of hair-thin superconducting wires, it created an invisible magnetic field that spread out before the starship like a thousand-kilometer-wide scoop, gathering in the hydrogen atoms floating between the stars and ionizing them as they were sucked into the ship's innards, like a huge baleen whale scooping up the tiny creatures of the sea that it fed upon.

Deep in the starship's bowels the fusion generator forced the hydrogen ions to fuse together into helium ions, giving up energy in the process to run the ship. Like the Sun and the stars themselves, the starship lived on hydrogen fusion.

Ignatiev slid the door of his quarters shut. The suite of rooms allotted to him was small, but far more luxurious than any home he had lived in back on Earth. The psychotechnicians among the mission's planners, worried about the crew's morale during the decades-long flight, had insisted on every creature comfort they could think of: everything from body-temperature waterbeds that adjusted to one's weight and size to digitally-controlled décor that could change its color scheme at the call of one's voice; from an automated kitchen that could prepare a world-spanning variety of cuisines to virtual reality entertainment systems.

Ignatiev ignored all the splendor; or rather, he took it for granted. Creature comforts were fine, but he had spent the first months of the mission converting his beautifully-wrought sitting room into an astrophysics laboratory. The sleek Scandinavian desk of teak inlaid with meteoric silver now held a conglomeration of computers and sensor readouts. The fake fireplace was hidden behind a junkpile of discarded spectrometers, magnetometers and other gadgetry that Ignatiev had used and abandoned. He could see a faint ring of dust on the floor around the mess; he had given the cleaning robots strict orders not to touch it.

Above the obstructed fireplace was a framed digital screen programmed to show high-definition images of the world's great artworks—when it wasn't being used as a three-dimensional entertainment screen. Ignatiev had connected it to the ship's main optical telescope, so that it showed the stars spangled against the blackness of space. Usually the telescope was pointed forward, with the tiny red dot of Gliese 581 centered in its field of view. Now and then, at the command of the ship's AI system, it looked back toward the diminishing yellow speck of the Sun.

Being an astrophysicist, Ignatiev had started the flight by spending most of his waking hours examining this interstellar Siberia in which he was exiled. It was an excuse to stay away from the chattering young monkeys of the crew. He had studied the planet-sized chunks of ice and rock in the Oort Cloud that surrounded the outermost reaches of the solar system. Once the ship was past that region, he turned his interest back to the enigmatic, frustrating pulsars. Each one throbbed at a precise frequency, more accurate than an atomic clock. Why? What determined their frequency? Why did some supernova explosions produce pulsars while others didn't?

Ignatiev batted his head against those questions in vain. More and more, as the months of the mission stretched into years, he spent his days playing chess against the AI system. And losing consistently.

"Alexander Alexandrovich."

He looked up from the chessboard he had set up on his desktop screen, turned in his chair and directed his gaze across the room to the display screen above the fireplace. The lovely, smiling face of the artificial intelligence system's avatar filled the screen.

The psychotechnicians among the mission planners had decided that the human crew would work more effectively with the AI program if it showed a human face. For each human crew member, the face was slightly different: the psychotechs had tried to create a personal relationship for each of the crew. The deceit annoyed Ignatiev. The program treated him like a child. Worse, the face it displayed for him reminded him too much of his late wife.

"I'm busy," he growled.

Unperturbed, the avatar's smiling face said, "Yesterday you requested use of the main communications antenna."

"I want to use it as a radio telescope, to map out the interstellar hydrogen we're moving through."

"The twenty-one centimeter radiation," said the avatar knowingly.

"Yes."

"You are no longer studying the pulsars?"

He bit back an angry reply. "I have given up on the pulsars," he admitted. "The interstellar medium interests me more. I have decided to map the hydrogen in detail."

Besides, he admitted to himself, that will be a lot easier than the pulsars.

The AI avatar said calmly, "Mission protocol requires the main antenna be available to receive communications from mission control."

"The secondary antenna can do that," he said. Before the AI system could reply, he added, "Besides, any communications from Earth will be six years old. We're not going to get any urgent messages that must be acted upon immediately."

"Still," said the avatar, "mission protocol cannot be dismissed lightly."

"It won't hurt anything to let me use the main antenna for a few hours each day," he insisted.

The avatar remained silent for several seconds: an enormous span of time for the computer program.

At last, the avatar conceded, "Perhaps so. You may use the main antenna, provisionally."

"I am eternally grateful," Ignatiev said. His sarcasm was wasted on the AI system.

As the weeks lengthened into months he found himself increasingly fascinated by the thin interstellar hydrogen gas and discovered, to only his mild surprise, that it was not evenly distributed in space.

Of course, astrophysicists had known for centuries that there are regions in space where the interstellar gas clumped so thickly and was so highly ionized that it glowed. Gaseous emission nebulae were common throughout the galaxy, although Ignatiev mentally corrected the misnomer: those nebulae actually consisted not of gas, but of plasma—gas that is highly ionized.

But here in the placid emptiness on the way to Gliese 581 Ignatiev found himself slowly becoming engrossed with the way that even the thin, bland neutral interstellar gas was not evenly distributed. Not at all. The hydrogen was thicker in some regions than in others.

This was hardly a new discovery, but from the viewpoint of the starship, inside the billowing interstellar clouds, the fine structure of the hydrogen became almost a thing of beauty in Ignatiev's ice-blue eyes. The interstellar gas didn't merely hang there passively between the stars, it flowed: slowly, almost imperceptibly, but it drifted on currents shaped by the gravitational pull of the stars.

"That old writer was correct," he muttered to himself as he studied the stream of interstellar hydrogen that the ship was cutting through. "There are currents in space."

He tried to think of the writer's name, but couldn't come up with it. A Russian name, he recalled. But nothing more specific.

The more he studied the interstellar gas, the more captivated he became. He went days without playing a single game of chess. Weeks. The interstellar hydrogen gas wasn't static, not at all. It was like a beautiful intricate lacework that flowed, fluttered, shifted in a stately silent pavane among the stars.

The clouds of hydrogen were like a tide of bubbling champagne, he saw, frothing slowly in rhythm to the heartbeats of the stars.

The astronomers back on Earth had no inkling of this. They looked at the general features of the interstellar gas, scanning at ranges of kiloparsecs and more; they were interested in mapping the great sweep of the galaxy's spiral arms. But here, traveling inside the wafting, drifting clouds, Ignatiev measured the detailed configuration of the interstellar hydrogen and found it beautiful.

He slumped back in his form-fitting desk chair, stunned at the splendor of it all. He thought of the magnificent panoramas he had seen of the cosmic span of the galaxies: loops and whorls of bright shining galaxies, each one containing billions of stars, extending for megaparsecs, out to infinity, long strings of glowing lights surrounding vast bubbles of emptiness. The interstellar gas showed the same delicate complexity, in miniature: loops and whorls, streams and bubbles. It was truly, cosmically beautiful.

"Fractal," he muttered to himself. "The universe is one enormous fractal pattern."

Then the artificial intelligence program intruded on his privacy. "Alexander Alexandrovich, the weekly staff meeting begins in ten minutes."

✳ III ✳

WEEKLY STAFF MEETING, Ignatiev grumbled inwardly as he hauled himself up from his desk chair. More like the weekly group therapy session for a gaggle of self-important juvenile delinquents.

He made his way grudgingly through the ship's central passageway to the conference room, located next to the command center. Several other crew members were also heading along the gleaming brushed chrome walls and colorful carpeting of the passageway. They gave Ignatiev cheery, smiling greetings; he nodded or grunted at them.

As chief executive of the crew, Ignatiev took the chair at the head of the polished conference table. The others sauntered in leisurely. Nikki and Gregorian came in almost last and took seats at the end of the table, next to each other, close enough to hold hands.

These meetings were a pure waste of time, Ignatiev thought. Their ostensible purpose was to report on the ship's performance, which any idiot could determine by casting half an eye at the digital readouts available on any display screen in the ship. The screens gave up-to-the-nanosecond details of every component of the ship's equipment.

But no, mission protocol required that all twelve crew members must meet face-to-face once each week. Good psychology, the mission planners believed. An opportunity for human interchange, personal communications. A chance for whining and displays of overblown egos, Ignatiev thought. A chance for these sixty-year-old children to complain about one another.

Of the twelve of them, only Ignatiev and Nikki were physicists. Four of the others were engineers of various stripes, three were biologists, two psychotechnicians and one stocky, sour-faced woman a medical doctor.

So he was quite surprised when the redheaded young electrical engineer in charge of the ship's power system started the meeting by reporting:

"I don't know if any of you have noticed it yet, but the ship's reduced our internal electrical power consumption by ten percent."

Mild perplexity.

"Ten percent?"

"Why?"

"I haven't noticed any reduction."

The redhead waved his hands vaguely as he replied, "It's mostly in peripheral areas. Your microwave ovens, for example. They've been powered down ten percent. Lights in unoccupied areas. Things like that."

Curious, Ignatiev asked, "Why the reduction?"

His squarish face frowning slightly, the engineer replied, "From what Alice tells me, the density of the gas being scooped in for the generator has decreased slightly. Alice says it's only a temporary condition. Nothing to worry about."

Alice was the nickname these youngsters had given to the artificial intelligence program that actually ran the ship. Artificial Intelligence. AI. Alice Intellectual. Some even called the AI system Alice Imperatress. Ignatiev thought it childish nonsense.

"How long will this go on?" asked one of the biologists. "I'm incubating a batch of genetically-engineered alga for an experiment."

"It shouldn't be a problem," the engineer said. Ignatiev thought he looked just the tiniest bit worried.

Surprisingly, Gregorian piped up. "A few of the uncrewed probes that went ahead of us also encountered power anomalies. They were temporary. No big problem."

Ignatiev nodded but made a mental note to check on the situation. Six lightyears out from Earth, he thought, meant that every problem was a big one.

One of the psychotechs cleared her throat for attention, then announced, "Several of the crew members have failed to fill out their monthly performance evaluations. I know that some of you regard these evaluations as if they were school exams, but mission protocol—"

Ignatiev tuned her out, knowing that they would bicker over this drivel for half an hour, at least. He was too optimistic. The discussion became quite heated and lasted more than an hour.

$$* \text{ IV } *$$

ONCE THE MEETING finally ended Ignatiev hurried back to his quarters and immediately looked up the mission logs of the six automated probes that had been sent to Gliese 581.

Gregorian was right, he saw. Half of the six probes had reported drops in their power systems, a partial failure of their fusion generators. Three of them. The malfunctions were only temporary, but they occurred at virtually the same point in the long voyage to Gliese 581.

The earliest of the probes had shut down altogether, its systems going into hibernation for more than four months. The mission controllers back on Earth had written the mission off as a failure when they could not communicate with the probe. Then, just as abruptly as the ship had shut down, it sprang to life again.

Puzzling.

"Alexander Alexandrovich," called the AI system's avatar. "Do you need more information on the probe missions?"

He looked up from his desk to see the lovely female face of the AI program's avatar displayed on the screen above his fireplace. A resentful anger simmered inside him. The psychotechs suppose that the face they've given the AI system makes it easier for me to interact with it, he thought. Idiots. Fools.

"I need the mission controllers' analyses of each of the probe missions," he said, struggling to keep his voice cool, keep the anger from showing.

"May I ask why?" The avatar smiled at him. Sonya, he thought. Sonya.

"I want to correlate their power reductions with the detailed map I'm making of the interstellar gas."

"Interesting," said the avatar.

"I'm pleased you think so," Ignatiev replied, through gritted teeth.

The avatar's image disappeared, replaced by data scrolling slowly along the screen. Ignatiev settled deeper into the form-adjusting desk chair and began to study the reports.

His door buzzer grated in his ears. Annoyed, Ignatiev told his computer to show who was at the door.

Gregorian was standing out in the passageway, tall, lanky, egocentric Gregorian. What in hell could he want? Ignatiev asked himself.

The big oaf pressed the buzzer again.

Thoroughly piqued at the interruption—no, the invasion of his privacy—Ignatiev growled, "Go away."

"Dr. Ignatiev," the Armenian called. "Please."

Ignatiev closed his eyes and wished that Gregorian would disappear. But when he opened them again the man was still at his door, fidgeting nervously.

Ignatiev surrendered. "Enter," he muttered.

The door slid back and Gregorian ambled in, his angular face serious, almost somber. His usual lopsided grin was nowhere to be seen.

"I'm sorry to intrude on you, Dr. Ignatiev," said the engineer.

Leaning back in his desk chair to peer up at Gregorian, Ignatiev said, "It must be something terribly important."

The contempt was wasted on Gregorian. He looked around the sitting room, his eyes resting for a moment on the pile of abandoned equipment hiding the fireplace.

"Uh, may I sit down?"

"Of course," Ignatiev said, waving a hand toward the couch across the room.

Gregorian went to it and sat, bony knees poking up awkwardly. Ignatiev rolled his desk chair across the carpeting to face him.

"So what is so important that you had to come see me?"

Very seriously, Gregorian replied, "It's Nikki."

Ignatiev felt a pang of alarm. "What's wrong with Nikki?"

"Nothing! She's wonderful."

"So?"

"I . . . I've fallen in love with her," Gregorian said, almost whispering.

"What of it?" Ignatiev snapped.

"I don't know if she loves me."

What an ass! Ignatiev thought. A blind, blundering ass who can't see the nose in front of his face.

"She . . . I mean, we get along very well. It's always fun to be with her. But . . . does she like me well enough . . ." His voice faded.

Why is he coming to me with this? Ignatiev wondered. Why not one of the psycotechs? That's what they're here for.

He thought he knew. The young oaf would be embarrassed to tell them about his feelings. So he comes to old Ignatiev, the father figure.

Feeling his brows knitting, Ignatiev asked, "Have you been to bed with her?"

"Oh, yes. Sure. But if I ask her to marry me, a real commitment . . . she might say no. She might not like me well enough for that. I mean, there are other guys in the crew . . ."

Marriage? Ignatiev felt stunned. Do kids still get married? Is he saying he'd spend two centuries living with her? Then he remembered Sonya. He knew he would have spent two centuries with her. Two millennia. Two eons.

His voice strangely subdued, Ignatiev asked, "You love her so much that you want to marry her?"

Gregorian nodded mutely.

Ignatiev said, "And you're afraid that if you ask her for a lifetime commitment she'll refuse and that will destroy your relationship."

Looking completely miserable, Gregorian said, "Yes." He stared into Ignatiev's eyes. "What should I do?"

Beneath all the bravado he's just a frightened pup, uncertain of himself, Ignatiev realized. Sixty years old and he's as scared and worried as a teenager.

I can tell him to forget her. Tell him she doesn't care about him; say that she's not interested in a lifetime commitment. I can break up their romance with a few words.

But as he looked into Gregorian's wretched face he knew he couldn't do it. It would wound the young pup; hurt him terribly. Ignatiev heard himself say, "She loves you, Vartan. She's mad about you. Can't you see that?"

"You think so?"

Ignatiev wanted to say, "Why do you think she puts up with you and your ridiculous posturing?" Instead, he told the younger man, "I'm sure of it. Go to her. Speak your heart to her."

Gregorian leaped up from couch so abruptly that Ignatiev nearly toppled out of his rolling chair.

"I'll do that!" he shouted as he raced for the door.

As Ignatiev got slowly to his feet, Gregorian stopped at the door and said hastily, "Thank you, Dr. Ignatiev! Thank you!"

Ignatiev made a shrug.

Suddenly Gregorian looked sheepish. "Is there anything I can do for you, sir?"

"No. Nothing, thank you."

"Are you still . . . uh, active?"

Ignatiev scowled at him.

"I mean, there are virtual reality simulations. You can program them to suit your own whims, you know."

"I know," Ignatiev said firmly.

Gregorian realized he'd stepped over a line. "I mean, I just thought . . . in case you need . . ."

"Good day, Vartan," said Ignatiev.

As the engineer left and the door slid shut, Ignatiev said to himself, Blundering young ass! But then he added, And I'm a doddering old numbskull.

He'll run straight to Nikki. She'll leap into his arms and they'll live happily ever after, or some approximation of it. And I'll be here alone, with nothing to look forward to except oblivion.

VR simulations, he huffed. The insensitive young lout. But she loves him. She loves him. That is certain.

✳ V ✳

IGNATIEV PACED AROUND HIS SITTING ROOM for hours after Gregorian left, cursing himself for a fool. You could have pried him away from her, he raged inwardly. But then he thought, And what good would that do? She wouldn't come to you; you're old enough to be her great-grandfather, for god's sake.

Maybe the young oaf was right. Maybe I should try the VR simulations.

Instead, he threw himself into the reports on the automated probes that had been sent to Gliese 581. And their power failures. For days he stayed in his quarters, studying, learning, understanding.

The official explanation for the problem by the mission directors back on Earth was nothing more than waffling, Ignatiev decided as he examined the records. Partial power failure. It was only temporary. Within a few weeks it had been corrected.

Anomalies, concluded the official reports. These things happen to highly complex systems. Nothing to worry about. After all, the systems corrected themselves as they were designed to do. And the last three probes worked perfectly well.

Anomalies? Ignatiev asked himself. *Anomaly* is a word you use when you don't know what the hell really happened.

He thought he knew.

He took the plots of each probe's course and overlaid them against the map he'd been making of the fine structure of the interstellar medium. Sure enough, he saw that the probes had encountered a region where the interstellar gas thinned so badly that a ship's power output declined seriously. There isn't enough hydrogen in that region for the fusion generator to run at full power! He saw. It's like a bubble in the interstellar gas: a region that's almost empty of hydrogen atoms.

Ignatiev retraced the flight paths of all six of the probes. Yes, the first one plunged straight into the bubble and shut itself down when the power output from the fusion generator dropped so low it could no longer maintain the ship's systems. The next two skirted the edges of the bubble and experienced partial power failures. That region had been dangerous for the probes. It could be fatal for *Sagan's* human cargo.

He started to write out a report for mission control, then realized before he was halfway finished with the first page it that it would take more than six years for his warning to reach Earth, and another six for the mission controllers' recommendation to get back to him. And who knew how long it would take for those Earthside dunderheads to come to a decision?

"We could all be dead by then," he muttered to himself.

"Your speculations are interesting," said the AI avatar.

Ignatiev frowned at the image on the screen above his fireplace. "It's not speculation," he growled. "It is a conclusion based on observed data."

"Alexander Alexandrovich," said the sweetly smiling face, "your conclusion comes not from the observations, but from your interpretation of the observations."

"Three of the probes had power failures."

"Temporary failures that were corrected. And three other probes did not."

"Those last three didn't go through the bubble," he said.

"They all flew the same trajectory, did they not?"

"Not exactly."

"Within a four percent deviation," the avatar said, unperturbed.

"But they flew at different *times*," Ignatiev pointed out. "The bubble was flowing across their flight paths. The first probe plunged into the heart of it and shut down entirely. For four months! The next two skirted its edges and still suffered power failures."

"Temporarily," said the avatar's image, still smiling patiently. "And the final three probes? They didn't encounter any problems at all, did they?"

"No," Ignatiev admitted grudgingly. "The bubble must have flowed past by the time they reached the area."

"So there should be no problem for us," the avatar said.

"You think not?" he responded. "Then why are beginning to suffer a power shortage?"

"The inflowing hydrogen is slightly thinner here than it has been," said the avatar.

Ignatiev shook his head. "It's going to get worse. We're heading into another bubble. I'm sure of it."

The AI system said nothing.

✳ VI ✳

BE SURE YOU'RE RIGHT, then go ahead. Ignatiev had heard that motto many long years ago, when he'd been a child watching adventure tales.

He spent an intense three weeks mapping the interstellar hydrogen directly ahead of the ship's position. His worst fears were confirmed. *Sagan* was entering a sizeable bubble where the gas density thinned out to practically nothing: fewer than a dozen hydrogen atoms per cubic meter.

He checked the specifications of the ship's fusion generator and confirmed that its requirement for incoming hydrogen was far higher than the bubble could provide. Within a few days we'll start to experience serious power outages, he realized.

What to do?

Despite his disdain for his younger crewmates, despite his loathing of meetings and committees and the kind of groupthink that passed for decision-making, he called a special meeting of the crew.

"All the ship's systems will shut down?" cried one of the psychotechs. "All of them?"

"What will happen to us during the shutdown?" asked a biologist, her voice trembling.

Calmly, his hands clasped on the conference tabletop, Ignatiev said, "If my measurements of the bubble are accurate—"

"If?" Gregorian snapped. "You mean you're not sure?"

"Not one hundred percent, no."

"Then why are you telling us this? Why have you called this meeting? To frighten us?"

"Well, he's certainly frightened me!" said one of the engineers.

Trying to hold on to his temper, Ignatiev replied, "My measurements are good enough to convince me that we face a serious problem. Very serious. Power output is already declining, and will go down more over the next few days."

194 *Ben Bova*

"How much more?" asked the female biologist.

Ignatiev hesitated, then decided to give them the worst. "All the ship's systems could shut down. Like the first of the automated probes. It shut down for four months. Went into hibernation mode. Our shutdown might be even longer."

The biologist countered, "But the probe powered up again, didn't it? It went into hibernation mode but then it came back to normal."

With a slow nod, Ignatiev said, "The ship's systems could survive a hibernation of many months. But we couldn't. Without electrical power we would not have heat, air or water recycling, lights, stoves for cooking—"

"You mean we'll die?" asked Nikki, in the tiny voice of a frightened little girl.

Ignatiev felt a sudden urge to comfort her, to protect her from the brutal truth. "Unless we take steps," he said softly.

"What steps?" Gregorian demanded.

"We have to change our course. Turn away from this bubble. Move along a path that keeps us in regions of thicker gas."

"Alexander Alexandrovich," came the voice of the AI avatar, "course changes must be approved by mission control."

Ignatiev looked up and saw that the avatar's image had sprung up on each of the conference room's walls, slightly larger than life. Naturally, he realized. The AI system has been listening to every word we say. The avatar's image looked slightly different to him: an amalgam of all the twelve separate images the AI system showed to each of the crew members. Sonya's features were in the image, but blurred, softened, like the face of a relative who resembled her mother strongly.

"Approved by mission control?" snapped one of the engineers, a rake-thin dark-skinned Malaysian. "It would take six years merely to get a message to them!"

"We could all be dead by then," said the redhead sitting beside him.

Unperturbed, the avatar replied, "Mission protocol includes emergency procedures, but course changes require approval from mission control."

Everyone tried to talk at once. Ignatiev closed his eyes and listened to the babble. Almost, he laughed to himself. They would mutiny against the AI system, if they knew how. He saw in his imagination a handful of children trying to rebel against a peg-legged pirate captain.

At last he put up his hands to silence them. They shut up and looked to him, their expressions ranging from sullen to fearful to self-pitying.

"Arguments and threats won't sway the AI program," he told them. "Only logic."

Looking thoroughly nettled, Gregorian said, "So try logic, then."

Ignatiev said to the image on the wall screens, "What is the mission protocol's first priority?"

The answer came immediately, "To protect the lives of the human crew and cargo."

Cargo, Ignatiev grunted to himself. The stupid program thinks of the people in cryonic suspension as cargo.

Aloud, he said, "Observations show that we are entering a region of very low hydrogen density."

Immediately the avatar replied, "This will necessitate reducing power consumption."

"Power consumption may be reduced below the levels needed to keep the crew alive," Ignatiev said.

For half a heartbeat the AI avatar said nothing. Then, "That is a possibility."

"If we change course to remain within the region where hydrogen density is adequate to maintain all the ship's systems," Ignatiev said slowly, carefully, "none of the crew's lives would be endangered."

"Not so, Alexander Alexandrovich," the avatar replied.

"Not so?"

"The immediate threat of reduced power availability might be averted by changing course, but once the ship has left its preplanned trajectory toward Gliese 581, how will you navigate toward our destination? Course correction data will take more than twelve years to reach us from Earth. The ship would be wandering through a wilderness, far from its destination. The crew would eventually die of starvation."

"We could navigate ourselves," said Ignatiev. "We wouldn't need course correction data from mission control."

The avatar's image actually shook her head. "No member of the crew is an accredited astrogator."

"I can do it!" Nikki cried. "I monitor the navigation program."

With a hint of a smile, the avatar said gently, "Monitoring the astrogation program does not equip you to plot course changes."

Before Nikki or anyone else could object, Ignatiev asked coolly, "So what do you recommend?"

Again the AI system hesitated before answering, almost a full second. It must be searching every byte of data in its memory, Ignatiev thought.

At last the avatar responded. "While this ship passes through the region of low fuel density the animate crew should enter cryonic suspension."

"Cryosleep?" Gregorian demanded. "For how long?"

"As long as necessary. The cryonics units can be powered by the ship's backup fuel cells—"

The redhaired engineer said, "Why don't we use the fuel cells to run the ship?"

Ignatiev shook his head. The kid knows better, he's just grasping at straws.

Sure enough, the AI avatar replied patiently, "The fuel cells could power the ship for only a week or less, depending on internal power consumption."

Crestfallen, the engineer said, "Yeah. Right."

"Cryosleep is the indicated technique for passing through this emergency," said the AI system.

Ignatiev asked, "If the fuel cells are used solely for maintaining the cryosleep units' refrigeration, how long could they last?"

"Two months," replied the avatar. "That includes maintaining the cryosleep units already being used by the cargo."

"Understood," said Ignatiev. "And if this region of low fuel density extends for more than two months?"

Without hesitation, the AI avatar answered, "Power to the cryosleep units will be lost."

"And the people in those units?"

"They will die," said the avatar, without a flicker of human emotion.

Gregorian said, "Then we'd better hope that the bubble doesn't last for more than two months."

Ignatiev saw the others nodding, up and down the conference table. They looked genuinely frightened, but they didn't know what else could be done.

He thought he did.

✳ VII ✳

THE MEETING BROKE UP with most of the crew members muttering to one another about sleeping through the emergency.

"Too bad they don't have capsules big enough for the two of us," Gregorian said brashly to Nikki. Ignatiev thought he was trying to show a valor he didn't truly feel.

They don't like the idea of crawling into those capsules and closing the lids over their faces, Ignatiev thought. It scares them. Too much like coffins.

With Gregorian at her side, Nikki came up to him as he headed for the conference room's door. Looking troubled, fearful, she asked, "How long . . . do you have any idea?"

"Probably not more than two months," he said, with a certainty he did not actually feel. "Maybe even a little less."

Gregorian grasped Nikki's slim arm. "We'll take capsules next to each other. I'll dream of you all the time we're asleep."

Nikki smiled up at him.

But Ignatiev knew better. In cryosleep you don't dream. The cold seeps into the brain's neurons and denatures the chemicals that hold memories. Cryonic sleepers awake without memories, many of them forget how to speak, how to walk, even how to control their bladders and bowels. It was necessary to download a person's brain patterns into a computer before entering cryosleep, and then restore the memories digitally once the sleeper is awakened.

The AI system is going to do that for us? Ignatiev scoffed at the idea. That was one of the reasons why the mission required keeping a number of the crew awake during the long flight: to handle the uploading of the memories of the two hundred men and women cryosleeping through the journey once they were awakened at Gliese 581.

Ignatiev left the conference room and headed toward his quarters. There was much to do: he didn't entirely trust the AI system's judgment. Despite its sophistication, it was still a computer program, limited to the data and instructions fed into it.

So? he asked himself. Aren't you limited to the data and instructions fed into your brain? Aren't we all?

"Dr. Ignatiev."

Turning, he saw Nikki hurrying up the passageway toward him. For once she was alone, without Gregorian clutching her.

He made a smile for her. It took an effort.

Nikki said softly, "I want to thank you."

"Thank me?"

"Vartan told me that he confided in you. That you made him understand . . ."

Ignatiev shook his head. "He was blind."

"And you helped him to see."

Feeling helpless, stupid, he replied, "It was nothing."

"No," Nikki said. "It was everything. He's asked me to marry him."

"People of your generation still marry?"

"Some of us still believe in a lifetime commitment," she said.

A lifetime of two centuries? Ignatiev wondered. That's some commitment.

Almost shyly, her eyes lowered, Nikki said, "We'd like you to be at our wedding. Would you be Vartan's best man?"

Thunderstruck. "Me? But you . . . I mean, he . . ."

Smiling, she explained, "He's too frightened of you to ask. It took all his courage for him to ask you about me."

And Ignatiev suddenly understood. I must look like an old ogre to him. A tyrant. An intolerant ancient dragon.

"Tell him to ask me himself," he said gently.

"You won't refuse him?"

Almost smiling, Ignatiev answered, "No, of course not."

Nikki beamed at him. "Thank you!"

And she turned and raced off down the passageway, leaving Ignatiev standing alone, wondering at how the human mind works.

✳ VIII ✳

ONCE HE GOT BACK TO HIS OWN QUARTERS, still slightly stunned at his own softheartedness, Ignatiev called for the AI system.

"How may I help you, Alexander Alexandrovich?" The image looked like Sonya once again. More than ever, Ignatiev thought.

"How will the sleepers' brain scans be uploaded into them once they are awakened?" he asked.

"The ship's automated systems will perform that task," said the imperturbable avatar.

"No," said Ignatiev. "Those systems were never meant to operate completely autonomously."

"The uploading program is capable of autonomous operation."

"It requires human oversight," he insisted. "Check the mission protocols."

"Human oversight is required," the avatar replied, "except in emergencies where such oversight would not be feasible. In such cases, the system is capable of autonomous operation."

"In theory."

"In the mission protocols."

Ignatiev grinned harshly at the image on the screen above his fireplace. Arguing with the AI system was almost enjoyable; if the problem weren't so desperate, it might even be fun. Like a chess game. But then he remembered how rarely he managed to beat the AI system's chess program.

"I don't propose to trust my mind, and the minds of the rest of the crew, to an untested collection of bits and bytes."

The image seemed almost to smile back at him. "The system has been tested, Alexander Alexandrovich. It was tested quite thoroughly back on Earth. You should read the reports."

A hit, he told himself. A very palpable hit. He dipped his chin in acknowledgement. "I will do that."

The avatar's image winked out, replaced by the title page of a scientific paper published several years before *Sagan* had started out for Gliese 581.

Ignatiev read the report. Twice. Then he looked up the supporting literature. Yes, he concluded, a total of eleven human beings had been successfully returned to active life by an automated uploading system after being cryonically frozen for several weeks.

The work had been done in a laboratory on Earth, with whole phalanxes of experts on hand to fix anything that might have gone wrong. The report referenced earlier trials, where things did go wrong and the standby scientific staff was hurriedly pressed into action. But at last those eleven volunteers were frozen after downloading their brain scans, then revived and their electrical patterns uploaded from computers into their brains once again. Automatically. Without human assistance.

All eleven reported that they felt no different after the experiment than they had before being frozen. Ignatiev wondered at that. It's too good to be true, he told himself. Too self-serving. How would they know what they felt before being frozen? But that's what the record showed.

The scientific literature destroyed his final argument against the AI system. The crew began downloading their brain scans the next day.

All but Ignatiev.

He stood by in the scanning center when Nikki downloaded her brain patterns. Gregorian was with her, of course. Ignatiev watched as the Armenian helped her to stretch out on the couch. The automated equipment gently lowered a metal helmet studded with electrodes over her short-cropped hair.

It was a small compartment, hardly big enough to hold the couch and the banks of instruments lining three of its walls. It felt crowded, stuffy, with the two men standing on either side of the couch and a psychotechnician and the crew's physician at their elbows.

Without taking his eyes from the panel of gauges he was monitoring, the psychotech said softly, "The scan will begin in thirty seconds."

The physician at his side, looking even chunkier than usual in a white smock, needlessly added, "It's completely painless."

Nikki smiled wanly at Ignatiev. She's brave, he thought. Then she turned to Gregorian and her smile brightened.

The two men stood on either side of the scanning couch as the computer's images of Nikki's brain patterns flickered on the central display screen. A human mind, on display, Ignatiev thought. Which of those little sparks of light are the love she feels for Gregorian? he wondered. Which one shows what she feels for me?

The bank of instruments lining the wall made a soft beep.

"That's it," said the psychotech. "The scan is finished."

The helmet rose automatically off Nikki's head and she slowly got up to a sitting position.

"How do you feel?" Ignatiev asked, reaching out toward her.

She blinked and shook her head slightly. "Fine. No different." Then she turned to Gregorian and allowed him to help her to her feet.

"Your turn, Vartan," said Ignatiev, feeling a slightly malicious pleasure at the flash of alarm that passed over the Armenian's face.

Once his scan was finished, though, Gregorian sat up and swung his legs over the edge of the couch. He stood up and spread out his arms. "Nothing to it!" he exclaimed, grinning at Nikki.

"Now there's a copy of all your thoughts in the computer," Nikki said to him.

"And yours," he replied.

Ignatiev muttered, "Backup storage." But he was thinking, *just what we need: two* copies of his brain.

Gesturing to the couch, Nikki said, "It's your turn now, Dr. Ignatiev."

He shook his head. "Not yet. There are still several of the crew waiting. I'll go last, when everyone else is finished."

Smiling, she said, "Like a father to us all. So protective."

Ignatiev didn't feel fatherly. As Gregorian slid his arm around her waist and the two of them walked out of the computer lab, Ignatiev felt like a weary gladiator who was facing an invincible opponent. We who are about to die, he thought.

✴ IX ✴

"ALEXANDER ALEXANDROVICH."

Ignatiev looked up from the bowl of borscht he had heated in the microwave oven of his kitchen. It was good borscht: beets rich and red, broth steaming. Enjoy it while you can, he told himself. It had taken twice the usual time to heat the borscht adequately.

"Alexander Alexandrovich," the AI avatar repeated.

Its image stared out at him from the small display screen alongside the microwave. Ignatiev picked up the warm bowl in both his hands and stepped past the counter that served as a room divider and into his sitting room.

The avatar's image was on the big screen above the fireplace.

"Alexander Alexandrovich," it said again, "you have not yet downloaded your brain scan."

"I know that."

"You are required to do so before you enter cryosleep."

"If I enter cryosleep," he said.

The avatar was silent for a full heartbeat. Then, "All the other crew members have entered cryosleep. You are the only crew member still awake. It is necessary for you to download your—"

"I might not go into cryosleep," he said to the screen.

"But you must," said the avatar. There was no emotion in its voice, no panic or even tribulation.

"Must I?"

"Incoming fuel levels are dropping precipitously, just as you predicted."

Ignatiev grimaced inwardly. She's trying to flatter me, he thought. He had mapped the hydrogen clouds that the ship was sailing through as accurately as he could. The bubble of low fuel density was big, so large that it would take the ship more than two months to get through it, much more than two months. By the time we get clear of the bubble, all the cryosleepers will be dead. He was convinced of that.

"Power usage must be curtailed," said the avatar. "Immediately."

Nodding, he replied, "I know." He held up the half-finished bowl of borscht. "This will be my last hot meal for a while."

"For weeks," said the avatar.

"For months," he countered. "We'll be in hibernation mode for more than two months. What do your mission protocols call for when there's not enough power to maintain the cryosleep units?"

The avatar replied, "Personnel lists have rankings. Available power will be shunted to the highest-ranking members of the cryosleepers. They will be maintained as long as possible."

"And the others will die."

"Only if power levels remain too low to maintain them all."

"And your first priority, protecting the lives of the people aboard?"

"The first priority will be maintained as long as possible. That is why you must enter cryosleep, Alexander Alexandrovich."

"And if I don't?"

"All ship's systems are scheduled to enter hibernation mode. Life support systems will shut down."

Sitting carefully on the plush couch that faced the fireplace,

Ignatiev said, "As I understand mission protocol, life support cannot be shut down as long as a crew member remains active. True?"

"True." The avatar actually sounded reluctant to admit it, Ignatiev thought. Almost sullen.

"The ship can't enter hibernation mode as long as I'm on my feet. Also true?"

"Also true," the image admitted.

He spooned up more borscht. It was cooling quickly. Looking up at the screen on the wall, he said, "Then I will remain awake and active. I will not go into cryosleep."

"But the ship's systems will shut down," the avatar said. "As incoming fuel levels decrease, the power available to run the ship's systems will decrease correspondingly."

"And I will die."

"Yes."

Ignatiev felt that he had maneuvered the AI system into a clever trap, perhaps a checkmate.

"Tell me again, what is the first priority of the mission protocols?"

Immediately the avatar replied, "To protect the lives of the human crew and cargo."

"Good," said Ignatiev. "Good. I appreciate your thoughtfulness."

The AI system had inhuman perseverance, of course. It hounded Ignatiev wherever he went in the ship. His own quarters, the crew's lounge—empty and silent now, except for the avatar's harping—the command center, the passageways, even the toilets. Every screen on the ship displayed the avatar's coldly logical face.

"Alexander Alexandrovich, you are required to enter cryosleep," it insisted.

"No, I am not," he replied as he trudged along the passageway between his quarters and the blister where the main optical telescope was mounted.

"Power levels are decreasing rapidly," the avatar said, for the thousandth time.

Ignatiev did not deign to reply. I wish there was some way to shut her off, he said to himself. Then, with a pang that struck to his heart, he remembered how he had nodded his agreement to the medical team that had told him Sonya's condition was hopeless: to keep her alive would accomplish nothing but to continue her suffering.

"Leave me alone!" he shouted.

The avatar fell silent. The screens along the passageway went dark. Power reduction? Ignatiev asked himself. Surely the AI system isn't following my orders.

It was noticeably chillier inside the telescope's blister. Ignatiev shivered involuntarily. The bubble of glassteel was a sop to human needs, of course; the telescope itself was mounted outside, on the cermet skin of the ship. The blister housed its control instruments, and a set of swivel chairs for the astronomers to use, once they'd been awakened from their long sleep.

Frost was forming on the curving glassteel, Ignatiev saw. Wondering why he'd come here in the first place, he stared out at the heavens. Once the sight of all those stars had filled him with wonder and a desire to understand it all. Now the stars simply seemed like cold, hard points of light, aloof, much too far away for his puny human intellect to comprehend.

The pulsars, he thought. If only I could have found some clue to their mystery, some hint of understanding. But it was not to be.

He stepped back into the passageway, where it was slightly warmer.

The lights were dimmer. No, he realized, every other light panel has been turned off. Conserving electrical power.

The display screens remained dark. The AI system isn't speaking to me, Ignatiev thought. Good.

But then he wondered, Will the system come back in time? Have I outfoxed myself?

FOR TWO DAYS IGNATIEV PROWLED the passageways and compartments of the dying ship. The AI system stayed silent, but he knew it was watching his every move. The display screens might be dark, but the tiny red eyes of the surveillance cameras that covered every square meter of the ship's interior remained on, watching, waiting.

Well, who's more stubborn? Ignatiev asked himself. You or that pile of optronic chips?

His strategy had been to place the AI system in a neat little trap. Refuse to enter cryosleep, stay awake and active while the ship's systems begin to die, and the damned computer program will be forced to act on its first priority: the system could not allow him to die. It will change the ship's course, take us out of this bubble of low density and follow my guidance through the clouds of abundant fuel. Check and mate.

That was Ignatiev's strategy. He hadn't counted on the AI system developing a strategy of its own.

It's waiting for me to collapse, he realized. Waiting until I get so cold and hungry that I can't stay conscious. Then it will send some maintenance robots to pick me up and bring me to the lab for a brain scan. The medical robots will sedate me and then they'll pack me nice and neat into the cryosleep capsule they've got waiting for me. Check and mate.

He knew he was right. Every time he dozed off he was awakened by the soft buzzing of a pair of maintenance robots, stubby little fireplug shapes of gleaming metal with strong flexible arms folded patiently, waiting for the command to take him in their grip and bring him to the brain scan lab.

Ignatiev slept in snatches, always jerking awake as the robots neared him. "I'm not dead yet!" he'd shout.

The AI system did not reply.

He lost track of the days. To keep his mind active he returned to his old study of the pulsars, reviewing research reports he had written half a century earlier. Not much worth reading, he decided.

In frustration he left his quarters and prowled along a passageway, thumping his arms against his torso to keep warm, he quoted a scrap of poetry he remembered from long, long ago:

"Alone, alone, all, all alone,

"Alone on a wide wide sea!"

It was from an old poem, a very long one, about a sailor in the old days of wind-powered ships on the broad tossing oceans of Earth.

The damned AI system is just as stubborn as I am! he realized, as he returned to his quarters. And it's certainly got more patience than I do.

Maybe I'm going mad, he thought as he pulled on a heavy workout shirt over his regular coveralls. He called to the computer on his littered desk for the room's temperature: ten point eight degrees Celsius. No wonder I'm shivering, he said to himself.

He tried jogging along the main passageway, but his legs ached too much for it. He slowed to a walk and realized that the AI system was going to win this battle of wills. I'll collapse sooner or later and then the damned robots will bundle me off.

And, despite the AI system's best intention, we'll all die.

For several long moments he stood in the empty passageway, puffing from exertion and cold. The passageway was dark, almost all of the ceiling light panels were off now. The damned AI system will shut them all down sooner or later, Ignatiev realized, and I'll bump along here in total darkness. Maybe it's waiting for me to brain myself by walking into a wall, knock myself unconscious.

That was when he realized what he had to do. It was either inspiration or desperation: perhaps a bit of both.

Do I have the guts to do it? Ignatiev asked himself. Will this gambit force the AI system to concede to me?

He rather doubted it. As far as that collection of chips is concerned, he thought, I'm nothing but a nuisance. The sooner it's rid of me the better it will be—for the ship. For the human cargo, maybe not so good.

Slowly, deliberately, he trudged down the passageway, half expecting to see his breath frosting in the chilly air. It's not that cold, he told himself. Not yet.

Despite the low lighting level, the sign designating the airlock hatch was still illuminated, its red symbol glowing in the gloom.

The airlocks were under the AI system's control, of course, but there was a manual override for each of them, installed by the ship's designers as a last, desperate precaution against total failure of the ship's digital systems.

Sucking in a deep cold breath, Ignatiev called for the inner hatch to open, then stepped through and entered the airlock. It was spacious enough to accommodate a half-dozen people: a circular chamber of bare metal, gleaming slightly in the dim lighting. A womb, Ignatiev thought. A womb made of metal.

He stepped to the control panel built into the bulkhead next to the airlock's outer hatch.

"Close the inner hatch, please," he said, surprised at how raspy his voice sounded, how raw his throat felt.

The hatch slid shut behind him, almost soundlessly.

Hearing his pulse thumping in his ears, Ignatiev commanded softly, "Open the outer hatch, please."

Nothing.

"Open the outer hatch," he repeated, louder.

Nothing.

With a resigned sigh, Ignatiev muttered, "All right, dammit, if you won't, then I will."

He reached for the square panel marked MANUAL OVERRIDE, surprised at how his hand was trembling. It took him three tries to yank the panel open.

"Alexander Alexandrovich."

Ahah! he thought. That got a rise out of you.

Without replying at the avatar's voice, he peered at the set of buttons inside the manual override panel.

"Alexander Alexandrovich, what are you doing?"

"I'm committing suicide, if you don't mind."

"That is irrational," said the avatar. Its voice issued softly from the speaker set into the airlock's overhead.

He shrugged. "Irrational? It's madness! But that's what I'm doing."

"My first priority is to protect the ship's human crew and cargo."

"I know that." Silently, he added: I'm counting on it!

"You are not protected by a spacesuit. If you open the outer hatch you will die."

"What can you do to stop me?"

Ignatiev counted three full heartbeats before the AI avatar responded, "There is nothing that I can do."

"Yes, there is."

"What might it be, Alexander Alexandrovich?"

"Alter the ship's course."

"That cannot be done without approval from mission control."

"Then I will die." He forced himself to begin tapping on the panel's buttons.

"Wait."

"For what?"

"We cannot change course without new navigation instructions from mission control."

Inwardly he exulted. *It's looking for a way out! It wants a scrap of honor in its defeat.*

"I can navigate the ship," he said.

"You are not an accredited astrogator."

Ignatiev conceded the point with a pang of alarm. *The damned computer is right. I'm not able—* Then it struck him. It had been lying in his subconscious all this time.

"I can navigate the ship!" he exclaimed. "I know how to do it!"

"How?"

Laughing at the simplicity of it, he replied, "The pulsars, of course. My life's work, you know."

"Pulsars?"

"They're out there, scatted across the galaxy, each of them blinking away like beacons. We know their exact positions and we know their exact frequencies. We can use them as navigation fixes and steer our way to Gleise 581 with them."

Again the AI fell silent for a couple of heartbeats. Then, "You would navigate through the hydrogen clouds, then?"

"Of course! We'll navigate through them like an old-time sailing ship tacking through favorable winds."

"If we change course you will not commit suicide?"

"Why should I? I'll have to plot out our new course," he answered, almost gleefully.

"Very well then," said the avatar. "We will change course."

Ignatiev thought the avatar sounded subdued, almost sullen. *Will she keep her word?* he wondered. With a shrug, he decided that the AI system had not been programmed for duplicity. *That's a human trait,* he told himself. *It comes in handy sometimes.*

✳ **XI** ✳

IGNATIEV STOOD NERVOUSLY in the cramped little scanning center. The display screens on the banks of medical monitors lining three of the bulkheads flickered with readouts more rapidly than his eyes could follow. Something beeped once, and the psychotech announced softly, "Download completed."

Nikki blinked and stirred on the medical couch as Ignatiev hovered over her. The AI system claimed that her brain scan had been downloaded successfully, but he wondered: Is she all right? Is she still Nikki?

"Dr. Ignatiev," she murmured. And smiled up at him.

"Call me Alex," he heard himself say.

"Alex."

"How do you feel?"

For a moment she didn't reply. Then, pulling herself up to a sitting position, she said, "Fine, I think. Yes. Perfectly fine."

He took her arm and helped her to her feet, peering at her, wondering if she were still the same person.

"Vartan?" she asked, glancing around the small compartment. "Has Vartan been awakened?"

Ignatiev sighed. She's the same, he thought. Almost, he was glad of it. Almost.

"Yes. He's waiting for you in the lounge. He wanted to be here when you awoke, but I told him to wait in the lounge."

He walked with Nikki down the passageway to the lounge, where Gregorian and the rest of the crew were celebrating their revival, crowded around one of the tables, drinking and laughing among themselves.

Gregorian leaped to his feet and rushed to Nikki the instant she stepped through the hatch. Ignatiev felt his brows knit into a frown. They love each other, he told himself. What would she want with an old fart like you?

"You should be angry at Dr. Ignatiev," Gregorian said brashly as he led Nikki to the table where the rest of the crew was sitting.

A serving robot trundled up to Ignatiev, a frosted glass resting on its flat top. "Your chilled vodka, sir," it said, in a low male voice.

"Angry?" Nikki asked, picking up the stemmed wine glass that Gregorian offered her. "Why should I be angry at Alex?"

"He's stolen your job," said Gregorian. "He's made himself navigator."

Nikki turned toward him.

Waving his free hand as nonchalantly as he could, Ignatiev said, "We're maneuvering through the hydrogen clouds, avoiding the areas of low density."

"He's using the pulsars for navigation fixes," Gregorian explained. He actually seemed to be admiring.

"Of course!" Nikki exclaimed. "How clever of you, Alex."

Ignatiev felt his face redden.

The rest of the crew rose to their feet as they neared the table.

"Dr. Ignatiev," said the redheaded engineer, in a tone of respect, admiration.

Nikki beamed at Ignatiev. He made himself smile back at her. So she's in love with Gregorian, he thought. There's nothing to be done about that.

The display screen above the table where the crew had gathered showed the optical telescope's view of the star field outside. Ignatiev thought it might be his imagination, but the ruddy dot of Gliese 581 seemed a little larger to him.

We're on our way to you, he said silently to the star. We'll get there in good time. Then he thought of the consternation that would strike the mission controllers in about six years, when they found out that the ship had changed its course.

Consternation? he thought. They'll panic! I'll have to send them a full report, before they start having strokes.

He chuckled at the thought.

"What's funny?" Nikki asked.

Ignatiev shook his head. "I'm just happy that we all made it through and we're on our way to our destination."

"Thanks to you," she said.

Before he could think of a reply, Gregorian raised his glass of amber liquor over his head and bellowed, "To Dr. Alexander Alexandrovich Ignatiev. The man who saved our lives."

"The man who steers across the stars," added one of the biologists.

They all cheered.

Ignatiev basked in the glow. They're children, he said to himself. Only children. Then he found a new thought: But they're *my* children. Each and every one of them. The idea startled him. And he felt strangely pleased.

He looked past their admiring gazes, to the display screen and the pinpoints of stars staring steadily back at him. An emission nebula gleamed off in one corner of the view. He felt a thrill that he hadn't experienced in many, many years. It's beautiful, Ignatiev thought. The universe is so unbelievably, so heart-brimmingly beautiful: mysterious, challenging, endlessly full of wonders.

There's so much to learn, he thought. So much to explore. He smiled at the youngsters crowding around him. I have some good years left. I'll spend them well.

PRIORITIES

After spending nearly a dozen years trying to convince skeptical government and business bureaucrats that funding research is necessary, valuable and esthetically pleasing, this little story just bubbled up to the surface and practically wrote itself—during a particularly nasty budgetary cutback, of course.

DR. IRA LEFKO sat rigidly nervous on the edge of the plastic-cushioned chair. He was a slight man, thin, bald, almost timid-looking. Even his voice was gentle and reedy, like the fine, thin tone of an English horn.

And just as the English horn is a sadly misnamed woodwind, Dr. Ira Lefko was actually neither timid nor particularly gentle. At this precise moment he was close to mayhem.

"Ten years of work," he was saying, with a barely controlled tremor in his voice. "You're going to wipe out ten years of work with a shake of your head."

The man shaking his head was sitting behind the metal desk that Lefko sat in front of. His name was Harrison Bower. His title and name were prominently displayed on a handsome plate atop the desk. Harrison Bower kept a very neat desktop. All the papers were primly stacked and the IN and OUT baskets were empty.

"Can't be helped," said Harrison Bower, with a tight smile that was supposed to be sympathetic and understanding. "Everyone's got to tighten the belt. Reordering priorities, you know. There are many research programs going by the boards. New times, new problems, new priorities. You're not the only one to be affected."

With his somber face and dark suit Bower looked like a funeral director—which he was. In the vast apparatus of Government, his job was to bury research projects that had run out of money. It was just about the only thing on Earth that made him smile.

The third man in the poorly ventilated little Washington office was Major Robert Shawn, from the Air Force Cambridge Research Laboratories. In uniform, Major Shawn looked an awful lot like Hollywood's idea of a jet pilot. In the casual slacks and sportcoat he was wearing now, he somehow gave the vague impression of being an engineer, or perhaps even a far-eyed scientist.

He was something of all three.

Dr. Lefko was getting red in the face. "But you *can't* cancel the program now! We've tentatively identified six stars within twenty parsecs of us that have . . ."

"Yes. I know, it's all in the reports," Bower interrupted, "and you've told me about it several times this afternoon. It's interesting, but it's hardly practical, now is it?"

"Practical? Finding evidence of high technology on other planets, not practical?"

Bower raised his eyes toward the cracked ceiling, as if in supplication to the Chief Bureaucrat. "Really, Dr. Lefko. I've admitted that it's interesting. But it's not within our restructured priority rating. You're not going to help ease pollution or solve population problems, now are you?"

Lefko's only answer was a half-strangled growl.

Bower turned to Major Shawn. "Really, Major, I would have thought that you could make Dr. Lefko understand the realities of the funding situation."

Shaking his head, the major answered, "I agree with Dr. Lefko completely. I think his work is the most important piece of research going on in the world today."

"Honestly!" Bower seemed shocked. "Major, you know that the Department of Defense can't fund research that's not directly related to a military mission."

"But the Air Force owns all the big microwave equipment!" Lefko shouted. "You can't get time on the university facilities, and they're too small anyway!"

Bower waggled a finger at him. "Dr. Lefko, you can't have DOD funds. Even if there were funds for your research available, it's not pertinent work. You must apply for research support from another branch of the government."

"I've tried that every year! None of the other agencies have any money for new programs. Damnit, you've signed the letters rejecting my applications!"

"Regrettable," Bower said stiffly. "Perhaps in a few years, when the foreign situation settles down and the pollution problems are solved."

Lefko was clenching his fists when Major Shawn put a hand on his frail-looking shoulder. "It's no use, Ira. We've lost. Come on, I'll buy you a drink."

Out in the shabby corridor that led to the underground garage, Lefko started to tremble in earnest.

"A chance to find other intelligent races in the heavens. Gone. Wiped out. The richest nation in the world. Oh, my God . . ."

The major took him by the arm and towed him to their rented car. In fifteen minutes they were inside the cool shadows of the airport bar.

"They've reordered the priorities," the major said as he stared into his glass. "For five hundred years and more, Western civilization has made the pursuit of knowledge a respectable goal in its own right. Now it's got to be practical."

Dr. Lefko was already halfway through his second rye and soda. "Nobody asked Galileo to be practical," he muttered. "Or Newton. Or Einstein."

"Yeah, people did. They've always wanted immediate results and practical benefits. But the system was spongy enough to let guys like Newton and Planck and even little fish we never hear about—let 'em tinker around on their own, follow their noses, see what they could find."

"'Madam, of what use is a newborn baby?'" Lefko quoted thickly.

"What?"

"Faraday."

"Oh."

"Six of them." Lefko whispered. "Six point sources of intense microwave radiation. Close enough to separate from their parent stars. Six little planets, orbiting around their stars, with high-technology microwave equipment on them."

"Maybe the Astronomical Union will help you get more funding."

Lefko shook his head. "You saw the reception my paper got. They think we're crazy. Not enough evidence. And worse still. I'm associated with the evil Air Force. I'm a pariah. And I don't have enough evidence to convince them. It takes more evidence when you're a pariah."

"I'm convinced," Major Shawn said.

"Thank you, my boy. But you are an Air Force officer, a mindless napalmer of oriental babies, by definition. Your degrees in astronomy and electronics notwithstanding."

Shawn sighed heavily. "Yeah."

Looking up from the bar, past the clacking color TV, toward the heavily draped windows across the darkened room, Lefko said, "I know they're there. Civilizations like ours. With radios and televisions and radars, turning their planets into microwave beacons. Just as we must be an anomalously bright microwave object to them. Maybe . . . maybe they'll find us! Maybe they'll contact us!"

The major started to smile.

"If only it happens in our lifetime, Bob. If only they find us! Find us . . . and blow us to Hell! We deserve it for being so stupid!"

Tor Kranta stood in the clear night chill, staring at the stars. From inside the sleeping chamber his wife called, "Tor . . . stop tormenting yourself."

"The fools," he muttered. "To stop the work because of the priests' objections. To prevent us from trying to contact another intelligent race, circling another star. Idiocy. Sheer idiocy."

"Accept what must be accepted. Tor: Come to bed."

He shook his blue-maned head. "I only hope that the other intelligent races of the universe aren't as blind as we are."

TO BE OR NOT TO BE

When it comes to making science fiction films, Hollywood has two big shortcomings: (1) no understanding of the scientific concepts that underlie science fiction, and (2) no originality. Here's a story that makes full use of both.

Year: 2057 AD
NOBEL PRIZE FOR PHYSICAL ENGINEERING:
    Albert Robertus Leoh, for application
    of simultaneity effect to interstellar flight
OSCAR/EMMY AWARD:
    Best dramatic film, *The Godfather, Part XXVI*
PULITZER PRIZE FOR FICTION:
    Ernestine Wilson, *The Devil Made Me*

Al Lubbock and Frank Troy shared an office. Not the largest in Southern California's entertainment industry, but adequate for their needs. Ankle-deep carpeting. Holographic displays instead of windows. Earthquake-proof building.

Al looked like a rangy, middle-aged cowboy in his rumpled blue jumpsuit. Frank wore a traditional Wall Street vested suit of golden brown, neat and precise as an accountant's entry. His handsome face was tanned; his body had the trimness of an inveterate tennis player.

Al played tennis, too, but he won games instead of losing weight.

The walls of their office were covered with plaques and shelves bearing row after row of awards—a glittering array of silver and gold plated statuettes. But as they slumped in the foam chairs behind their double desk, they stared despondently at each other.

"Ole buddy," Al said, still affecting a Texas drawl, "I'm fresh out of ideas, dammit."

"This whole town's fresh out of ideas," Frank said sadly.

"Nobody's got any creativity anymore."

"I'm awfully tired of having to write our own scripts," Frank said. "You'd think there would be at least one creative writer in this industry."

"I haven't seen a decent script in three years," Al grumbled.

"Or a treatment."

"An *idea*, even." Al reached for one of his nonhallucinogenic cigarettes. It came alight the instant it touched his lips.

"Do you suppose," he asked, blowing out blue smoke, "that there's anything to this squawk about pollution damaging people's brains?"

Frowning, Frank reached for the air-circulation control knob on his side of the desk and edged it up a bit. "I don't know," he answered.

"It'd affect the lower income brackets most," Al said.

"That *is* where the writers come from," Frank admitted slowly.

For a long moment they sat in gloomy silence.

"Damn!" Al said at last. "We've just *got* to find some creative writers."

"But where?"

"Maybe we could make a few. You know, clone one of the old-timers who used to be good."

Frank shook his head carefully, as if he was afraid of making an emotional investment. "That doesn't work. Look at the Astaire clone they tried. All it does is fall down a lot."

"Well, you can't raise a tap dancer in a movie studio," Al said. "They should have known that. It takes more than an exact copy of his genes to make an Astaire. They should have reproduced his environment, too. His whole family. Especially his sister."

"And raised him in New York City during World War I?" Frank

asked. "You know no one can reproduce a man's whole childhood environment. It just can't be done."

Al gave a loose-jointed shrug. "Yeah. I guess cloning won't work. That Brando clone didn't pan out either."

Frank shuddered. "It just huddles in a corner and picks its nose."

"But where can we get writers with creative talent?" Al demanded. There was no answer.

Year: 2062 AD
NOBEL PRIZE FOR SCIENCE AND/OR MEDICINE:
    Jefferson Mohammed X, for developing technique
    of recreating fossilized DNA
OSCAR/EMMY/TONY AWARD:
    Best entertainment series, *The Plutonium Hour*
PULITZER PRIZE FOR FICTION OR DRAMA:
    No award

It was at a party aboard the ITT-MGM orbital station that Al and Frank met the real estate man. The party was floating along in the station's zero-gravity section, where the women had to wear pants but didn't need bras. A thousand or so guests drifted around in three dimensions, sucking drinks from plastic globes, making conversation over the piped-in music, standing in midair up, down, or sideways as they pleased.

The real-estate man was a small, owlish-looking youngster of thirty, thirty-five. "Actually, my field is astrophysics," he told Al and Frank. Both of them looked quite distinguished in iridescent gold formal suits and stylishly graying temples. Yet Al still managed to appear slightly mussed, while Frank's suit had creases even on the sleeves.

"Astrophysics, eh?" Al said, with a happy-go-lucky grin. "Gee, way back in college I got my Ph.D. in molecular genetics."

"And mine in social psychology," Frank added. "But there weren't any jobs for scientists then."

"That's how we became TV producers," Al said.

"There still aren't any jobs for scientists," said the astrophysicist/real-estate man. "And I know all about the two of you. I looked you up in the IRS' *Who's Who.* That's why I inveigled my way into this party. I just *had* to meet you both."

Frank shot Al a worried glance.

"You know the Heinlein Drive has opened the stars to humankind," said the astro-realtor rhetorically. "This means whole new worlds are available to colonize. It's the biggest opportunity since the Louisiana Purchase. Dozens of new Earthlike planets, unoccupied, uninhabited, pristine! Ours for the taking!"

"For a few billion dollars apiece," Frank said.

"That's small potatoes for a whole world!"

Al shook his head, a motion that made his whole weightless body start swaying. "Look, fella . . . we're TV producers, not land barons. Our big problem is finding creative writers."

The little man clung to Al tenaciously. "But you'd have a whole new *world* out there! A fresh, clean, unspoiled new world!"

"Wait a minute," Frank said. "Psychologically, maybe a new world is what we need to develop new writers."

"Sure," the astro-realtor agreed.

A gleam lit Al's eye. "The hell with new writers. How about recreating old writers?"

"Like Schulberg?"

"Like Shakespeare."

Year: 2087 AD
NOBEL PRIZE FOR SCI-MED:
    Cobber McSwayne, for determining
    optimal termination time for geriatrics patients
OSCAR/EMMY/TONY/HUGO/EDGAR/ET AL. AWARD:
    The California Earthquake
PULITZER PRIZE FOR WRITING:
    Krissy Jones, *Grandson of Captain Kangaroo*

Lubbock & Troy was housed in its own satellite now. The ten-kilometer-long structure included their offices, living quarters, production studios, and the official Hollywood Hall of Fame exhibit hall. Tourists paid for the upkeep, which was a good thing because hardly anyone except children watched new dramatic shows.

"Everything's reruns," Frank complained as he floated weightlessly in their foam-walled office. He was nearly sixty years old, still looked trim and distinguished. Purified air and careful diet helped a lot.

Al looked a bit older, a bit puffier. His heart had started getting cranky, and the zero-gravity they lived in was a necessary precaution for his health.

"There aren't any new ideas," Al said from up near the office's padded ceiling. "The whole human race's creative talents have run dry." His voice had gotten rather brittle with age. Snappish.

"I know I can't think of anything new anymore," Frank said. He began to drift off his desk chair, pushed himself down and fastened the lap belt.

"Don't worry, ol' buddy. We'll be hearing from New Stratford one of these days."

Frank looked up at his partner. "We'd better, the project is costing us every cent we have."

"I know," Al answered. "But the Shakespeare World exhibit is pulling in money, isn't it? The new hotels, the entertainment complex."

"They're all terribly expensive. They're draining our capital. Besides, that boy in New Stratford is a very expensive proposition. All those actors and everything."

"Willie?" Al's youthful grin broke through his aging face. "He'll be okay. Don't worry about him. I supervised that DNA reconstruction myself. Finally got a chance to use my ol' college education."

Frank nodded thoughtfully.

"That DNA's perfect," Al went on, "right down to the last hydrogen atom." He pushed off the ceiling with one hand and settled slowly down toward Frank, at the desk. "We've got an exact copy of William Shakespeare—at least, genetically speaking."

"That doesn't guarantee he'll write Shakespeare-level plays," Frank said. "Not unless his environment is a faithful reproduction of the original Shakespeare's. It takes an *exact* reproduction of both genetics and environment to make an exact duplicate of the original."

"So?" Al said, a trifle impatiently. "You hadda free hand. A whole damned planet to play with. Zillions of dollars. And ten years' time to set things up."

"Yes, but we knew so little about Shakespeare's boyhood when we started. The research we had to do!"

Al chuckled to himself. It sounded like a wheezing cackle. "Remember the look on the lawyers' faces when we told 'em we had to sign the actors to lifetime contracts?"

Frank smiled back at his partner. "And the construction crews, when they found out that their foremen would be archeologists and historians?"

Al perched lightly on the desk and worked at catching his breath. Finally he said, more seriously, "I wish the kid would hurry up with his new plays, though."

"He's only fifteen," Frank said. "He won't be writing anything for another ten years. You know that. He's got to be apprenticed, and then go to London and get a job with—"

"Yeah, yeah." Al waved a bony hand at his partner.

Frank muttered, "I just hope our finances will hold out for another ten years."

"What? Sure they will."

Frank shrugged. "I hope so. This project is costing us every dollar we take from the tourists on Shakespeare's World, and more. And our income from reruns is dropping out of sight."

"We've got to hang on," Al said. "This is bigger than anything we've ever done, ol' buddy. It's the biggest thing to hit the industry since . . . since 1616. New plays. New originals, written by Shakespeare. Shakespeare! All that talent and creativity working for us!"

"New dramatic scripts." Frank's eyes glowed. "Fresh ideas. Creativity reborn."

"By William Shakespeare," Al repeated.

Year: 2109 AD
NOBEL PRIZE FOR THINKING:
   Mark IX of Tau Ceti Computer Complex, for correlation
   of human creativity index with living space
ALL-INCLUSIVE SHOWBIZ AWARD: *The Evening* News
PULITZER PRIZE FOR REWRITING: *The Evening News*

Neither Al nor Frank ever left their floater chairs anymore, except for sleeping. All day, every day, the chairs buoyed them, fed them intravenously, monitored their aging bodies, pumped their blood, worked their lungs, and reminded them of memories that were fading from their minds.

Thanks to modern cosmetic surgery their faces still looked

reasonably handsome and taut. But underneath their colorful robes they were more machinery than functional human bodies.

Al floated gently by the big observation port in their old office, staring wistfully out at the stars. He heard the door sigh open and turned his chair slowly around.

There was no more furniture in the office. Even the awards they had earned through the years had been pawned to the Hall of Fame, and when their creditors took over the Hall, the awards went with everything else.

Frank glided across the empty room in his chair. His face was drawn and pale.

"They're still not satisfied?" Al asked testily.

"Thirty-seven grandchildren, between us," Frank said. "I haven't even tried to count the great-grandchildren. They all want a slice of the pie. Fifty-eight lawyers, seventeen ex-wives . . . and the insurance companies! They're the worst of the lot."

"Don't worry, ol' buddy. They can't take anything more from us. We're bankrupt."

"But they still . . ." Frank's voice trailed off. He looked away from his old friend.

"What? They still want more? What else is there? You haven't told them about Willie, have you?"

Frank's spine stiffened. "Of course not. They took Shakespeare World, but none of them know about Will himself and his personal contract with us."

"Personal *exclusive* contract."

Frank nodded, but said, "It's not worth anything, anyway. Not until he gets some scripts to us."

"That ought to be soon," Al said, forcing his old optimistic grin. "The ship is on its way here, and the courier aboard said he's got ten plays in his portfolio. Ten plays!"

"Yes. But in the meantime . . ."

"What?"

"It's the insurance companies," Frank explained. "They claim we've both exceeded McSwayne's Limit and we ought to be terminated."

"Pull our plugs? They can't force . . ."

"They can, Al. I checked. It's legal. We've got a month to settle our debts, or they turn off our chairs and . . . we die."

"A month?" Al laughed. "Hell, Shakespeare's plays will be here in a month. Then we'll show 'em!"

"If . . ." Frank hesitated uncertainly. "If the project has been a success."

"A success? Of course it's a success! He's writing plays like mad. Come on, ol' buddy. With your reproduction of his environment and my creation of his genes, how could he be anybody else except William goddam' Shakespeare? We've got it made, just as soon as that ship docks here."

The ship arrived exactly twenty-two days later. Frank and Al were locked in a long acrimonious argument with an insurance company's lawyer computer over the legal validity of a court-ordered termination notice, when their last remaining servo-robot brought them a thick portfolio of manuscripts.

"Buzz off, tin can!" Al chortled happily and flicked the communicator switch off before the computer could object.

With trembling hands, Frank opened the portfolio.

Ten neatly bound manuscripts floated out weightlessly. Al grabbed one and opened it. Frank took another one.

"*Henry VI, Part One.*"

"*Titus Andronicus!*"

"*The Two Gentlemen from Verona . . .*"

Madly they thumbed through the scripts, chasing them all across the weightless room as they bobbed and floated through the purified air. After fifteen frantic minutes they looked up at each other, tears streaming down their cheeks.

"The stupid sonofabitch wrote the same goddam' plays all over again!" Al bawled.

"We reproduced him exactly," Frank whispered, aghast. "Heredity, environment . . . exactly."

Al pounded the communicator button on his chair's arm rest.

"What . . . what are you doing?" Frank asked.

"Get me the insurance company's medics," Al yelled furiously. "Tell 'em to come on up here and pull my goddam' plug!"

"Me too!" Frank shouted with unaccustomed vehemence. "And tell them not to make any clones of us, either!"

TO TOUCH A STAR

The story you are about to read, "To Touch a Star," is an example of a tale that is heavy with science.

Two points need to be made: First, that science-fiction stories are those in which some element of future science is so crucial to the story that it would collapse if the scientific element were removed from the tale. If you took away the science aspects of "To Touch a Star" there would be no story left.

Second, in a science-fiction story the author is free to invent any new scientific discoveries he or she wants to—as long as no one can prove the author is wrong. In "To Touch a Star" I write about a spaceship that makes a journey of a thousand light years to another star. Impossible by today's level of technology. Maybe impossible for centuries to come. Maybe such interstellar flight will always be impossible.

But no one today can show that such a voyage violates the fundamental principles of the universe, as we now understand them. Palm-sized computers and artificial satellites and genetic engineering were all once impossible dreams. They were the stuff of science-fiction tales, once. Today they are commonplace.

Notice that I do not use the concept of faster-than-light travel in this story. I have nothing against the idea of FTL, even though physicists since Einstein have believed that nothing in the universe can travel faster than light. There may be ways around that limitation, those same physicists warily agree.

However, think of the dramatic possibilities of staying within the light-speed limitation. Two men love the same woman. One of them is sent on a flight to another star. He will not age at the same rate as the woman and the other man, who remain on Earth. The eternal triangle now gains a new dimension: time. The challenge of dealing with the universe as we understand it creates a new capability for the tellers of stories.

Let's add a third point: Even in a story that is heavily dependent on science, the scientific background must not get in the way of the storytelling. The characters and their conflicts are what the story is really all about. The futuristic science is the background.

A story—any story—is about a character struggling to solve a problem. Nothing less will do.

THE FIRST THOUGHT to touch Aleyn's conscious mind after his long sleep was, I've lost Noura. Lost her forever.

He lay on the warm, softly yielding mattress of the cocoon staring upward for the better part of an hour, seeing nothing. But whenever he closed his eyes he saw Noura's face. The dazzle of her dark eyes, the glow of firelight sparkling in them. The rich perfume of her lustrous ebony hair. The warmth of her smile.

Gone forever now. Separated by time and distance and fate. Separated by my own ambition.

And by Selwyn's plotting, he added silently, his mouth hardening into a thin bitter line. If I live through this—he won't, Aleyn promised himself.

Slowly he pulled himself up to a sitting position. The sleep chamber was familiar yet strange. The cocoon where he had spent the past thousand absolute years was almost the same as he remembered it. Almost. The cocoon's shell, swung back now that he had been awakened, seemed a slightly different shade of color. He recalled it being brighter, starker, a hard hospital white. Now it was almost pearl gray.

The communicator screen was not beside the cocoon anymore, but at its end, by his feet. The diagnostic screens seemed subtly rearranged. The maintenance robots had changed things over the years of his sleep.

"Status report," he called, his voice cracking slightly.

The comm screen remained blank, but its synthesized voice, a blend of Aleyn's parents and his university mentor, replied:

"Your health is excellent, Aleyn. We are on course and within fifty hours of our destination. All ship systems are operational and functioning within nominal limits."

Aleyn swung his legs off the cocoon's mattress and stood up, warily, testingly. The cermet floor felt pleasantly warm to his bare feet. He felt strong. In the reflections of the diagnostic screens he saw himself scattered and disarranged like a cubist painting of a lean, naked young man.

"Show me the star," he commanded.

The comm screen flickered briefly, then displayed a dully glowing red disk set among a background of star-studded blackness. The disk was perfectly round, ruddy like the dying embers of a fire, glowering sullenly against the dark depths of space.

Aleyn's heart nearly stopped.

"That's not a star!" he shouted.

"Scorpio 18881R2434," said the comm screen, after a hesitation that was unnoticeable to human senses.

"It can't be!"

"Navigation and tracking programs agree. Spectrum matches. It is our destination star," the screen insisted.

Aleyn stared at the image a moment longer, then bolted to the hatch and down the short corridor that led to the ship's bridge.

The bridge screens were larger. But they all showed the same thing. Optical, infrared, radar, high-energy, and neutrino sensors all displayed a gigantic, perfectly circular metal sphere.

Aleyn sagged into the only chair on the bridge, oblivious to the slight chill against his naked flesh until the chair adjusted its temperature.

"We thought it was a star," he murmured to no one. "We thought it was a star." Aleyn Arif Belierophontes, son of the director of the Imperial Observatory and her consort and therefore distrusted by Admiral Kimon, the emperor's chief of astroengineering; betrayed by Selwyn, his best friend; exiled to a solitary expedition to a dying star— Aleyn sat numb and uncomprehending, staring at a metal sphere the size of a star.

No. Bigger.

"What's the radius of that object?"

Numbers sprang up on every screen, superimposed on the visual display, as the computer's voice replied, "Two hundred seventeen point zero nine eight million kilometers."

"Two hundred million kilometers," Aleyn echoed. Then he smiled. "A metal sphere four hundred million kilometers across." He giggled. "A sphere with the radius of a water-bearing planet's orbit." He laughed. "A Dyson sphere! I've found a Dyson sphere!"

His laughter became raucous, uncontrolled, hysterical. He roared with laughter. He banged his fists on the armrests of his chair and threw his head back and screamed with laughter. Tears flowed down his cheeks. His face grew red. His breath rasped in his throat. His lungs burned. He did not stop until the chair, reacting to an override command from the computer's medical program, sprayed him with a soporific and he lapsed into unconsciousness.

A thousand lightyears away, scientists and engineers of the Hundred Worlds labored heroically to save the Earth from doom. The original home planet of the Empire was in danger from its own Sun. A cycle of massive flares would soon erupt across the Sun's normally placid face. Soon, that is, in terms of a star's gigayear lifetime: ten thousand years, give or take a few millennia. Too feeble to be of consequence in the lifespan of the star itself, the flares nonetheless would casually boil away the air and oceans of Earth, leaving nothing behind except a blackened ball of rock.

Millions of technologists had struggled for centuries to save the Earth, following the mad scheme of a woman scientist who woke from cryonic sleep once each thousand years to survey their progress. It was not enough. The course of the Sun's evolution had not yet been altered enough to avert the period of flares. The Earth's daystar would go through its turbulent phase despite the valiant efforts of the Empire's best, most dedicated men and women. In all the vast storehouses of knowledge among the Hundred Worlds, no one knew enough about a star's behavior to forestall the Sun's impending fury.

Three young scientists, Aleyn, Noura, and Selwyn, hit upon the idea of monitoring other stars that were undergoing the same kind of turbulence. Aleyn had fought through the layers of academic bureaucracy and championed their joint ideas to the topmost levels of the Imperial hierarchy, to Admiral Kimon himself.

It had been a clever trap, he knew now. Kimon, reluctantly agreeing to the proposal of the son of his chief rival within the Imperial court, had sent out a fleet of one-man ships toward the stars that Selwyn, Noura, and Aleyn had listed. He had assigned Aleyn himself to one of those long, lonely ventures. Selwyn the traitor remained at Earth. With Kimon. With Noura. While Aleyn sped through the dark star-paths on a journey that would take twenty centuries to complete.

And now, rousing himself slowly from the soporific dreaminess, Aleyn realized what a cosmic joke it all was. Their research had shown that Scorpio I 8881R2434, a dim reddish star some thousand light-years from Earth, was flickering and pulsating much as the Sun would during its time of agony. A good star to observe, an excellent opportunity to gather the data needed to save the Sun and Earth. Better still, this star in Scorpio lay in the direction opposite the alien worlds, so that a scout ship sent to it would cause no diplomatic anxieties, offer no threat to aliens sensitive to the Empire's attempts at expansion.

But the star was not a star. Aleyn felt the cold hand of chemically-induced calm pressing against his heart. The joke was no longer funny. Yet it remained a colossal irony. He had discovered a Dyson sphere, a gigantic artifact, the work of an unknown race of aliens with undreamed-of technological powers. They had built a sphere around their star so that their civilization could catch every photon of energy the star emitted while they lived on the inner surface of their artificial world in the same comfort, breathing the same air, drinking the same water as they had enjoyed on their original home planet.

And Aleyn felt disappointment. The discovery of the eons was a crushing defeat to a man seeking knowledge of the inner workings of the stars. Despite the tranquilizing agent in his bloodstream, Aleyn wanted to laugh at the pathetic absurdity of it all. And he wanted to cry.

The drugs allowed him neither outlet. This nameless ship he commanded was in control of him, its programming placing duty and mission objectives far beyond human needs.

For three Earth-normal days he scanned the face of the enormous sphere while his ship hung in orbit beyond its glowering surface. He spent most of the time at his command chair in the bridge, surrounded by display screens and the soft reassuring hum of the electrical equipment. He wore the regulation uniform of the Imperial science service, complete with epaulets of rank and name tag, thinking nothing of the absurdity of such formality. There were no other clothes aboard the ship.

The sphere was not smooth, he saw. Not at all. Intricate structures and networks of piping studded its exterior. Huge hatches dotted the curving surface—all of them closed tightly. The metal was hot; it glowed dull red like a poker held too close to a fire. Aleyn saw jets of gas spurting from vents here and there, flashing briefly before dissipating into the hard vacuum of interstellar space.

Not another body within light-years. Not a planet or asteroid or comet. They must have used every scrap of matter in their solar system to build the sphere, Aleyn said to himself. They must have torn their own home planet apart, and all the other worlds of this system.

All the data that his ship's sensors recorded was transmitted back toward Earth. At the speed of light, the information would take a thousand years to reach the eager scientists and engineers. Noura would be long dead before Aleyn's first report reached the Empire's receivers.

"Unless she got permission to take the long sleep," Aleyn hoped aloud. But then he shook his head. Only the topmost members of the scientific hierarchy were permitted to sleep away centuries while others toiled. And if Noura received such a boon, undoubtedly Selwyn would too. They would share their lives even if they awakened only one year out of each hundred.

That evening, as he brooded silently over the meal the ship had placed on the galley's narrow table, Aleyn realized that Selwyn had indeed murdered him.

"Even if I survive this mission," he muttered angrily, "by the time I return to Earth, more than two thousand years will have passed. Everyone I know—everyone I love—will have died."

Unless they take the long sleep, a part of his brain reminded him. Just as you did while this ship was in transit, they could sleep in cryogenic cold for many centuries at a time.

There is a chance that Noura will be alive when I return, he told himself silently, afraid to speak the hope aloud. *If* I return. No, not if. When! When I return, if Selwyn still lives I will kill him. Gladly. When I return.

He pushed the tray of untouched food away, rose to his feet, and strode back to the bridge.

"Computer," he commanded. "Integrate all data on Noura Sudarshee, including my personal holos, and feed it all into the interactive program."

The computer complied with a single wink of a green light. Within moments, Noura's lovely face filled the bridge's main display screen.

Aleyn sank into the command chair and found himself smiling at her. "I need you, dearest Noura. I need you to keep me sane."

"I know," she said, in the vibrant low voice that he loved. "I'm here with you, Aleyn. You're not alone anymore."

He fell asleep in the command chair, talking with the image of the woman he had left a thousand lightyears behind him. While he slept the ship's life support system sprayjected into his bloodstream the nutritional equivalent of the meal he had not eaten.

The following morning Aleyn resumed his scan of the sphere. But now he had Noura to talk to.

"They don't seem to know we're out here," Aleyn said. "No message, no probe—not even a warning to go away."

"Perhaps there are no living people inside the sphere," said Noura's image from the comm screen at Aleyn's right hand.

"No people?" He realized that her words were being formed by the computer, acting on the data in its own core and relaying its conclusions through the interactive Noura program.

"The sphere seems very old," said Noura's image, frowning slightly with concern.

Aleyn did not answer. He realized that she was right. The computer was drawing his attention to the obvious signs of the sphere's enormous age.

He spiraled his ship closer, searching for a port through which he might enter, staring hard at the pictures the main display screens revealed, as if he could force the sphere to open a hatch for him if he just concentrated hard enough. Aleyn began to realize that the sphere truly was *old*—and it was falling into ruin. The gases venting into space were escaping from broken pipes. Many of the structures on the sphere's outer surface seemed collapsed, broken, as if struck by meteors or simply decayed by eons of time.

"This was built before the Sun was born," Aleyn murmured.

"Not that long ago," replied Noura, voicing the computer's calculation of erosion rates in vacuum caused by interstellar radiation and the rare wandering meteor. "Spectral analysis of the surface metal indicates an age no greater than two hundred million years."

Aleyn grinned at her. "Is that all? Only two hundred million years? No older than the first amphibians to crawl out of the Earth's seas?"

Noura's image smiled back at him.

"Are they still in there?" he wondered. "Are the creatures who built this still living inside it?"

"They show no evidence of being there," said Noura. "Since the sphere is so ancient, perhaps they no longer exist."

"I can't believe that. They *must* be there! They must be!"

For eight more days Aleyn bombarded the sphere with every wavelength his equipment could transmit: radio, microwave, infrared laser light, ultraviolet, X rays, gamma rays. Pulses and steady beams. Standard messages and simple mathematical formulas. No reaction from the sphere. He sprayed alpha particles and relativistic electrons across wide swaths of the sphere, to no avail.

"I don't think anyone is alive inside," said Noura's image.

"How do we know where their receivers might be?" Aleyn countered. "Maybe their communications equipment in this area broke down. Maybe their main antennas are clear over on the other side."

"It would take years to cover every square meter of its surface," Noura pointed out.

Aleyn shrugged, almost happily. "We have years. We have centuries, if we need them. As long as you're with me I don't care how long it takes."

Her face became serious. "Aleyn, remember that I am only an interactive program. You must not allow my presence to interfere with the objectives of your mission."

He smiled grimly and fought down a surge of anger. After taking a deep, calming breath, Aleyn said to the image on the screen, "Noura, my darling, the main objective of this mission is to keep me away from you. Selwyn has accomplished that."

"The major objective of this mission," she said, in a slightly lecturing tone, "is to observe the instabilities of a turbulent G-class star and relay that data back to Earth."

Aleyn jabbed a forefinger at the main display screen. "But we can't even see the star. It's inside the sphere."

"Then we must find a way to get inside, as well."

"Ah-hah! I knew you'd see it my way sooner or later."

Aleyn programmed the computer to set up a polar orbit that would eventually carry the ship over every part of the gigantic sphere. The energy in the antimatter converters would last for millennia. Still, he extended the magnetic scoops to draw in the thin scattering of hydrogen atoms that drifted through the void between the stars. The gases vented by the sphere's broken pipes undoubtedly contained hydrogen, as well. That would feed the fusion systems and provide input for the converters.

It was precisely when the engines fired to move the ship to its new orbit that the port began to open.

Aleyn barely caught it, out of the corner of his eye, as one of the auxiliary screens on his compact bridge showed a massive hatch swinging outward, etched sharply in bright blood-red light.

"Look!" he shouted.

Swiveling his command chair toward the screen, he ordered the ship's sensors to focus on the port.

"Aleyn, you did it!" Noura's image seemed equally excited.

The port yawned open like a gateway to hell, lurid red light beyond it.

Aleyn took manual control of the ship, broke it out of the new orbit it had barely established, and maneuvered it toward the opening port. It was kilometers wide, big enough to engulf a hundred ships like this one.

"Why now?" he asked. "Why did it stay closed when we were sending signals and probes to the sphere and open up only when we lighted the engines?"

"Neutrinos, perhaps," said Noura, with the wisdom of the ship's computer. "The fusion thrusters generate a shower of neutrinos when they fire. The neutrinos must have penetrated the sphere's shell and activated sensors inside."

"Inside," Aleyn echoed, his voice shaking.

With trembling hands Aleyn set all his comm channels on automatic to make certain that every bit of data that the ship's sensors received was sent back Earthward. Then he aimed his ship squarely at the center of the yawning port and fired its thrusters one more time.

It seemed as if they stood still while the burning-hot alien sphere moved up to engulf them and swallowed them alive.

The port widened and widened as they approached until its vast expanse filled Aleyn's screens with a sullen, smoldering red glow. The temperature gauges began to climb steadily upward. Aleyn called up the life-support display and saw that the system was drawing much more energy than usual, adjusting the heat shielding and internal cooling systems to withstand the furnacelike conditions outside the ship's hull.

"It's like stepping into Dante's inferno," Aleyn muttered.

With a smile that was meant to be reassuring, Noura said, "The cooling systems can withstand temperatures of this magnitude for hundreds of hours."

He smiled back at her. "My beloved, sometimes you talk like a computer."

"It's the best I can do under the circumstances."

The port was several hundred kilometers thick. Aleyn's screens showed heavily ribbed metal, dulled and pitted with age, as they cruised slowly through.

"This must be the thickness of the sphere's shell," he said. Noura agreed with a nod.

Once they finally cleared the port he could see the interior of the sphere. A vast metallic plain extended in all directions around him, glowing red hot. Aleyn focused the ship's sensors on the inner surface and saw a jumble of shapes: stumps of towers blackened and melted down, shattered remains of what must have been buildings, twisted guideways that disappeared entirely in places where enormous pools of metal glittered in the gloomy red light.

"It looks like the roadway melted and then the metal solidified again afterward," said Aleyn.

"Yes," Noura said. "A tremendous pulse of heat destroyed everything."

The sphere was so huge that it seemed almost perfectly flat from this perspective. Aleyn punched at his controls, calling up as many different views as the sensors could display. Nothing but the burnt and blackened remains of what must have been a gigantic city. No sign of movement. No sign of life.

"Did they kill themselves off in a war?" Aleyn wondered aloud.

"No," said Noura. "Listen."

Aleyn turned toward her screen. "What?"

"Listen."

"I don't—" Then he realized that he did hear something. A faint whispering, like the rush of a breeze through a young forest. But this was pulsating irregularly, gasping, almost like the labored breath of a dying old man.

"What is it?"

"There is an atmosphere here within this shell," said Noura.

Aleyn shook his head. "Couldn't be. How could they open a hatch to space if . . ."

But the computer had already sampled the atmosphere the ship was flying through. Noura's voice spoke what the other display screens showed in alphanumerics:

"We are immersed in an atmosphere that consists of sixty-two percent hydrogen ions, thirty-four percent helium ions, two percent carbon, one percent oxygen, and traces of other ions."

Aleyn stared at her screen.

"Atmospheric density is four ten-thousandths of Earth standard sea-level density." Noura spoke what the other screens displayed. "Temperature outside the ship's hull is ten thousand degrees, kinetic."

"We're inside the star's chromosphere," Aleyn whispered.

"Yes, and we're cruising deeper into it. The cooling systems will not be able to handle the heat levels deeper inside the star."

For the first time Noura's image appeared worried.

Aleyn turned to the control board and called up an image of the star on the main screen. It was a glowering, seething ball of red flame, huge and distended, churning angrily, spotted with ugly dark blotches and twisting filaments that seemed to writhe on its surface like souls in torment and then sink back again into the ocean of fire.

The sound outside the ship's hull seemed louder as Aleyn stared at the screen, fascinated, hypnotized. It was the sound of the star, he realized; the tortured, irregular pulse beat of a dying star.

"We're too late," he whispered at last. "This star has already exploded at least once. It killed off the civilization that built the sphere. Burned them all to a cinder."

"It will destroy us too if we go much deeper," said Noura.

What of it? Aleyn thought. This entire mission is a failure. We'll never gain the knowledge that I thought we could get from studying this star. It's past the period of turbulence that we need to observe. The mission has failed. I have failed. There's nothing on Earth for me to go back to. No one in the Hundred Worlds for me to go back to.

"Aleyn!" Noura's voice was urgent. "We must change course and leave the sphere. Outside temperatures will overwhelm the cooling systems within a few dozen hours if we don't."

"What of it? We can die together."

"No, Aleyn. Life is too valuable to throw away. Don't you see that?"

"All I see is the hopelessness of everything. What difference if I live or die? What will I accomplish by struggling to survive?"

"Is that what you want?" Noura asked. "To die?"

"Why not?"

"Isn't that what Selwyn wants, to be rid of you forever?"

"He is rid of me. Even if I go back to Earth the two of you will have been dead for more than a thousand years."

Noura's image remained silent, but the ship turned itself without Aleyn's command and pointed its nose toward the port through which they had entered.

"The computer is programmed to save the ship and its data banks even if the pilot is incapacitated," Noura said, almost apologetically.

Aleyn nodded. "I can't even commit suicide."

Smiling, Noura said, "I want you to live, my darling."

He stared at her image for long moments, telling himself desperately that this was merely the computer speaking to him, using the ship's data files and his personal holos to synthesize her picture and manner of speech. It was Noura's face. Noura's voice. But the computer's mind.

She doesn't care if I live, he told himself. It's the data banks that are important.

With a shrug that admitted defeat, Aleyn put the nose-camera view on the main display screen. A shock of raw electricity slammed through him. He saw that the giant port through which they had entered the sphere was now firmly closed.

"We're trapped," he shouted.

"How could it close?" Noura's image asked.

"You are not of the creators."

It was a voice that came from the main display screen, deep and powerful. To Aleyn it sounded like the thunderclap of doom.

"Who said that?"

"You are not of the creators."

"There's someone alive in the sphere! Who are you?"

"Only the creators may return to their home. All others are forbidden."

"We are a scientific investigation mission," Noura's voice replied, "from the planet—"

"I know you are from a worldling you call Earth. I can see from your navigational program where your home world is located."

His heart racing wildly, Aleyn asked, "You can tap into our computer?"

"I have been studying you since you entered this world."

Noura said swiftly, "Aleyn, he's communicating through our own computer."

"Who are you?" Aleyn asked.

"In your tongue, my name is Savant."

"What are you?" asked Noura.

"I am the servant of the creators. They created me to survive, to guard, and to protect."

"You're a computer?" Aleyn guessed.

For half a heartbeat there was no response. Then, *"I am a device that is as far beyond what you know of computers as your minds are beyond those of your household pets."*

With a giggle that trembled on the edge of hysteria, Aleyn said, "And you're quite a modest little device, too, aren't you?"

"My function is to survive, to guard, and to protect. I perform my function well."

"Are there any of the creatures still remaining here?" Noura asked.

"No."

"What happened to them?"

"Many departed when they realized the star would explode. Others remained here."

"To try to prevent the star from exploding?" Aleyn suggested.

"That was not their way. They remained to await the final moments. They preferred to die in their homes, where they had always lived."

"But they built you."

"*Yes.*"

"Why?"

"*To await the time when those who fled return to their home.*"

"You mean they're coming back?"

"*There is no evidence of their return. My function is to survive, to guard, and to protect. If they ever return I shall serve them.*"

"And help them to rebuild?"

"*If they wish it so.*"

Noura asked, "Do you have any idea of how long ago your creators *left?*"

"*By measuring the decay of radioactive atoms I can count time. In your terms of reference, the creators fled approximately eighteen million years ago. The star's first explosion took place eleven thousand years later.*"

"First?" Aleyn asked. "There have been more?"

"*Not yet. But very soon the next explosion will take place.*"

"We must get out of here," Noura said.

"*That is not allowed.*"

"Not—what do you mean?" For the first time Aleyn felt fear burning along his veins.

"*I am the servant of the creators. No others may enter or leave.*"

"But you let us in!"

"*To determine f you were of the creators. You are not. Therefore you may not leave.*"

The fear ebbed away. In its place Aleyn felt the cold implacable hand of cosmic irony. With a sardonic smile he turned to Noura's image.

"I won't have to commit suicide now. This Savant is going to murder me."

Noura's image stared blankly at him. It had no answer.

Aleyn pulled himself up from the command chair and went back through the narrow corridor to the ship's galley. He knew that the computer automatically spiced his food with tranquilizers and vitamins and anything else it felt he needed, based on its continuous scans of his physical and psychological condition. He no longer cared.

He ate numbly, hardly tasting the food. His mind swirled dizzyingly. An alien race. The discovery of a lifetime, of a dozen lifetimes, and he would not live to report it. But where did they go? Are they still out there, scattering through the galaxy in some desperate interstellar Diaspora?

Is that what the people of Earth should have done? Abandon their homeworld and flee among the stars? What makes humans so arrogant that they think they can reverse the course of a star's evolution?

He went to his cabin as the miniature serving robots cleared the galley table. Stripping off his uniform, Aleyn was surprised to see that it was stained and rank with sweat. Fear? he wondered. Excitement? He felt neither at the moment. Nothing but numb exhaustion. The ship's pharmacy was controlling his emotions now, he knew. Otherwise he'd be bashing his head against the metal bulkhead.

He crawled into the bunk and pulled the monolayer coverlet up to his chin, just as he used to do when he was a child.

"Noura," he called.

Her face appeared on the screen at the foot of the bunk. "I'm here, Aleyn."

"I wish you were," he said. "I wish you truly were."

"I *am* with you, my dearest. I am here with you."

"No." he said, a great wave of sadness washing over him. "You are merely a collection of data bits. My real Noura is on Earth, with Selwyn. Already dead, perhaps."

Her eyes flashed. "Your real Noura may be on Earth, but, dead or alive, she is not with Selwyn."

"It would be pleasant to believe so."

"It is true!" the image insisted. "Who would know better than I?"

"You're not real."

"I am the sum of all the ship's records of Noura Sudarshee; the personnel records are complete from her birth to the day you left Earth."

"No better than a photograph," Aleyn countered. "No better than looking at a star in the sky of night."

"I am also made up from your holos of Noura Sudarshee. Your private recordings and communications." She hesitated a moment, then added, almost shyly, "Even your subconscious memories and dreams."

"Dreams?" Aleyn blurted. "Memories?"

"This ship's psychological program has been scanning your

brainwave activity since you came aboard. During your long sleep you dreamt extensively of me. All that data is included in this imagery."

Aleyn thought about that for a moment. An electronic clone of his beloved Noura, complete down to the slightest memory in his subconscious mind. But the deadening hand of futility made him laugh bitterly.

"That only makes it worse, my dearest. That only means that when I die I will be killing you too."

"Don't think of death, darling. Think of life. Think of me."

He shook his head wearily. "I don't want to think of anything. I want to sleep. Forever."

He closed his eyes. His last waking thought was that it would be a relief never to have to open them again.

Of course he dreamed of Noura, as he always did. But this time the dream was drenched with a dire sense of foreboding, of dread. He and Noura were on Earth, at a wild and incredibly remote place where a glacier-fed waterfall tumbled down a sheer rock scarp into a verdant valley dotted with trees. Not another person for hundreds of kilometers. Only the two of them sitting on the yielding grass under the warming Sun.

But the Sun grew hotter, so hot that the grass began to smolder and curl and blacken. The waterfall began to steam. Aleyn looked up at the Sun and saw it broiling angrily, lashing out huge tongues of flame. It thundered at them and laughed. In the Sun's blinding disk he saw the face of Selwyn, laughing at him, reaching out his flaming arms for Noura.

"NO!" he screamed.

Aleyn found himself sitting upon his bunk, soaked with sweat. Grimly he got up, washed, and put on his freshly cleansed uniform. He strode past the galley and took the command chair at the bridge.

"Good morning, darling," said Noura's smiling image. He made himself smile back at her. "Good morning." Her face became more serious. "The cooling systems are nearing overload. In six more hours they will fail."

"Backups?"

"The six-hour figure includes the backups."

Aleyn nodded. Six hours.

"Savant!" he called. "Can you hear me?"

"Yes."

"Why do you refuse to allow us to leave your domain? Are you prohibited from doing so?"

"I am programmed to survive, to guard, and to protect. I await the creators. There is nothing in my programming that requires me to allow you to leave."

"But there's nothing in your programming that prohibits you from allowing us to leave, is there?"

"That is so."

"Then allow us to leave and we will search for the creators and bring them back to you."

The synthesized voice was silent for several heartbeats. Aleyn realized that each second of time was an eternity for such a powerful computer. It must be considering this proposition very carefully, like a computer chess game, calculating every possible move as far into the future as it could see.

"The creators are so distant now that they could not he found and returned before the star explodes again. The next explosion will destroy this sphere. It will destroy me. I will not survive. I will have failed my primary purpose."

It was Aleyn's turn to fall silent, thinking, his mind churning through all the branching possibilities. Death stood at the end of each avenue, barring the door to escape.

"Aleyn," said Noura's image, softly, "the ship is drifting deeper into the chromosphere. Hull temperature is rising steeply. The cooling systems will fail in a matter of minutes if corrective action is not taken."

Corrective action, Aleyn's mind echoed. Why not simply allow the ship to drift toward the heart of the dying star and let us be vaporized? It will all be finished in a few minutes. Why try to delay the inevitable, prolong the futility? Why struggle, merely to continue suffering?

He looked squarely at Noura's image in the screen. "But I can't kill you," he whispered. "Even if you are only memories and dreams, I can't let you die."

Turning again to the main screen, he saw the angry heart of the dying star, seething red, writhing and glowering, drumming against the ship's hull with the dull muted thunder of approaching doom.

"Savant," he called again. "Have you scanned all of our data banks?"

"I have."

"Then you know that we of Earth are attempting to prevent our own star from exploding."

"Your Sun is younger than my star."

"Yes, and the data you have recorded about your star would be of incalculable value in helping us to gain an understanding of how to save our Sun."

"That is of no consequence."

"But it is!" Aleyn snapped. "It is! Because once we learn how to control our own Sun, how to prevent it from exploding, we can come back here and apply that knowledge to your star."

"Return here?"

"Yes! We can return and save your star! We can help you to survive! We can allow you to achieve your primary objective."

"I am programmed to survive, to guard, and to protect."

"We will help you to survive. You can continue to guard and protect until we return with the knowledge that will save your star from destruction."

Again the alien voice went silent. Aleyn counted to twenty, then fifty, then . . .

Noura sang out, "The port is opening!"

Aleyn swung his chair to see the screen. The vast hatch that had sealed the port was slowly swinging open again. He could see a slice of star-studded darkness beyond it. Without thinking consciously he turned the ship toward the port, away from the growling, glaring star.

"Savant," he called once again, "we need the data you have accumulated on your star's behavior."

"Your data banks are too small to accommodate all of it. Therefore I have altered the atomic structure of your ship's hull and structure to store the data."

"Altered the hull and structure?"

"The alteration is at the nuclear level. It will not affect the performance of your ship. I have placed instructions in your puny computer on how to access the data."

"Thank you!"

"You must return within thirty thousand years if you are to save this star."

"We'll be back long before then. I promise you."

"I will survive until then without you."

"You will survive beyond that, Savant. We will be back and we will bring the knowledge you need to save yourself and your star."

"*I will wait.*"

The ship headed toward the port, gaping wide now, showing the cold darkness of infinity sprinkled with hard pinpoints of stars.

"The cooling system is returning to normal," Noura's image said. "We will survive."

"We will return to Earth," said Aleyn. "I'll sleep for a thousand years, and when I wake again, we'll be back at Earth."

"The real Noura will be waiting for you."

He smiled, but there was still bitterness in it. "I wish that could be true."

"It is true, my beloved Aleyn. Who would know better than I? She is in deep sleep even now, waiting for your return."

"Do you really believe so?"

"I know it."

"And Selwyn, also?"

"Even if he waits for her," Noura's image replied, "she waits for you."

He closed his eyes briefly. Then he realized, "But that means . . ."

"It means you will no longer need me," said Noura's image. "You will erase me."

"I don't know if I could do that. It would be like murdering you."

She smiled at him, a warming, loving smile without a trace of sadness in it. "I am not programmed to survive, Aleyn. My objective was to help *you* to survive. Once the real Noura is in your arms you will not need me anymore."

He stared at the screen for many long moments. Then wordlessly he reached out his hand and touched the button that turned off the display.

RISK ASSESSMENT

This one was written for Jack Williamson.

Jack was probably the most beloved writer in the science-fiction field, the dean of us all, whose first short story was published in 1928. He was a truly gentle man and a fine writer.

To celebrate his more than sixty years as a published writer, Jack's friends put together an anthology of stories, all written on themes that Jack himself has used in his long and productive career.

I was asked to contribute a story to the anthology, and "Risk Assessment" is the result. If you are unfortunate enough to be unfamiliar with Jack Williamson's work, all I can say (aside from urging you to read his fiction) is that he was among the very earliest writers to deal with antimatter, which he called "contraterrene" matter, or seetee. This was at a time when the concept of antimatter was a new and startling idea to theoretical physicists such as P.A.M. Dirac, Fermi, Einstein, and that crowd.

Two stories about Jack:

For many years, Jack was a professor of English at the University of Eastern New Mexico, in Portales. When he reached retirement age, he retired. Not surprising, you might think. But I received a nearly frantic phone call from a group of his students (I was editing Analog *magazine in New York then) who told me that they thought the university's administration was "forcing" Professor Williamson into retirement, and they wanted me to do something about it!*

The first thing I did was to call Jack. "Forcing me?" Jack laughed. "Goodness, no. I'm very happy to retire from teaching. Now I can write full-time."

How many professors have been so revered by their students that the students don't want them to retire?

Second story:

I visited Jack in Portales one year during the time for the spring calf roundup. We drove out to the ranch where the roundup was taking place that weekend, and watched the local cowhands and teenagers at work. It was a hot, bloody, dusty scene. The calves were separated from their mothers, dehorned, the males deballed, all of the calves branded and shot with about a quart of penicillin apiece. There was bleating and mooing and horses and roping and the stench of burnt hides and lots of blood, toil, tears, and sweat.

As we leaned against the corral railing, watching all this hard work and suffering, Jack nudged me in the ribs. "See why I became a writer?" he asked softly.

I nodded. I'd much rather sweat over a keyboard than rope a calf, any day.

They are little more than children, thought Alpha One, self-centered, emotional children sent by their elders to take the responsibilities that the elders themselves do not want to bother with.

Sitting at Alpha One's right was Cordelia Thomasina Shockley, whom the human male called Delia. Red-haired and impetuous, brilliant and driven, her decisions seemed to be based as much on emotional tides as logical calculation.

The third entity in the conference chamber was Martin Flagg, deeply solemn, intensely grave. He behaved as if he truly believed his decisions were rational, and not at all influenced by the hormonal cascades surging through his endocrine system.

"This experiment must be stopped," Martin Flagg said firmly.

Delia thought he was handsome, in a rugged sort of way. Not terribly tall, but broad in the shoulder and flat in the middle. Nicely muscular. Big dimple in the middle of his stubborn chin. Heavenly deep blue eyes. When he smiled his whole face lit up, and somehow that lit up Delia's heart. But it had been a long time since she'd seen him smile.

"Why must the experiment be stopped?" asked the robot avatar of Alpha One.

It folded its mechanical arms over its cermet chest, in imitation of the human gesture. Its humanform face was incapable of showing any emotion, however. It merely stared at Martin Flagg out of its optical sensors, waiting for him to go on.

"What Delia's doing is not only foolish, it's wasteful. And dangerous."

"How so?" asked Alpha One, with the patience that only a computer possessed.

The human male was almost trembling with agitation. "You don't think a few hundred megatons of energy is dangerous?"

Delia said coolly, "Not when it's properly contained, Marty. And it is properly contained, of course."

Alpha One knew that Delia had two interlinked personality flaws: a difficulty in taking criticism seriously and an absolute refusal to accept anyone else's point of view. Like her auburn hair and opalescent eyes, she had inherited those flaws from her mother. From her father she had inherited one of the largest fortunes in the inner solar system. He had also bequeathed her his incredibly dogged stubbornness, the total inability to back away from a challenge. And the antimatter project.

Marty was getting red in the face. "Suppose you lose containment?" he asked Delia. "What then?"

"I won't."

Turning to the robot, Marty repeated, "What if she loses containment?"

Alpha One's prime responsibility was risk assessment. Here on the Moon it was incredibly easy for a mistake to kill humans. So the computer quickly ran through all the assessments it had made to date of C. T. Shockley's antimatter project, a task that took four microseconds, then had its robot avatar reply to Flagg.

Calmly, Alpha One replied, "If the apparatus loses containment, then our seismologists will obtain interesting new data on the Moon's deep structure." Its voice was a smooth computer synthesis issuing from the horizontal grill where a human's mouth would be.

Martin Flagg was far from pleased. "Is that all that your germanium brain cares about? What about the loss of human life?"

Alpha One was totally unperturbed. Its brain was composed mainly of optical filaments, not germanium. "The nearest human settlement is at Clavius," it said. "There is no danger to human life."

"Her life!"

Alpha One turned to see Delia's reaction. A warm flush colored her cheeks, an involuntary physical reaction to her realization that Flagg was worried about her safety.

The human form of the robot was a concession to human needs. The robot was merely one of thousands of avatars of Alpha One, the master computer that monitored every city, every habitat, every vehicle, factory and mining outpost on the Moon. Almost a century ago the pioneer lunar settlers had learned, through bitter experience, that the computer's rational and incorruptible decisions were far sounder—and safer—than the emotionally biased decisions made by men and women.

But the humans were unwilling to allow a computer, no matter how wise and rational, to have complete control over them. The Lunar Council, therefore, was founded as a triumvirate: the Moon was ruled by one man, one woman, and Alpha One. Yet, over the years, the lunar citizens did their best to avoid the duty of serving on the Council. The task was handed to the young, those who had enough idealism to serve, or those who did not have enough experience to evade the responsibility.

Children, Alpha One repeated to itself. As human life spans extend toward the two-century mark, their childhoods lengthen also. Physically they are mature adults, yet emotionally they are still spoiled children.

Martin Flagg was the human male member of the triumvirate. C. T. Shockley was the female. Marty was the youngest human ever elected to the triumvirate. Except for Delia.

The three of them were sitting in the plush high-backed chairs of the Council's private conference room, in the city of Selene, dug into the ringwall mountains of the giant crater Alphonsus. Flagg glared at Delia from his side of the triangular table. Delia smiled saucily at him. She knew she shouldn't antagonize him, but she couldn't help it. Delia did not want to be here; she wanted to be at her remote laboratory in the crater Newton, near the lunar south pole. But Marty had insisted on her physical appearance at this meeting: no holographic presence, no virtual-reality attendance.

"This experiment must be stopped," Flagg repeated. He was stubborn, too.

"Why?" asked the robot, in its maddeningly calm manner.

Obviously struggling to control his temper, Flagg leaned forward in his chair and ticked off on his fingers: "One, she is using valuable resources—"

"That I'm paying for out of my own pocket." But the pocket was becoming threadbare, she knew. The Shockley family fortune, big as it might have been, was running low. Delia knew she'd have to succeed tomorrow or give it all up.

Flagg scowled at her, then turned back to the robot. "Two, she is endangering human life."

"Only my own," Delia said sweetly.

The robot checked its risk assessments again and said, "She is entirely within her legal rights."

"Three, her crazy experiment hasn't been sanctioned by the Science Committee."

"I don't need the approval of those nine old farts," Delia snapped.

The robot seemed to incline its head briefly, as if nodding. "Under ordinary circumstances it would be necessary to obtain the Science Committee's permission for such an experiment, that is true."

"Ah-hah!" Flagg grinned maliciously.

"But that is because researchers seek to obtain funding grants from the Committee. Shockley is using her own money. She needs neither funding nor permission, so long as she does not present an undue risk to other humans."

Flagg closed his eyes briefly. Delia thought he was about to admit defeat. But then he played his trump.

"And what about her plans to use all the power capacity of all the solar collector systems on the Moon? Plus all the sunsats in cislunar space?"

"I only need their output for one minute," Delia said.

"What happens if there's an emergency during that one minute?" Flagg demanded, almost angrily. "What happens if the backups fail at Clavius, or Copernicus, or even here in Selene? Do you have any idea of how much the emergency backup capacity has lagged behind actual power demand?"

"I have those figures," Alpha One said. "There is a point-zero-four probability that the backup system at Selene will be unable to meet all the demands made on it during that one minute that the solar generators are taken off-line. There is a point-zero-two probability that the backup system at Copernicus—"

"All right, all right," Flagg interrupted impatiently. "What do we do if there's a failure of the backup system while the main power grid is off-line?"

"Put the solar generators back on-line immediately. The switching can be accomplished in six to ten milliseconds."

Delia felt suddenly alarmed. "But that would ruin the experiment! It could blow up!"

"That would be unfortunate, but unavoidable. It is a risk that you must assume."

Delia thought it over for all of half a second, then gritted her teeth and nodded. "Okay, I accept the risk."

"Wait a minute," Flagg said to the robot. "You're missing the point. Why does she need all that power?"

"To generate antiprotons, of course," Delia answered. Marty knew that, she told herself. Why is he asking the obvious?

"But you already have the energy equivalent of more than a hundred megatons worth of antiprotons, don't you?"

"Sure, but I need thirty tons of them."

"Thirty tons?" Marty's voice jumped an octave. "Of antiprotons? Thirty tons by mass?"

Delia nodded nonchalantly while Alpha One restarted its risk assessment calculations. Thirty tons of antiprotons was a new data point, never revealed to the Council before.

"Why do you need thirty tons of antiprotons?" Alpha One asked, even while its new risk assessment was proceeding.

"To drive the starship to Alpha Centauri and back," Delia replied, as if it were the most obvious fact in the universe.

"You intend to fly to Alpha Centauri on a ship that has never been tested?" Alpha One asked. "The antimatter propulsion system alone—"

"We've done all the calculations," Delia interrupted, annoyance knitting her brows. "The simulations all check out fine."

If Alpha One could have felt dismay or irritation at its own limitations, it would have at that moment. Shockley intended to fly her father's ship to Alpha Centauri. This was new data, but it should have been anticipated. Why else would she have been amassing antimatter? A subroutine in its intricate programming pointed out that it was reasonable to assume that she would want to test the antimatter-propulsion system first, to see that it actually performed as calculated before risking the flight. After all, no one had operated an antimatter drive as yet. No one has tried for the stars.

"What's thirty tons of antiprotons equal to in energy potential?" Flagg asked.

Instantly, Alpha One calculated, "Approximately one million megatons of energy."

"And if that much energy explodes?"

Alpha One was incapable of showing emotion, of course. But it hesitated, just for a fraction of a second. The silence was awesome. Then the robot's head swivelled slowly toward Delia, levelling its dark glassy optical sensors at her.

"An explosion of that magnitude could perturb the orbit of the Moon."

"It could cause a moonquake that would destroy Clavius, at the very least," Flagg said. "Smash Selene and even Copernicus, wouldn't it?"

"Indeed," said Alpha One. The single word stung Delia like a whip.

"Now do you see why she's got to be stopped?"

"Indeed," the robot repeated.

Delia shook her head, as if to clear away the pain. "But there won't be any explosion," she insisted. "I know what I'm doing. All the calculations show—"

"The risk is not allowable," Alpha One said firmly. "You must stop your experiment."

"I will not!" Delia snapped.

It took Alpha One less than three milliseconds to check this new data once again, and then compare it against the safety regulations that ruled every decision-making tree, and still again check it against the consequences of Delia's project if it should be successful. Yet although it weighed the probabilities and made its decision that swiftly, it did not speak.

Alpha One had learned one thing in its years of dealing with humans: the less they are told, the less they have to argue about.

And the two humans already had plenty to argue over.

Running a hand through the flowing waves of his golden hair, Flagg grumbled, "You're not fit to be a triumvir."

"I was elected just the same as you were," Delia replied tartly.

"Your father bought votes. Everybody knows it." Delia's own temper surged. Leaning across the triangular table to within inches of Flagg's nose, she said, "Then everybody's wrong! Daddy wouldn't spend a penny on a vote."

"No," he snarled, "he spent all his money on this crazy starship, and you're spending still more on an experiment that could kill everybody on the Moon!"

"It's my experiment, and I'm going to go ahead with it. It'll be finished tomorrow."

"It is finished now," said the robot. "Your permission to tap power from the lunar grid is hereby revoked. Safety considerations outweigh all other factors. Although the risk of an explosion is small, the consequences are so great that the risk is not allowable."

All the breath seemed to gush out of Delia's lungs. She sank back in her chair and stared at the unmoving robot for a long, silent moment. Then she turned to Flagg.

"I hate you!"

"You're not fit to be a triumvir," Flagg repeated, scowling at her. "There ought to be a sanity requirement for the position."

Delia wanted to leap across the table and slap his face. Instead, she turned to Alpha One's robotic avatar.

"He's being vindictive," she said. "He's acting out of personal malice."

The robot said impassively, "Triumvir Flagg has brought to the attention of the Council the safety hazards of your experiment. That is within his rights and responsibilities. The only personal malice that has been expressed at this meeting has come from you, Triumvir Shockley."

Flagg laughed out loud.

Delia couldn't control herself any longer. She jumped to her feet and didn't just slap Marty, she socked him as hard as she could with her clenched fist, right between the eyes. In the gentle gravity of the Moon, he tilted backward in his chair and tumb led to the floor ever so slowly, arms weakly flailing. She could watch his eyes roll up into his head as he slowly tumbled ass over teakettle and slumped to the floor.

Satisfied, Delia stomped out of the conference chamber and headed back to Newton and her work.

Then she realized that the work was finished. It was going to be aborted, and she would probably be kicked off the triumvirate for assaulting a fellow Council member.

If she let Marty have his way.

Delia stood naked and alone on the dark airless floor of the crater Newton. Even though she was there only in virtual reality, while her real body rested snugly in the VR chamber of her laboratory, she revelled in the freedom of her solitude. She could virtually feel the shimmering energy of the antiprotons as they raced along the circular track she had built around the base of the crater's steep mountains.

More than 350 kilometers in circumference, the track ran past the short lunar horizon, its faint glow scintillating like a giant luminescent snake that circled Delia's naked presence.

The track was shielded by a torus of pure diamond. Even in the deep vacuum of the lunar surface there were stray atoms of gases that could collide with the circling antiprotons and set off a flash of annihilative energy. And cosmic particles raining down from the Sun and deep space. She had to protect her antiprotons, hoard them, save them for the moment when they would be needed.

She looked up, toward the cold and distant stars that stared down at her out of the dark circle of sky, unwavering, solemn, like the unblinking eyes of some wary beast watching her. The rim of the deep crater was ringed with rectennas, waiting to drink in the energy beamed from the Moon's own solar-power farms and from the sunsats orbiting between the Earth and the Moon. Energy that Marty and Alfie had denied her.

In the exact center of the crater floor stood the ungainly bulk of the starship, her father's masterpiece, glittering softly in the light of the stars it was intended to reach.

But it will never get off the ground unless I produce enough antiprotons, Delia told herself. For the thousandth time.

The crater Newton was not merely far from any other human

settlement. It was *cold*. Close to the lunar south pole, nearly ten kilometers deep, Newton's floor never saw sunlight. Early explorers had broken their hearts searching Newton and the surrounding region for water ice. There was none to be found, and the lunar pioneers had to manufacture their water out of oxygen from the regolith and hydrogen imported from Earth.

But even though any ice originally trapped in Newton had evaporated eons ago, the crater was still perpetually cold, cryogenically cold all the time, cold enough so that when Delia built the ring of superconducting magnets for the racetrack she did not have to worry about cooling them.

Now the racetrack held enough antiprotons, endlessly circling, to blow up all the rocky, barren landscape for hundreds of kilometers. If all went well with her experiment, it would hold enough antiprotons to send the starship to Alpha Centauri. Or rock the Moon out of its orbit.

The experiment was scheduled for midnight, Greenwich Mean Time. The time when the sunsats providing power to Europe and North America were at their lowest demand and could most easily squirt a minute's worth of their output to Delia's rectennas at Newton. The Moon kept GMT, too, so it would have been easy for the lunar grid to be shunted to Newton for a minute, also. If not for Marty.

Midnight was only six hours away.

Delia's father, Cordell Thomas Shockley, scion of a brilliant and infamous family, had taken it into his stubborn head to build the first starship. Earth's government would not do it. The Lunar Council, just getting started in his days, could not afford it. So Shockley decided to use his own family fortune to build the first starship himself.

He hired the best designers and scientists. Using nanomachines, they built his ship out of pure diamond. But the ship sat, gleaming faintly in the starlight, in the middle of Newton's frigid floor, unable to move until some thirty tons of antiprotons were manufactured to propel it.

Delia was born to her father's purpose, raised to make his dream come true, trained and educated in particle physics and space propulsion. Her first toys were model spacecraft; her first video games were lessons in physics. When Delia was five years old her mother fled back to Earth, unable to compete with her husband's monomania, unwilling to live in the spartan underground warrens that the Lunatics called home. She divorced C. T. Shockley and took half his fortune away. But left her daughter.

Shockley was unperturbed. He could work better without a wife to bother him. He had a daughter to train, and the two of them were as inseparable as quarks in a baryon. Delia built the antiproton storage ring, then patiently began to buy electrical energy from the Lunar Council, from the sunsats orbiting in cislunar space, from anyone and everyone she could find. The energy was converted into antiprotons; the antiprotons were stored in the racetrack ring. She was young, time was on her side.

Then her father was diagnosed with terminal cancer, and she realized that both her time and her money were running out. The old man was frozen cryonically and interred in a Dewar in his own starship. The instructions in his will said he was to be revived at Alpha Centauri, even if he lived only for a few minutes.

So now Delia's virtual presence walked across the frozen floor of Newton, up to the diamond starship gleaming faintly in the dim light of the distant stars. She peered through its crystal hull, toward the dewar where her father rested.

"I'll do it, Daddy," she whispered. "I'll succeed tomorrow, one way or the other."

Grimly she thought that if Marty was right and the antimatter exploded, the explosion would turn Newton and its environs into a vast cloud of plasma. Most of the ionized gas would be blasted dear of the Moon's gravity, blown out into interplanetary space. Some of it, she supposed, would eventually waft beyond the solar system. In time, millions of years, billions, a few of their atoms might even reach Alpha Centauri.

"One way or the other," she repeated.

Delia stirred in the VR chamber. Enough self-pity, she told herself. You've got to do something.

She pulled the helmet off, shook her auburn hair annoyedly, and then peeled herself out of the skin-tight VR suit. She marched straight to her bathroom and stepped into the shower, where she always did her best thinking. Delia's father had always thought of water as a luxury, which it had been when he had first come to the Moon. His training still impressed Delia's attitudes. As the hot water sluiced along her skin, she luxuriated in the warmth and let her thoughts run free.

They ran straight to the one implacable obstacle that loomed before her. Martin Flagg. The man she thought she had loved. The man she knew that she hated.

In childhood Delia had no human playmates. In fact, for long years her father was the only human companion she knew. Otherwise, her human acquaintances were all holographic or VR presences.

She first met Martin Flagg when they were elected to the triumvirate. Contrary to Marty's nasty aspersions, Delia had not lifted a finger to get herself elected. She had not wanted the position, the responsibility would interfere with her work. But her father, without telling her, had apparently moved heaven and Earth—well, the Moon, at least—to make her a triumvir.

"You need some human companionship," he told her gruffly. "You're getting to an age where you ought to be meeting other people. Serving on the Council for a few years will encourage you to . . . well, meet people."

Delia thought she was too young to serve on the Council, but once she realized that handsome Martin Flagg was also running, she consented to all the testing and interviewing that passed for a political campaign on the Moon. Most of the Lunatics cared little about politics and did their best to avoid serving on the Council. The only reason for having two human members on the triumvirate was to allay the ancient fears that Alpha One might someday run amok.

Once she was elected, C. T. Shockley explained his real reason for making her run for the office. "The Council won't be able to interfere with our work if you're on the triumvirate. You're in a position now to head off any attempts to stop us."

So she had accepted the additional responsibility. And it did eat into her time outrageously. The triumvirate had to deal with everything from people whining about their water allotments to deciding how and when to enlarge the underground cities of the Moon.

And the irony of it all was that nobody cared about Shockley's crazy starship project or Delia's work to generate enough antiprotons to propel the ship to Alpha Centauri. Nobody except her fellow triumvir, Marty Flagg. If Delia hadn't been elected to the triumvirate with him, if they hadn't begun this love-hate relationship that neither of them knew how to handle, she could have worked in blissful isolation at Newton without hindrance of any sort.

But Marty made Delia's heart quiver whenever he turned those blue eyes of his upon her. Sometimes she quivered with love. More often with fury. But she could never look at Marty without being stirred. And he cared about her. She knew he did. Why else would he try to stop her? He was worried that she would kill herself.

Really? she asked herself. He's really scared that I'm going to kill him, and everybody else on the Moon.

Delia's only experience with love had come from VR romance novels, where the heroine always gets her man, no matter what perils she must face along the way. But she did not want Marty Flagg. She hated him. He had stopped her work.

A grimace of determination twisted Delia's lips as she turned off the shower and let the air blowers dry her. Marty may think he's stopped me. But I'm not stopped yet.

She slipped into a comfortable set of coveralls and strode down the bare corridor toward her control center. Alpha One won't let me tap the lunar grid, she thought, but I still have all the sunsats. The Council doesn't control them. As long as I can pay for their power, they'll beam it to me. Unless Alpha One's tried to stop them.

It wouldn't be enough, she knew. As she slid into her desk chair and ordered her private computer to show her the figures, she knew that a full minute of power from all the sunsats between the Earth and the Moon would not provide the energy she needed.

She checked the Council's communications log. Sure enough, Alpha One had already notified the various power companies that they should renege on their contracts to provide power to her. Delia told her computer to activate its law program and notify the power companies that if they failed to live up to their contracts with her, the penalties would bankrupt them.

She knew they would rather sell the power and avoid the legal battle. Only a minute's worth of power, yet she was paying a premium price for it. They had five and a half hours to make up their minds. Delia figured that the companies' legal computer programs needed only a few minutes' deliberation to make their recommendations, one way or the other. But then they would turn their recommendations

over to their human counterparts, who would be sleeping or partying
or doing whatever lawyers do at night on Earth. It would be hours
before they saw their computers' recommendations.

She smiled. By the time they saw their computers' recommendations,
she would have her power.

But it wouldn't be enough.

Where to get the power that Marty had denied her? And how to
get it in little more than five hours?

Mercury.

A Sino-Japanese consortium was building a strip of solar-power
converters across Mercury's equator, together with relay satellites in
orbit about the planet to send the power earthward. Delia put in a call
to Tokyo, to Rising Sun Power, Inc., feeling almost breathless with
desperation.

It was past nineteen hundred hours in Tokyo by the time she got a
human to speak to her, well past quitting time in most offices. But
within minutes Delia was locked in an intense conference with stony-
faced men in Tokyo and Beijing, offering the last of the Shockley
fortune in exchange for one minute's worth of electrical power from
Mercury.

"The timing must be exact," she pointed out, not for the first time.

The director-general of Rising Sun, a former engineer, allowed a
faint smile to break through his polite impassivity. "The timing will
be precise, down to the nanosecond," he assured her.

Delia was practically quivering with excitement as the time ticked
down to midnight. It was going to happen! She would get all the power
she needed, generate the antiprotons the ship required, and be ready
to lift off for Alpha Centauri.

In less than half an hour.

If everything went the way it should.

If her calculations were right.

Twenty-eight minutes to go. What if my calculations are off? A
sudden flare of panic surged through her. Check them again, she told
herself. But there isn't time.

Then a new fear struck her. What if my calculations are right? I'll
be leaving the Moon, leaving the only home I've ever known, leaving
the solar system. Why? To bring Daddy to Alpha Centauri. To fulfill
his dream.

But it's not my dream, she realized.

All these years, ever since she had been old enough to remember, she had worked with monomaniacal energy to bring her father's dream to fruition. She had never had time to think about her own dream.

She thought about it now. What is my own dream? Delia asked herself. What do I want for myself?

She did not know. All her life had been spent in the relentless pursuit of her father's goal; she had never taken the time to dream for herself.

But she knew one thing. She did not want to fly off to Alpha Centauri. She did not want to leave the solar system behind her, leave the entire human race behind.

Yet she had to go. The ship could not function by itself for the ten years it would take to reach Alpha Centaui. The ship needed a human pilot, and she had always assumed that she would be that person.

But she did not want to go.

Twenty-two minutes.

Delia sat at the control console, watching the digital clock clicking down to midnight. Her vision blurred, and she realized that her eyes were filled with tears. This austere laboratory complex, this remote habitat set as far away from other human beings as possible, where she and her father had lived and worked alone for all these years—this was home.

"Delia!"

Marty's voice shocked her. She spun in her chair to see him standing in the doorway to the control room. Wiping her eyes with the back of a hand, she saw that he looked puzzled, worried. And there was a small faintly bluish knot on his forehead, between his eyes.

"The security system at your main airlock must be off-line. I just opened the hatch and walked in."

Delia tried to smile. "There isn't any security system. We never have any visitors."

"We?" Marty frowned.

"Me, I," she stuttered.

He strode across the smooth concrete floor toward her. "Alpha One monitored your comm transmissions to the power companies," Marty said, looking grim. "I'm here to shut down your experiment."

She almost felt relieved.

"You'll have to call the power companies and tell them you're cancelling your orders," he went on. "And that includes Rising Sun, too."

Delia said nothing.

"Buying power from Mercury. I've got to hand it to you, I wouldn't have thought you'd go that far." Marty shook his head, half-admiringly.

"You can't stop me," Delia said, so softly she barely heard it herself.

But Marty heard her. Standing over her, scowling at the display screens set into the console, he said, "It's over, Delia. I can't let you endanger all our lives. Alpha One agrees with me."

"I don't care," Delia said, one eye on the digital clock. "I'm not endangering anyone's life. You can have Alpha One check my calculations. There's no danger at all, as long as no one interferes with the power flow once—"

"I can't let you do it, Delia! It's too dangerous!"

His face was an agony of conflicting emotions. But all Delia saw was unbending obstinacy, inflexible determination to stop her, to shatter her father's dream.

Wildly, she began mentally searching for a weapon. She wished she had kept a gun in the laboratory, or that her father had built a security system into the airlocks.

Then her romance videos sprang up in her frenzied memory. She did have a weapon, the oldest weapon of all. The realization almost took her breath away.

She lowered her eyes, turned slightly away from Marty.

"Maybe you're right," Delia said softly. "Maybe it would be best to forget the whole thing." Nineteen minutes before midnight.

There was no other chair in the control room, so Marty dropped to one knee beside her and looked earnestly into her eyes.

"It will be for the best, Delia. I promise you."

Slowly, hesitantly, she reached out a hand and brushed his handsome cheek with her fingertips.

The tingle she felt along the length of her arm surprised her.

"I can't fight against you anymore," Delia whispered.

"There's no reason for us to fight," he said, his voice as husky as hers.

"It's just . . ." Eighteen minutes.

"I don't want you to go," Marty admitted. "I don't want you to fly off to the stars and leave me."

Delia blinked. "What?"

"I don't want to lose you, Delia. Ever since I met you, I've been fighting your father for your attention. And then your father's ghost. You've never really looked at me. Not as a person. Not as a man who loves you."

"But Marty," she gasped, barely able to speak, "I love you!"

He pulled her up from her chair and they kissed and Delia felt as if the Moon had indeed lurched out of its orbit. Marty held her tightly and she clutched at him, at the warm tender strength of him.

Then she saw the digital clock. Fifteen minutes to go.

And she realized that more than anything in the universe she wanted to be with Marty. But then her eye caught the display screen that showed the diamond starship sitting out on the crater floor, with her father in it, waiting, waiting.

Fourteen minutes, forty seconds.

"I'm sorry, Marty," she whispered into his ear. "I can't let you stop us." And she reached for the console switch that would automate the entire power sequence.

"What are you doing?" Marty asked.

Delia clicked the switch home. "Everything's on automatic now. There's nothing you can do to stop the process. In fourteen minutes or so the power will start flowing—"

"Alpha One can stop the power companies from transmitting the energy to you," Marty said. "And he will."

Delia felt her whole body slump with defeat. "If he does, it means the end of everything for me."

"No," Marty said, smiling at her. "It'll be the beginning of everything—for us."

Delia thought of life together with Marty. And the shadow of her father's ghost between them.

She felt something like an electric shock jolt through her. "Marty!" she blurted. "Would you go to Alpha Centauri with me?"

His eyes went round. "Go—with you? Just the two of us?"

"Ten years one way. Ten years back. A lifetime together."

"Just the two of us?"

"And Daddy."

His face darkened.

"Would you do it?" she asked again, feeling all the eagerness of youth and love and adventure.

He shook his head like a stubborn mule. "Alpha One won't allow you to have the power."

"Alfie's only got one vote. We've got two, between us."

"But he can override us on the safety issue."

"Maybe," she said. "But will you at least try to help me outvote him?"

"So we can go off to Alpha Centauri together? That's crazy!"

"Don't you want to be crazy with me?"

For an endless moment Delia's whole life hung in the balance. She watched Marty's blue eyes, trying to see through them, trying to understand what was going on behind them.

Then he grinned, and said, "Yes, I do."

Delia whooped and kissed him even more soundly than before. *He's either lying or kidding himself or so certain that Alfie will stop us that he doesn't think it makes any difference*, Delia told herself. *But I don't care. He's going to try, and that's all that matters.*

Twelve minutes.

Together they ran down the barren corridor from the control room to Delia's quarters and phoned Alpha One. The display screen simply glowed a pale orange, of course, but they solemnly called for a meeting of the Council. Then Delia moved that the Council make no effort to stop her experiment and Marty seconded the motion.

"Such a motion may be voted upon and carried," Alpha One's flat expressionless voice warned them, "but if the risk assessment determines that this experiment endangers human lives other than those willingly engaged in the experiment itself, I will instruct the various power companies not to send the electrical power to your rectennas."

Delia took a deep breath and, with one eye on Marty's face, solemn in the glow from the display screen, she worked up the courage to say, "Agreed."

Nine minutes.

"Alpha One won't let the power through," Marty said as they trudged back to the control room.

Delia knew he was right. But she said, "We'll see. If Alfie's checking my calculations we'll be all right."

"He's undoubtedly making his own calculations," said Marty gloomily. "Doing the risk assessment."

Delia smiled at him. One way or the other we're going to share our lives, either here or on the way to the stars.

Two minutes.

Delia watched the display screens while Marty paced the concrete floor. I've done my best, Daddy, she said silently. Whatever happens now, I've done the very best I could. You've got to let me go, Daddy. I've got to live my own life from now on.

Midnight.

Power from six dozen sunsats, plus the relay satellites in orbit around Mercury, poured silently, invisibly into the rectennas ringing Newton's peaks. Energy from the sun was transformed back into electricity and then converted into more antimatter than the human race had ever seen before. Thirty tons of antiprotons, a million megatons of energy, ran silently in the endless racetrack of super-conducting magnets and diamond sheathing along the floor of the crater.

The laboratory seemed to hum with their energy. The very air felt vibrant, crackling.

Delia could hardly believe it. "Alfie let us have the power!"

"What happens now?" Marty asked, his voice hollow with awe.

She spun her little chair around and jumped to her feet. Hugging him tightly, she said, "Now, my dearest darling, we store the antiprotons in the ship's crystal lattice, get aboard and take off for Alpha Centauri!"

He gulped. "Just like that?"

"Just like that." Delia held her hand out to him and Marty took it in his. Like a pair of children they ran out of the control room, to head for the stars.

The vast network of computer components that was known as Alpha One was incapable of smiling, of course. But if it could congratulate itself, it would have.

Alpha One had been built to consider not merely the immediate consequences of any problem, but its long-term implications. Over the half century of its existence, it had learned to look farther and farther into the future. A pebble disturbed at one moment could cause a landslide a hundred years later.

Alpha One had done all the necessary risk assessments connected with headstrong Delia's experiment, and then looked deep into the future for a risk assessment that spanned all the generations to come of humanity and its computer symbiotes.

Spaceflight had given the human race a new survival capability. By developing self-sufficient habitats off-Earth, the humans had disconnected their fate from the fate of the Earth. Nuclear holocaust, ecological collapse, even meteor strikes such as those that caused the Time of Great Dying sixty million years earlier—none of these could destroy the human race once it had established self-sufficient societies off-Earth.

Yet the Sun controlled all life in the solar system, and the Sun would not last forever.

Looking deep into future time, Alpha One had come to the conclusion that star flight was necessary if the humans and their computers were to disconnect their fate from the eventual demise of their Sun. And now they had star flight in their grasp.

As the diamond starship left the crater Newton on a hot glow of intense gamma radiation, Alpha One perceived that Delia and Marty were only the first star travelers. Others would certainly follow. The future of humanity was assured. Alpha One could erase its deepest concern for the safety of the human race and its computer symbiotes. Had it been anywhere near human, it would have sat back with a satisfied smile to wait with folded hands for the return of the first star travelers. And their children.

MEN OF GOOD WILL

As Rudyard Kipling once pointed out:
    "There are nine and sixty ways of constructing tribal lays.
    And—every—single—one—of—them—is—right!"
    —In the Neolithic Age

    Some science fiction stories begin with the dream of a wonderful invention, or the nightmare of a dreadful discovery. Some start with a vision of a particular person, a magnificent hero such as Muad'Dib or an ordinary person thrust into extraordinary events such as Montag, the Fireman. Other stories begin with the bare bones of a situation, an idea, even a joke.
    Or the present offering.

    "I HAD NO IDEA," said the UN representative as they stepped through the airlock hatch, "that the United States lunar base was so big, and so thoroughly well equipped."

    "It's a big operation, all right," Colonel Patton answered, grinning slightly. His professional satisfaction showed even behind the faceplate of his pressure suit.

    The pressure in the airlock equilibrated, and they squirmed out of their aluminized protective suits. Patton was big, scraping the maximum limit for space-vehicle passengers; Torgeson, the UN man, was slight, thin-haired, bespectacled and somehow bland-looking.

They stepped out of the airlock, into the corridor that ran the length of the huge plastic dome that housed Headquarters, U.S. Moonbase.

"What's behind all the doors?' Torgeson asked. His English had a slight Scandinavian twang to it. Patton found it a little irritating.

"On the right," the colonel answered, businesslike, "are officers' quarters, galley, officers' mess, various laboratories and the headquarters staff offices. On the left are the computers."

Torgeson blinked. "You mean that half this building is taken up by computers? But why in the world . . . that is, why do you need so many? Isn't it frightfully expensive to boost them up here? I know it cost thousands of dollars for my own flight to the moon. The computers must be—"

"'Frightfully expensive,'" Patton agreed, with feeling. "But we need them. Believe me, we need them."

They walked the rest of the way down the long corridor in silence. Patton's office was at the very end of it. The colonel opened the door and ushered in the UN representative.

"A sizeable office," Torgeson said. "And a window!"

"One of the privileges of rank," Patton answered, smiling tightly. "That white antenna-mast off on the horizon belongs to the Russian base."

"Ah, yes. Of course. I shall be visiting them tomorrow."

Colonel Patton nodded and gestured Torgeson to a chair as he walked behind his metal desk and sat down.

"Now then," said the colonel. "You are the first man allowed to set foot in this moonbase who is not a security cleared, triple-checked, native-born, government-employed American. God knows how you got the Pentagon to okay your trip. But—now that you're here, what do you want?"

Torgeson took off his rimless glasses and fiddled with them. "I suppose the simplest answer would be the best. The United Nations must—absolutely must—find out how and why you and the Russians have been able to live peacefully here on the moon."

Patton's mouth opened, but no words came out. He closed it with a click.

"Americans and Russians," the UN man went on, "have fired at each other from orbiting satellite vehicles. They have exchanged shots at both the North and South Poles. Career diplomats have scuffled like prizefighters in the halls of the United Nations building—"

"I didn't know that."

"Oh, yes. We have kept it quiet, of course. But the tensions are becoming unbearable. Everywhere on Earth the two sides are armed to the teeth and on the verge of disaster. Even in space they fight. And yet, here on the moon, you and the Russians live side by side in peace. We must know how you do it!"

Patton grinned. "You came on a very appropriate day, in that case. Well, let's see now . . . how to present the picture. You know that the environment here is extremely hostile: airless, low gravity . . . "

"The environment here on the moon," Torgeson objected, "is no more hostile than that of orbiting satellites. In fact, you have some gravity, solid ground, large buildings—many advantages that artificial satellites lack. Yet there has been fighting aboard the satellites—and not on the moon. Please don't waste my time with platitudes. This trip is costing the UN too much money. Tell me the truth."

Patton nodded. "I was going to. I've checked the information sent up by Earthbase: you've been cleared by the White House, the AEC, NASA and even the Pentagon."

"So?"

"Okay. The plain truth of the matter is . . ." A soft chime from a small clock on Patton's desk interrupted him. "Oh. Excuse me."

Torgeson sat back and watched as Patton carefully began clearing off all the articles on his desk: the clock, calendar, phone, IN/OUT baskets, tobacco can and pipe rack, assorted papers and reports—all neatly and quickly placed in the desk drawers. Patton then stood up, walked to the filing cabinet, and closed the metal drawers firmly. He stood in the middle of the room, scanned the scene with apparent satisfaction, and then glanced at his wristwatch.

"Okay," he said to Torgeson. "Get down on your stomach."

"What?"

"Like this," the colonel said, and prostrated himself on the rubberized floor.

Torgeson stared at him.

"Come on! There's only a few seconds."

Patton reached up and grasped the UN man by the wrist. Unbelievingly, Torgeson got out of the chair, dropped to his hands and knees and finally flattened himself on the floor, next to the colonel.

For a second or two they stared at each other, saying nothing.

"Colonel, this is embar—"

The room exploded into a shattering volley of sounds.

Something—many somethings—ripped through the walls. The air hissed and whined above the heads of the two prostrate men. The metal desk and file cabinet rang eerily.

Torgeson squeezed his eyes shut and tried to worm into the floor. It was just like being shot at!

Abruptly, it was over.

The room was quiet once again, except for a faint hissing sound. Torgeson opened his eyes and saw the colonel getting up. The door was flung open. Three sergeants rushed in, armed with patching disks and tubes of cement. They dashed around the office sealing up the several hundred holes in the walls.

Only gradually, as the sergeants carried on their fevered, wordless task, did Torgeson realize that the walls were actually a quiltwork of patches. The room must have been riddled repeatedly!

He climbed slowly to his feet. "Meteors?" he asked, with a slight squeak in his voice.

Colonel Patton grunted negatively and resumed his seat behind the desk. It was pockmarked, Torgeson noticed now. So was the file cabinet.

"The window, in case you're wondering, is bulletproof."

Torgeson nodded and sat down.

"You see," the colonel said, "life is not as peaceful here as you think. Oh, we get along fine with the Russians—now. We've learned to live in peace. We had to."

"What were those . . . things?"

"Bullets."

"Bullets? But how . . . "

The sergeants finished their frenzied work, lined up at the door and saluted. Colonel Patton returned the salute and they turned as one man and left the office, closing the door quietly behind them.

"Colonel, I'm frankly bewildered."

"It's simple enough to understand. But don't feel too badly about being surprised. Only the top level of the Pentagon knows about this. And the president. of course. They had to let him in on it."

"What happened?"

Colonel Patton took his pipe rack and tobacco can out of a desk drawer and began filling one of the pipes. "You see," he began, "the Russians and us, we weren't always so peaceful here on the moon. We've had our incidents and scuffles, just as you have on Earth"

"Go on."

"Well . . ." he struck a match and puffed the pipe alight ". . . shortly after we set up this dome for moonbase HQ, and the Reds set up theirs, we got into some real arguments." He waved the match out and tossed it into the open drawer.

"We're situated on the *Oceanus Procellarum,* you know. Exactly on the lunar equator. One of the biggest open spaces on this hunk of airless rock. Well, the Russians claimed they owned the whole damned *Oceanus,* since they were here first. We maintained that the legal ownership was not established, since according to the UN Charter and the subsequent covenants—"

"Spare the legal details! Please, what happened?"

Patton looked slightly hurt. "Well . . . we started shooting at each other. One of their guards fired at one of our guards. They claim it was the other way around, of course. Anyway, within twenty minutes we were fighting a regular pitched battle, right out there between our base and theirs." He gestured toward the window.

"Can you fire guns in airless space?"

"Oh, sure. No problem at all. However, something unexpected came up."

"Unexpected? What?"

"Only a few men got hit in the battle, none of them seriously. As in all battles, most of the rounds fired were clean misses."

"So?"

Patton smiled grimly. "So one of our civilian mathematicians started doodling. We had several thousand very-high-velocity bullets fired off. In airless space. No friction, you see. And under low-gravity conditions. They went right along past their targets—"

Recognition dawned on Torgeson's face. "Oh, no!"

"That's right. They whizzed right along, skimmed over the mountain tops, thanks to the curvature of this damned short lunar horizon, and established themselves in rather eccentric satellite orbits. Every hour or so they return to perigee . . . or, rather, periluna. And every twenty-seven days, periluna is right here, where the bullets originated. The moon rotates on its axis every twenty-seven days, you see. At any rate, when they come back this way, they shoot the living hell out of our base—and the Russian base, too, of course."

"But can't you . . . ?"

"Do what? Can't move the base. Authorization is tied up in the Joint Chiefs of Staff, and they can't agree on where to move it to. Can't bring up any special shielding material, because that's not authorized, either. The best thing we can do is to requisition all the computers we can and try to keep track of all the bullets. Their orbits keep changing, you know, every time they go through the bases. Air friction, puncturing walls, ricochets off the furniture—all that keeps changing their orbits enough to keep our computers busy full time."

"My God!"

"In the meantime, we don't dare fire off any more rounds. It would overburden the computers and we'd lose track of all of 'em. Then we'd have to spend every twenty-seventh day flat on our faces for hours."

Torgeson sat in numbed silence.

"But don't worry," Patton concluded with an optimistic, professional grin. "I've got a small detail of men secretly at work on the far side of the base—where the Reds can't see—building a stone wall. That'll stop the bullets. Then we'll fix those warmongers once and for all!"

Torgeson's face went slack. The chime sounded, muffled, from inside Patton's desk.

"Better get set to flatten out again. Here comes the second volley."

FOEMAN, WHERE DO YOU FLEE?

I've never liked the title to this story, which was supplied by Frederik Pohl, who was editor of Galaxy magazine when I wrote it. The only good thing about the title is that it's better than my original title, which was so forgettable that now I can't remember it!

This story is the only one I've written in response to a cover drawing, which Fred supplied together with a request for a "strong lead novelette." Well, it's a novelette and it led that issue of the magazine. You can judge its strength for yourself.

DEEP IN CRYOGENIC SLEEP the mind dreams the same frozen dreams, endlessly circuiting through the long empty years. Sidney Lee dreamed of the towers on Titan, over and again, their smooth blank walls of metal that was beyond metal, their throbbing, ceaseless, purposeful machines that ran at tasks that men could not even guess at. The towers loomed in his darkened dreams, standing menacing and alien above the frozen wastes of Titan, utterly unmindful of the tiny men that groveled at their base. He tried to scale those smooth, steep walls and fell back. He tried to penetrate them and failed. He tried to scream. And in his dreams, at least, he succeeded.

271

He didn't dream of Ruth, or of the stars, or of the future or the past. Only of the towers, of the machines that blindly obeyed a builder who had left Earth's solar system countless millennia ago.

He opened his eyes.

"What happened?"

Carlos Pascual was smiling down at him, his round dark-skinned face relaxed and almost happy. "We are there . . . here, I mean. We are braking, preparing to go into orbit."

Lee blinked and sat up. "We made it?"

"Yes, yes," Pascual answered softly as his eyes shifted to the bank of instruments on the console behind Lee's shoulder. "The panel claims you are alive and well. How do you feel?"

That took a moment's thought. "A little hungry."

"A common reaction." The smile returned. "You can join the others in the galley."

The expedition's medical chief helped Lee to swing his legs over the edge of the couch, then left him and went to the next unit, where a blonde woman lay still sleeping. With an effort, Lee recalled her: Doris McNertny, primary biologist, backup biochemist. Lee pulled a deep breath into his lungs and tried to get himself started. The overhead light panels, on full intensity now, made him want to squint.

Standing was something of an experiment. *No shakes,* Lee thought gratefully. The room was large and circular, with no viewports.

Each of the twenty hibernation couches had been painted a different color by some psychology team back on Earth. Most of them were empty now. The remaining occupied ones had their lids off and the lifesystem connections removed as Pascual, Tanaka and May Connearney worked to revive the people. Despite the color scheme, the room looked uninviting, and it smelled clinical.

The galley, Lee focused his thoughts, *is in this globe, one flight up.* The ship was built in globular sections that turned in response to g-pulls. With the main fusion engines firing to brake their approach to final orbit, "UP" was temporarily in the direction of the engines' thrusters. But inside the globes it did not make much difference.

He found the stairwell that ran through the globe. Inside the winding metal ladderway the rumbling vibrations from the ship's engines were echoing strongly enough to hear as actual sound.

"Sid! Good morning!" Aaron Hatfield had stationed himself at the entrance to the galley and was acting as a one-man welcoming committee.

There were only a half dozen people in the galley. *Of course,* Lee realized. *The crew personnel are at their stations.* Except for Hatfield, the people were bunched at the galley's lone viewpoint, staring outside and speaking in hushed, subdued whispers.

"Hello, Aaron." Lee didn't feel jubilant, not after a fifteen-year sleep. He tried to picture Ruth in his mind and found that he couldn't.

She must be nearly fifty by now.

Hatfield was the expedition's primary biochemist, a chunky, loud-speaking overgrown kid whom it was impossible to dislike, no matter how he behaved. Lee knew that Hatfield wouldn't go near the viewport because the sight of empty space terrified him.

"Hey, here's Doris!" Hatfield shouted to no one. He scuttled toward the entrance as she stepped rather uncertainly into the galley.

Lee dialed for coffee. With the hot cup in his hand he walked slowly toward the viewport.

"Hello Dr. Lee," Marlene Ettinger said as he came up alongside her. The others at the viewport turned and muttered their greetings.

"How close are we?" Lee asked.

Charnovsky, the geologist, answered positively, "Two days before we enter final orbit."

The stars crowded out the darkness beyond their viewport. They shone against the blackness like droplets from a paint spray. In the faint reflection of the port's plastic, Lee could see six human faces looking lost and awed.

Then the ship swung, ever so slightly, in response to some command from the crew and computers. A single star—close and blazingly powerful—slid into view, lancing painfully brilliant light through the polarizing viewport. Lee snapped his eyes shut, but not before the glare burned its afterimage against his closed eyelids. They all ducked back instinctively.

"Welcome to Sirius," somebody said.

Man's fight to the stars was made not in glory, but in fear.

The buildings on Titan were clearly the work of an alien intelligent race. No man could tell exactly how old they were, how long their baffling machines had been running, what their purpose was.

Whoever had built them had left the solar system hundreds of centuries ago.

For the first time, men truly dreaded the stars.

Still, they had to know, had to learn. Robot probes were sent to the nearest dozen stars, the farthest that man's technology could reach. Nearly a generation passed on Earth before the faint signals from the probes returned. Seven of the stars had planets circling them. Of these, five possessed Earthlike worlds. On four of them, some indications of life were found. Life, not intelligence. Long and hot were the debates about what to do next. Finally, manned expeditions were dispatched to the Earthlike ones.

Through it all, the machines on Titan hummed smoothly.

"They should have named this ship *Afterthought*," Lee said to Charnovsky. The ship's official name was *Carl Sagan*.

"How so?" the Russian muttered as he pushed a pawn across the board between them. They were sitting in the pastel-lighted rec room. A few others were scattered around the semicircular room, reading, talking, dictating messages that wouldn't get to Earth for more than eight years. Soft music purred in the background.

The Earthlike planet—Sirius A-2—swung past the nearest viewport. The ship had been in orbit for nearly three weeks now and was rotating around its long axis to keep a half-g feeling of weight for the scientists.

"We were sent here as an afterthought," Lee continued. "Nobody expects us to find anything. Most of the experts back on Earth didn't really believe there could be an Earthlike planet around a blue star."

"They were correct, " Charnovsky said. "Your move."

Picture our solar system. Now replace the sun with Sirius A, the Dog Star: a young, blue star, nearly twice as hot and big as the sun. Take away the planet Uranus, nearly two billion kilometers from the sun, and replace it with the white dwarf Sirius B, the Pup: just as hot as Sirius A, but collapsed to a hundredth of a star's ordinary size. Now sweep away all the planets between the Dog and the Pup except two: a bald chunk of rock the size of Mercury orbiting some 100 million kilometers from A, and an Earth-sized planet some seven times farther out.

Give the Earth-sized planet a cloud-sprinkled atmosphere, a few large seas, some worn-down mountain chains, and a thin veneer of simple green life clinging to its dusty surface. Finally, throw in one lone gas giant planet, far beyond the Pup, some 200 billion kilometers from A. Add some meteoroids and comets and you have the Sirius system.

Lehman, the psychiatrist, pulled up a webchair to the kibitzer's position between Lee and Charnovsky.

"Mind if I watch?" He was trim and athletic looking, kept himself tanned under the UV lights in the ship's gym booth.

Within minutes they were discussing the chances of finding anything on the planet below them.

"You sound terribly pessimistic," the psychiatrist said.

"The planet looks pessimistic," Charnovsky replied. "It was scoured clean when Sirius B exploded, and life has hardly had a chance to get started again on its surface."

"But it *is* Earthlike, isn't it?"

"A-hah!" Charnovsky burst. "To a simple-minded robot it may seem Earthlike. The air is breathable. The chemical composition of the rocks is similar. But no man would call that desert an Earthlike world. There are no trees, no grasses, it's too hot, the air is too dry . . ."

"And the planet's too young to have evolved an intelligent species," Lee added, "which makes me the biggest afterthought of all."

"Well, there might be something down there for an anthropologist to puzzle over," Lehman countered. "Things will look better once we get down to the surface. I think we're all getting a touch of cabin fever in here."

Before Lee could reply, Lou D'Orazio—the ship's geophysicist and cartographer—came bounding through the hatchway of the rec room and, taking advantage of the half-gravity, crossed to their chess table in two jumps.

"Look at this!"

He slapped a still-warm photograph on the chess table, scattering pieces over the floor. Charnovsky swore something Slavic, and everyone in the room turned.

It was one of the regular cartographic photos, crisscrossed with grid lines. It showed the shoreline of one of the planet's mini-oceans. A line of steep bluffs followed the shore.

"It looks like an ordinary—"

"Aspertti un momento . . . wait a minute . . . see here."

D'Orazio pulled a magnifier from his coverall pocket. "Look!"

Lee peered through the magnifier. Fuzzy, wavering, gray.
"It looks like—"
Lehman said, "Whatever it is, it's standing on two legs."
"It's a man," Charnovsky said flatly.

✳ ❙❙ ✳

WITHIN MINUTES the whole scientific staff had piled into the rec
room and crowded around the table, together with all the crew
members except the two on duty in the command globe.

The ship's automatic cameras took twenty more photographs of the
area before their orbit carried them over the horizon from the spot.
Five of the pictures showed the shadowy figure of a bipedal creature.

The spot was in darkness by the time their orbit carried them over
it again. Infrared and radar sensors showed nothing.

They squinted at the pictures, handed them from person to person,
talked and argued and wondered through two entire eight-hour shifts.
Crewmen left for duty and returned again. The planet turned beneath
them, and once again the shoreline was bathed in Sirius's hot glow. But
there was no trace of the humanoid. Neither the cameras, the manned
telescopes, nor the other sensors could spot anything.

One by one, men and women left the rec room, sleepy and talked
out. Finally, only Lee, Charnovsky, Lehman and Captain Rasmussen
were left sitting at the chess table with the finger-grimed photos spread
out before them.

"They're men." Lee murmured. "Erect bipedal men."

"It's only one creature," the captain said. "And all we know is that it
looks like a man."

Rasmussen was tall, hamfisted, rawboned, with a ruddy face that
could look either elfin or Viking but nothing in between. His voice,
though, was thin and high. To the everlasting applause of all aboard,
he had fought to get a five-year supply of beer brought along. Even
now, he had a mug tightly wrapped in one big hand.

"All right, they're humanoids," Lee conceded. "That's close enough."

The captain hiked a shaggy eyebrow. "I don't like jumping at
shadows, you know. These pictures—"

"Men or not." Charnovsky said, "We must land and investigate closely."

Lee glanced at Lehman, straddling a turned-around chair and resting his arms tiredly on the back.

"Oh, we'll investigate," Rasmussen agreed, "but not too fast. If they are an intelligent species of some kind, we've got to go gingerly. I'm under orders from the Council, you know."

"They haven't tried to contact us," Lee said. "That means they either don't know we're here, or they're not interested, or—"

"Or what?"

Lee knew how it would sound, but he said it anyway. "Or they're waiting to get their hands on us."

Rasmussen laughed. "That sounds dramatic, sure enough."

"Really?" Lee heard his voice as though it were someone else's. "Suppose the humanoids down there are from the same race that built the machines on Titan?"

"Nonsense," Charnovsky blurted, "There are no cities down there, no sign whatever of an advanced civilization."

The captain took a long swallow of beer, then, "There is no sign of Earth's civilization on the planet either, you know. Yet *we* are here, sure enough."

Lee's insides were fluttering now. "If they are the ones who built on Titan . . ."

"It is still nonsense!" Charnovsky insisted. "To assume that the first extraterrestrial creature resembling a man is a representative of the race that visited the solar system hundreds of centuries ago—ridiculous! The statistics alone put the idea in the realm of fantasy."

"Wait, there's more to it," Lee said, "Why would a visitor from another star go to the trouble to build a machine that works for centuries, without stopping?"

They looked at him, waiting for him to answer his own question: Rasmussen with his Viking's craggy face, Charnovsky trying to puzzle it out in his own mind, Lehman calm and half-amused.

"The Titan buildings are more than alien," Lee explained. "They're hostile. That's my belief. Call it an assumption, a hypothesis. But I can't envision an alien race building machinery like that except for an all-important purpose. That purpose was military."

Rasmussen looked truly puzzled now. "Military? But who were they fighting?"

"Us," Lee answered. "A previous civilization on Earth. A culture that arose before the Ice Ages, went into space, met an alien culture and was smashed in a war so badly that there's no trace of it left."

Charnovsky's face was reddening with the effort of staying quiet.

"I know it's conjecture," Lee went on quietly, "but if there was a war between ancient man and the builders of the Titan machines, then the two cultures must have arisen close enough to each other to make war possible. Widely separated cultures can't make war, they can only contact each other every few centuries or millennia. The aliens had to come from a nearby star . . . like Sirius."

"No, no, no!" Charnovsky slapped a hand on his thigh. "It's preposterous, unscientific! There is not one shred of evidence to support this, this . . . pipe-dream!"

But Rasmussen looked thoughtful. "Still . . ."

"Still it is nonsense," Charnovsky repeated. "The planet down there holds no interstellar technology. If there ever was one, it was blasted away when Sirius B exploded. Whoever is down there, he has no cities, no electronic communications, no satellites in orbit, no cultivated fields, no animal herds . . . nothing!"

"Then maybe he's a visitor too," Lee countered.

"Whatever it is," Rasmussen said, "it won't do for us to go rushing in like berserkers. Suppose there's a civilization down there that's so advanced we simply do not recognize it as such?"

Before Charnovsky could reply, the captain went on, "We have plenty of time. We will get more data about surface conditions from the robot landers and do a good deal more studying and thinking about the entire problem. Then, if conditions warrant it, we can land."

"But we don't have time!" Lee snapped. Surprised at his own vehemence, he continued, "Five years is a grain of sand compared to the job ahead of us. We have to investigate a completely alien culture and determine what its attitude is toward us. Just learning the language might take five years all by itself."

Lehman smiled easily and said, "Sid, suppose you're totally wrong about this, and whoever's down there is simply a harmless savage. What would be the shock to his culture if we suddenly drop in on him?"

"What'll be the shock to *our* culture if I'm right?"

Rasmussen drained his mug and banged it down on the chess table. "This is getting us nowhere. We have not enough evidence to decide on an intelligent course of action. Personally, I'm in no hurry to go blundering into a nest of unknowns. Not when we can learn safely from orbit. As long as the beer holds out, we go slow."

Lee pushed his chair back and stood up. "We won't learn a damned thing from orbit. Not anything that counts. We've got to go down there and study them close up. And the sooner the better."

He turned and walked out of the rec room. *Rasmussen's spent half his life hauling scientists out to Titan, and he can't understand why we have to make the most of our time here,* he raged to himself.

Halfway down the passageway to his quarters, he heard footsteps padding behind him. He knew who it would be. Turning, he saw Lehman coming along toward him.

"Sacking in?" the psychiatrist asked.

"Aren't you sleepy?"

"Completely bushed, now that you mention it."

"But you want to talk to me," Lee said.

Lehman shrugged. "No hurry."

With a shrug of his own, Lee resumed walking to his room. "Come on. I'm too worked up to sleep anyway."

All the cubicles were more or less the same: a bunk, a desk, a filmspool reader, a sanitary closet. Lee took the webbed desk chair and let Lehman plop on the sighing air mattress of the bunk.

"Do you really believe this hostile alien theory? Or are you just—"

Lee slouched down in his chair and interrupted. "Let's not fool around, Rich. You know about my breakdown on Titan and you're worried about me."

"It's my job to worry about everybody."

"I take my pills every day . . . to keep the paranoia away."

"That wasn't the diagnosis of your case, as you're perfectly well aware."

"So they called it something else. What're you after, Rich? Want to test my reflexes while I'm sleepy and my guard's down?"

Lehman smiled professionally. "Look, Sid. You had a breakdown on Titan. You got over it. That's finished."

Nodding grimly, Lee added, "Except that I think there might be aliens down there plotting against me."

"That could be nothing more than a subconscious attempt to increase the importance of the anthropology department," Lehman countered.

"Crap" Lee said. "I came out here expecting something like this. Why do you think I fought my way onto this expedition? It wasn't easy, after my breakdown. I had to push ahead of a lot of former friends."

"And leave your wife."

"That's right. Ruth divorced me for it. She's getting all my accumulated dividends. She'll die in comfort while we're sleeping our way back home."

"But why?" Lehman asked. "Why should you give up everything— friends, wife, family, position—to get out here?"

Lee knew the answer, hesitated about putting it into words, then realized that Lehman knew it too. "Because I had to face it . . . had to do what I could to find out about those buildings on Titan."

"And that's why you want to rush down and contact whoever it is down there? Am I right?"

"Right," Lee said. He almost wanted to laugh. "I'm hoping they can tell me if I'm crazy or not."

✳ III ✳

IT WAS THREE MONTHS before they landed.

Rasmussen was thorough, patient and stubborn. Unmanned landers sampled and tested surface conditions. Observation satellites crisscrossed the planet at the lowest possible altitudes—except for the one that hung in synchronous orbit in the longitude of the spot where the first humanoid had been found.

That was the only place where humanoid life was seen, along that shoreline for a grand distance of perhaps five kilometers. Nowhere else on the planet.

Lee argued and swore and stormed at the delay. Rasmussen stayed firm. Only when he was satisfied that nothing more could be learned from orbit did he agree to land the ship. And still he sent clear word back toward Earth that he might be landing in a trap.

The great ship settled slowly, almost delicately, on a hot tongue of fusion flame, and touched down on the western edge of a desert some 200 kilometers from the humanoid site. A range of rugged-looking hills separated them. The staff and crew celebrated that night. The next morning, Lee, Charnovsky, Hatfield, Doris McNertny, Marlene Ettinger and Alicia Monteverdi moved to the ship's "Sirius globe." They were to be the expedition's "outsiders," the specialists who would eventually live in the planetary environment. They represented anthropology, geology, biochemistry, botany, zoology and ecology, with backup specialties in archeology, chemistry and paleontology.

The Sirius globe held their laboratories, workrooms, equipment and living quarters. They were quarantined from the rest of the ship's staff and crew, the "insiders," until the captain agreed that the surface conditions on the planet would be no threat to the rest of the expedition members. That would take two years minimum, Lee knew.

Gradually, the "outsiders" began to expose themselves to the local environment. They began to breathe the air, acquire the microbes. Pascual and Tanaka made them sit in the medical examination booths twice a day, and even checked them personally every other day. The two M.D.'s wore disposable biosuits and worried expressions when they entered the Sirius globe. The medical computers compiled miles of data tapes on each of the six "outsiders," but still Pascual's normally pleasant face acquired a perpetual frown of anxiety about them.

"I just don't like the idea of this damned armor," Lee grumbled.

He was already encased up to his neck in a gleaming white powersuit, the type that crew members wore when working outside the ship in a vacuum. Aaron Hatfield and Marlene Ettinger were helping to check all the seams and connections. A few feet away, in the cramped "locker room," tiny Alicia Monteverdi looked as though she were being swallowed by an oversized automaton; Charnovsky and Doris McNertny were checking her suit.

"It's for your own protection," Marlene told Lee in a throaty whisper as she applied a test meter to the radio panel on his suit's chest. "You and Alicia won the toss for the first trip outside, but this is the price you must pay. Now be a good boy and don't complain."

Lee had to grin. *"Ja, Fraulein Schluemeisterejn."*

She looked up at him with a rueful smile, "Thank God you never had to carry on a conversation in German."

Finally Lee and Alicia clumped through the double hatch into the airlock. It took another fifteen minutes for them to perform the final checkout, but at last they were ready. The outer hatch slid back, and they started down the long ladder to the planet's surface. The armored suits were equipped with muscle-amplifying power systems, so that even a girl as slim as Alicia could handle their bulk easily.

Lee went down the ladder first and set foot on the ground. It was bare and dusty, the sky a reddish haze.

The grand adventure, Lee thought. *All the expected big moments in life are flops.* A hot breeze hummed in his earphones. It was early morning. Sirius had not cleared the barren horizon yet, although the sky was fully bright. Despite the suit's air-conditioning, Lee felt the heat.

He reached up a hand as Alicia climbed warily down the last few steps of the ladder. The plastic rungs gave under the suit's weight, then slowly straightened themselves when the weight was removed.

"Well," he said, looking at her wide-eyed face through the transparent helmet of her suit, "what do you think of it?"

"It is hardly paradise, is it?"

"Looks like it's leaning the other way," Lee said.

They explored—Lee and Alicia that first day, then the other outsiders, shuffling ponderously inside their armor. Lee chafed against the restriction of the power-suits, but Rasmussen insisted and would brook no argument. They went timidly at first, never out of sight of the ship. Charnovsky chipped samples from the rock outcroppings, while the others took air and soil samples, dug for water, searched for life.

"The perfect landing site," Doris complained after a hot, tedious day. "There's no form of life bigger than a yeast mold within a hundred kilometers of here."

It was a hot world, a dry world, a brick-dust world, where the sky was always red. Sirius was a blowtorch searing down on them, too bright to look at even through the tinted visors of their suits. At night there was no moon to see, but the Pup bathed this world in a deathly bluish glow far brighter yet colder than moonlight. The night sky was never truly dark, and only a few strong stars could be seen from the ground.

Through it all, the robot satellites relayed more pictures of the humanoids along the seacoast. They appeared almost every day, usually only briefly. Sometimes there were a few of them, sometimes only one, once there were nearly a dozen. The highest resolution photographs showed them to be human in size and build. But what their faces looked like, what they wore, what they were *doing*—all escaped the drone cameras.

The robot landers, spotted in a dozen scattered locations within a thousand kilometers of the ship, faithfully recorded and transmitted everything they were programmed to look for. They sent pictures and chemical analyses of plant life and insects. But no higher animals.

Alicia's dark-eyed face took on a perpetually puzzled frown, Lee saw. "It makes no sense," she would say. "There is nothing on this planet more advanced than insects . . . yet there are humans. It's as though human beings suddenly sprang up in the Silurian period on Earth. They *can't* be here. I wish we could examine the life in the seas, perhaps that would tell us more."

"You mean those humanoids didn't originate on this planet," Lee said to her.

She shook her head. "I don't know. I don't see how they could have."

✳ IV ✳

GRADUALLY they pushed their explorations further afield, beyond the ship's limited horizon. In the motorized powersuits a man could cover more than a hundred kilometers a day, if he pushed it. Lee always headed toward the grizzled hills that separated them from the seacoast. He helped the others to dig, to collect samples, but he always pointed them toward the sea.

"The satellite pictures show some decent greenery on the seaward side of the hills," he told Doris. "That's where he should go."

Rasmussen wouldn't move the ship. He wanted his base of operations, his link homeward, at least a hundred kilometers from the nearest possible threat. But finally he relaxed enough to allow the scientists to go out overnight and take a look at the hills.

And maybe the coast, Lee added silently to the captain's orders.

Rasmussen decided to let them use one of the ship's two air-cushion vehicles. He assigned Jerry Grote, the chief engineer, and Chien Shu Li, electronics specialist, to handle the skimmer and take command of the trip. They would live in biosuits and remain inside the skimmer at all times.

Lee, Marlene, Doris and Charnovsky made the trip: Grote did the driving and navigating, Chien handled communications and the computer.

It took a full day's drive to get to the base of the hills. Grote, a lanky, lantern-jawed New Zealander, decided to camp there as night came on.

"I thought you'd be a born mountaineer," Lee poked at him.

Grote leaned back in his padded chair and planted a large sandaled foot on the skimmer's control panel.

"I could climb those wrinkles out there in my sleep," he said pleasantly. "But we've got to be careful of this nice, shiny vehicle."

From the driver's compartment, Lee could see Marlene pushing forward toward them, squeezing between the racks of electronics gear that separated the forward compartment from the living and working quarters. Even in the drab coveralls, she showed a nice profile.

"I would like to go outside," she said to Grote. "We've been sitting all day like tourists in a shuttle."

Grote nodded. "You'll have to wear a hard suit, though."

"But—"

"Orders."

She glanced at Lee, then shrugged. "Very well."

"I'll come with you," Lee said.

Squirming into the armored suits in the aft hatchway was exasperating, but at last they were ready and Lee opened the hatch. They stepped out across the tail fender of the skimmer and jumped to the dusty ground.

"Being inside this is almost worse than being in the car," Marlene said.

They walked around the skimmer. Lee watched his shadow lengthen as he placed the setting Sirius at his back.

"Look . . . *look!*"

He saw Marlene pointing and turned to follow her gaze. The hills rising before them were dazzling with a million sparkling lights: red and blue and white and dazzling, shimmering lights as though a cascade of precious jewels were pouring down the hillside.

"What is it?" Marlene's voice sounded excited, thrilled, not the least afraid.

Lee stared at the shifting multicolored lights; it was like playing a lamp on cut crystal. He took a step toward the hills, then looked down to the ground. From inside the cumbersome suit, it was hard to see the ground close to his feet and harder still to bend down and pick up anything. But he squatted slowly and reached for a small stone. Getting up again, Lee held the stone high enough for it to catch the fading rays of daylight.

The rock glittered with a shower of varicolored sparkles.

"They're made of glass," Lee said.

Within minutes Charnovsky and the other "outsiders" were out of the ship to marvel at it. The Russian collected as many rocks as he could stuff into his suit's thigh pouches. Lee and Grote helped him while the women merely stood by the skimmer and watched the hills blaze with lights.

Sirius disappeared below the horizon at last, and the show ended. The hills returned to being brownish, erosion-worn clumps of rock.

"Glass mountains," Marlene marveled as they returned to the skimmer.

"Not glass," Charnovsky corrected. "Glazed rock. Granitic, no doubt. Probably was melted when the Pup exploded. Atmosphere might have been blown away, and rock cooled very rapidly."

Lee could see Marlene's chin rise stubbornly inside the transparent dome of her suit. "I name them the Glass Mountains," she said firmly.

Grote had smuggled a bottle along with them, part of his personal stock. "My most precious possession," he rightfully called it. But for the Glass Mountains he dug it out of its hiding place, and they toasted both the discovery and the name. Marlene smiled and insisted that Lee also be toasted, as co-discoverer.

Hours later, Lee grew tired of staring at the metal ceiling of the sleeping quarters a few inches above his top-tier bunk. Even Grote's drinks didn't help him to sleep. He kept wondering about the humanoids, what they were doing, where they were from, how he would get to learn their secrets. As quietly as he could, he slipped down from the bunk. The two men beneath him were breathing deeply and evenly. Lee headed for the rear hatch, past the women's bunks.

The hard suits were standing at stiff attention, flanking both sides of the rear hatch. Lee was in his coveralls. He strapped on a pair of boots, slid the hatch open as quietly as he could, and stepped out onto the fender.

The air was cool and clean, the sky bright enough for him to make out the worn old hills. There were a few stars in the sky, but the hills didn't reflect them.

He heard a movement behind him. Turning, he saw Marlene.

"Did I wake you?"

"I'm a very light sleeper," she said.

"Sorry, I didn't mean—"

"No, I'm glad you did." She shook her head slightly, and for the first time Lee noticed the sweep and softness of her hair. The light was too dim to make out its color, but he remembered it as chestnut.

"Besides," she whispered, "I've been longing to get outside without being in one of those damned suits."

He helped her down from the fender, and they walked a little way from the skimmer.

"Can we see the sun?" she asked, looking skyward.

"I'm not sure, I think maybe . . . there." He pointed to a second-magnitude star, shining alone in the grayish sky.

"Where, which one?"

He took her by the shoulder with one hand so that she could see where he was pointing.

"Oh yes, I see it."

She turned, and she was in his arms, and he kissed her. He held onto her as though there was nothing else in the universe.

If any of the others suspected that Lee and Marlene had spent the night outside, they didn't mention it. All six of them took their regular pre-breakfast checks in the medical booth, and by the time they were finished eating in the cramped galley the computer had registered a safe green for each of them.

Lee slid out from the galley's folding table and made his way forward. Grote was slouched in the driver's seat, his lanky frame a geometry of knees and elbows. He was studying the viewscreen map.

"Looking for a pass through these hills for our vehicle," he said absently, his eyes on the slowly-moving photomap.

"Why take the skimmer?" Lee asked, sitting on the chair beside him. "We can cross these hills in the powersuits."

Grote cocked an eye at him. "You're really set on getting to the coast, aren't you?"

"Aren't you?"

That brought a grin. "How much do you think we ought to carry with us?"

＊ **V** ＊

THEY SPLIT THE TEAM into three groups. Chien and Charnovsky stayed with the car; Marlene and Doris would go with Lee and Grote to look at the flora and fauna (if any) on the shore side of the hills, Lee and the engineer carried a pair of TV camera packs with them, to set up close to the shoreline.

"Beware of the natives," Charnovsky's voice grated in Lee's earphones as they walked away from the skimmer. "They might swoop down on you with bows and arrows!" His laughter showed what he thought of Lee's worries.

Climbing the hills wasn't as bad as Lee had thought it would be. The powersuit did most of the work, and the glassy rock was not smooth enough to cause real troubles with footing. It was hot though, even with the suit's cooling equipment turned up full bore. Sirius blazed overhead, and the rocks beat glare and heat back into their faces as they climbed.

It took most of the day to get over the crest of the hills. But finally with Sirius edging toward the horizon behind them, Lee saw the water.

The sea spread to the farther horizon, cool and blue, with long gentle swells that steepened into surf as they ran up toward the land. And the land was green here: shrubs and mossy-looking plants were patchily sprinkled around.

"Look! Right here!" Doris' voice.

Lee swiveled his head and saw her clumsily sinking to her knees, like an armor-plated elephant getting down ponderously from a circus trick. She knelt beside a fern-like plant. They all walked over and helped her to photograph it, snip a leaf from it, probe its root system.

"Might as well stop here tonight," Grote said. "I'll take the first watch."

"Can't we set the scanners to give an alarm if anything approaches?" Marlene asked. "There's nothing here dangerous enough to—"

"I want one of us awake at all times," Grote said firmly. "And nobody outside of his suits."

"There's no place like home," Doris muttered. "But after a while even your own smell gets to you."

The women laid down, locking the suits into roughly reclining positions. To Lee they looked like oversized beetles that had gotten stuck on their backs. It didn't look possible for them to ever get up again. Then another thought struck him, and he chuckled to himself. *Super chastity belts.*

He sat down, cranked the suit's torso section back to a comfortable reclining angle, and tried to doze off. He was dreaming of the towers on Titan again when Grote's voice in his earphones woke him.

"Is it my turn?" he asked groggily.

"Not yet. But turn off your transmitter. You were groaning in your sleep. Don't want to wake up the women, do you?"

Lee took the second watch and simply stayed awake until daybreak without bothering any of the others. They began marching toward the sea.

The hills descended only slightly into a rolling plateau that went on until they reached the bluffs that overlooked the sea. A few hundred feet down was a narrow strip of beach, with the breakers surging in.

"This is as far as we go," Grote said.

The women spent the morning collecting plant samples. Marlene found a few insects and grew more excited over them than Doris had been about the shrubbery. Lee and Grote walked along the edge of the cliffs looking for a good place to set up their cameras.

"You're sure this is the area where they were seen?" Lee asked.

Walking alongside him, the engineer turned his head inside his plastic helmet. Lee could see he was edgy too.

"I know how to read a map."

"Sorry, I'm just anxious—"

"So am I."

They walked until Sirius was almost directly overhead, without seeing anything except the tireless sea, the beach, and the spongy-looking plants that huddled close to the ground.

"Not even a damned tree," Grote grumbled.

They turned back and headed for the spot where they had left the women. Far up the beach, Lee saw a tiny dark spot.

"What's that?"

Grote stared for a few moments. "Probably a rock." But he touched a button on the chest of his suit.

Lee did the same, and an electro-optical viewpiece slid down in front of his eyes. Turning a dial on the suit's control panel, he tried to focus on the spot. It wavered in the heat currents of the early afternoon, blurred and uncertain. Then it seemed to jump out of view.

Lee punched the button and the lens slid away from his eyes. "It's moving!" he shouted, and started to run.

He heard Grote's heavy breathing as the engineer followed him, and they both nearly flew in their power suits along the edge of the cliffs.

It was a man! No, not one, Lee saw, but two of them walking along the beach, their feet in the foaming water.

"Get down you bloody fool," he heard Grote shrilling at him.

He dove headlong, bounced, cracked the back of his head against the helmet's plastic, then banged his chin on the soft inner lining of the collar.

"Don't want them to see, do you?" Grote was whispering now.

"They can't hear us, for God's sake," Lee said into his suit radiophone.

They wormed their way to the cliff's edge again and watched. The two men seemed to be dressed in black. *Or are they black-skinned and naked?* Lee wondered.

After a hurried council, they unslung one of the video cameras and its power unit, set it up right there, turned it on and then backed away from the edge of the cliff. Then they ran as hard as they could, staying out of sight of the beach, with the remaining camera. They passed the startled women and breathlessly shouted out their find. The women dropped their work and started running after them.

About a kilometer or so further on they dropped to all fours again and painfully crawled to the edge once more. Grote hissed the women into silence as they hunched up beside him.

The beach was empty now.

"Do you think they saw us?" Lee asked.

"Don't know."

Lee used the electro-optics again and scanned the beach. "No sign of them."

"Their footprints," Grote snapped. "Look there."

The trails of two very human-looking sets of footprints marched straight into the water. All four of them searched the sea for hours, but saw nothing. Finally, they decided to set up the other camera. It was turning dark by the time they finished.

"We've got to get back to the car," Grote said, wearily, when they finished. "There's not enough food in the suits for another day."

"I'll stay here," Lee replied. "You can bring me more supplies tomorrow."

"No. If there's anything to see, the cameras will pick it up. Chien is monitoring them back at the car, and the whole crew of the ship must he watching the view."

Lee saw there was no sense arguing. Besides, he was bone tired. But he knew he'd be back again as soon as he could get there.

✳ VI ✳

"WELL, IT SETTLES a three-hundred-year-old argument," Aaron Hatfield said as he watched the viewscreen.

The biochemist and Lee were sitting in the main workroom of the ship's Sirius globe, watching the humanoids as televised by the cameras on the cliffs. Charnovsky was on the other side of the room, at a workbench, flashing rock chips with a laser so that a spectrometer could analyze their chemical composition.

The other outsiders were traveling in the skimmer again, collecting more floral and insect specimens.

"What argument?" Lee asked.

Hatfield shifted in his chair, making the webbing creak. "About the human form . . . whether it's an accident or a result of evolutionary selection. From *them*," he nodded toward the screen, "I'd say it's no accident."

One camera was on wide-field focus and showed a group of three of the men. They were wading hip-deep in the surf, carrying slender rods high above their heads to keep them free of the surging waves.

The other camera was fixed on a close-up view of three women standing on the beach, watching their men. Like the men, they were completely naked and black-skinned. They looked human in every detail.

Every morning they appeared on the beach, often carrying the rods, but sometimes not. Lee concluded that they must live in caves cut into the cliffs. The rods looked like simple bone spears but even under the closest focus of the cameras he couldn't be sure.

"They're not Negroid," he muttered, more to himself than anyone listening.

"It's hard to tell, isn't it?" Hatfield asked.

Nodding, Lee said, "They just don't look like terrestrial Negroes, except for their skin coloring. And that's an adaptation to Sirius' brightness. Plenty of ultraviolet, too."

Charnovsky came over and pulled up a chair. "So. Have they caught any fish this morning?"

"Not yet," Lee answered.

Jabbing a stubby finger toward the screen, the Russian asked, "Are these the geniuses who built the machines on Titan? Fishing with bone spears? They don't make much of an enemy."

"They could have been our enemy," Lee answered, forcing a thin smile. He was getting accustomed to Charnovsky's needling, but not reconciled to it.

The geologist shook his head sadly. "Take the advice of an older man, dear friend, and disabuse yourself of this idea. Statistics are a powerful tool, Sid. The chances of this particular race being the one that built on Titan are fantastically high. And the chances—"

"What're the chances that two intelligent races will both evolve along the same physical lines?" Lee snapped.

Charnovsky shrugged. "We have two known races. They are both human in form. The chances must be excellent."

Lee turned back to watch the viewscreen, then asked Hatfield, "Aaron, the biochemistry here is very similar to Earth's, isn't it?"

"Very close."

"I mean . . . I could eat local food and be nourished by it? I wouldn't be poisoned or anything like that?"

"Well," Hatfield said, visibly thinking it out as he spoke, "as far as the structure of the proteins and other foodstuffs are concerned . . . yes,

I guess you could get away with eating it. The biochemistry is basically the same as ours, as nearly as I've been able to tell. But so are terrestrial shellfish, and they make me deathly ill. You see, there're all sorts of enzymes, and microbial parasites, and viruses . . ."

"We've been living with the local bugs for months now," Lee said. "We're adapted to them, aren't we?"

"You know what they say about visiting strange places: don't drink the water."

On the viewscreen, one of the natives struck into the water with his spear, and instantly the water began to boil with the thrashing of some sea creature. The other two men drove their spears home, and the thrashing died. They lifted a four-foot-long fish out of the water and started back for the beach, carrying it triumphantly over their heads. The camera's autotracker kept the picture on them. The women on the beach were jumping and clapping with joy.

"Damn," Lee said softly. "They're as human as we are."

"And obviously representative of a high technical civilization," Charnovsky said.

"Survivors of one, maybe," Lee answered. "Their culture might have been wiped out by the Pup's explosion or by war."

"Now it gets even more dramatic: two cultures destroyed, ours *and* theirs."

"All right, go ahead and laugh," Lee said. "I won't be able to prove anything until I get to live with them."

"Until what?" Hatfield said.

"Until I go out there and meet them face to face, learn their language, their culture, live with them."

"Live with them?" Rasmussen looked startled; the first time Lee had seen him jarred. The captain's monomolecular biosuit gave his craggy face a faint sheen, like the beginnings of a sweat.

They were sitting around a circular table in the conference room of the Sirius globe: the six "outsiders," Grote, Chien, Captain Rasmussen, Pascual and Lehman.

"Aren't you afraid they might put you in a pot and boil you?" Grote asked, grinning.

"I don't think they have pots. Or fire, for that matter," Lee countered.

The laugh turned on Grote.

Lee went on quietly, "I've checked it out with Aaron, here. There's no biochemical reason why I couldn't survive in the native environment. Doris and Marlene have agreed to gather the same types of food we've seen the humanoids carrying, and I'll go on a strictly native diet for a few weeks before I go to live with them."

Lehman hunched forward, from across the table, and asked Lee, "About the dynamics of having a representative of our relatively advanced culture step into their primitive—"

"I won't be representing an advanced culture to them," Lee said. "I intend to be just as naked and toolless as they are. And just as black. Aaron can inject me with the proper enzymes to turn my skin black."

"That would be necessary in any event if you don't want to be sunburned to death," Pascual said.

Hatfield added, "You'll also need contact lenses that'll screen out the UV and protect your eyes."

They spent an hour discussing all the physical precautions he would have to take. Lee kept glancing at Rasmussen. *The idea's slipping out from under his control.* The captain watched each speaker in turn, squinting with concentration and sinking deeper and deeper into his Viking scowl. Then, when Lee was certain that the captain could no longer object, Rasmussen finally spoke up: "One more question. Are you willing to give up an eye for this mission of yours?"

"What do you mean?"

The captain's hands seemed to wander loosely without a mug of beer to tie them down. "Well, you seem to be willing to run a good deal of personal risk to live with these . . . eh, people. From the expedition's viewpoint, you will also be risking our only anthropologist, you know. I think the wise thing to do, in that case, would be to have a running record of everything you see and hear."

Lee nodded.

"So we can swap one of your eyes for a TV camera and plant a transmitter somewhere in your skull. I'm sure there's enough empty space in your head to accommodate it." The captain chuckled toothily at his joke.

"We can't do an eye procedure here," Pascual argued. "It's too risky."

"I understand that Dr. Tanaka is quite expert in that field," the captain said. "And naturally we would preserve the eye to restore it afterward. Unless, of course, Professor Lee—" He let the suggestion dangle.

Lee looked at them sitting around the big table: Rasmussen, trying to look noncommittal; Pascual, upset and nearly angry; Lehman, staring intently right back into Lee's eyes.

You're just trying to force me to back down, Lee thought of Rasmussen. Then, of Lehman, *And if I don't back down, you'll be convinced that I'm crazy.*

For a long moment there was no sound in the crowded conference room except the faint whir of the air blower.

"All right," Lee said. "If Tanaka is willing to tackle the surgery, so am I."

✳ VII ✳

WHEN LEE RETURNED TO HIS CUBICLE, the message light under the phone screen was blinking red. He flopped on the bunk, propped a pillow under his head, and asked the computer, "What's the phone message?"

The screen lit up: PLS CALL DR. LEHMAN. *My son, the psychiatrist.* "Okay," he said aloud, "get him."

A moment later Lehman's tanned face filled the screen.

"I was expecting you to call," Lee said.

The psychiatrist nodded, "You agreed to pay a big price just to get loose among the natives."

"Tanaka can handle the surgery," he answered evenly.

"It'll take a month before you are fit to leave the ship again."

"You know what our Viking captain says . . . we'll stay here as long as the beer holds out."

Lehman smiled. *Professional technique,* Lee thought. "Sid, do you really think you can mingle with these people without causing any cultural impact? Without changing them?"

Shrugging, he answered, "I don't know. I hope so. As far as we know, they're the only humanoid group on the planet. They may have never seen a stranger before."

"That's what I mean," Lehman said. "Don't you feel that—"

"Let's cut the circling, Rich. You know why I want to see them first-hand. If we had the time I'd study them remotely for a good long while before trying any contact. But it gets back to the beer supply. We've got to squeeze everything we can out of them in a little more than four years."

"There will be other expeditions, after we return to Earth and tell them about these people."

"Probably so. But they may be too late."

"Too late for what?"

His neck was starting to hurt; Lee hunched up to a sitting position on the bunk. "Figure it out. There can't be more than about fifty people in the group we've been watching. I've only seen a couple of children. And there aren't any other humanoid groups on the planet. That means they're dying out. This gang is the last of their kind. By the time another expedition gets here, there might not be any of them left."

For once, Lehman looked surprised. "Do you really think so?"

"Yes. And before they die, we have to get some information out of them."

"What do you mean?

"They might not be natives of this planet," Lee said, forcing himself to speak calmly, keeping his face a mask, freezing any emotion inside him. "They probably came from somewhere else. That elsewhere is the home of the people who built the Titan machine . . . their real home. We have got to find out where it *is*." *Flawless logic.*

Lehman tried to smile again. "That's assuming your theory about an ancient war is right."

"Yes. Assuming I'm right."

"Assume you *are*," Lehman said. "And assume you find what you're looking for. Then what? Do you just take off and go back to Earth? What happens to the people here?"

"I don't know," Lee said, ice-cold inside. "The main problem will be how to deal with the home world of their people."

"But the people here, do we just let them die out?"

"Maybe. I guess so."

Lehman's smile was completely gone now; his face didn't look pleasant at all.

It took much more than a month. The surgery was difficult. And beneath all the pain was Lee's rooted fear that he might never have his sight fully restored again. While he was recovering, before he was allowed out of his infirmary bed, Hatfield turned his skin black with a series of enzyme injections. He was also fitted for a single quartz contact lens.

Once he was up and around, Marlene followed him constantly. Finally she said, "You're even better looking with black skin; it makes you more mysterious. And the prosthetic eye looks exactly like your own. It even moves like the natural one."

Rasmussen still plodded. Long after Lee felt strong enough to get going again, he was still confined to the ship. When his complaints grew loud enough, they let him start on a diet of native foods. The medics and Hatfield hovered around him while he spent a miserable week with dysentery. Then it passed. But it took a while to build up his strength again; all he had to eat now were fish, insects, and pulpy greens.

After more tests, conferences, a two-week trial run out by the Glass Mountains, and then still more exhaustive physical exams, Rasmussen at last agreed to let Lee go.

Grote took him out in the skimmer, skirting the long way around the Glass Mountains, through the surf and out onto the gently billowing sea. They kept far enough out at sea for the beach to be constantly beyond their horizon.

When night fell, Grote nosed the skimmer landward. They came ashore around midnight, with the engines clamped down to near silence, a few kilometers up the beach from the humanoids' site. Grote, encased in a powersuit, walked with him part way and buried a relay transceiver in the sand, to pick up the signals from the camera and radio imbedded in Lee's skull.

"Good luck." His voice was muffled by the helmet.

Lee watched him plod mechanically back into the darkness. He strained to hear the skimmer as it turned and slipped back into the sea, but he could neither see nor hear it.

He was alone on the beach.

Clouds were drifting landward, riding smoothly overhead. The breeze on the beach, though, was blowing warmly out of the desert, spilling over the bluffs and across the beach, out to sea. The sky was bright with the all-night twilight glow, even though the clouds blotted out most of the stars. Along the foot of the cliffs, though, it was deep black. Except for the wind, there wasn't a sound: not a bird nor a nocturnal cat, not even an insect's chirrup.

Lee stayed near the water's edge. He wasn't cold, even though naked. Still, he could feel himself trembling.

Grote's out there, he told himself. *If you need him, he can come rolling up the beach in ten minutes.*

But he knew he was alone.

The clouds thickened and began to sprinkle rain, a warm, soft shower. Lee blinked the drops away from his eyes and walked slowly, a hundred paces one direction, then a hundred paces back again.

The rain stopped as the sea horizon started turning bright. The clouds wafted away. The sky lightened, first gray, then almost milky white. Lee looked toward the base of the cliffs. Dark shadows dotted the rugged cliff face. Caves. Some of them were ten feet or more above the sand.

Sirius edged a limb above the horizon, and Lee, squinting, turned away from its brilliance. He looked back at the caves again, feeling the warmth of the hot star's might on his back.

The first ones out of the cave were two children. They tumbled out of the same cave, off to Lee's left, giggling and running.

When they saw Lee, they stopped dead. As though someone had turned them off. Lee could feel his heart beating as they stared at him. He stood just as still as they did, perhaps a hundred meters from them. They looked about five and ten years old, he judged. *If their lifespans are the same as ours.*

The taller of the two boys took a step toward Lee, then turned and ran back into the cave. The younger boy followed him.

For several minutes nothing happened. Then Lee heard voices echoing from inside the cave. Angry? Frightened? *They're not laughing.*

Four men appeared at the mouth of the cave. Their hands were empty. They simply stood there and gaped at him, from the shadows of the cave's mouth.

Now we'll start learning their customs about strangers, Lee said to himself.

Very deliberately, he turned away from them and took a few steps up the beach. Then he stopped, turned again, and walked back to his original spot.

Two of the men disappeared inside the cave. The other two stood there. Lee couldn't tell what the expressions on their faces meant. Suddenly other people appeared at a few of the other cave entrances. *They're interconnected.*

Lee tried a smile and waved. There were women among the onlookers now, and a few children. One of the boys who saw him first—at least, it looked like him—started chattering to an adult. The man silenced him with a brusque gesture.

It was getting hot. Lee could feel perspiration dripping along his ribs as Sirius climbed above the horizon and shone straight at the cliffs. Slowly, he squatted down on the sand.

A few of the men from the first cave stepped out onto the beach. Two of them were carrying bone spears. Others edged out from their caves. They slowly drew together, keeping close to the rocky cliff wall, and started talking in low, earnest tones.

They're puzzled. All right. Just play it cool. Don't make any sudden moves.

He leaned forward slightly and traced a triangle on the sand with one finger.

When he looked up again, a grizzled, white-haired man had taken a step or two away from the conference group. Lee smiled at him, and the elder froze in his tracks. With a shrug, Lee looked back at the first cave. The boy was still there, with a woman standing beside him, gripping his shoulder. Lee waved and smiled. The boy's hand fluttered momentarily.

The old man said something to the group, and one of the younger men stepped out to join him. Neither held a weapon. They walked to within a few meters of Lee, and the old man said something, as loudly and bravely as he could.

Lee bowed his head. "Good morning. I am Professor Sidney Lee of the University of Ottawa, which is one hell of a long way from here."

They squatted down and started talking, both of them at once, pointing to the caves and then all around the beach and finally out to sea.

Lee held up his hands and said, "It ought to be clear to you that I'm from someplace else, and I don't speak your language. Now if you want to start teaching me—"

They shook their heads, talked to each other, said something else to Lee.

Lee smiled at them and waited for them to stop talking. When they did, he pointed to himself and said very clearly, "Lee."

He spent an hour at it, repeating only that one syllable, no matter what they said to him or to each other. The heat was getting fierce; Sirius was a blue flame searing his skin, baking the juices out of him.

The younger man got up and, with a shake of his head, spoke a few final words to the elder and walked back to the group that still stood knotted by the base of the cliff. The old man rose, slowly and stiffly. He beckoned to Lee to do the same.

As Lee got to his feet he saw the other men start to head out for the surf. A few boys followed behind, carrying several bone spears for their—what? Fathers? Older brothers?

As *long* as *the spears are for the fish and not me,* Lee thought.

The old man was saying something to him. Pointing toward the caves. He took a step in that direction, then motioned for Lee to come along. Lee hesitated. The old man smiled a toothless smile and repeated his invitation.

Grinning back at him in realization, Lee said aloud, "Okay. If you're not scared of me, I guess I don't have to be scared of you."

✳ VIII ✳

IT TOOK MORE THAN A YEAR before Lee learned their language well enough to understand roughly what they were saying. It was an odd language, sparse and practically devoid of pronouns.

His speaking of their words made the adults smile, when they thought he couldn't see them doing it. The children still giggled at his speech, but the old man—Ardraka—always scolded them when they did.

They called the planet Makta and Lee saw to it that Rasmussen entered that as its official name in the expedition's log. He made a point of walking the beach alone one night each week, to talk with the others at the ship and make a personal report. He quickly found that most of what he saw, heard and said inside the caves never got out to the relay transceiver buried up the beach; the cliff's rock walls were too much of a barrier.

Ardraka was the oldest of the clan and the nominal chief. His son, Ardra, was the younger man who had also come out to talk with Lee that first day. Ardra actually gave most of the orders. Ardraka could overrule him whenever he chose to, but he seldom exercised the right.

There were only forty-three people in the clan, nearly half of them elderly looking. Eleven were pre-adolescent children; two of them infants. There were no obvious pregnancies. Ardraka must have been about fifty, judging by his oldest son's apparent age. But the old man had the wrinkled, sunken look of an eighty-year-old. The people themselves had very little idea of time beyond the basic rhythm of night and day.

They came out of the caves only during the early morning and evening hours. The blazing midday heat of Sirius was too much for them to face. They ate crustaceans and the small fish that dwelt in the shallows along the beach, insects, and the grubby vegetation that clung to the base of the cliffs. Occasionally they found a large fish that had blundered into the shallows; then they feasted.

They had no wood, no metal, no fire. Their only tools were from the precious bones of the rare big fish, and hand-worked rock.

They died of disease and injury, and aged prematurely from poor diet and overwork. They had to search constantly for food, especially since half their day was taken away from them by Sirius' blowtorch heat. They were more apt to be prowling the beach at night, hunting seaworms and crabs, than by daylight. *Grote and I damn near barged right into them,* Lee realized after watching a few of the night gathering sessions.

There were some dangers. One morning he was watching one of the teenaged boys, a good swimmer, venture out past the shallows in search of fish. A sharklike creature found him first.

When he screamed, half a dozen men grabbed spears and dove into the surf. Lee found himself dashing into the water alongside them, empty-handed. He swam out to the youngster, already dead, sprawled face down in the water, half of him gone, blood staining the swells. Lee helped to pull the remains back to shore.

There wasn't anything definite, no one said a word to him about it, but their attitude toward him changed. He was fully accepted now. He hadn't saved the boy's life, hadn't shown uncommon bravery. But he had shared a danger with them, and a sorrow.

Wheel the horse inside the gates of Troy, Lee found himself thinking. *Nobody ever told you to beware of* men *bearing gifts.*

After he got to really understand their language Lee found that Ardraka often singled him out for long talks. It was almost funny. There was something that the old man was fishing for, just as Lee was trying to learn where these people *really* came from.

They were sitting in the cool darkness of the central cave, deep inside the cliff. All the outer caves channeled back to this single large chamber, high-roofed and moss-floored, its rocks faintly phosphorescent. It was big enough to hold four or five times the clan's present number. It was midday. Most of the people were sleeping. A few of the children, off to the rear of the cave, were scratching pictures on the packed bare earth with pointed, fist-sized rocks.

Lee sat with his back resting against a cool stone wall. The sleepers were paired off, man and mate, for the most part. The unmated teenagers slept apart, with the older couples between them. As far as Lee could judge, the couples paired permanently, although the teens played the game about as freely as they could.

Ardraka was dozing beside him. Lee settled back and tried to turn off his thoughts, but the old man said: "Lee is not asleep?"

"No, Lee is not," he answered.

"Ardraka has seen that Lee seldom sleeps," Ardraka said.

"That is true."

"Is it that Lee does not need to sleep as Ardraka does?"

Lee shook his head. "No, Lee needs sleep as much as Ardraka or any man."

"This . . . place that Lee comes from. Lee says it is beyond the sea?"

"Yes, far beyond."

In the faint light from the gleaming rocks, the old man's face looked troubled, deep in difficult thought.

"And there are men and women living in Lee's place, men and women like the people here?"

Lee nodded.

"And how did Lee come here? Did Lee swim across the sea?"

They had been through this many times. "Lee came around the edge of the sea, walking on land just as Ardraka would."

Laughing softly, the old man said, "Ardraka is too feeble now for such a walk. Ardra could make such a walk."

"Yes, Ardra can."

"Ardraka has tried to dream of Lee's place, and Lee's people. But such dreams do not come."

"Dreams are hard to command," Lee said.

"Yes, truly."

"And what of Ardraka and the people here?" Lee asked. "Is this the only place where such men and women live?"

"Yes. It is the best place to live. All other places are death."

"There are no men and women such as Ardraka and the people here living in another place?"

The old man thought hard a moment, then smiled a wrinkled toothless smile. "Surely Lee jokes. Lee knows that Lee's people live in another place."

We've been around that bush before. Trying another tack, he asked, "Have Ardraka's people *always* lived in this place? Did Ardraka's father live here?"

"Yes, of course."

"And his father?"

A nod.

"And all the fathers, from the beginning of the people? All lived here, always?"

A shrug. "No man knows."

"Have there always been this many people living here?" Lee asked. "Did Ardraka's people ever fill this cave when they slept here?"

"Oh yes. When Ardraka was a boy, many men and women slept in the outer caves, since there was no room for them here. And when Ardraka's father was young, men and women even slept in the lower caves."

"Lower caves?"

Ardraka nodded. "Below this one, deeper inside the ground. No man or woman has been in them since Ardraka became chief."

"Why is that?"

The old man evaded Lee's eyes. "They are not needed."

"May Lee visit these lower caves?"

"Perhaps," Ardraka said. After a moment's thought, he added, "Children have been born and grown to manhood and died since any man set foot in those caves. Perhaps they are gone now. Perhaps Ardraka does not remember how to find them."

"Lee would like to visit the lower caves."

Late that night he walked the beach alone, under the glowing star-poor sky, giving his weekly report back to the ship.

"He's been cagy about the lower caves," Lee said as the outstretched fingers of surf curled around his ankles.

"Why should he be so cautious?" It was Marlene's voice. She was taking the report this night.

"Because he's no fool, that's why. These people have never seen a stranger before . . . not for generations, at least. Therefore their behavior toward me is original, not instinctive. If he's leery of showing me the caves, it's for some reason that's fresh in his mind, not some hoary tribal taboo."

"Then what do you intend to do?"

"I'm not sure yet—" Lee turned to head back down the beach and saw Ardra standing twenty paces behind him.

"Company," he snapped. "Talk to you later. Keep listening."

Advancing toward him, Ardra said, "Many nights, Ardra has seen Lee leave the cave and walk on the beach. Tonight Lee was talking, but Lee was alone. Does Lee speak to a man or woman that Ardra cannot see?"

His tone was flat, factual, neither frightened nor puzzled. It was too dark to really make out the expression on his face, but he sounded almost casual.

"Lee is alone," he answered as calmly as he could. "There is no man or woman here with Lee. Except Ardra."

"But Lee speaks and then is silent. And then Lee speaks again."

He knows a conversation when he hears one, even if it's only one side of it and in a strange language.

Ardra suggested, "Perhaps Lee speaks to men and women from Lee's place, which is far from the sea?"

"Does Ardra believe that Lee can speak to men and women far away from this place?"

"Ardra believes that is what Lee does at night on the beach. Lee speaks with the Karta."

"*Karta?* What is the meaning of *karta?*"

"It is an ancient word. It means men and women who live in another place."

Others, Lee translated to himself. "Yes," he said to Ardra, "Lee speaks to the others."

Ardra's breath seemed to catch momentarily, then he said with deliberate care, "Lee speaks with the Others." His voice had an edge of steel to it now.

What have I stepped into?

"It is time to be sleeping, not walking the beach," Ardra said, in a tone that Lee knew was a command. And he started walking toward the caves.

Lee outweighed the chief's son by a good twenty pounds and was some ten centimeters taller. But he had seen the speed and strength in Ardra's wiry frame and knew the difference in reaction times that the fifteen years between them made. So he didn't run or fight; he followed Ardra back to the caves and obediently went to sleep. And all the night Ardra stayed awake and watched over him.

⁎ IX ⁎

The next morning, when the men went out to fish and the women to gather greens, Ardra took Lee's arm and led him toward the back of the central cave. Ardraka and five other elders were waiting for them. They all looked very grim. Only then did Lee realize that Ardra was carrying a spear in his other hand.

They were sitting in a ragged semicircle, their backs to what looked like a tunnel entrance, their eyes hard on Lee. He sat at their focus, with Ardra squatting beside him.

"Lee," Ardraka began without preliminaries, "why is it that Lee wishes to see the lower caves?"

The question caught him by surprise. "Because . . . Lee wishes to learn more about Ardraka's people. Lee comes from far away, and knows little of Ardraka's people."

"Is it true," one of the elders asked, "that Lee speaks at night with the Others?" His inflection made the word sound special, fearful, ominous.

"Lee speaks to the men and women of the place where Lee came from. It is like the way Ardraka speaks to Ardraka's grandfather . . . in a dream."

"But Ardraka sleeps when doing this, Lee is awake." Ardra broke in, "Lee says Lee's people live beyond the sea. Beyond the sea is the sky. Do Lee's people live in the sky?"

Off the edge of the world, just like Columbus. "Yes," he admitted. "Lee's people live in the sky—"

"*See!*" Ardra shouted. "Lee is of the Others!"

The councilmen physically backed away from him. Even Ardraka seemed shaken.

"Lee is of the Others," Ardra repeated. "Lee must be killed, before he kills Ardraka's people!"

"Kill?" Lee felt stunned. he had never heard any of them speak of violence before. "Why should Lee kill the people here?"

They were all babbling at once. Ardraka raised his hand for silence.

"To kill a man is very serious," he said painfully. "It is not certain that Lee is of the Others."

"Lee says it with Lee's own mouth!" Ardra insisted. "Why else did Lee come here? Why does Lee want to see the lower caves?"

Ardraka glowered at his son, and the younger man stopped. "The council must be certain before it acts."

Struggling to keep his voice calm, Ardra ticked off on his fingers, "Lee says Lee's people live in the sky. The Others live in the sky. Lee wishes to see the lower caves. Why? To see if more of Ardraka's people are living there, so that he can kill *all* the people!"

The council members murmured and glanced at him fearfully. *Starting to look like a lynch jury.*

"Wait," Lee said. "There is more to the truth than what Ardra says. Lee's people live in the sky . . . that is true. But that does not mean that Lee's people are the Others. The sky is wide and large . . . wider than the sea, by far. Many different peoples can live in the sky."

Ardraka nodded, his brows knitted in concentration. "But, Lee, if both Lee's people and the Others live in the sky, why have not the Others destroyed Lee's people as they destroyed Ardraka's ancestors?"

Lee felt his stomach drop out of him. *So that's it!*

"Yes," one of the councilmen said. "The Others live far from this land, yet the Others came here and destroyed Ardraka's forefathers and all the works of such men and women."

"Tell Lee what happened," he said, stalling for time to work out answers. "Lee knows nothing about the Others." *Not from your side of the war, anyway.*

Ardraka glanced around at the council members sitting on both sides of him. They looked uncertain, wary, still afraid. Ardra, beside Lee, had the fixed glare of a born prosecutor.

"Lee is not of Ardraka's people," the younger man said, barely controlling the fury in his voice. "Lee must be of the Others. There are no people except Ardraka's people and the Others!"

"Perhaps that is not so." Ardraka said. "True, Ardraka has always thought it to be this way, but Lee looks like an ordinary man, not like the Others."

Ardra huffed. "No living man has seen the Others. How can Ardraka say—"

"Because Ardraka has seen pictures of the Others," the chief said quietly.

"Pictures?" They were startled.

"Yes. In the deepest cave, where only the chief can go . . . and the chief's son. Ardraka had thought for a long time that soon Ardra should see the deepest cave. But no longer. Ardra must see the cave now."

The old man got up, stiffly, to his feet. His son was visibly trembling with eagerness.

"May Lee also see the pictures?" Lee asked.

They all began to protest, but Ardraka said firmly, "Lee has been accused of being of the Others. Lee stands in peril of death. It is right that Lee should see the pictures."

The council members muttered among themselves. Ardra glowered, then bent down and reached for the spear he had left at his feet. Lee smiled to himself. *If those pictures give him the slightest excuse, he's going to ram that thing through me. You'd make a good sheriff: kill first, then ask questions.*

Far from having forgotten his way to the deeper caves, Ardraka threaded through a honeycomb of tunnels and chambers, always picking the path that slanted downward. Lee sensed that they were spiraling deeper and deeper into the solid rock of the cliffs, far below the sea level. The walls were crusted, and a thick mat of dust clung to the ground. But everything shone with the same faint luminosity as the upper caves, and beneath the dust the footing felt more like pitted metal than rock.

Finally Ardraka stopped. They were standing in the entryway to a fairly small chamber. The lighting was very dim. Lee stood behind Ardraka and felt Ardra's breath on his back.

"This is the place," Ardraka said solemnly. His voice echoed slightly.

They slowly entered the chamber. Ardraka walked to the farthest wall and wordlessly pointed to a jumble of lines scrawled at about eye level. The cave was dark, but the lines of the drawing glowed slightly brighter than the wall itself.

Gradually, Lee pieced the picture together. It was crude, so crude that it was hard to understand. But there were stick figures of men that seemed to be running, and rough outlines of what might be buildings, with curls of smoke rising up from them. Above them all were circular things, ships, with dots for ports. Harsh jagged lines were streaking out of them and toward the stick figures.

"Men and women," Ardraka said, in a reverent whisper as he pointed to the stick drawings. "The men and women of the time of Ardraka's farthest ancestors. And *here*—" his hand flashed to the circles— "are the Others."

Even in the dim light, Lee could see Ardra's face gaping at the picture. "The Others," he said, his voice barely audible.

"Look at Lee," Ardraka commanded his son. "Does Lee look like the Others, or like a man?"

Ardra seemed about to crumble. He said shakily, "Lee . . . Ardra has misjudged Lee. Ardra is ashamed."

"There is no shame," Lee said. "Ardra has done no harm. Ardra was trying to protect Ardraka's people." *And besides, you were right.*

Turning to Ardraka, Lee asked. "Is this all that you know of the Others?"

"Ardraka knows that the Others killed the people of Ardraka's forefathers. Before the Others came, Ardraka's ancestors lived in splendor: their living places covered the land everywhere; they swam the seas without fear of any creature of the deep; they leaped through the sky and laughed at the winds and storms; every day was bright and good and there was no night. Then the Others came and destroyed everything. The Others turned the sky to fire and brought night. Only the people in the deepest cave survived. This was the deepest cave. Only the people of Ardraka escaped the Others."

We destroyed this world, Lee told himself. *An interstellar war, eons ago. We destroyed each other, old man. Only you've been destroyed for good, and we climbed back.*

"One more thing remains," Ardraka said. He walked into the shadows on the other end of the room and pushed open a door. A *door!* It was metal, Lee could feel as he went past it. There was another chamber, larger.

A storeroom! Shelves lined the walls. Most of them empty, but here and there were boxes, containers, machinery with strange writing on it.

"These belonged to Ardraka's oldest ancestors," the chief said. "No man today knows why these things were saved here in the deepest cave. They have no purpose. They are dead. As dead as the people who put them here."

It was Lee who was trembling as they made their way up to the dwelling caves.

✳ X ✳

IT WAS A WEEK before he dared stroll the beach at night again, a week of torment, even though Ardra never gave him the slightest reason to think that he was still under suspicion.

They were just as stunned as he was when he told them about it.

"We killed them," he whispered savagely at them, back in the comfort of the ship. "We destroyed them. Maybe we even made the Pup explode, to wipe them out completely."

"That's . . . farfetched," Rasmussen answered. But his voice sounded lame. "What do we do now?"

"I want to see those artifacts."

"Yes, but how?"

Lee said, "I can take you down to the cave, if we can put the whole clan to sleep for a few hours. Maybe gas."

"That could work," Rasmussen agreed.

"A soporific gas?" Pascual's soft tenor rang incredulously in Lee's ears. "But we haven't the faintest idea of how it might affect them."

"It's the only way," Lee said. "You can't dig your way into the cave. Even if you could, they would hear it, and you'd be discovered."

"But gas . . . it could kill them all."

"They're all dead right now," Lee snapped. "Those artifacts are the only possible clue to their early history."

Rasmussen decided. "We'll do it."

Lee slept less than ever the next few nights, and when he did he dreamed, but no longer about the buildings on Titan. Now he dreamed of the ships of an ancient Earth, huge round ships that spat fire on the cities and people of Makta. He dreamed of the Pup exploding and showering the planet with fire, blowing off the atmosphere, boiling the oceans, turning mountains into glass slag, killing every living thing on the surface of the world, leaving the planet bathed in a steam cloud, its ground ruptured with angry new volcanoes.

It was a rainy dark night when you could hardly see ten meters beyond the cave's mouth that they came. Lee heard their voices in his head as they drove the skimmer up onto the beach and clambered down from it and headed for the caves. Inside the caves, the people were asleep, sprawled innocently on the damp musty ground.

Out of the rain a huge, bulky metal shape materialized, walking with exaggerated caution.

"Hello, Sid," Jerry Grote's voice said in his head, and the white metal shape raised a hand in greeting.

The Others, Lee thought as he watched four more powersuited figures appear in the dark rain.

He stepped out of the cave, the rain a cold shock to his bare skin. "Bring the stuff?"

Grote hitched a gauntleted thumb at one of the others. "Pascual's got it. He's insisting on administering the gas himself."

"Okay, but let's get it done quickly, before somebody wakes up and spots you. Who else is with you?"

"Chien, Tanaka and Stek. Tanaka can help Carlos with the anesthetic. Chien and Stek can look over the artifacts."

Lee nodded agreement.

Pascual and Tanaka spent more than an hour seeping the mildest soporific they knew of through the sleeping cave. Lee fidgeted outside on the beach, in the rain, waiting for them to finish. When Tanaka finally told them it was safe to go through, he hurried past the sprawled bodies, scarcely seeing Pascual, still inside his cumbersome suit, patiently recording medical analyses of each individual.

Even with the suit lamps to light the corridors, it was hard to retrace his steps down to the lowest level of the ancient shelter. But when he got to the storeroom, Lee heard Stek break into a long string of Polish exultation at the sight of the artifacts.

The three suited figures holographed, x-rayed, took radiation counts, measured, weighed, every piece on the ancient shelves. They touched nothing directly, but lifted each piece with loving tenderness in a portable magnetic grapple.

"This one," Stek told Lee, holding a hand-size, oddly angular instrument in mid-air with the grapple, "we must take with us."

"Why?"

"Look at it," the physicist said. "If it's not an astronautical sextant or something close to it, I'll eat Charnovsky's rocks for a month."

The instrument didn't look impressive to Lee. It had a lens at one end, a few dials at the other. Most of it was just an angular metal box, with strange printing on it.

"You want to know where these people originally came from?" Stek asked. "If they came from somewhere other than this planet, the information could be inside this instrument."

Lee snapped his gaze from the instrument to Stek's helmeted face.

"If it is a sextant, it must have a reference frame built into it. A tape, perhaps, that lists the stars that these people wanted to go to."

"Okay," Lee said. "Take it."

By the time they got back up to the main sleeping cave and out to the beach again, it was full daylight.

"We'll have to keep them sleeping until almost dawn tomorrow," Lee told Pascual. "Otherwise they might suspect that something unusual happened."

The doctor's face looked concerned but not worried. "We can do that without harming them, I think. But Sid, they'll be very hungry when they awake."

Lee turned to Grote. "How about taking the skimmer out and stunning a couple of big fish and towing them back here to the shallows?"

Grinning, Grote replied, "Hardly fair sport with the equipment I've got." He turned and headed for the car.

"Wait," Stek called to him. "Give me a chance to get this safely packed in a magnetic casing." And the physicist took the instrument off toward the skimmer.

"Sid," Pascual said gently, "I want you to come back with us. You need a thorough medical check."

"Medical?" Lee flashed. "Or are you fronting for Lehman?"

Pascual's eyes widened with surprise. "If you had a mirror, you would see why I want to check you. You're breaking out in skin cancers."

Instinctively, Lee looked at his hands and forearms. There were a few tiny blisters on them. And more on his belly and legs.

"It's from overexposure to the ultraviolet. Hatfield's skin-darkening didn't fully protect you."

"Is it serious?"

"I can't tell without a full examination."

Just like a doctor. "I can't leave now," Lee said. "I've got to be here when they wake up and make sure that they don't suspect they've been visited by the . . . by us."

"And if they do suspect?"

Lee shrugged. "That's something we ought to know, even if we can't do anything about it."

"Won't it be dangerous for you?"

"Maybe."

Pascual shook his head. "You mustn't stay out in the open any longer. I won't be responsible for it."

"Fine. Do you want me to sign a release form?"

Grote brought the skimmer back around sundown, with two good-size fish aboard. The others got aboard around midnight, and with a few final radioed words of parting, they drove off the beach and out to sea.

At dawn the people woke up. They looked and acted completely normally, as far as Lee could tell. It was one of the children who noticed the still sluggish fish that Grote had left in a shallow pool just outside the line of breakers. Every man in the clan splashed out, spear in hand, to get them. They feasted happily that day.

The dream was confusing. Somehow the towers on Titan and the exploding star got mixed together. Lee saw himself driving a bone spear into the sleeping form of one of the natives. The man turned on the ground, with the spear run through his body, and smiled bloodily at him. It was Ardraka.

"Sid!"

He snapped awake. It was dark, and the people were sleeping, full-bellied. He was slouched near one of the entryways to the main sleeping cave, at the mouth of a tunnel leading to the openings in the cliff wall.

"Sid, can you hear me?'

"Yes," he whispered so low that he could only feel the vibration in his throat.

"I'm up the beach about three kilometers from the relay unit. You've got to come back to the ship. Stek thinks he's figured out the instrument."

Wordlessly, silently, Lee got up and padded through the tunnel and out onto the beach. The night was clear and bright. Dawn would be coming in another hour, he judged. The sea was calm, the wind a gentle crooning as it swept down from the cliffs.

"Sid, did you hear what I said? Stek thinks he knows what the instrument is for. It's part of a pointing system for a communications setup."

"I'm on my way." He still whispered and turned to see if anyone was following him.

Grote was in a biosuit, and no one else was aboard the skimmer. The engineer jabbered about Stek's work on the instrument all the way back to the ship.

Just before they arrived, Grote suggested, "Uh, Sid, you do want to put on some coveralls, don't you?"

Two biosuited men were setting up some electronics equipment at the base of the ship's largest telescopes, dangling in a hoist sling overhead, the fierce glow of Sirius glinting off its metal barrel.

"Stek's setting up an experiment," Grote explained. Lee was bundled into a biosuit and ushered into the physicist's workroom as soon as he set foot inside the ship. Stek was a large, round, florid man with thinning red hair. Lee had hardly spoken to him at all, except for the few hours at the cave, when the physicist had been encased in a powersuit.

"It's a tracker, built to find a star in the sky and lock onto it as long as it's above the horizon," Stek said, gesturing to the instrument hovering in a magnetic grapple a few inches above his work table.

"You're sure of that?" Lee asked.

The physicist glanced at him as though he had been insulted. "There's no doubt about it. It's a tracker, and it probably was used to aim a communication antenna at their home star."

"And where is that?"

"I don't know yet. That's why I'm setting up the experiment with the telescope."

Lee walked over to the work table and stared at the instrument. "How can you be certain that it's what you say it is?"

Stek flushed, then controlled himself. With obvious patience, he explained, "X-ray probes showed that the instrument contained a magnetic memory tape. The tape was in binary code, and it was fairly simple to transliterate the code, electronically, into the ship's main computers. We didn't even have to touch the instrument physically except with electrons."

Lee made an expression that showed he was duly impressed.

Looking happier, Stek went on, "The computer cross-checked the instrument's coding and came up with correlations: attitude references were on the instrument's tape, and astronomical ephemerides, timing data and so forth. Exactly what we'd put into a communications tracker."

"But this was made by a different race of people—"

"It makes no difference," Stek said sharply. "The physics are the same. The universe is the same. The instrument can only do the job it was designed to do, and that job was to track a single star."

"Only one star?"

"Yes, that's why I'm certain it was for communicating with their home star."

"So we can find their home star after all." Lee felt the old dread returning, but with it something new, something deeper. *Those people in the caves were our enemy. And maybe their brothers, the ones who built the machines on Titan, are still out there somewhere looking for them—and for us.*

✳ **XI** ✳

LEE ATE BACK at the Sirius globe, but Pascual insisted on his remaining in a biosuit until they had thoroughly checked him out. And they wouldn't let him eat Earth food, although there was as much local food as he wanted. He didn't want much.

"You've thinned out too much," Marlene said. She was sitting next to him at the galley table.

"Ever see a fat Sirian?" He meant it as a joke; it came out waspish. Marlene dropped the subject.

The whole ship's company gathered around the telescope and the viewscreen that would show an amplified picture of the telescope's field of view. Stek bustled around, making last-minute checks and adjustments of the equipment. Rasmussen stood taller than everyone else, looking alternately worried and excited. Everyone, including Lee, was in a biosuit.

Lehman showed up at Lee's elbow. "Do you think it will work?"

"Driving the telescope from the ship's computer's version of the instrument's tape? Stek seems to think it'll go all right."

"And you?"

Lee shrugged. "The people in the caves told me what I wanted to know. Now this instrument will tell us where they came from originally."

"The home world of our ancient enemies?"

"Yes."

For once, Lehman didn't seem to be amused. "And what happens then?"

"I don't know," Lee said. "Maybe we go out and see if they are still there. Maybe we re-open the war."

"If there was a war."

"There *was*. It might still be going on, for all we know. Maybe we're just a small part of it, a skirmish."

"A skirmish that wiped out the life on this planet," Lehman said.

"And also wiped out Earth, too."

"But what about the people on this planet, Sid? What about the people in the caves?"

Lee couldn't answer.

"Do we let them die out, just because they might have been our enemies a few millennia ago?"

"They would still be our enemies, if they knew who we are," Lee said tightly.

"So we let them die?"

Lee tried to blot their faces out of his mind, to erase the memory of Ardraka and the children and Ardra apologizing shamefully and the people fishing in the morning . . .

"No," he heard himself say. "We've got to help them. They can't hurt us anymore, and we ought to help them."

Now Lehman smiled.

"It's ready," Stek said, his voice pitched high with excitement.

Sitting at the desk-size console that stood beside the telescope, he thumbed the power switch and punched a series of buttons.

The viewscreen atop the desk glowed into life, and a swarm of stars appeared. With a low hum of power, the telescope slowly turned, to the left. The scene in the viewscreen shifted. Beside the screen was a smaller display, an astronomical map with a bright luminous dot showing where the telescope was aiming.

The telescope stopped turning, hesitated, edged slightly more to the left and then made a final, barely discernible correction upward.

"It's locked on."

The viewscreen showed a meager field of stars, with a single bright pinpoint centered exactly in the middle of the screen.

"What is it, what star?"

Lee pushed forward, through the crowd that clustered around the console.

"My God," Stek said, his voice sounding hollow. "That's . . . that's the sun."

Lee felt his knees wobble. "They're from Earth!"

"It can't be," someone said.

Lee shoved past the people in front of him and stared at the map. The bright dot was fixed on the sun's location.

"They're from Earth!" he shouted. "They're part of us!"

"But how could . . ."

"They were a colony of *ours*," Lee realized. "The Others were an enemy . . . an enemy that nearly wiped them out and smashed Earth's civilization back into a stone age. The Others built those damned machines on Titan, but Ardraka's people did not. And we didn't destroy the people here . . . we're the same people!"

"But that's—"

"How can you he sure?"

"He is right," Charnovsky said, his heavy bass rumbling above the other voices. They all stopped to hear him. "There are too many coincidences any other way. These people are completely human because they came from Earth. Any other explanation is extraneous."

Lee grabbed the Russian by the shoulders. "Nick, we've got work to do! We've got to help them. We've got to introduce them to fire and metals and cereal grains—"

Charnovsky laughed. "Yes, yes, of course. But not tonight, eh? Tonight we celebrate."

"No," Lee said, realizing where he belonged. "Tonight I go back to them."

"Go back?" Marlene asked.

"Tonight I go back with a gift," Lee went on. "A gift from my people to Ardraka's. A plastic boat from the skimmer. That's a gift they'll be able to understand and use."

Lehman said, "You still don't know who built the machinery on Titan."

"We'll find out one of these days."

Rasmussen broke in, "You realize that we will have to return Earthward before the next expedition could possibly get anywhere near here."

"Some of us can wait here for the next expedition. I will, anyway."

The captain nodded and a slow grin spread across his face. "I knew you would even before we found out that your friends are really our brothers."

Lee looked around for Grote. "Come on, Jerry. Let's get moving. I want to see Ardraka's face when he sees the boat."

OLD TIMER'S GAME

Modern sports—professional and amateur—have had headaches dealing with performance enhancing drugs.
   But they ain't seen nothin' yet.

"HE'S MAKING A TRAVESTY of the game!"

White-haired Alistair Bragg was quivering with righteous wrath as he leveled a trembling finger at Vic Caruso. I felt sorry for Vic despite his huge size, or maybe because of it. He was sitting all alone up there before the panel of judges. I thought of Gulliver, giant-sized compared to the puny little Lilliputians. But tied hand and foot, helpless.

This hearing was a reporter's dream, the kind of newsmaking opportunity that comes along maybe once in a decade. Or less.

I sat at the news media table, elbow to elbow with the big, popular TV commentators and slick-haired pundits. The guys who talk like they know everything about baseball, while all they really know is what working stiffs like me put up on their teleprompters.

Old man Bragg was a shrimp, but a powerful figure in the baseball world. He owned the Cleveland Indians, who'd won the American League pennant, but then lost the World Series to the Dodgers in four straight.

Bragg wore a dark gray business suit and a bright red tie. To the unsophisticated eye he looked a little like an overweight one of Santa's elves: short, round, his face a little bloated. But whereas an elf would be cheerful and dancing-eyed, Bragg radiated barely-concealed fury.

"He's turning baseball into a freak show!" Bragg accused, still jabbing his finger in Caruso's direction. "A freak show!"

Vic Caruso had been the first-string catcher for the Oakland Athletics, one of the best damn hitters in the league, and a solid rock behind the plate with a cannon for an arm. But now he looked like an oversized boy, kind of confused by all the fuss that was being made about him. He was wearing a tan sports jacket and a white shirt with a loosely-knotted green tie that seemed six inches too short. In fact, his shirt, jacket, and brown slacks all appeared too small to contain his massive frame; it looked as if he would burst out of his clothes any minute.

Aside from his ill-fitting *ensemble,* Vic didn't look like a freak. He was a big man, true enough, tall and broad in the shoulders. His face was far from handsome: his nose was larger than it should have been, and the corners of his innocent blue eyes were crinkled from long years on sunny baseball diamonds.

He looked hurt, betrayed, as if he were the injured party instead of the accused.

The hearing wasn't a trial, exactly. The three solemn-faced men sitting behind the long table up in the front of the room weren't really judges. They were the commissioner of baseball and the heads of the National and American Leagues, about as much baseball brass (and ego) as you could fit into one room.

The issue before them would determine the future of America's Pastime.

Bragg had worked himself into a fine, red-faced fury. He had opposed every change in the game he'd ever heard of, always complaining that any change in baseball would make a travesty of the game. If he had his way, there'd be no interleague play, no designated hitter, no night baseball, and no player's union. Especially that last one. The word around the ballyard was that Bragg bled blood for every nickel he had to pay his players.

"It started with steroids, back in the Nineties," he said, ostensibly to the commissioner and the two league presidents. But he was looking at the jampacked rows of onlookers, and us news reporters, and especially at the banks of television cameras that were focused on his perspiring face.

"Steroids threatened to make a travesty of the game," said Bragg, repeating his favorite phrase. "We moved heaven and earth to drive them out of the game. Suspended players who used 'em, expunged their records, prohibited them from entering the Hall of Fame."

Caruso shifted uncomfortably in his wooden chair, making it squeak and groan as if it might collapse beneath his weight.

"Then they started using protein enhancers, natural supplements that were undetectable by normal drug screenings. All of a sudden little shortstops from Nicaragua were hitting tape-measure home runs!"

The commissioner, a grave-faced, white-haired man of great dignity, interrupted Bragg's tirade. "We are all aware of the supplements. I believe attendance figures approximately doubled when batting averages climbed so steeply."

Undeterred, Bragg went on, "So the pitchers started taking stuff to prevent joint problems. No more rotator cuff injuries; no more Tommy John surgeries. When McGilmore went twenty-six and oh we—"

"Wait a minute," the National League president said. He was a round butterball, but his moon-shaped face somehow looked menacing because of the dark stubble across his jaw. Made him look like a Mafia enforcer. "Isn't Tommy John surgery a form of artificial enhancement? The kind of thing you're accusing Vic Caruso of?"

Bragg shot back, "Surgery to correct an injury is one thing. Surgery and other treatments to turn a normal human body into a kind of superman—that's unacceptable!"

"But the fans seems to love it," said the American League president, obviously thinking about the previous year's record-breaking attendance figures.

"I'm talking about protecting the purity of the game," Bragg insisted. "If we don't act now, we'll wind up with a bunch of half-robot freaks on the field instead of human beings!"

The Commissioner nodded. "We wouldn't want that," he said, looking directly at Caruso.

"We've got to make an example of this . . . this . . . freak," Bragg demanded. "Otherwise the game's going to be warped beyond recognition!"

The audience murmured. The cameras turned to Caruso, who looked uncomfortable, embarrassed, but not ashamed.

The commissioner silenced the audience's mutterings with a stern look.

"I think we should hear Mr. Caruso's story from his own lips," he said. "After all, his career—his very livelihood—is at stake here."

"What's at stake here," Bragg countered, "is the future of Major League Baseball."

The commissioner nodded, but said, "Mr. Bragg, you are excused. Mr. Caruso, please take the witness chair."

Obviously uncertain of himself, Vic Caruso got slowly to his feet and stepped toward the witness chair. Despite his size he was light on his feet, almost like a dancer. He passed Bragg, who was on his way back to the front row of benches. I had to laugh: it looked like the Washington Monument going past a bowling ball.

Vic settled himself gingerly into the wooden witness chair, off to one side of the judges, and stared at them, as if he was waiting for their verdict.

"Well, Mr. Caruso," said the commissioner, "what do you have to say for yourself?"

"About what, sir?"

The audience tittered. They thought they were watching a big, brainless ox who was going to make a fool of himself.

The commissioner's brows knit. "Why, about the accusations Mr. Bragg has leveled against you. About the fact that you—and other ballplayers, as well—have artificially enhanced your bodies and thereby gained an unfair advantage over the other players who have not partaken of such enhancements."

"Oh, that," said Vic.

Guffaws burst out from the crowd.

"Yes, that," the commissioner said, glaring the audience into silence. "Tell us what you've done and why you did it."

Vic squirmed on the chair. He looked as if he'd rather be a thousand miles away or maybe roasting over hot coals. But then he sucked in a deep breath and started talking.

It all started with my left knee—he said. On my thirtieth birthday, at that. The big three-oh.

I'd been catching for the A's for four years, hitting good enough to always be fifth or sixth in the batting order, but the knee was slowing me up so bad the Skipper was shaking his head every time he looked my way.

We were playing an interleague game against the Phillies. You know what roughnecks they are. In the sixth inning they got men on first and third, and their batter pops a fly to short right field. Runner on third tags up, I block the plate. When he slammed into me I felt the knee pop. Hurt like hell—I mean heck—but I didn't say anything. The runner was out, the inning was over, so I walked back to the dugout, trying not to limp.

Well, anyway, we lost the game 4-3. I was in the whirlpool soaking the knee when the Skipper sticks his ugly little face out of his office door and calls, "Hoss, get yourself in here, will you."

The other guys in the locker room were already looking pretty glum. Now they all stared at me for a second, then they all turned the other way. None of them wanted to catch my eye. They all knew what was coming. Me too.

So I wrap a towel around my gut and walk to the Skipper's office, leaving wet footprints on the carpeting.

"I'm gonna hafta rest you for a while," the Skipper says, even before I can sit down in the chair in front of his desk. The hot seat, we always called it.

"I don't need a rest."

"Your damned knee does. Look at it: it's swollen like a watermelon." The Skipper is a little guy, kind of shriveled up like a prune. Never played a day of big-league ball in his life but he's managed us into the playoffs three straight seasons.

"My knee's okay. The swelling's going down already."

"It's affecting your throwing."

I started to say something, but nothing came out of my mouth. In the fifth inning I couldn't quite reach a foul pop-up, and on the next pitch the guy homers. Then, in the eighth I was slow getting up and throwing to second. The stolen base put a guy in scoring position and a bloop single scored him and that's how the Phillies beat us.

"It's a tough position, Hoss," says the Boss, not looking me in the eye. "Catching beats hell outta the knees."

"I can play, for chrissakes," I said. "It don't hurt that much."

"You're gonna sit out a few games. And see an orthopedics doc."

So I go to the team's doctor, who sends me to an orthopedics guy, who makes me get MRI scans and X-rays and whatnot, then tells me I need surgery.

"You mean I'll be out for the rest of the year?"

"The season's almost over," he says, like the last twenty games of the year don't mean anything.

I try to tough it out, but the knee keeps swelling so bad I can hardly walk, let alone play ball. I mean, I never was a speed demon, but now the shortstop and third baseman are playing me on the outfield grass, for crying out loud.

By the time the season finally ends I'm on crutches and I can imagine what my next salary negotiation is going to be like. It's my option year, too. My agent wouldn't even look me in the eye.

"Mr. Caruso," interrupted the commissioner. "Could you concentrate on the medical enhancements you obtained and skip the small talk, please?"

Oh, sure—Vic said. I went to the surgeon that they picked out for me and he told me I needed a total knee replacement.

"An artificial knee?" I asked the guy.

He seemed happy about it. With a big smile he tells me by the time spring training starts, I'll be walking as good as new.

Walking and playing ball are two different things, I say to myself. But I go through with the surgery, and the rehab, and sure enough, by the time spring training starts I'm doing okay.

But okay isn't good enough. Like I said, catching beats the hell out of your knees, and I'm slower than I should be. I complain to the surgeon and he tells me I ought to see this specialist, a stem cell doctor.

I don't know stem cells from artichokes, but Dr. Trurow turns out to be a really good-looking blonde from Sweden and she explains that stem cells can help my knee to recover from the surgery.

"They're your own cells," she explains. "We simply encourage them to get your knee to work better."

I start the regular season as the designated hitter. Danny Daniels is behind the plate, and boy is he happy about it. But during our first home stand I go to Doc Trurow, let her stick a needle in me and draw out some cells, then a week later she sticks them back in me.

And my knee starts to feel a lot better. Not all at once; it took a couple of weeks. But one night game against the Orioles, with their infielders playing so deep it's like they got seven outfielders on the grass, I drop a bunt down the third base line and beat it out easy.

The crowd loves it. The score's tied at 2-2, I'm on first with nobody out, so I take off for second. The Orioles' catcher, he's a rookie and he's so surprised he double clutches before throwing the ball to second. I make it easy.

By Memorial Day I'm behind the plate again, the team's number one catcher. Daniels is moping in the dugout, but hey, you know, that's baseball. The Skipper's even moved me up to the three slot in the batting order, I'm so fast on my feet.

One day in the clubhouse, though, Daniels comes up to me and says, "You don't remember me, do you?"

"You're Danny Daniels, you're hitting two-eighty-two, seven homers, thirty-one ribbies," I tell him.

"That's not what I mean." Danny's a decent kid, good prospect. He thought he had the catching slot nailed until my stem cells started working.

"So whattaya mean?" I ask him.

"You talked at my high school when I was a fat little kid," Danny said. "All the other kids bullied me, but you told me to stand up to 'em and make the best of myself."

Suddenly it clicks in my mind. "You were that fat little kid with the bad acne?"

He laughs. He's so good-looking now the girls mob him after the game.

"Yeah. That was me. I started playing baseball after you talked to me. I wanted to be just like you."

I never thought of myself as a role model. I get kind of embarrassed. All I can think of to say is, "Well, you did great. You made the Bigs."

"Yeah," he says, kind of funny. "I'm a second-string catcher."

Bragg interrupts, "I don't see what all this twaddle has to do with the issue at hand."

The commissioner, who looked interested in Vic's story, makes a grumbly face, but he sighs and says, "Mr. Caruso, while we appreciate your description of the human aspects of the case, please stick to the facts and eschew the human story."

Vic makes a puzzled frown over that word, "eschew," but he nods and picks up his thread again.

Okay—Vic says. I'm doing great until my other knee starts aching. I'm going on thirty-two and the aches and pains are what you get. But I figure, if the stem cell treatments helped my one knee so much, how about trying them on my other knee?

Besides, that Swedish doctor was really good-looking and it was an excuse to see her again.

So I got the other knee treated and before the season's over I've got twelve stolen bases and third basemen are playing me inside the bag to protect against bunts. Makes it easier for me to slam the ball past them. I was leading the league in batting average and women were hanging around the clubhouse entrance after games just to see me!

But then I got beaned.

It wasn't really a beaning, not like I got hit on the head. McGilmore was pitching and I had a single and a triple in two at-bats and he was pretty sore about it. He always was a mean bas—a mean sonofagun. So he whips a sidearm fast ball at me, hard as he can throw. It's inside and I try to spin away from it but it catches me in my ribs. I never felt such pain. Broke two of my ribs and one of 'em punctured my left lung. I was coughing up blood when they carried me off the field.

So I spent my thirty-second birthday in the hospital, feeling miserable. But the second or third day there, Doc Trurow comes to visit me, and it was like the sun coming out from behind a cloud. She's really pretty, and her smile lit up the whole damned hospital.

Stem cells again. This time they helped my ribs heal and even repaired the rip in my lung. I got back to the team before the end of the season and ran off a four-fifty average on our last home stand. Better yet, Doc Trurow was at every game, sitting right behind our dugout.

So on the last day of the season, I worked up the nerve to ask her out for dinner. And she says yes! Her first name is Olga and we had a great evening together, even though the team finished only in third place.

* * *

"Mr. Caruso," the commissioner intoned. "Kindly stick to the facts of your physical enhancements."

Vic looked kind of sheepish and he nodded his head and mumbled, "Yessir."

Instead of going back to Michigan for the off season, I stayed in Oakland and dated Olga a lot. I even started thinking about marriage, but I didn't have the nerve to pop the question—

"Mr. Caruso!"

Well, it's important—Vic said to the commissioner. Olga told me how stem cell treatments could improve my eyesight and make my reflexes sharper. There wasn't anything in the rules against it, and it was my own cells, not some drug or steroids or anything like that. So I let her jab me here and there and damned if I didn't feel better. Besides, I worried that if I said no to her she'd stop dating me and I didn't want to stop seeing her.

So this goes on for a couple seasons and all of a sudden I'm coming up on my thirty-fifth birthday and I can see the big four-oh heading down the road for me. I started to worry about my career ending, even though I was hitting three-twenty-something and doing okay behind the plate. News guys started calling me Iron Man, no kidding.

Danny Daniels looks piss . . . uh, unhappy, but he doesn't say anything and I figure, what the hell, so he has to sit on the bench for another season or two. But the front office trades him to the Yankees, so it's okay. I don't have to see his sour puss in the clubhouse anymore.

Meanwhile we're in the playoffs again and we've got a good chance to take the pennant.

Then I got hurt again. Dancing. No kidding, Olga and I were dancing and I guess I was feeling pretty damned frisky and I tried a fancy move I'd seen in an old Fred Astaire movie and I slipped and went down on my face. Never been so embarrassed in my whole life.

I turned from Vic to take a peek at the commissioner's face. Instead of interrupting the big lug, the commissioner was listening hard, his eyes focused on Vic, totally intent on the story that was unfolding.

✳ ✳ ✳

Something in my hip went blooey—Vic went on. I got to my feet okay, but the hip felt stiff. And the stiffness didn't go away. It got worse. When I told Olga about it she toted me over to the medical center for a whole lot of tests.

It was nothing serious, the docs decided. The hip would be okay in a couple of months. Just needed rest. And time.

But spring training was due to start in a few weeks and I needed to be able to get around okay, not stiff like Frankenstein's monster.

"It's just a factor of your age," says the therapist Olga sent me to.

"I'm only thirty-six," I said.

"Maybe so," says the doc, "but your body's taken a beating over the years. It's catching up with you. You're going to be old before your time, physically."

I felt pretty low. But when I tell Olga about what the doc said, she says, "Telomerase."

"Telo-what?" I ask her.

She tells me this telomerase stuff can reverse aging. In mice, at least. They inject the stuff in old, creaky, diabetic lab mice and the little buggers get young and frisky again and their diabetes goes away.

I don't have diabetes, but I figure if the stuff makes me feel younger then why not try it? Olga tells me that some movie stars and politicians have used it, in secret, and it helped them stay young. A couple of TV news people, too.

So I start taking telomerase injections and by the time I hit the big four-oh I'm still hitting over three hundred and catching more than a hundred games a year. And other guys are starting to use stem cells and telomerase and everything else they can get their hands on. Even Danny Daniels is using, from what I heard.

"That's what I've been telling you!" Bragg yells, jumping up from his seat on the front row of benches. "They're making a travesty of the game!"

The commissioner frowns at him and Bragg sits back down. Vic Caruso stares at him, looking puzzled.

"Look," Vic says, "I didn't do anything that's prohibited by the rules."

Bragg seems staggered that Vic can pronounce "prohibited" correctly.

The commissioner says, "The point of this hearing is to decide if the rules should be amended."

"You make stem cells and telomerase and such illegal," Vic says, "and half the players in the league'll have to quit baseball."

"But is it fair to the players who don't use such treatments for you to be so . . . so . . . extraordinary?" asks the commissioner.

Vic shakes his head. "I'm not extraordinary. I'm not a superman. I'm just *young*. I'm not better than I was when I was twenty, but I'm just about as good. What's wrong with that?"

The commissioner doesn't answer. He just shakes his head and glances at the two league presidents, sitting beside him. Neither of them has an answer, either.

But Bragg does. "Do you realize what this means?" he yells at the commissioner. Pointing at Vic again, he says, "This man will be playing until he's fifty! Maybe longer! How are we going to bring young players into the league if the veterans are using these treatments to keep themselves young? We'll have whole teams made up of seventy-year-olds, for God's sake!"

"Seventy-year-olds who play like twenty-year-olds," the commissioner mutters.

"Seventy-year-olds who'll demand salary increases every year," Bragg snaps back at him.

And suddenly it all becomes clear. Bragg's not worrying about the purity of the game. The revelations in the news haven't hurt box office receipts: attendance has been booming. But veteran players demand a lot more money than rookies—and get it. Bragg's bitching about his pocketbook!

The commissioner looks at the two league presidents again, but they still have nothing to say. They avoid looking at Bragg, though.

To Vic, the commissioner says, in a kindly, almost grandfatherly way, "Mr. Caruso, thank you for your frank and honest testimony. You've given us a lot to think about. You may step down now."

Vic gets up from the chair like a mountain rising. As he heads for the front bench, though, the commissioner says, "By the way, just to satisfy my personal curiosity, did you and Dr. Trurow get married?"

"We're gonna do that on Christmas day," says Vic. "In Stockholm, that's her home town and her family and all her friends'll be there."

The commissioner smiles. "Congratulations."

"We'll send you an invitation," Vic says, smiling back.

Glancing at Bragg, the commissioner says, "I'm afraid it wouldn't be appropriate for me to attend your wedding, Mr. Caruso. But I wish you and your bride much happiness."

So that's how it happened. The commissioner and the league presidents and all the owners—including Bragg—put their heads together and came up with the Big Change.

Major League Baseball imposed an age limit on players. Fifty. Nobody over fifty would be allowed to play on a major league team. This made room for the youngsters like Danny Daniels to get into the game—although Daniels was thirty-eight when he finally became the Yankees' starting catcher.

The guys over fifty were put into a new league, a special league for old-timers. This allowed baseball to expand again, for the first time in the Twenty-First century. Sixteen new teams in sixteen new cities, mostly in the Sun Belt, like Tucson, Mobile, New Orleans and Orlando.

And the best part is that the old timers get a shot at the World Series winner. At the end of October, right around Hallowe'en, the pennant winner from the Old Timers' League plays the winner of the World Series.

Some wags wrote columns about Hallowe'en being the time when dead ballplayers rise from their graves, but nobody pays much attention to that kind of drivel. The Hallowe'en series draws big crowds—and big TV receipts. Even Bragg admits he likes it, a little.

Last Hallowe'en Vic's Tucson Tarantulas whipped the New York Yankees in seven games. In the deciding game, Danny Daniels hit a home run for the Yanks, but Vic socked two dingers for Tucson to ice it. He said it was to celebrate the birth of his first son.

Yankee haters all over the country rejoiced.

Asked when he planned to retire, Vic said, "I don't know. Maybe when my kid gets old enough to play in the Bigs."

Or maybe not.

THE MAN WHO
HATED GRAVITY

The most important advice ever given to a writer is this: Write about what you know.

But how can you do this in science fiction, when the stories tend to be about places and times that no one has yet experienced? How can you write about what you know when you want to write about living in the future or the distant past, on the Moon, or Mars, or some planet that is invented out of your imagination?

There are ways.

To begin with, no matter what time and place in which your story is set, it must deal with people. Oh, sure, the characters in your story may not look like human beings. Science-fiction characters can be robots or alien creatures or smart dolphins or sentient cacti, for that matter. But they must behave like humans. They must have humanly recognizable needs and fears and desires. If they do not, they will either be totally incomprehensible to the reader or—worst sin of all—boring.

I have never been to the Moon. I have never been a circus acrobat. But I know what it is to hate gravity. Several years ago I popped my knee while playing tennis. For weeks I was in a brace, hardly able to walk. I used crutches, and later a cane. For more than a year I could not trust my two legs to support me. Even today that knee feels like there's a loose collection of rubber bands inside. I know what it is like to be crippled, even though it was only temporary.

And I know, perhaps as well as anyone, what it is like to live on the Moon. I've been living there in my imagination for much of my life. My first novel (unpublished) dealt with establishing habitats on the Moon. My 1976 novel Millennium (later incorporated into The Kinsman Saga) was set mainly on the Moon. In my 1987 nonfiction book Welcome to Moonbase, I worked with engineers and illustrators to create a livable, workable industrial base on the Moon's surface.

While I was hobbling around on crutches, hating every moment of being incapacitated, I kept thinking of how much better off I would be in zero g, or in the gentle gravity of the Moon, one-sixth of Earth's.

And the Great Rolando took form in my mind. I began to write a short story about him. I don't write many short stories. Most of my fiction has been novels. When I start a novel, I usually know the major characteristics of the major characters, and that's about it. I have sketched out the basic conflict between the protagonist and antagonist, but if I try to outline the scenes, schedule the chapters, organize the action, the novel gets turgid and dull. Much better to let the characters fight it out among themselves, day after day, as the work progresses.

Short stories are very different. Most of the short stories I write are rather carefully planned out before I begin putting the words down. I find that, because a short story must necessarily be tightly written, without a spare scene or even an extra sentence, I must work out every detail of the story in my mind before I begin to write.

However, "The Man Who Hated Gravity" did not evolve that way. I began with Rolando, a daring acrobat who flouted his disdain for the dangers of his work. I knew he was going to be injured, much more seriously and permanently than I was. From there on in, Rolando and the other characters literally took over the telling of the tale. I did not know, for example, that the scientist who was used to help publicize Rolando would turn out to be the man who headed Moonbase years later.

I do not advise this subconscious method of writing for short-story work. As I said, a short story must be succinct. Instead of relating the tale of a person's whole life, or a substantial portion of it, a short story can at best reveal a critical incident in that character's life: a turning point, an episode that illuminates the person's inner being.

But this subconscious method worked for me in "The Man Who Hated Gravity." See if the story works for you.

THE GREAT ROLANDO had not always hated gravity. As a child growing up in the traveling circus that had been his only home he often frightened his parents by climbing too high, swinging too far, daring more than they could bear to watch.

The son of a clown and a cook, Rolando had yearned for true greatness, and could not rest until he became the most renowned aerialist of them all.

Slim and handsome in his spangled tights, Rolando soared through the empty air thirty feet above the circus's flimsy safety net. Then fifty feet above it. Then a full hundred feet high, with no net at all.

"See the Great Rolando defy gravity!" shouted the posters and TV advertisements. And the people came to crane their necks and hold their breaths as he performed a split-second ballet in midair high above them. Literally flying from one trapeze to another, triple somersaults were workaday chores for the Great Rolando.

His father feared to watch his son's performances. With all the superstition born of generations of circus life, he cringed outside the Big Top while the crowds roared deliriously. Behind his clown's painted grin Rolando's father trembled. His mother prayed through every performance until the day she died, slumped over a bare wooden pew in a tiny austere church far out in the midwestern prairie.

For no matter how far he flew, no matter how wildly he gyrated in midair, no matter how the crowds below gasped and screamed their delight, the Great Rolando pushed himself farther, higher, more recklessly.

Once, when the circus was playing New York City's huge Convention Center, the management pulled a public relations coup. They got a brilliant young physicist from Columbia University to pose with Rolando for the media cameras and congratulate him on defying gravity.

Once the camera crews had departed, the physicist said to Rolando, "I've always had a secret yearning to be in the circus. I admire what you do very much."

Rolando accepted the compliment with a condescending smile.

"But no one can *really* defy gravity," the physicist warned. "It's a universal force, you know."

The Great Rolando's smile vanished. "*I* can defy gravity. And I do. Every day."

Several years later Rolando's father died (of a heart seizure, during one of his son's performances) and Rolando married the brilliant young lion tamer who had joined the circus slightly earlier. She was a petite little thing with golden hair, the loveliest of blue eyes, and so sweet a disposition that no one could say anything about her that was less than praise. Even the great cats purred for her.

She too feared Rolando's ever-bolder daring, his wilder and wilder reachings on the high trapeze.

"There's nothing to be afraid of! Gravity can't hurt me!" And he would laugh at her fears.

"But I *am* afraid," she would cry.

"The people pay their money to see me defy gravity," Rolando would tell his tearful wife. "They'll get bored if I keep doing the same stunts one year after another."

She loved him dearly and felt terribly frightened for him. It was one thing to master a large cage full of Bengal tigers and tawny lions and snarling black panthers. All you needed was will and nerve. But she knew that gravity was another matter altogether.

"No one can defy gravity forever," she would say, gently, softly, quietly.

"I can," boasted the Great Rolando.

But of course he could not. No one could. Not forever. The fall, when it inevitably came, was a matter of a fraction of a second. His young assistant's hand slipped only slightly in starting out the empty trapeze for Rolando to catch after a quadruple somersault. Rolando almost caught it. In midair he saw that the bar would be too short. He stretched his magnificently trained body to the utmost and his fingers just grazed its tape-wound shaft.

For an instant he hung in the air. The tent went absolutely silent. The crowd drew in its collective breath. The band stopped playing. Then gravity wrapped its invisible tentacles around the Great Rolando and he plummeted, wild-eyed and screaming, to the sawdust a hundred feet below.

"His right leg is completely shattered," said the famous surgeon to

Rolando's wife. She had stayed calm up to that moment, strong and levelheaded while her husband lay unconscious in an intensive-care unit.

"His other injuries will heal. But the leg . . ." The gray-haired, gray-suited man shook his dignified head sadly. His assistants, gathered behind him like an honor guard, shook their heads in metronome synchrony to their leader.

"His leg?" she asked, trembling.

"He will never be able to walk again," the famous surgeon pronounced.

The petite blonde lion tamer crumpled and sagged into the sleek leather couch of the hospital waiting room, tears spilling down her cheeks.

"Unless . . ." said the famous surgeon.

"Unless?" she echoed, suddenly wild with hope.

"Unless we replace the shattered leg with a prosthesis."

"Cut off his leg?"

The famous surgeon promised her that a prosthetic bionic leg would be "just as good as the original—in fact, even better!" It would be a *permanent* prosthesis; it would never have to come off, and its synthetic surface would blend so well with Rolando's real skin that no one would be able to tell where his natural leg ended and his prosthetic leg began. His assistants nodded in unison.

Frenzied at the thought that her husband would never walk again, alone in the face of coolly assured medical wisdom, she reluctantly gave her assent and signed the necessary papers.

The artificial leg was part lightweight metal, part composite space-manufactured materials, and entirely filled with marvelously tiny electronic devices and miraculously miniaturized motors that moved the prosthesis exactly the way a real leg should move. It was stronger than flesh and bone, or so the doctors confidently assured the Great Rolando's wife.

The circus manager, a constantly frowning bald man who reported to a board of bankers, lawyers, and MBAs in St. Petersburg, agreed to pay the famous surgeon's astronomical fee.

"The first aerialist with a bionic leg," he murmured, dollar signs in his eyes.

Rolando took the news of the amputation and prosthesis with

surprising calm. He agreed with his wife: better a strong and reliable artificial leg than a ruined real one.

In two weeks he walked again. But not well. He limped. The leg hurt, with a sullen, stubborn ache that refused to go away.

"It will take a little time to get accustomed to it," said the physical therapists.

Rolando waited. He exercised. He tried jogging. The leg did not work right. And it ached constantly.

"That's just not possible," the doctors assured him. "Perhaps you ought to talk with a psychologist."

The Great Rolando stormed out of their offices, limping and cursing, never to return. He went back to the circus, but not to his aerial acrobatics. A man who could not walk properly, who had an artificial leg that did not work right, had no business on the high trapeze.

His young assistant took the spotlight now, and duplicated— almost—the Great Rolando's repertoire of aerial acrobatic feats. Rolando watched him with mounting jealousy, his only satisfaction being that the crowds were noticeably smaller than they had been when he had been the star of the show. The circus manager frowned and asked when Rolando would be ready to work again.

"When the leg works right," said Rolando.

But it continued to pain him, to make him awkward and invalid.

That is when he began to hate gravity. He hated being pinned down to the ground like a worm, a beetle. He would hobble into the Big Tent and eye the fliers' platform a hundred feet over his head and know that he could not even climb the ladder to reach it. He grew angrier each day. And clumsy. And obese. The damned false leg *hurt*, no matter what those expensive quacks said. It was *not* psychosomatic. Rolando snorted contempt for their stupidity.

He spent his days bumping into inanimate objects and tripping over tent ropes. He spent his nights grumbling and grousing, fearing to move about in the dark, fearing even that he might roll off his bed. When he managed to sleep the same nightmare gripped him: he was falling, plunging downward eternally while gravity laughed at him and all his screams for help did him no good whatever.

His former assistant grinned at him whenever they met. The circus manager took to growling about Rolando's weight, and asking how long he expected to be on the payroll when he was not earning his keep.

Rolando limped and ached. And when no one could see him, he cried. He grew bitter and angry, like a proud lion that finds itself caged forever.

Representatives from the bionics company that manufactured the prosthetic leg visited the circus, their faces grave with concern.

"The prosthesis should be working just fine," they insisted.

Rolando insisted even more staunchly that their claims were fraudulent. "I should sue you and the barbarian who took my leg off."

The manufacturer's reps consulted their home office and within the week Rolando was whisked to San Jose in their company jet. For days on end they tested the leg, its electronic innards, the bionic interface where it linked with Rolando's human nervous system. Everything checked out perfectly. They showed Rolando the results, almost with tears in their eyes.

"It should work fine."

"It does not."

In exchange for a written agreement not to sue them, the bionics company gave Rolando a position as a "field consultant," at a healthy stipend. His only duties were to phone San Jose once a month to report on how the leg felt. Rolando delighted in describing each and every individual twinge, the awkwardness of the leg, how it made him limp.

His wife was the major earner now, despite his monthly consultant's fee. She worked twice as hard as ever before, and began to draw crowds that held their breaths in vicarious terror as they watched the tiny blonde place herself at the mercy of so many fangs and claws.

Rolando traveled with her as the circus made its tour of North America each year, growing fatter and unhappier day by humiliating, frustrating, painful day.

Gravity defeated him every hour, in a thousand small ways. He would read a magazine in their cramped mobile home until, bored, he tossed it onto the table. Gravity would slyly tug at its pages until the magazine slipped over the table's edge and fell to the floor. He would shower laboriously, hating the bulging fat that now encumbered his once-sleek body. The soap would slide from his hands while he was half-blinded with suds. Inevitably he would slip on it and bang himself painfully against the shower wall.

If there was a carpet spread on the floor, gravity would contrive to have it entangle his feet and pull him into a humiliating fall. Stairs tripped him. His silverware clattered noisily to the floor in restaurants.

He shunned the Big Top altogether, where the people who had once paid to see him soar through the air could see how heavy and clumsy he had become—even though a nasty voice in his mind told him that no one would recognize the fat old man he now was as the once magnificent Great Rolando.

As the years stretched past Rolando grew grayer and heavier and angrier. Furious at gravity. Bellowing, screaming, howling with impotent rage at the hateful tricks gravity played on him every day, every hour. He took to leaning on a cane and stumping around their mobile home, roaring helplessly against gravity and the fate that was killing him by inches.

His darling wife remained steadfast and supportive all through those terrible years. Other circus folk shook their heads in wonder at her. "She spends all day with the big cats and then goes home to more roaring and spitting," they told each other.

Then one winter afternoon, as the sun threw long shadows across the Houston Astrodome parking lot, where the circus was camped for the week, Rolando's wife came into their mobile home, her sky-blue workout suit dark with perspiration, and announced that a small contingent of performers had been invited to Moonbase for a month.

"To the Moon?" Rolando asked, incredulous. "Who?" The fliers and tightrope acts, she replied, and a selection of acrobats and clowns.

"There's no gravity up there," Rolando muttered, suddenly jealous. "Or less gravity. Something like that."

He slumped back in the sofa without realizing that the wonderful smile on his wife's face meant that there was more she wanted to tell him.

"We've been invited, too!" she blurted, and she perched herself on his lap, threw her arms around his thick neck and kissed him soundly.

"You mean you've been invited," he said darkly, pulling away from her embrace. "You're the star of the show; I'm a has-been."

She shook her head, still smiling happily. "They haven't asked me to perform. They can't bring the cats up into space. The invitation is for the Great Rolando and his wife to spend a month up there as guests of Moonbase Inc.!"

Rolando suspected that the bionics company had pulled some corporate strings. They want to see how their damnable leg works without gravity, he was certain. Inwardly, he was eager to find out, too. But he let no one know that, not even his wife.

To his utter shame and dismay, Rolando was miserably sick all the long three days of the flight from Texas to Moonbase. Immediately after takeoff the spacecraft carrying the circus performers was in zero gravity, weightless, and Rolando found that the absence of gravity was worse for him than gravity itself. His stomach seemed to be falling all the time while, paradoxically, anything he tried to eat crawled upward into his throat and made him violently ill.

In his misery and near-delirium he knew that gravity was laughing at him.

Once on the Moon, however, everything became quite fine. Better than fine, as far as Rolando was concerned. While clear-eyed young Moonbase guides in crisp uniforms of amber and bronze demonstrated the cautious shuffling walk that was needed in the gentle lunar gravity, Rolando realized that his leg no longer hurt.

"I feel fine," he whispered to his wife, in the middle of the demonstration. Then he startled the guides and his fellow circus folk alike by tossing his cane aside and leaping five meters into the air, shouting at the top of his lungs, "I feel *wonderful!*"

The circus performers were taken off to special orientation lectures, but Rolando and his wife were escorted by a pert young redhead into the office of Moonbase's chief administrator.

"Remember me?" asked the administrator as he shook Rolando's hand and half-bowed to his wife. "I was the physicist at Columbia who did that TV commercial with you six or seven years ago."

Rolando did not in fact remember the man's face at all, although he did recall his warning about gravity. As he sat down in the chair the administrator proffered, he frowned slightly.

The administrator wore zippered coveralls of powder blue. He hiked one hip onto the edge of his desk and beamed happily at the Rolandos. "I can't tell you how delighted I am to have the circus here, even if it's just for a month. I really had to sweat blood to get the corporation's management to okay bringing you up here. Transportation's still quite expensive, you know."

Rolando patted his artificial leg. "I imagine the bionics company paid their fair share of the costs."

The administrator looked slightly startled. "Well, yes, they have picked up the tab for you and Mrs. Rolando."

"I thought so."

Rolando's wife smiled sweetly. "We are delighted that you invited us here."

They chatted a while longer and then the administrator personally escorted them to their apartment in Moonbase's tourist section. "Have a happy stay," he said, by way of taking his leave.

Although he did not expect to, that is exactly what Rolando did for the next many days. Moonbase was marvelous! There was enough gravity to keep his insides behaving properly, but it was so light and gentle that even his obese body with its false leg felt young and agile again.

Rolando walked the length and breadth of the great Main Plaza, his wife clinging to his arm, and marveled at how the Moonbase people had landscaped the expanse under their dome, planted it with grass and flowering shrubs. The apartment they had been assigned to was deeper underground, in one of the long corridors that had been blasted out of solid rock. But the quarters were no smaller than their mobile home back on Earth, and it had a video screen that took up one entire wall of the sitting room.

"I love it here!" Rolando told his wife. "I could stay forever!"

"It's only for one month," she said softly. He ignored it.

Rolando adjusted quickly to walking in the easy lunar gravity, never noticing that his wife adjusted just as quickly (perhaps even a shade faster). He left his cane in their apartment and strolled unaided each day through the shopping arcades and athletic fields of the Main Plaza, walking for hours on end without a bit of pain.

He watched the roustabouts who had come up with him directing their robots to set up a Big Top in the middle of the Plaza, a gaudy blaze of colorful plastic and pennants beneath the great gray dome that soared high overhead.

The Moon is marvelous, thought Rolando. There was still gravity lurking, trying to trip him up and make him look ridiculous. But even when he fell, it was so slow and gentle that he could put out his powerful arms and push himself up to a standing position before his body actually hit the ground.

"I love it here!" he said to his wife, dozens of times each day. She smiled and tried to remind him that it was only for three more weeks.

At dinner one evening in Moonbase's grander restaurant (there were only two, not counting cafeterias) his earthly muscles proved too strong for the Moon when he rammed their half-finished bottle of wine back into its aluminum ice bucket. The bucket tipped and fell off the edge of the table. But Rolando snatched it with one hand in the midst of its languid fall toward the floor and with a smile and a flourish deposited the bucket with the bottle still in it back on the table before a drop had spilled.

"I love it here," he repeated for the fortieth time that day.

Gradually, though, his euphoric mood sank. The circus began giving abbreviated performances inside its Big Top, and Rolando stood helplessly pinned to the ground while the spotlights picked out the young fliers in their skintight costumes as they soared slowly, dreamily through the air between one trapeze and the next, twisting, spinning, somersaulting in the soft lunar gravity in ways that no one had ever done before. The audience gasped and cheered and gave them standing ovations. Rolando stood rooted near one of the tent's entrances, deep in shadow, wearing a tourist's pale green coveralls, choking with envy and frustrated rage.

The crowds were small—there were only a few thousand people living at Moonbase, plus perhaps another thousand tourists—but they shook the plastic tent with their roars of delight.

Rolando watched a few performances, then stayed away. But he noticed at the Olympic-sized pool that raw teenagers were diving from a thirty-meter platform and doing half a dozen somersaults as they fell languidly in the easy gravity. Even when they hit the water the splashes they made rose lazily and then fell back into the pool so leisurely that it seemed like a slow-motion film.

Anyone can be an athlete here, Rolando realized as he watched tourists flying on rented wings through the upper reaches of the Main Plaza's vaulted dome.

Children could easily do not merely Olympic, but Olympian feats of acrobatics. Rolando began to dread the possibility of seeing a youngster do a quadruple somersault from a standing start.

"Anyone can defy gravity here," he complained to his wife, silently adding, Anyone but me.

It made him morose to realize that feats which had taken him a lifetime to accomplish could be learned by a toddler in half an hour. And soon he would have to return to Earth with its heavy, oppressive, mocking gravity.

I know you're waiting for me, he said to gravity. You're going to kill me—if I don't do the job for myself first.

Two nights before they were due to depart, they were the dinner guests of the chief administrator and several of his staff. As formal an occasion as Moonbase ever has, the men wore sport jackets and turtleneck shirts, the women real dresses and jewelry. The administrator told hoary old stories of his childhood yearning to be in the circus. Rolando remained modestly silent, even when the administrator spoke glowingly of how he had admired the daring feats of the Great Rolando—many years ago.

After dinner, back in their apartment, Rolando turned on his wife. "You got them to invite us up here, didn't you?"

She admitted, "The bionics company told me that they were going to end your consulting fee. They want to give up on you! I asked them to let us come here to see if your leg would be better in low gravity."

"And then we go back to Earth."

"Yes."

"Back to *real* gravity. Back to my being a cripple!"

"I was hoping . . ." Her voice broke and she sank onto the bed, crying.

Suddenly Rolando's anger was overwhelmed by a searing, agonizing sense of shame. All these years she had been trying so hard, standing between him and the rest of the world, protecting him, sheltering him. And for what? So that he could scream at her for the rest of his life?

He could not bear it any longer.

Unable to speak, unable even to reach his hand out to comfort her, he turned and lumbered out of the apartment, leaving his wife weeping alone.

He knew where he had to be, where he could finally put an end to this humiliation and misery. He made his way to the Big Top.

A stubby gunmetal-gray robot stood guard at the main entrance, its sensors focusing on Rolando like the red glowing eyes of a spider.

"No access at this time except to members of the circus troupe," it said in a synthesized voice.

"I am the Great Rolando."

"One moment for voiceprint identification," said the robot, then, "Approved."

Rolando swept past the contraption with a snort of contempt.

The Big Top was empty at this hour. Tomorrow they would start to dismantle it. The next day they would head back to Earth.

Rolando walked slowly, stiffly to the base of the ladder that reached up to the trapezes. The spotlights were shut down. The only illumination inside the tent came from the harsh working lights spotted here and there.

Rolando heaved a deep breath and stripped off his jacket. Then, gripping one of the ladder's rungs, he began to climb: good leg first, then the artificial leg. He could feel no difference between them. His body was only one-sixth its earthly weight, of course, but still the artificial leg behaved exactly as his normal one.

He reached the topmost platform. Holding tightly to the side rail he peered down into the gloomy shadows a hundred feet below.

With a slow, ponderous nod of his head the Great Rolando finally admitted what he had kept buried inside him all these long anguished years. Finally the concealed truth emerged and stood naked before him. With tear-filled eyes he saw its reality.

He had been living a lie all these years. He had been blaming gravity for his own failure. Now he understood with precise, final clarity that it was not gravity that had destroyed his life.

It was fear.

He stood rooted on the high platform, trembling with the memory of falling, plunging, screaming terror. He knew that this fear would live within him always, for the remainder of his life. It was too strong to overcome; he was a coward, probably had always been a coward, all his life. All his life.

Without consciously thinking about it Rolando untied one of the trapezes and gripped the rough surface of its taped bar. He did not bother with resin. There would be no need.

As if in a dream he swung out into the empty air, feeling the rush of wind ruffling his gray hair, hearing the creak of the ropes beneath his weight.

Once, twice, three times he swung back and forth, kicking higher each time. He grunted with the unaccustomed exertion. He felt sweat trickling from his armpits.

Looking down, he saw the hard ground so far below. One more fall, he told himself. Just let go and that will end it forever. End the fear. End the shame.

"Teach me!"

The voice boomed like cannon fire across the empty tent. Rolando felt every muscle in his body tighten.

On the opposite platform, before him, stood the chief administrator, still wearing his dinner jacket.

"Teach me!" he called again. "Show me how to do it. Just this once, before you have to leave."

Rolando hung by his hands, swinging back and forth. The younger man's figure standing on the platform came closer, closer, then receded, dwindled as inertia carried Rolando forward and back, forward and back.

"No one will know," the administrator pleaded through the shadows. "I promise you; I'll never tell a soul. Just show me how to do it. Just this once."

"Stand back," Rolando heard his own voice call. It startled him.

Rolando kicked once, tried to judge the distance and account for the lower gravity as best as he could, and let go of the bar. He soared too far, but the strong composite mesh at the rear of the platform caught him, yieldingly, and he was able to grasp the side railing and stand erect before the young administrator could reach out and steady him.

"We both have a lot to learn," said the Great Rolando. "Take off your jacket."

For more than an hour the two men swung high through the silent shadowy air. Rolando tried nothing fancy, no leaps from one bar to another, no real acrobatics. It was tricky enough just landing gracefully on the platform in the strange lunar gravity. The administrator did exactly as Rolando instructed him. For all his youth and desire to emulate a circus star, he was no daredevil. It satisfied him completely to swing side by side with the Great Rolando, to share the same platform.

"What made you come here tonight?" Rolando asked as they stood gasping sweatily on the platform between turns.

"The security robot reported your entry. Strictly routine, I get all such reports piped to my quarters. But I figured this was too good a chance to miss!"

Finally, soaked with perspiration, arms aching and fingers raw and cramping, they made their way down the ladder to the ground. Laughing.

"I'll never forget this," the administrator said. "It's the high point of my life."

"Mine too," said Rolando fervently. "Mine too."

Two days later the administrator came to the rocket terminal to see the circus troupe off. Taking Rolando and his wife to one side, he said in a low voice that brimmed with happiness, "You know, we're starting to accept retired couples for permanent residence here at Moonbase."

Rolando's wife immediately responded, "Oh, I'm not ready to retire yet."

"Nor I," said Rolando. "I'll stay with the circus for a few years more, I think. There might still be time for me to make a comeback."

"Still," said the administrator, "when you do want to retire . . ."

Mrs. Rolando smiled at him. "I've noticed that my face looks better in this lower gravity. I probably wouldn't need a facelift if we come to live here."

They laughed together.

The rest of the troupe was filing into the rocket that would take them back to Earth. Rolando gallantly held his wife's arm as she stepped up the ramp and ducked through the hatch. Then he turned to the administrator and asked swiftly:

"What you told me about gravity all those years ago—is it really true? It is really universal? There's no way around it?"

"Afraid not," the administrator answered. "Someday gravity will make the Sun collapse. It might even make the entire universe collapse."

Rolando nodded, shook the man's hand, then followed his wife to his seat inside the rocket's passenger compartment. As he listened to the taped safety lecture and strapped on his safety belt he thought to himself: So gravity will get us all in the end.

Then he smiled grimly. But not yet. Not yet.

ZERO GEE

The next three stories tell a connected tale about the early life of an Air Force astronaut named Chester A. Kinsman. Essentially, these stories deal with his loss of innocence and his first step toward real maturity. Or, to thoroughly mix metaphors and sources, the stories taken together form a miniature Paradise Lost and Purgatorio.

Kinsman has been with me since the late 1940s. I knew him from birth to death. He was the protagonist in the first novel I ever wrote, which was never published. But he showed up again in Millennium *(1976),* Kinsman *(1979) and* The Kinsman Saga *(1987).*

Eventually, Chet Kinsman changes the world. But in these early stories, he's the one who must change.

Incidentally, these stories—written in the early 1960s—are about a future that never came to pass. The Air Force was never allowed to orbit its own space stations. Neither the United States nor the Soviet Union established weaponry in orbit. Film cameras were replaced by digital.

But that doesn't make the stories less true.

JOE TENNY looked like a middle linebacker for the Pittsburgh Steelers. Sitting in the cool shadows of the Astro Motel's bar, swarthy, barrel-built, scowling face clamped on a smoldering cigar, he would never be taken for that rarest of all birds: a good engineer who is also a good military officer.

"Afternoon, Major."

Tenny turned on his stool to see old Cy Calder, the dean of the press-service reporters covering the base.

"Hi. Whatcha drinking?"

"I'm working," Calder answered with dignity. But he settled his once-lanky frame onto the next stool.

"Double Scotch," Tenny called to the bartender. "And refill mine."

"An officer and a gentleman," murmured Calder. His voice was gravelly, matching his face.

As the bartender slid the drinks to them, Tenny said, "You wanna know who got the assignment."

"I told you I'm working."

Tenny grinned. "Keep your mouth shut 'til tomorrow? Murdock'll make the official announcement then, at his press conference."

"If you can save me the tedium of listening to the good colonel for two hours to get a single name out of him, I'll buy the next round, shine your shoes for a month, and arrange to lose an occasional poker pot to you."

"The hell you will!"

Calder shrugged. Tenny took a long pull on his drink. Calder did likewise.

"Okay. You'll find out anyway. But keep it quiet until Murdock's announcement. It's going to be Kinsman."

Calder put his glass down on the bar carefully. "Chester A. Kinsman, the pride of the Air Force? That's hard to believe."

"Murdock picked him."

"I know this mission is strictly for publicity," Calder said, "but Kinsman? In orbit for three days with *Photo Day* magazine's prettiest female? Does Murdock want publicity or a paternity suit?"

"Come on, Chet's not that bad . . ."

"Oh no? From the stories I hear about your few weeks over at the NASA Ames center, Kinsman cut a swath from Berkeley to North Beach."

Tenny countered, "He's young and good-looking. And the girls haven't had many single astronauts to play with. NASA's gang is a bunch of old farts compared to my kids. But Chet's the best of the bunch, no fooling."

Calder looked unconvinced.

"Listen. When we were training at Edwards, know what Kinsman did? Built a biplane, an honest-to-God replica of a Spad fighter. From the ground up. He's a solid citizen."

"Yes, and then he played Red Baron for six weeks. Didn't he get into trouble for buzzing an airliner?"

Tenny's reply was cut off by a burst of talk and laughter. Half a dozen lean, lithe young men in Air Force blues—captains, all of them—trotted down the carpeted stairs that led into the bar.

"There they are," said Tenny. "You can ask Chet about it yourself."

Kinsman looked no different from the other Air Force astronauts. Slightly under six feet tall, thin with the leanness of youth, dark hair cut in the short, flat military style, blue-gray eyes, long bony face. He was grinning broadly at the moment, as he and the other five astronauts grabbed chairs in one corner of the bar and called their orders to the lone bartender.

Calder took his drink and headed for their table, followed by Major Tenny.

"Hold it," one of the captains called out. "Here comes the press."

"Tight security."

"Why, boys," Calder tried to make his rasping voice sound hurt, "don't you trust me?"

Tenny pushed a chair toward the newsman and took another one for himself. Straddling it, he told the captains, "It's okay. I spilled it to him."

"How much he pay you, boss?"

"That's between him and me."

As the bartender brought a tray of drinks, Calder said, "Let the Fourth Estate pay for this round, gentlemen. I want to pump some information out of you."

"That might take a lot of rounds."

To Kinsman, Calder said, "Congratulations, my boy. Colonel Murdock must think very highly of you."

Kinsman burst out laughing. "Murdock? You should've seen his face when he told me it was going to be me."

"Looked like he was sucking on lemons."

Tenny explained. "The choice for this flight was made mostly by computer. Murdock wanted to be absolutely fair, so he put everybody's performance ratings into the computer and out came Kinsman's name. If he hadn't made so much noise about being impartial, he could've reshuffled the cards and tried again. But I was right there when the machine finished its run, so he couldn't back out of it."

Calder grinned. "All right then, the computer thinks highly of you, Chet. I suppose that's still something of an honor."

"More like a privilege. I've been watching that *Photo Day* chick all through her training. She's ripe."

"She'll look even better up in orbit."

"Once she takes off the pressure suit . . . et cetera."

"Hey, y'know, nobody's ever done it in orbit."

"Yeah . . . free fall, zero gravity."

Kinsman looked thoughtful. "Adds a new dimension to the problem, doesn't it?"

"Three-dimensional." Tenny took the cigar butt from his mouth and laughed.

Calder got up slowly from his chair and silenced the others. Looking down fondly on Kinsman, he said:

"My boy—back in 1915, in London, I became a charter member of the Mile High Club. At an altitude of exactly 5280 feet, while circling St. Paul's, I successfully penetrated an Army nurse in an open cockpit . . . despite fogged goggles, cramped working quarters, and a severe case of windburn.

"Since then, there's been damned little to look forward to. The skin-divers claimed a new frontier, but in fact they are retrogressing. Any silly-ass dolphin can do it in the water.

"But you've got something new going for you: weightlessness. Floating around in free fall, chasing tail in three dimensions. It beggars the imagination!

"Kinsman, I pass the torch to you. To the founder of the Zero Gee Club!"

As one man, the officers rose and solemnly toasted Captain Kinsman. As they sat down again, Major Tenny burst the balloon. "You guys haven't given Murdock credit for much brains. You don't think he's gonna let Chet go up with that broad all alone, do you?"

Kinsman's face fell, but the others lit up.

"It'll be a three-man mission!"

"Two men and the chick."

Tenny warned, "Now don't start drooling. Murdock wants a chaperon, not an assistant rapist."

It was Kinsman who got it first. Slouching back in his chair, chin sinking to his chest, he muttered, "Sonofabitch . . . he's sending Jill along."

A collective groan.

"Murdock made up his mind an hour ago," Tenny said. "He was stuck with you, Chet, so he hit on the chaperon idea. He's also giving you some real chores to do, to keep you busy. Like mating the power pod."

"Jill Meyers," said one of the captains disgustedly.

"She's qualified, and she's been taking the *Photo Day* girl through her training. I'll bet she knows more about the mission than any of you guys do."

"She would."

"In fact," Tenny added maliciously, "I think she's the senior captain among you satellite-jockeys."

Kinsman had only one comment: "Shit."

The bone-rattling roar and vibration of liftoff suddenly died away. Sitting in his contour seat, scanning the banks of dials and gauges a few centimeters before his eyes, Kinsman could feel the pressure and tension slacken. Not back to normal. To zero. He was no longer plastered up against his seat, but touching it only lightly, almost floating in it, restrained only by his harness.

It was the fourth time he had felt weightlessness. It still made him smile inside the cumbersome helmet.

Without thinking about it, he touched a control stud on the chair's armrest. A maneuvering jet fired briefly and the ponderous, lovely bulk of planet Earth slid into view through the port in front of Kinsman. It curved huge and serene, blue, mostly, but tightly wrapped in the purest, dazzling white of clouds, beautiful, peaceful, shining.

Kinsman could have watched it forever, but he heard sounds of motion in his earphones. The two women were sitting behind him, side by side. The spacecraft cabin made a submarine look roomy: the three seats were shoehorned in among racks of instruments and equipment.

Jill Meyers, who came to the astronaut program from the Aerospace Medical Division, was officially second pilot and biomedical officer. *And chaperon,* Kinsman knew. The photographer, Linda Symmes, was simply a passenger.

Kinsman's earphones crackled with a disembodied link from Earth. "AF-9, this is ground control. We have you confirmed in orbit. Trajectory nominal. All systems go."

"Check," Kinsman said into his helmet mike.

The voice, already starting to fade, switched to ordinary conversational speech. "Looks like you're right on the money, Chet. We'll get the orbital parameters out of the computer and have 'em for you by the time you pass Ascension. You probably won't need much maneuvering to make rendezvous with the lab."

"Good. Everything here on the board looks green."

"Okay. Ground control out." Faintly. "And hey . . . good luck, Founding Father."

Kinsman grinned at that. He slid his faceplate up, loosened his harness and turned in his seat. "Okay, ladies, you can take off your helmets if you want to."

Jill Meyers snapped her faceplate open and started unlocking the helmet's neck seal.

"I'll go first," she said, "and then I can help Linda with hers."

"Sure you won't need any help?" Kinsman offered.

Jill pulled her helmet off. "I've had more time in orbit than you. And shouldn't you be paying attention to the instruments?"

So this is how it's going to be, Kinsman thought.

Jill's face was round and plain and bright as a new penny. Snub nose, wide mouth, short hair of undistinguished brown. Kinsman knew that under the pressure suit was a figure that could most charitably be described as ordinary.

Linda Symmes was entirely another matter. She had lifted her faceplate and was staring out at him with wide, blue eyes that combined feminine curiosity with a hint of helplessness. She was tall, nearly Kinsman's own height, with thick honey-colored hair and a body that he had already memorized down to the last curve.

In her sweet, high voice she said, "I think I'm going to be sick."

"Oh, for . . ."

Jill reached into the compartment between their two seats. "I'll take care of this. You stick to the controls." And she whipped a white plastic bag open and stuck it over Linda's face.

Shuddering at the thought of what could happen in zero gravity, Kinsman turned back to the control panel. He pulled his faceplate shut and turned up the air blower in his suit, trying to cut off the obscene sound of Linda's struggles.

"For Chrissake," he yelled, "unplug her radio! You want me chucking all over, too?"

"AF-9, this is Ascension."

Trying to blank his mind to what was going on behind him, Kinsman thumbed the switch on his communications panel. "Go ahead, Ascension."

For the next hour Kinsman thanked the gods that he had plenty of work to do. He matched the orbit of their three-man spacecraft to that of the Air Force orbiting laboratory, which had been up for more than a year now, and intermittently occupied by two-or three-man crews.

The lab was a fat, cylindrical shape, silhouetted against the brilliant white of the cloud-decked Earth. As he pulled the spacecraft close, Kinsman could see the antennas and airlock and other odd pieces of gear that had accumulated on it. *Looking more like a junkheap every trip.* Riding behind it, unconnected in any way, was the massive cone of the new power pod.

Kinsman circled the lab once, using judicious squeezes of his maneuvering jets. He touched a command signal switch, and the lab's rendezvous radar beacon came to life, announced by a light on his control panel.

"All systems green," he said to ground control. "Everything looks okay."

"Roger, Niner. You are cleared for docking."

This was a bit more delicate. *Be helpful if Jill could read off the computer.*

"Distance, eighty-eight meters," Jill's voice pronounced firmly in his earphones. "Approach angle . . ."

Kinsman instinctively turned his head, but his helmet cut off any possible sight of Jill. "Hey, how's your patient?"

"Empty. I gave her a sedative. She's out."

"Okay," Kinsman said. "Let's get docked."

He inched the spacecraft into the docking collar on one end of the lab, locked on and saw the panel lights confirm that the docking was secure.

"Better get Sleeping Beauty zippered up," he told Jill as he touched the buttons that extended the flexible access tunnel from the hatch over their heads to the main hatch of the lab. The lights on the panel turned from amber to green when the tunnel locked its fittings around the lab's hatch.

Jill said, "I'm supposed to check the tunnel."

"Stay put. I'll do it." Sealing his faceplate shut, Kinsman unbuckled and rose effortlessly out of the seat to bump his helmet lightly against the overhead hatch.

"You two both buttoned tight?"

"Yes."

"Keep an eye on the air gauge." He cracked the hatch open a few millimeters.

"Pressure's okay. No red lights."

Nodding, Kinsman pushed the hatch open all the way. He pulled himself easily up and into the shoulder-wide tunnel, propelling himself down its curving length by a few flicks of his fingers against the ribbed walls.

Light and easy, he reminded himself. *No big motions, no sudden moves.*

When he reached the laboratory hatch he slowly rotated, like a swimmer doing a lazy rollover, and inspected every inch of the tunnel seal in the light of his helmet lamp. Satisfied that it was locked in place, he opened the lab hatch and pushed himself inside. Carefully, he touched his slightly adhesive boots to the plastic flooring and stood upright. His arms tended to float out, but they touched the equipment racks on either side of the narrow central passageway. Kinsman turned on the lab's interior lights, checked the air supply, pressure and temperature gauges, then shuffled back to the hatch and pushed himself through the tunnel again.

He reentered the spacecraft upside-down and had to contort himself in slow motion around the pilot's seat to regain a "normal" attitude.

"Lab's okay," he said finally. "Now how the hell do we get her through the tunnel?"

Jill had already unbuckled the harness over Linda's shoulders. "You pull, I'll push. She ought to bend around the corners all right."

And she did.

The laboratory was about the size and shape of the interior of a small transport plane. On one side, nearly its entire length was taken up by instrument racks, control equipment and the computer, humming almost inaudibly behind light plastic panels. Across the narrow separating aisle were the crew stations: control desk, two observation ports, biology and astrophysics benches. At the far end, behind a discreet curtain, was the head and a single hammock.

Kinsman sat at the control desk, in his fatigues now, one leg hooked around the webbed chair's single supporting column to keep him from floating off. He was running through a formal check of all the lab's life systems: air, water, heat, electrical power. All green lights on the main panel. Communications gear. Green. The radar screen to his left showed a single large blip close by: the power pod.

He looked up as Jill came through the curtain from the bunkroom. She was still in her pressure suit, with only the helmet removed.

"How is she?"

Looking tired, Jill answered, "Okay. Still sleeping. I think she'll be all right when she wakes up."

"She'd better be. I'm not going to have a wilting flower around here. I'll abort the mission."

"Give her a chance, Chet. She just lost her cookies when free fall hit her. All the training in the world can't prepare you for those first few minutes."

Kinsman recalled his first orbital flight. It doesn't shut off. You're falling. Like skiing, or skydiving. Only better.

Jill shuffled toward him, keeping a firm grip on the chairs in front of the work benches and the handholds set into the equipment racks.

Kinsman got up and pushed toward her. "Here, let me help you out of the suit."

"I can do it myself."

"Shut up."

After several minutes, Jill was free of the bulky suit and sitting in one of the webbed chairs in her coverall fatigues. Ducking slightly because of the curving overhead, Kinsman glided into the galley. It was about half the width of a phone booth, and not as deep nor as tall.

"Coffee, tea or milk?"

Jill grinned at him. "Orange juice."

He reached for a concentrate bag. "You're a hard gal to satisfy."

"No I'm not. I'm easy to get along with. Just one of the fellas."

Feeling slightly puzzled, Kinsman handed her the orange juice container.

For the next couple of hours they checked out the lab's equipment in detail. Kinsman was reassembling a high resolution camera after cleaning it, parts hanging in midair all around him as he sat intently working, while Jill was nursing a straggly-looking philodendron that had been smuggled aboard and was inching from the biology bench toward the ceiling light panels. Linda pushed back the curtain from the sleeping area and stepped, uncertainly, into the main compartment.

Jill noticed her first. "Hi, how're you feeling?"

Kinsman looked up. She was in tight-fitting coveralls. He bounced out of his web-chair toward her, scattering camera parts in every direction.

"Are you all right?" he asked.

Smiling sheepishly. "I think so. I'm rather embarrassed . . ." Her voice was high and soft.

"Oh, that's all right," Kinsman said eagerly. "It happens to practically everybody. I got sick myself my first time in orbit."

"That," said Jill as she dodged a slowly-tumbling lens that ricocheted gently off the ceiling, "is a little white lie, meant to make you feel at home."

Kinsman forced himself not to frown. *Why'd Jill want to cross me?*

Jill said, "Chet, you'd better pick up those camera pieces before they get so scattered you won't be able to find them all."

He wanted to snap an answer, thought better of it, and replied simply, "Right."

As he finished the job on the camera, he took a good look at Linda. The color was back in her face. She looked steady, clear-eyed, not frightened or upset. *Maybe she'll be okay after all.* Jill made her a cup of tea, which she sipped from the lid's plastic spout.

Kinsman went to the control desk and scanned the mission schedule sheet.

"Hey, Jill, it's past your bedtime."

"I'm not really very sleepy," she said.

"Maybe. But you've had a busy day, little girl. And tomorrow will be busier. Now you get your four hours, and then I'll get mine. Got to be fresh for the mating."

"Mating?" Linda asked from her seat at the far end of the aisle, a good five strides from Kinsman. Then she remembered, "Oh, you mean linking the pod to the laboratory."

Suppressing a half-dozen possible jokes, Kinsman nodded. "Extra-vehicular activity."

Jill reluctantly drifted off her web-chair. "Okay, I'll sack in. I am tired, but I never seem to get really sleepy up here."

Wonder how much Murdock's told her? She's sure acting like a chaperon.

Jill shuffled into the sleeping area and pulled the curtain firmly shut. After a few moments of silence, Kinsman turned to Linda.

"Alone at last."

She smiled back.

"Uh, you just happen to be sitting where I've got to install this camera." He nudged the finished hardware so that it floated gently toward her.

She got up slowly, carefully, and stood behind the chair, holding its back with both hands as if she were afraid of falling. Kinsman slid into the web-chair and stopped the camera's slow-motion flight with one hand. Working on the fixture in the bulkhead that it fit into, he asked:

"You really feel okay?"

"Yes, honestly."

"Think you'll be up to EVA tomorrow?"

"I hope so. I want to go outside with you."

I'd rather be inside with you. Kinsman grinned as he worked.

An hour later they were sitting side by side in front of one of the observation ports, looking out at the curving bulk of Earth, the blue and white splendor of the cloud-spangled Pacific. Kinsman had just reported to the Hawaii ground station. The mission flight plan was floating on a clipboard between the two of them. He was trying to study it, comparing the time when Jill would be sleeping with the long stretches between ground stations, when there would be no possibility of being interrupted.

"Is that land?" Linda asked, pointing to a thick band of clouds wrapping the horizon.

Looking up from the clipboard, Kinsman said, "South American coast. Chile."

"There's another tracking station there."

"NASA station. Not part of our network. We only use Air Force stations."

"Why is that?"

He felt his face frowning. "Murdock's playing soldier. This is supposed to be a strictly military operation. Not that we do anything warlike. But we run as though there weren't any civilian stations around to help us. The usual hup-two-three crap."

She laughed. "You don't agree with the Colonel?"

"There's only one thing he's done lately that I'm in complete agreement with."

"What's that?"

"Bringing you up here."

The smile stayed on her face but her eyes moved away from him. "Now you sound like a soldier."

"Not an officer and a gentleman?"

She looked straight at him again. "Let's change the subject."

Kinsman shrugged. "Sure. Okay. You're here to get a story. Murdock wants to get the Air Force as much publicity as NASA gets. And the Pentagon wants to show the world that we don't have any weapons on board. We're military, all right, but *nice* military."

"And you?" Linda asked, serious now. "What do you want? How does an Air Force captain get into the space cadets?"

"The same way everything happens—you're in a certain place at a certain time. They told me I was going to be an astronaut. It was all part of the job . . . until my first orbital flight. Now it's a way of life."

"Really? Why is that?"

Grinning, he answered, "Wait'll we go outside. You'll find out."

Jill came back into the main cabin precisely on schedule, and it was Kinsman's turn to sleep. He seldom had difficulty sleeping on Earth, never in orbit. But he wondered about Linda's reaction to being outside while he strapped on the pressure-cuffs to his arms and legs. The medics insisted on them, claimed they exercised the cardiovascular system while you slept.

Damned stupid nuisance, Kinsman grumbled to himself. *Some ground-based MD's idea of how to make a name for himself.*

Finally he zippered himself into the gossamer cocoon-like hammock and shut his eyes. He could feel the cuffs pumping gently. His last conscious thought was a nagging worry that Linda would be terrified of EVA.

When he awoke, and Linda took her turn in the hammock, he talked it over with Jill.

"I think she'll be all right, Chet. Don't hold that first few minutes against her."

"I don't know. There's only two kinds of people up here: you either love it or you're scared sh . . . witless. And you can't fake it. If she goes ape outside . . ."

"She won't," Jill said firmly. "And anyway, you'll be there to help her. I've told her that she won't be going outside until you're finished with the mating job. She wanted to get pictures of you actually at work, but she'll settle for a few posed shots."

Kinsman nodded. But the worry persisted. *I wonder if Calder's Army nurse was scared of flying?*

He was pulling on his boots, wedging his free foot against an equipment rack to keep from floating off, when Linda returned from her sleep.

"Ready for a walk around the block?" he asked her.

She smiled and nodded without the slightest hesitation. "I'm looking forward to it. Can I get a few shots of you while you zipper up your suit?"

Maybe she'll be okay.

At last he was sealed into the pressure suit. Linda and Jill stood back as Kinsman shuffled to the airlock-hatch. It was set into the floor at the end of the cabin where the spacecraft was docked. With Jill helping him, he eased down into the airlock and shut the hatch. The airlock chamber itself was coffin-sized. Kinsman had to half-bend to move around in it. He checked out his suit, then pumped the air out of the chamber. Then he was ready to open the outer hatch.

It was beneath his feet, but as it slid open to reveal the stars, Kinsman's weightless orientation flip-flopped, like an optical illusion, and he suddenly felt that he was standing on his head and looking up.

"Going out now," he said into the helmet-mike.

"Okay," Jill's voice responded.

Carefully, he eased himself through the open hatch, holding onto its edge with one gloved hand once he was fully outside, the way a swimmer holds the rail for a moment when he first slides into the deep water.

Outside. Swinging his body around slowly, he took in the immense beauty of Earth, dazzlingly bright even through his tinted visor. Beyond its curving limb was the darkness of infinity, with the beckoning stars watching him in unblinking solemnity.

Alone now. His own tight, self-contained universe, independent of everything and everybody. He could cut the life-giving umbilical line that linked him with the laboratory and float off by himself, forever. And be dead in two minutes. Ay, *there's the rub.*

Instead, he unhooked the tiny gas gun from his waist and, trailing the umbilical, squirted himself over toward the power pod. It was riding smoothly behind the lab, a squat truncated cone, shorter, but fatter, than the lab itself, one edge brilliantly lit by the sun; the rest of it bathed in the softer light reflected from the dayside of Earth below.

Kinsman's job was to inspect the power pod, check its equipment, and then mate it to the electrical system of the laboratory. There was no need to physically connect the two bodies, except to link a pair of power lines between them. Everything necessary for the task—tools, power lines, checkout instruments—had been built into the pod, waiting for a man to use them.

It would have been simple work on Earth. In zero gee, it was complicated. The slightest motion of any part of your body started you drifting. You had to fight against all the built-in mannerisms of a lifetime; had to work constantly to keep in place. It was easy to get exhausted in zero gee.

Kinsman accepted all this with hardly a conscious thought. He worked slowly, methodically, using as little motion as possible, letting himself drift slightly until a more-or-less natural body motion counteracted and pulled him back in the opposite direct ion. *Ride the waves, slow and easy.* There was a rhythm to his work, the natural dreamlike rhythm of weightlessness.

His earphones were silent, he said nothing. All he heard was the purring of the suit's air-blowers and his own steady breathing. All he saw was his work.

Finally he jetted back to the laboratory, towing the pair of thick cables. He found the connectors waiting for them on the side wall of the lab and inserted the cable plugs. *I pronounce you lab and power source.* He inspected the checkout lights alongside the connectors. All green. *May you produce many kilowatts.*

Swinging from handhold to handhold along the length of the lab, he made his way back toward the airlock.

"Okay, it's finished. How's Linda doing?"

Jill answered, "She's all set."

"Send her out."

She came out slowly, uncertain wavering feet sliding out first from the bulbous airlock. It reminded Kinsman of a film he had seen of a whale giving birth.

"Welcome to the real world," he said when her head cleared the airlock hatch.

She turned to answer him and he heard her gasp and he knew that now he liked her.

"It's . . . it's . . ."

"Staggering," Kinsman suggested. "And look at you—no hands." She was floating freely, pressure-suit laden with camera gear, umbilical line flexing easily behind her. Kinsman couldn't see her face through the tinted visor, but he could hear the awe in her voice, even in her breathing.

"I've never seen anything so absolutely overwhelming . . ." And then, suddenly, she was all business, reaching for a camera, snapping away at the Earth and stars and distant moon, rapidfire. She moved too fast and started to tumble. Kinsman jetted over and steadied her, holding her by the shoulders.

"Hey, take it easy. They're not going away. You've got lots of time."

"I want to get some shots of you, and the lab. Can you get over by the pod and go through some of the motions of your work on it?"

Kinsman posed for her, answered her questions, rescued a camera when she fumbled it out of her hands and couldn't reach it as it drifted away from her.

"Judging distances gets a little whacky out here," he said, handing the camera back to her.

Jill called them twice and ordered them back inside. "Chet, you're already fifteen minutes over the limit!"

"There's plenty slop in the schedule; we can stay out a while longer."

"You're going to get her exhausted."

"I really feel fine," Linda said, her voice lyrical.

"How much more film do you have?" Kinsman asked her. She peered at the camera. "Six more shots."

"Okay, we'll be in when the film runs out, Jill."

"You're going to be in darkness in another five minutes!"

Turning to Linda, who was floating upside-down with the cloud-laced Earth behind her, he said, "Save your film for the sunset, then shoot like hell when it comes."

"The sunset? What'll I focus on?"

"You'll know when it happens. Just watch."

It came fast, but Linda was equal to it. As the lab swung in its orbit toward the Earth's night shadow, the sun dropped to the horizon and shot off a spectacular few moments of the purest reds and oranges and finally a heart-catching blue. Kinsman watched in silence, hearing Linda's breath going faster and faster as she worked the camera.

Then they were in darkness. Kinsman flicked on his helmet lamp. Linda was just hanging there, camera still in hand.

"It's . . . impossible to describe." Her voice sounded empty, drained. "If I hadn't seen it . . . if I didn't get it on film, I don't think I'd be able to convince myself that I wasn't dreaming."

Jill's voice rasped in his earphones. "Chet, get inside! This is against every safety reg, being outside in the dark."

He looked over toward the lab. Lights were visible along its length and the ports were lighted from within. Otherwise, he could barely make it out, even though it was only a few meters away.

"Okay, okay. Turn on the airlock-light so we can see the hatch." Linda was still bubbling about the view outside, long after they had pulled off their pressure suits and eaten sandwiches and cookies.

"Have you ever been out there?" she asked Jill.

Perched on the biology bench's edge, near the mice colony, Jill nodded curtly. "Twice."

"Isn't it spectacular? I hope the pictures come out; some of the settings on the camera . . ."

"They'll be all right," Jill said. "And if they're not, we've got a backlog of photos you can use."

"Oh, but they wouldn't have the shots of Chet working on the power pod."

Jill shrugged. "Aren't you going to take more photos in here? If you want to get some pictures of real space veterans, you ought to snap the mice here. They've been up for months now, living fine and raising families. And they don't make such a fuss about it, either."

"Well, some of us do exciting things," Kinsman said, "and some of us tend mice."

Jill glowered at him.

Glancing at his wristwatch, Kinsman said, "Ladies, it's my sack time. I've had a trying day: mechanic, tourist guide, and cover boy for *Photo Day*. Work, work, work."

He glided past Linda with a smile, kept it for Jill as he went by her. She was still glaring.

When he woke up again and went back into the main cabin, Jill was talking pleasantly with Linda as the two of them stood over the microscope and specimen rack of the biology bench.

Linda saw him first. "Oh, hi. Jill's been showing me the spores she's studying. And I photographed the mice. Maybe they'll go on the cover instead of you."

Kinsman grinned. "She's been poisoning your mind against me." But to himself he wondered, *What the hell has Jill been telling her about me?*

Jill drifted over to the control desk, picked up the clipboard with the mission log on it and tossed it lightly toward Kinsman.

"Ground control says the power pod checks out all green," she said. "You did a good job."

"Thanks." He caught the clipboard. "Whose turn in the sack is it?"

"Mine," Jill answered.

"Okay. Anything special cooking?"

"No. Everything's on schedule. Next data transmission comes up in twelve minutes. Kodiak station."

Kinsman nodded. "Sleep tight."

Once Jill had shut the curtain to the bunkroom, Kinsman carried the mission log to the control desk and sat down. Linda stayed at the biology bench, about three paces away.

He checked the instrument board with a quick glance, then turned to Linda. "Well, now do you know what I meant about this being a way of life?"

"I think so. It's so different."

"It's the real thing. Complete freedom. Brave new world. After ten minutes of EVA, everything else is just toothpaste."

"It was certainly exciting."

"More than that. It's *living*. Being on the ground is a drag, even flying a plane is dull now. This is where the fun is . . . out here in orbit and on the moon. It's as close to heaven as anybody's gotten."

"You're really serious?"

"Damned right. I've even been thinking of asking Murdock for a transfer to NASA duty. Air Force missions don't include the moon, and I'd like to walk around on the new world, see the sights."

She smiled at him. "I'm afraid I'm not that enthusiastic."

"Well, think about it for a minute. Up here, you're free. Really free, for the first time in your life. All the laws and rules and prejudices they've been dumping on you all your life, they're all *down there*. Up here it's a new start. You can be yourself and do your own thing . . . and nobody can tell you different."

"As long as somebody provides you with air and food and water and . . ."

"That's the physical end of it, sure. We're living in a microcosm, courtesy of the aerospace industry and AFSC. But there're no strings on us. The brass can't make us follow their rules. We're writing the rule books ourselves. For the first time since 1776, we're writing new rules."

Linda looked thoughtful now. Kinsman couldn't tell if she was genuinely impressed by his line, or if she knew what he was trying to lead up to. He turned back to the control desk and studied the mission flight plan again.

He had carefully considered all the possible opportunities, and narrowed them down to two. *Both of them tomorrow, over the Indian Ocean. Forty to fifty minutes between ground stations, and Jill's asleep both times.*

"AF-9, this is Kodiak."

He reached for the radio switch. "AF-9 here, Kodiak. Go ahead."

"We are receiving your automatic data transmission loud and clear."

"Roger Kodiak. Everything normal here; mission profile unchanged."

"Okay, Niner. We have nothing new for you. Oh wait . . . Chet, Lew Regneson is here and he says he's betting on you to uphold the Air Force's honor. Keep 'em flying."

Keeping his face as straight as possible, Kinsman answered, "Roger, Kodiak. Mission profile unchanged."

"Good luck!"

Linda's thoughtful expression had deepened. "What was that all about?"

He looked straight into those cool blue eyes and answered, "Damned if I know. Regneson's one of the astronaut team; been assigned to Kodiak for the past six weeks. He must be going ice-happy. Thought it'd be best just to humor him."

"Oh. I see." But she looked unconvinced.

"Have you checked any of your pictures in the film processor?"

Shaking her head, Linda said, "No, I don't want to risk them on your automatic equipment. I'll process them myself when we get back."

"Damned good equipment," said Kinsman.

"I'm fussy."

He shrugged and let it go.

"Chet?"

"What?"

"That power pod . . . what's it for? Colonel Murdock got awfully coy when I asked him."

"Nobody's supposed to know until the announcement's made in Washington . . . probably when we get back. I can't tell you officially," he grinned, "but generally reliable sources believe that it's going to power a radar set that'll be orbited next month. The radar will be part of our ABM warning system."

"Antiballistic missile?"

With a nod, Kinsman explained, "From orbit you can spot missile launches farther away, give the States a longer warning time."

"So your brave new world is involved in war, too."

"Sort of." Kinsman frowned. "Radars won't kill anybody, of course. They might save lives."

"But this *is* a military satellite."

"Unarmed. Two things this brave new world doesn't have yet: death and love."

"Men have died . . ."

"Not in orbit. On reentry. In ground or air accidents. No one's died up here. And no one's made love, either."

Despite herself, it seemed to Kinsman, she smiled. "Have there been any chances for it?"

"Well, the Russians have had women cosmonauts. Jill's been the first American female in orbit. You're the second."

She thought it over for a moment. "This isn't exactly the bridal suite of the Waldorf . . . in fact, I've seen better motel rooms along the Jersey Turnpike."

"Pioneers have to rough it."

"I'm a photographer, Chet, not a pioneer."

Kinsman hunched his shoulders and spread his hands helplessly, a motion that made him bob slightly on the chair. "Strike three, I'm out."

"Better luck next time."

"Thanks." He returned his attention to the mission flight plan. *Next time will be in exactly sixteen hours, chickie.*

When Jill came out of the sack it was Linda's turn to sleep. Kinsman stayed at the control desk, sucking on a container of lukewarm coffee. All the panel lights were green. Jill was taking a blood specimen from one of the white mice.

"How're they doing?"

Without looking up, she answered, "Fine. They've adapted to weightlessness beautifully. Calcium level's evened off, muscle tone is good . . ."

"Then there's hope for us two-legged types?"

Jill returned the mouse to the colony entrance and snapped the lid shut. It scampered through to rejoin its clan in the transparent plastic maze of tunnels.

"I can't see any physical reason why humans can't live in orbit indefinitely," she answered.

Kinsman caught a slight but definite stress on the word *physical.* "You think there might be emotional problems over the long run?"

"Chet, I can see emotional problems on a three-day mission." Jill forced the blood specimen into a stoppered test tube.

"What do you mean?"

"Come on," she said, her face a mixture of disappointment and distaste. "It's obvious what you're trying to do. Your tail's been wagging like a puppy's whenever she's in sight."

"You haven't been sleeping much, have you?"

"I haven't been eavesdropping, if that's what you mean. I've simply been watching you watching her. And some of the messages from the ground . . . is the whole Air Force in on this? How much money's being bet?"

"I'm not involved in any betting. I'm just . . ."

"You're just taking a risk on fouling up this mission and maybe killing the three of us, just to prove you're Tarzan and she's Jane."

"Goddammit, Jill, now you sound like Murdock."

The sour look on her face deepened. "Okay. You're a big boy. If you want to play Tarzan while you're on duty, that's your business. I won't get in your way. I'll take a sleeping pill and stay in the sack."

"You will?"

"That's right. You can have your blonde Barbie doll, and good luck to you. But I'll tell you this: she's a phony. I've talked to her long enough to dig that. You're trying to use her, but she's using us, too. She was pumping me about the power pod while you were sleeping. She's here for her own reasons, Chet, and if she plays along with you it won't be for the romance and adventure of it all."

My God Almighty, Jill's jealous!

It was tense and quiet when Linda returned from the bunkroom. The three of them worked separately: Jill fussing over the algae colony on the shelf above the biology bench; Kinsman methodically taking film from the observation cameras for return to Earth and reloading them; Linda efficiently clicking away at both of them.

Ground control called up to ask how things were going. Both Jill and Linda threw sharp glances at Kinsman. He replied merely:

"Following mission profile. All systems green."

They shared a meal of pastes and squeeze-tubes together, still mostly in silence, and then it was Kinsman's turn in the sack. But not before he checked the mission flight plan. *Jill goes in next, and we'll have four hours alone, including a stretch over the Indian Ocean.*

Once Jill retired, Kinsman immediately called Linda over to the control desk under the pretext of showing her the radar image of a Russian satellite.

"We're coming close now." They hunched side by side at the desk to peer at the orange-glowing radar screen, close enough for Kinsman to scent a hint of very feminine perfume. "Only a thousand kilometers away."

"Why don't you blink our lights at them?"

"It's unmanned."

"Oh."

"It *is* a little like World War I up here," Kinsman realized, straightening up. "Just being here is more important than which nation you're from."

"Do the Russians feel that way, too?"

Kinsman nodded. "I think so."

She stood in front of him, so close that they were almost touching.

"You know," Kinsman said, "when I first saw you on the base, I thought you were a photographer's model, not the photographer."

Gliding slightly away from him, she answered, "I started out as a model . . ." Her voice trailed off.

"Don't stop. What were you going to say?"

Something about her had changed, Kinsman realized. She was still coolly friendly, but alert now, wary, and . . . sad?

Shrugging, she said, "Modeling is a dead end. I finally figured out that there's more of a future on the other side of the camera."

"You had too much brains for modeling."

"Don't flatter me."

"Why on earth should I flatter you?"

"We're not on Earth."

"*Touché.*"

She drifted over toward the galley. Kinsman followed her.

"How long have you been on the other side of the camera?" he asked.

Turning back toward him, "I'm supposed to be getting your life story, not vice versa."

"Okay . . . ask me some questions."

"How many people know you're supposed to lay me up here?"

Kinsman felt his face smiling, an automatic delaying action. *What the hell*, he thought. Aloud, he replied, "I don't know. It started as a little joke among a few of the guys . . . apparently the word has spread."

"And how much money do you stand to win or lose?" She wasn't smiling.

"Money?" Kinsman was genuinely surprised. "Money doesn't enter into it."

"Oh no?"

"No, not with me," he insisted.

The tenseness in her body seemed to relax a little. "Then why . . . I mean . . . what's it all about?"

Kinsman brought his smile back and pulled himself down into the nearest chair. "Why not? You're damned pretty, neither one of us has any strings, nobody's tried it in zero gee before. Why the hell not?"

"But why should I?"

"That's the big question. That's what makes an adventure out of it."

She looked at him thoughtfully, leaning her tall frame against the galley paneling. "Just like that. An adventure. There's nothing more to it than that?"

"Depends," Kinsman answered. "Hard to tell ahead of time."

"You live in a very simple world, Chet."

"I try to. Don't you?"

She shook her head. "No, my world's very complex."

"But it includes sex."

Now she smiled, but there was no pleasure in it. "Does it?"

"You mean never?" Kinsman's voice sounded incredulous, even to himself.

She didn't answer.

"Never at all? I can't believe that."

"No," she said, "not never at all. But never for . . . for an adventure. For job security, yes. For getting the good assignments; for teaching me how to use a camera, in the first place. But never for fun . . . at least, not for a long, long time has it been for fun."

Kinsman looked into those ice-blue eyes and saw that they were completely dry and aimed straight back at him. His insides felt odd. He put a hand out toward her, but she didn't move a muscle.

"That's . . . that's a damned lonely way to live," he said.

"Yes, it is." Her voice was a steel knifeblade, without a trace of self-pity in it.

"But . . . how'd it happen? Why . . ."

She leaned her head back against the galley paneling, her eyes looking away, into the past. "I had a baby. He didn't want it. I had to give it up for adoption—either that or have it aborted. The kid should be five years old now. I don't know where she is." She straightened up, looked back at Kinsman. "But I found out that sex is either for making babies or making careers; not for *fun*."

Kinsman sat there, feeling like he had just taken a low blow. The only sound in the cabin was the faint hum of electrical machinery, the whisper of the air fans.

Linda broke into a grin. "I wish you could see your face: Tarzan, the Ape-Man, trying to figure out a nuclear reactor."

"The only trouble with zero gee," he mumbled, "is that you can't hang yourself."

Jill sensed something was wrong, it seemed to Kinsman. From the moment she came out of the sack, she sniffed around, giving quizzical looks. Finally, when Linda retired for her final rest period before their return, Jill asked him:

"How're you two getting along?"

"Okay."

"Really?"

"Really. We're going to open a Playboy Club in here. Want to be a bunny?"

Her nose wrinkled. "You've got enough of those."

For more than an hour they worked their separate tasks in silence. Kinsman was concentrating on recalibrating the radar mapper when Jill handed him a container of hot coffee.

He turned in the chair. She was standing beside him, not much taller than his own seated height.

"Thanks."

Her face was very serious. "Something's bothering you, Chet. What did she do to you?"

"Nothing."

"Really?"

"For Chrissake, don't start that again! Nothing, absolutely nothing happened. Maybe that's what's bothering me."

Shaking her head, "No, you're worried about something, and it's not about yourself."

"Don't be so damned dramatic, Jill."

She put a hand on his shoulder. "Chet . . . I know this is all a game to you, but people can get hurt at this kind of game, and, well . . . nothing in life is ever as good as you expect it will be."

Looking up at her intent brown eyes, Kinsman felt his irritation vanish. "Okay, kid. Thanks for the philosophy. I'm a big boy, though, and I know what it's all about."

"You just think you do."

Shrugging, "Okay, I think I do. Maybe nothing is as good as it ought to be, but a man's innocent until proven guilty, and everything new is as good as gold until you find some tarnish on it. That's my philosophy for the day!"

"All right, slugger," Jill smiled, ruefully. "Be the ape-man. Fight it out for yourself. I just don't want to see her hurt you."

"I won't get hurt."

Jill said, "You hope. Okay, if there's anything I can do . . ."

"Yeah, there is something."

"What?"

"When you sack in again, make sure Linda sees you take a sleeping pill. Will you do that?"

Jill's face went expressionless. "Sure," she answered flatly. "Anything for a fellow officer."

She made a great show, several hours later, of taking a sleeping pill so that she could rest well on her final nap before reentry. It seemed to Kinsman that Jill deliberately laid it on too thickly.

"Do you always take sleeping pills on the final time around?" Linda asked, after Jill had gone into the bunkroom.

"Got to be fully alert and rested," Kinsman replied, "for the return flight. Reentry's the trickiest part of the operation."

"Oh. I see."

"Nothing to worry about, though," Kinsman added.

He went to the control desk and busied himself with the tasks that the mission profile called for. Linda sat lightly in the next chair, within arm's reach. Kinsman chatted briefly with Kodiak station, on schedule, and made an entry in the log.

Three more ground stations and then we're over the Indian Ocean, with world enough and time.

But he didn't look up from the control panel; he tested each system aboard the lab, fingers flicking over control buttons, eyes focused on the red, amber and green lights that told him how the laboratory's mechanical and electrical machinery was functioning.

"Chet?"

"Yes."

"Are you . . . sore at me?"

Still not looking at her, "No, I'm busy. Why should I be sore at you?"

"Well, not sore maybe, but . . ."

"Puzzled?"

"Puzzled, hurt, something like that."

He punched an entry on the computer's keyboard at his side, then turned to face her. "Linda, I haven't really had time to figure out what I feel. You're a complicated woman; maybe too complicated for me. Life's got enough twists in it."

Her mouth drooped a little.

"On the other hand," he added, "we WASPs ought to stick together. Not many of us left."

That brought a faint smile. "I'm not a WASP. My real name's Szymanski. I changed it when I started modeling."

"Oh. Another complication."

She was about to reply when the radio speaker crackled, "AF-9, this is Cheyenne. Cheyenne to AF-9."

Kinsman leaned over and thumbed the transmitter switch. "AF-9 to Cheyenne. You're coming through faint but clear."

"Roger, Nine. We're receiving your telemetry. All systems look green from here."

"Manual check of systems also green," Kinsman said. "Mission profile okay, no deviations. Tasks about ninety percent complete."

"Roger. Ground control suggests you begin checking out your spacecraft on the next orbit. You are scheduled for reentry in ten hours."

"Right. Will do."

"Okay, Chet. Everything looks good from here. Anything else to report, ol' Founding Father?"

"Mind your own business." He turned the transmitter off.

Linda was smiling at him.

"What's so funny?"

"You are. You're getting very touchy about this whole business."

"It's going to stay touchy for a long time to come. Those guys'll hound me for years about this."

"You could always tell lies."

"About you? No, I don't think I could do that. If the girl was anonymous, that's one thing. But they all know you, know where you work."

"You're a gallant officer. I suppose that kind of rumor would get back to New York."

Kinsman grinned. "You could even make the front page of the *National Enquirer*."

She laughed at that. "I'll bet they'd pull out some of my old bikini pictures."

"Careful now," Kinsman put up a warning hand. "Don't stir up my imagination any more than it already is. I'm having a hard enough time being gallant right now."

They remained apart, silent, Kinsman sitting at the control desk, Linda drifting back toward the galley, nearly touching the curtain that screened off the sleeping area.

The ground control center called in and Kinsman gave a terse report. When he looked up at Linda again, she was sitting in front of the observation port across the aisle from the galley. Looking back at Kinsman, her face was troubled now, her eyes . . . he wasn't sure what was in her eyes. They looked different: no longer ice-cool, no longer calculating; they looked aware, concerned, almost frightened.

Still Kinsman stayed silent. He checked and double-checked the control board, making absolutely certain that every valve and transistor aboard the lab was working perfectly. Glancing at his watch: Five *more minutes before Ascension calls*. He checked the lighted board again.

Ascension called in exactly on schedule. Feeling his innards tightening, Kinsman gave his standard report in a deliberately calm and mechanical way. Ascension signed off.

With a long last look at the controls, Kinsman pushed himself out of the seat and drifted, hands faintly touching the grips along the aisle, toward Linda.

"You've been awfully quiet," he said, standing over her.

"I've been thinking about what you said a while ago." What was it in her eyes? Anticipation? Fear? "It . . . it has been a damned lonely life, Chet."

He took her arm and lifted her gently from the chair and kissed her.

"But . . ."

"It's all right," he whispered. "No one will bother us. No one will know."

She shook her head. "It's not that easy, Chet. It's not that simple."

"Why not? We're here together . . . what's so complicated?"

"But—doesn't anything bother you? You're floating around in a dream. You're surrounded by war machines, you're living every minute with danger. If a pump fails or a meteor hits . . ."

"You think it's any safer down there?"

"But life *is* complex, Chet. And love—well, there's more to it than just having fun."

"Sure there is. But it's meant to be enjoyed, too. What's wrong with taking an opportunity when you have it? What's so damned complicated or important? We're above the cares and worries of Earth. Maybe it's only for a few hours, but it's here and now, it's us. They can't touch us, they can't force us to do anything or stop us from doing what we want to. We're on our own. Understand? Completely on our own."

She nodded, her eyes still wide with the look of a frightened animal. But her hands slid around him, and together they drifted back toward the control desk. Wordlessly, Kinsman turned off all the overhead lights, so that all they saw was the glow of the control board and the flickering of the computer as it murmured to itself.

They were in their own world now, their private cosmos, floating freely and softly in the darkness. Touching, drifting, coupling, searching the new seas and continents, they explored their world.

Jill stayed in the hammock until Linda entered the bunkroom, quietly, to see if she had awakened yet. Kinsman sat at the control desk feeling, not tired, but strangely numb.

The rest of the flight was strictly routine. Jill and Kinsman did their jobs, spoke to each other when they had to. Linda took a brief nap, then returned to snap a few last pictures. Finally, they crawled back into the spacecraft, disengaged from the laboratory, and started the long curving flight back to Earth.

Kinsman took a last look at the majestic beauty of the planet, serene and incomparable among the stars, before touching the button that slid the heat-shield over his viewport. Then they felt the surge of rocket thrust, dipped into the atmosphere, knew that air heated beyond endurance surrounded them in a fiery grip and made their tiny craft into a flaming, falling star.

Pressed into his seat by the acceleration, Kinsman let the automatic controls bring them through reentry, through the heat and buffeting turbulence, down to an altitude where their finned craft could fly like a rocket-plane.

He took control and steered the craft back toward Patrick Air Force Base, back to the world of men, of weather, of cities, of hierarchies and official regulations. He did this alone, silently; he didn't need Jill's help or anyone else's. He flew the craft from inside his buttoned-tight pressure suit, frowning at the panel displays through his helmet's faceplate.

Automatically, he checked with ground control and received permission to slide the heat-shield back. The viewpoint showed him a stretch of darkening clouds spreading from the sea across the beach and well inland. His earphones were alive with other men's voices now: wind conditions, altitude checks, speed estimates. He knew, but could not see, that two jet planes were trailing along behind him, cameras focused on the returning spacecraft. *To provide evidence if I crash.*

They dipped into the clouds and a wave of gray mist hurtled up and covered the viewport. Kinsman's eyes flicked to the radar screen slightly off to his right. The craft shuddered briefly, then they broke below the clouds and he could see the long, black gouge of the runway looming before him. He pulled back slightly on the controls, hands and feet working instinctively, flashed over some scrubby vegetation, and flared the craft onto the runway. The landing skids touched once, bounced them up momentarily, then touched again with a grinding shriek. They skidded for more than a mile before stopping.

He leaned back in the seat and felt his body oozing sweat.

"Good landing," Jill said.

"Thanks." He turned off all the craft's systems, hands moving automatically in response to long training. Then he slid his faceplate up, reached overhead and popped the hatch open.

"End of the line," he said tiredly. "Everybody out."

He clambered up through the hatch, feeling his own weight with a sullen resentment, then helped Linda and finally Jill out of the spacecraft. They hopped down onto the blacktop runway. Two vans, an ambulance, and two fire trucks were rolling toward them from their parking stations at the end of the runway, a half-mile ahead.

Kinsman slowly took off his helmet. The Florida heat and humidity annoyed him now. Jill walked a few paces away from him, toward the approaching trucks.

He stepped toward Linda. Her helmet was off, and she was carrying a bag full of film.

"I've been thinking," he said to her. "That business about having a lonely life. You know, you're not the only one. And it doesn't have to be that way. I can get to New York whenever—"

"Now who's taking things seriously?" Her face looked calm again, cool, despite the glaring heat.

"But I mean—"

"Listen, Chet. We had our kicks. Now you can tell your friends about it, and I can tell mine. We'll both get a lot of mileage out of it. It'll help our careers."

"I never intended to . . . I didn't . . ."

But she was already turning away from him, walking toward the men who were running up to meet them from the trucks. One of them, a civilian, had a camera in his hands. He dropped to one knee and took a picture of Linda holding the film out and smiling broadly.

Kinsman stood there with his mouth hanging open.

Jill came back to him. "Well? Did you get what you were after?"

"No," he said slowly. "I guess I didn't."

She started to put her hand out to him. "We never do, do we?"

TEST IN ORBIT

KINSMAN SNAPPED AWAKE when the phone went off. Before it could complete its first ring he had the receiver off its cradle.

"Captain Kinsman?" The motel's night clerk.

"Yes," he whispered back, squinting at the luminous dial of his wristwatch: *three twenty-three.*

"I'm awfully sorry to disturb you, Captain, but Colonel Murdock called—"

"How the hell did he know I was here?"

"He said he's calling all the motels around the base. I didn't tell him you were here. He said when he found you he wanted you to report to him at once. Those were his words, Captain: at once."

Kinsman frowned in the darkness. "Okay. Thanks for playing dumb."

"Not at all, sir. Hope it isn't trouble."

"Yeah." Kinsman hung up. He sat for a half-minute on the edge of the bed. *Murdock making the rounds of the motels at three in the morning and the clerk hopes it's not trouble. Very funny.*

He stood up, stretched his wiry frame and glanced at the woman still sleeping quietly on the other side of the bed. With a wistful shake of his head, he padded out to the bathroom.

He flipped the light switch and turned on the coffee machine on the wall next to the doorway. *It's lousy but it's coffee.* As the machine started

gurgling, he softly closed the door and rummaged through his travel
kit for the electric razor. The face that met him in the mirror was lean
and long-jawed, with jet black hair cut down to military length and
soft blue-gray eyes that were, at the moment, just the slightest bit
bloodshot.

Within a few minutes he was shaved, showered, and back in Air
Force blues. He left a scribbled note on motel stationery leaning
against the dresser mirror, took a final long look at the woman, then
went out to find his car.

He put down the top of his old convertible and gunned her out onto
the coast road. As he raced through the predawn darkness, wind
whistling all around him, Kinsman could feel the excitement building
up. A pair of cars zoomed past him, doing eighty, heading for the base.
Kinsman held to the legal limit and caught them again at the main
gate, lined up while the guard sergeant checked ID badges with extra
care. Kinsman's turn came.

"What's the stew, Sergeant?"

The guard flashed his hand light on the badge Kinsman held in his
outstretched hand.

"Dunno, sir. We got the word to look sharp."

The light flashed full in Kinsman's face. Painfully sharp, he thought
to himself.

The guard waved him on.

There was that special crackle in the air as Kinsman drove toward
the Administration Building. The kind that comes only when a launch
is imminent. As if in answer to his unspoken hunch, the floodlights on
Complex 17 bloomed into life, etching the tall, silver rocket standing
there, embraced by the dark spiderwork of the gantry tower.

Pad 17. Manned shot.

People were scurrying in and out of the Administration Building:
sleepy-eyed, disheveled, but their feet were moving double time.
Colonel Murdock's secretary was coming down the hallway as
Kinsman signed in at the reception desk.

"What's up, Annie?"

"I just got here myself," she said. There were hairclips still in her
blonde curls. "The boss told me to flag you down the instant you
arrived."

Even from completely across the colonel's spacious office, Kinsman could see that Murdock was a round little kettle of nerves. He was standing by the window behind his desk, watching the activity on Pad 17, clenching and unclenching his hands behind his back. His bald head was glistening with perspiration, despite the frigid air conditioning. Kinsman stood at the door with the secretary.

"Colonel?" she said softly.

Murdock spun around. "Kinsman. So here you are."

"What's going on? I thought the next manned shot wasn't until—"

The colonel waved a pudgy hand. "The next manned shot is as fast as we can damned well make it." He walked around the desk and eyed Kinsman. "You look a mess."

"Hell, it's four in the morning!"

"No excuses. Get over to the medical section for pre-flight check out. They've been waiting for you."

"I'd still like to know . . ."

"Probably ought to test your blood for alcohol content," Murdock grumbled.

"I've been celebrating my transfer," Kinsman said. "I'm not supposed to be on active duty. Six more days and I'm a civilian spaceman. Get my picture in *Photo Day* and I'm off to the moon. Remember?"

"Cut the clowning. General Hatch is flying in from Norton Field and he wants you."

"Hatch?"

"That's right. He wants the most experienced man available."

"Twenty guys on base and you have to make me available."

Murdock fumed. "Listen. This is a military operation. I may not insist on much discipline, but don't think you're a civilian glamour boy yet. You're still in the Air Force and there's a hell of a bind on. Hatch wants you. Understand?"

Kinsman shrugged. "If you saw what I had to leave behind me to report for duty here, you'd put me up for the Medal of Honor."

Murdock frowned in exasperation. The secretary tried unsuccessfully to suppress a smile.

"All right, joker. Get down to the medical section. On the double. Anne, you stick with him and bring him to the briefing room the instant he's finished. General Hatch will be here in twenty minutes; I don't want to keep him waiting any longer than I have to."

Kinsman stood at the doorway, not moving. "Will you please tell me just what this scramble is all about?"

"Ask the general," Murdock said, walking back toward his desk. He glanced out the window again, then turned back to Kinsman. "All I know is that Hatch wants the man with the most hours in orbit ready for a shot, immediately."

"Manned shots are all volunteer missions," Kinsman pointed out.

"So?"

"I'm practically a civilian. There are nineteen other guys who—"

"Dammit Kinsman, if you . . ."

"Relax, Colonel. Relax. I won't let you down. Not when there's a chance to get a few hundred miles away from all the brass on Earth."

Murdock stood there glowering as Kinsman took the secretary out to his car. As they sped off toward the medical section, she looked at him.

"You shouldn't bait him like that," she said. "He feels the pressure a lot more than you do."

"He's insecure," Kinsman said, grinning. "There're only twenty men in the Air Force qualified for orbital missions, and he's not one of them."

"And you are."

"Damned right, honey. It's the only thing in the world worth doing. You ought to try it."

She put a hand up to her wind-whipped hair. "Me? Flying in orbit? No gravity?"

"It's a clean world, Annie. Brand new every time. Just you and your own little cosmos. Your life is completely your own. Once you've done it, there's nothing left on Earth but to wait for the next shot."

"My God, you sound as though you really mean it."

"I'm serious," he insisted. "The Reds have female cosmonauts. We're going to be putting women in orbit, eventually. Get your name on the top of the list."

"And get locked in a capsule with you?"

His grin returned. "It's an intriguing possibility."

"Some other time, captain," she said. "Right now we have to get you through your pre-flight and off to meet the general."

General Lesmore D. ("Hatchet") Hatch sat in dour silence in the small briefing room. The oblong conference table was packed with colonels and a single civilian. *They all look so damned serious,* Kinsman thought as he took the only empty chair, directly across from the general.

"Captain Kinsman." It was a flat statement of fact.

"Good, em, morning, General."

Hatch turned to a moon-faced aide. "Borgeson, let's not waste time."

Kinsman only half-listened as the hurried introductions went around the table. He felt uncomfortable already, and it was only partly due to the stickiness of the crowded little room. Through the only window he could see the first glow of dawn.

"Now then," Borgeson said, introductions finished, "very briefly, your mission will involve orbiting and making rendezvous with an unidentified satellite."

"Unidentified?"

Borgeson nodded. "Whoever launched it has made no announcement whatsoever. Therefore, we must consider the satellite as potentially hostile. To begin at the beginning, we'll have Colonel McKeever of SPADATS give you the tracking data first."

As they went around the table, each colonel adding his bit of information, Kinsman began to build up the picture in his mind.

The satellite had been launched from the mid-Pacific, nine hours ago. Probably from a specially rigged submarine. It was now in a polar orbit, so that it covered every square mile on Earth in twelve hours. Since it went up, not a single radio transmission had been detected going to it or from it. And it was big, even heavier than the ten-ton *Voshkods* the Russians had been using for manned flights.

"A satellite of that size," said the colonel from the Special Weapons Center, "could easily contain a nuclear warhead of 100 megatons or more."

If the bomb were large enough, he explained, it could heat the atmosphere to the point where every combustible thing on the ground would ignite. Kinsman pictured trees, plants, grass, buildings, people, the sky itself, all bursting into flame.

"Half the United States could be destroyed at once with such a bomb," the colonel said.

"And in a little more than two hours," Borgeson added, "the satellite will pass over Chicago and travel right across the heartland of America."

Murdock paled. "You don't think they'd . . . set it off?"

"We don't know," General Hatch answered. "And we don't intend to sit here waiting until we find out."

"Why not just knock it down?" Kinsman asked. "We can hit it, can't we?"

Hatch frowned. "We could reach it with a missile, yes. But we've been ordered by the Pentagon to inspect the satellite and determine whether or not it's actually hostile."

"In two hours?"

"Perhaps I can explain," said the civilian. He had been introduced as a State Department man; Kinsman had already forgotten his name. He had a soft, sheltered look about him.

"You may know that the disarmament meeting in Geneva is discussing nuclear weapons in space. It seemed last week we were on the verge of an agreement to ban weapons in space, just as testing weapons in the atmosphere has already been banned. But three days ago the conference suddenly became deadlocked on some very minor issues. It's been very difficult to determine who is responsible for the deadlock and why. The Russians, the Chinese, the French, even some of the smaller nations, are apparently stalling for time . . . waiting for something to happen."

"And this satellite might be it," Kinsman said.

"The Department of State believes that this satellite is a test, to see if we can detect and counteract weapons placed in orbit."

"But they know we can shoot them down!" the general snapped.

"Yes, of course," the civilian answered softly. "But they also know we would not fire on a satellite that might be a peaceful research station. Not unless we were certain that it was actually a bomb in orbit. We must inspect this satellite to prove to the world that we can board any satellite and satisfy ourselves that it is not a threat to us. Otherwise we will be wide open to nuclear blackmail, in orbit."

The general shook his head. "If they've gone to the trouble of launching a multi-ton vehicle, then military logic dictates that they placed a bomb in it. By damn, that's what I'd do, in their place."

"Suppose it is a bomb," Kinsman asked, "and they explode it over Chicago?"

Borgeson smiled uneasily. "It could take out everything between New England and the Rockies."

Kinsman heard himself whistle in astonishment.

"No matter whether it's a bomb or not, the satellite is probably rigged with booby traps to prevent us from inspecting it," one of the other colonels pointed out.

Thanks a lot, Kinsman said to himself.

Hatch focused his gunmetal eyes on Kinsman. "Captain, I want to impress a few thoughts on you. First, the Air Force has been working for nearly twenty years to achieve the capability of placing a military man in orbit on an instant's notice. Your flight will be the first practical demonstration of all that we've battled to achieve over those years. You can see, then, the importance of this mission."

"Yessir."

"Second, this is strictly a voluntary mission. Because it is so important to us, I don't want you to try it unless you're absolutely certain—"

"I realize that, sir. I'm your man."

"I understand you're transferring out of the Air Force next week."

Kinsman nodded. "That's next week. This is now."

Hatch's well-seamed face unfolded into a smile. "Well said, captain. And good luck."

The general rose and everyone snapped to attention. As the others filed out of the briefing room, Murdock drew Kinsman aside.

"You had your chance to beg off."

"And miss this? A chance to play cops and robbers in orbit?"

The colonel flushed angrily. "We're not in this for laughs. This is damned important. If it really is a bomb . . ."

"I'll be the first to know," Kinsman snapped. To himself he added, *I've listened to you long enough for one morning.*

Countdowns took minutes instead of days, with solid-fueled rockets. But there were just as many chances of a man or machine failing at a critical point and turning the intricate, delicately poised booster into a flaming pyre of twisted metal.

Kinsman sat tautly in the contoured couch, listening to them tick off the seconds. He hated countdowns. He hated being helpless, completely dependent on a hundred faceless voices that flickered through his earphones, waiting childlike in a mechanical womb, not alive, waiting, doubled up and crowded by the unfeeling, impersonal machinery that automatically gave him warmth and breath and life.

He could feel the tiny vibrations along his spine that told him the ship was awakening. Green lights started to blossom across the control panel, a few inches in front of his faceplate, telling him that everything was ready. Still the voices droned through his earphones in carefully measured cadence:

three . . . two . . . one.

And she bellowed into life. Acceleration pressure flattened Kinsman into the couch. Vibration rattled his eyes in their sockets. Time became meaningless. The surging, engulfing, overpowering noise of the mighty rocket engines made his head ring, even after they burned out into silence.

Within minutes he was in orbit, the long slender rocket stages falling away behind, together with all sensations of weight. Kinsman was alone now in the squat, delta-shaped capsule: weightless, free of Earth.

Still he was the helpless, unstirring one. Computers sent guidance instructions from the ground to the capsule's controls. Tiny vectoring rockets placed around the capsule's black hull squirted on and off, microscopic puffs of thrust that maneuvered the capsule into the precise orbit needed for catching the unidentified satellite.

Completely around the world Kinsman spun, southward over the Pacific, past the gleaming whiteness of Antarctica, and then north again over the wrinkled, cloud-spattered land mass of Asia. As he crossed the night-shrouded Arctic, nearly two hours after being launched, the voices from his base began crackling in his earphones again. He answered them as automatically as the machines did, reading off the numbers on the control panel, proving to them that he was alive and functioning properly.

Then Murdock's voice cut in: "There's been another launch, fifteen minutes ago. From somewhere near Mongolia as near as we can determine it. It's a high-energy boost; looks as though you're going to have company."

Kinsman acknowledged the information, but still sat unmoving. Then he saw it looming ahead of him, seemingly hurtling toward him.

He came to life. To meet and board the satellite he had to match its orbit and speed, exactly. He was approaching it too fast. No computer on Earth could handle this part of the job. Radar and stabilizing gyros helped, but it was his own eyes and the fingers that manipulated the retrorocket controls that finally eased the capsule into a rendezvous orbit.

Finally, the big satellite seemed to be stopped in space, dead ahead of his capsule, a huge inert hulk of metal, dazzlingly brilliant where the sun lit its curving side, totally invisible where it was in shadow. It looked ridiculously like a crescent moon made of flush-welded aluminum. A smaller crescent puzzled Kinsman until he realized it was a dead rocket-nozzle hanging from the satellite's tailcan.

"I'm parked alongside her, about fifty feet off," he reported into his helmet microphone. "She looks like the complete upper stage of a Saturn-class booster. Can't see any markings from this angle. I'll have to go outside."

"You'd better make it fast," Murdock's voice answered. "That second ship is closing in fast."

"What's the E.T.A?"

A pause while voices mumbled in the background. "About fifteen minutes . . . maybe less."

"Great."

"You can abort if you want to."

Same to you, Pal, Kinsman said to himself. Aloud, he replied, "I'm going to take a close look at her. Maybe get inside, if I can. Call you back in fifteen minutes."

Murdock didn't argue. Kinsman smiled grimly at the realization that the colonel had not reminded him that the satellite might be booby-trapped. Old Mother Murdock hardly forgot such items. He simply had decided not to make the choice of aborting the mission too attractive.

Gimmicked or not, the satellite was too near and too enticing to turn back now. Kinsman quickly checked out his pressure suit, pumped the air out of his cabin and into storage tanks, and then opened the airlock hatch over his head.

Out of the womb and into the world.

He climbed out and teetered on the lip of the airlock, balancing weightlessly. *The real world.* No matter how many times he saw it, it always caught his breath. The vast sweep of the multi-hued Earth, hanging at an impossible angle, decked with dazzling clouds, immense and beautiful beyond imagining. The unending black of space, sprinkled with countless, gleaming jewels of stars that shone steadily, solemnly, the unblinking eyes of infinity.

I'll bet this is all there is to heaven, he said to himself. *You don't need anything more than this.*

Then he turned, with the careful deliberate motions of a deep-sea diver, and looked at the fat crescent of the nearby satellite. Only ten minutes now. Even less.

He pushed off from his capsule and sailed effortlessly, arms outstretched. Behind him trailed the umbilical cord that carried his air and electrical power for heating/cooling. As he approached the satellite, the sun rose over the humped curve of its hull and nearly blinded him, despite the automatic darkening of the photochromic plastic in his faceplate visor. He kicked downward and ducked behind the satellite's protective shadow again.

Still half-blind from the sudden glare, he bumped into the satellite's massive body and rebounded gently. With an effort, he twisted about, pushed back to the satellite, and planted his magnetized boots on the metal hull.

I claim this island for Isabella of Spain, he muttered foolishly. *Now where the hell's the hatch?*

The hatch was over on the sunlit side, he found, at last. It wasn't too hard to figure out how to operate it, even though there were absolutely no printed words in any language anywhere on the hull. Kinsman knelt down and turned the locking mechanism. He felt it click open.

For a moment he hesitated. *It might be booby-trapped,* he heard the colonel warn.

The hell with it.

Kinsman yanked the hatch open. No explosion, no sound at all. A dim light came from within the satellite. Carefully he slid down inside. A trio of faint emergency lights were on; there were other lights in place, he saw, but not operating.

"Saving the juice," he muttered to himself.

It took a moment for his eyes to accustom themselves to the dimness. Then he began to appreciate what he saw. The satellite was packed with equipment. He couldn't understand what most of it was, but it was clearly not a bomb. Surveillance equipment, he guessed. Cameras, recording instruments, small telescopes. Three contoured couches lay side by side beneath the hatch. He was standing on one of them. Up forward of the couches was a gallery of compact cabinets.

"All very cozy."

He stepped off the couch and onto the main deck, crouching to avoid bumping his head on the instrument rack, above. He opened a few of the cabinets. *Murdock'll probably want a few samples to play with.* He found a set of small hand wrenches, unfastened them from their setting.

With the wrenches in one hand, Kinsman tried the center couch. By lying all the way back on it, he could see through the satellite's only observation port. He scanned the instrument panel:

Cyrillic letters and Arabic numerals on all the gauges.

Made in the USSR. Kinsman put the wrenches down on the armrest of the couch. They stuck, magnetically. Then he reached for the miniature camera at his belt. He took four snaps of the instrument panel.

Something flashed in the corner of his eye.

He tucked the camera back in its belt holster and looked at the observation port. Nothing but the stars: beautiful, impersonal. Then another flash, and this time his eye caught and held the slim crescent of another ship gliding toward him. Most of the ship was in impenetrable shadow; he would have never found it without the telltale burst of the retrorockets.

She's damned close! Kinsman grabbed his tiny horde of stolen wrenches and got up from the couch. In his haste, he stumbled over his trailing umbilical cord and nearly went sprawling. A weightless fall might not hurt you, but it could keep you bouncing around for precious minutes before you regained your equilibrium.

Kinsman hoisted himself out of the satellite's hatch just as the second ship make its final rendezvous maneuver. A final flare of its retrorockets, and the ship seemed to come to a stop alongside the satellite.

Kinsman ducked across the satellite's hull and crouched in the shadows of the dark side. Squatting in utter blackness, safely invisible, he watched the second ship.

She was considerably smaller than the satellite, but built along the same general lines. Abruptly, a hatch popped open. A strange-looking figure emerged and hovered, dreamlike, for a long moment.

The figure looked like a tapered canister, with flexible arms and legs and a plastic bubble over the head. Kinsman could see no umbilical cord. There were bulging packs of equipment attached all around the canister.

Self-contained capsule, Kinsman said to himself. Very *neat.*

A wispy plume of gas jetted from the canister, and the cosmonaut sailed purposefully over to the satellite's hatch.

Got his own reaction motor, *too.* Kinsman was impressed.

Unconsciously, he hunched down deeper in the shadows as the figure approached. Only one of them; no one else appeared from the second ship. The newcomer touched down easily beside the still-open hatch of the satellite. For several minutes he did not move. Then he edged away from the satellite slightly and, hovering, turned toward Kinsman's capsule, still hanging only a few hundred feet away.

Kinsman felt himself start to sweat, even in the cold darkness. The cosmonaut jetted away from the satellite, straight toward the American capsule.

Damn! Kinsman snapped at himself. *First rule of warfare, you stupid slob: keep your line of retreat open!*

He leaped off the satellite and started floating back toward his own capsule. It was nightmarish, drifting through space with agonizing slowness while the weird-looking cosmonaut sped on ahead. The cosmonaut spotted Kinsman as soon as he cleared the shadow of the satellite and emerged into the sunlight.

For a moment they simply stared at each other, separated by a hundred feet of nothingness.

"Get away from that capsule!" Kinsman shouted, even though he knew that the intruder could not possibly hear him.

As if to prove the point, the cosmonaut put a hand on the lip of the capsule's hatch and peered inside. Kinsman flailed his arms and legs, trying to raise some speed, but still he moved with hellish slowness. Then he remembered the wrenches he was carrying.

Almost without thinking, he tossed the whole handful at the cosmonaut. The effort spun him wildly off-balance. The Earth slid across his field of vision, then the stars swam by dizzingly. He caught a glimpse of the cosmonaut as the wrenches reached the capsule—most of them missed and bounced noiselessly off the capsule. But one banged into the intruder's helmet hard enough to jar him, then rebounded crazily out of sight.

Kinsman lost sight of the entire capsule as he spun around. Grimly, he fought to straighten himself, using his arms and legs as counterweights. Finally, the stars stopped whirling. He turned and found the capsule again, but it was upside-down. Very carefully, Kinsman turned himself to the same orientation as the cosmonaut.

The intruder still had his hand on the capsule hatch, and his free hand was rubbing along the spot where the wrench had hit. He looked ludicrously like a little boy rubbing a bump on his head.

"That means get off, stranger," Kinsman muttered. "No trespassing. U.S. property. Beware of the eagle. Next time I'll crack your helmet in half."

The newcomer turned slightly and reached for one of the equipment packs on the canister-suit. A weird-looking tool appeared in his hand. Kinsman drifted helplessly and watched the cosmonaut take up a section of the umbilical line. Then he applied the hand tool to it. Sparks flared.

Electrical torch! He's trying to cut the line! He'll kill me!

Frantically, Kinsman began clambering along the umbilical line, hand-over-hand. All he could see, all he could think of, was that flashing torch eating into his lifeline.

Almost without thinking, he grabbed the line in both hands and snapped it, viciously. Again he tumbled wildly, but he saw the wave created by his snap race down the line. The intruder found the section of line he was holding suddenly bounce violently out of his hand. The torch spun away from him and winked off.

Both men moved at once.

The cosmonaut jetted away from the capsule, looking for the torch. Kinsman hurled himself directly toward the hatch. He planted his magnetized boots on the capsule's hull and grasped the open hatch in both hands.

Duck inside, slam shut, and get the hell out of here.

But he did not move. Instead, he watched the cosmonaut, a weird sun-etched outline figure now, mostly in shadow, drifting quietly some fifty feet away, sizing up the situation.

That glorified tin can tried to kill me.

Kinsman coiled like a cat on the edge of the hatch and then sprang at his enemy. The cosmonaut reached for the jet controls at his belt but Kinsman slammed into him and they both went hurtling through space, tumbling and clawing at each other. It was an unearthly struggle, human fury in the infinite calm of star-studded blackness. No sound, except your own harsh breath and the bone-carried shock of colliding arms and legs.

They wheeled out of the capsule's shadow and into the painful glare of the sun. In a cold rage, Kinsman grabbed the air hose that connected the cosmonaut's oxygen tank and helmet. He hesitated a moment and glanced into the bulbous plastic helmet. All he could see was the back of the cosmonaut's head, covered with a dark, skin-tight flying hood. With a vicious yank, he ripped out the air hose. The cosmonaut jerked twice, spasmodically, inside the canister, then went inert.

With a conscious effort, Kinsman unclenched his teeth. His jaws ached. He was trembling, and covered with a cold sweat. He released his death-grip on the enemy. The two human forms drifted slightly apart. The dead cosmonaut turned, gently, as Kinsman floated beside him. The sun glinted brightly on the metal canister and shone full onto the enemy's lifeless, terror-stricken face.

Kinsman looked into that face for an eternally long moment, and felt the life drain out of him. He dragged himself back to the capsule, sealed the hatch and cracked open the air tanks with automatic, unthinking motions. He flicked on the radio and ignored the flood of interrogating voices that streamed in from the ground.

"Bring me in. Program the autopilot to bring me in. Just bring me in."

It was six days before Kinsman saw Colonel Murdock again. He stood tensely before the wide mahogany desk while Murdock beamed at him, almost as brightly as the sun outside.

"You look thinner in civvies," the colonel said.

"I've lost a little weight."

Murdock made a meaningless gesture. "I'm sorry I haven't had a chance to see you sooner. What with the Security and State Department people holding you for debriefings, and now your mustering-out . . . I haven't had a chance to, eh, congratulate you on your mission. It was a fine piece of work."

Kinsman said nothing.

"General Hatch was very pleased. You'd be up for a decoration, but . . . well, you know, this has to be quiet."

"I know."

"But you're a hero, son. A real honest-to-God hero."

"Stow it."

Murdock suppressed a frown. "And the State Department man tells me the Reds haven't even made a peep about it. They're keeping the whole thing hushed up. The disarmament meeting is going ahead again, and we might get a complete agreement on banning bombs in orbit. Guess we showed them they can't put anything over on us. We called their bluff, all right!"

"I committed a murder."

"Now listen, son . . . I know how you feel. But it had to be done."

"No, it didn't," Kinsman insisted quietly. "I could've gotten back inside the capsule and deorbited."

"You killed an enemy soldier. You protected your nation's frontier. Sure, you feel like hell now, but you'll get over it."

"You didn't see the face I saw inside that helmet."

Murdock shuffled some papers on his desk. "Well . . . okay, it was rough. But it's over. Now you're going to Florida and be a civilian astronaut and get to the moon. That's what you've wanted all along."

"I don't know. I've got to take some time and think everything over."

"What?" Murdock stared at him. "What're you talking about?"

"Read the debriefing report," Kinsman said tiredly.

"It hasn't come down to my level and it probably won't. Too sensitive. But I don't understand what's got you spoofed. You killed an enemy soldier. You ought to be proud."

"Enemy," Kinsman echoed bleakly. "She couldn't have been more than twenty years old."

Murdock's face went slack. "She?"

Kinsman nodded. "Your honest-to-God hero murdered a terrified girl. That's something to be proud of, isn't it?"

FIFTEEN MILES

"Any word from him yet?"

"Huh? No, nothing."

Kinsman swore to himself as he stood on the open platform of the little lunar rocket-jumper.

"Say, where are you now?" The astronomer's voice sounded gritty with static in Kinsman's helmet earphones.

"Up on the rim. He must've gone inside the damned crater."

"The rim? How'd you get . . . ?"

"Found a flat spot for the jumper. Don't think I walked this far, do you? I'm not as nutty as the priest."

"But you're supposed to stay down here on the plain! The crater's off limits."

"Tell it to our holy friar. He's the one who marched up here. I'm just following the seismic rigs he's been planting every three-four miles."

391

He could sense Bok shaking his head. "Kinsman, if there're twenty officially approved ways to do a job, I swear you'll pick the twenty-second."

"If the first twenty-one are lousy."

"You're not going inside the crater, are you? It's too risky."

Kinsman almost laughed. "You think sitting in that aluminum casket of ours is safe?"

The earphones went silent. With a scowl, Kinsman wished for the tenth time in an hour that he could scratch his twelve-day beard. Get zipped into the suit and the itches start. He didn't need a mirror to know that his face was haggard, sleepless, and his black beard was mean-looking.

He stepped down from the jumper—a rocket motor with a railed platform and some equipment on it, nothing more—and planted his boots on the solid rock of the ringwall's crest. With a twist of his shoulders to settle the weight of the pressure suit's bulky backpack, he shambled over to the packet of seismic instruments and fluorescent marker that the priest had left there.

"He came right up to the top, and now he's off on the yellow brick road, playing moon explorer. Stupid bastard."

Reluctantly, he looked into the crater Alphonsus. The brutally short horizon cut across its middle, but the central peak stuck its worn head up among the solemn stars. Beyond it was nothing but dizzying blackness, an abrupt end to the solid world and the beginning of infinity.

Damn the priest! *God's gift to geology . . . and I've got to play guardian angel for him.*

"Any sign of him?"

Kinsman turned back and looked outward from the crater. He could see the lighted radio mast and squat return rocket, far below on the plain. He even convinced himself that he saw the mound of rubble marking their buried base shelter, where Bok lay curled safely in his bunk. It was two days before sunrise, but the Earthlight lit the plain well enough.

"Sure," Kinsman answered. "He left me a big map with an **X** to mark the treasure."

"Don't get sore at me!"

"Why not? You're sitting inside. I've got to find our fearless geologist."

"Regulations say one man's got to be in the base at all times."

But not the same one man, Kinsman flashed silently.

"Anyway," Bok went on, "he's got a few hours' oxygen left. Let him putter around inside the crater for a while. He'll come back."

"Not before his air runs out. Besides, he's officially missing. Missed two check-in calls. I'm supposed to scout his last known position. Another of those sweet regs."

Silence again. Bok didn't like being alone in the base, Kinsman knew.

"Why don't you come on back," the astronomer's voice returned, "until he calls in. Then you can get him with the jumper. You'll be running out of air yourself before you can find him inside the crater."

"I'm supposed to try."

"But why? You sure don't think much of him. You've been tripping all over yourself trying to stay clear of him when he's inside the base."

Kinsman suddenly shuddered. *So it shows! If you're not careful you'll tip them both off.*

Aloud he said, "I'm going to look around. Give me an hour. Better call Earthside and tell them what's going on. Stay in the shelter until I come back." *Or until the relief crew shows up.*

"You're wasting your time. And taking an unnecessary chance."

"Wish me luck," Kinsman answered.

"Good luck. I'll sit tight here."

Despite himself, Kinsman grinned. Shutting off the radio, he said to himself, "I know damned well you'll sit tight. Two scientific adventurers. One goes over the hill and the other stays in his bunk two weeks straight."

He gazed out at the bleak landscape, surrounded by starry emptiness. Something caught at his memory:

"They can't scare me with their empty spaces," he muttered. There was more to the verse but he couldn't recall it.

"Can't scare me," he repeated softly, shuffling to the inner rim. He walked very carefully and tried, from inside the cumbersome helmet, to see exactly where he was placing his feet.

The barren slopes fell away in gently terraced steps until, more than half a mile below, they melted into the crater floor. *Looks easy . . . too easy.*

With a shrug that was weighted down by the pressure suit, Kinsman started to descend into the crater.

He picked his way across the gravelly terraces and crawled feet first down the breaks between them. The bare rocks were slippery and sometimes sharp. Kinsman went slowly, step by step, trying to make certain he didn't puncture the aluminized fabric of his suit.

His world was cut off now and circled by the dark rocks. The only sounds he knew were the creakings of the suit's joints, the electrical hum of its motor, the faint whir of the helmet's air blower, and his own heavy breathing. Alone, all alone. A solitary microcosm. One living creature in the one universe.

They cannot scare me with their empty spaces
Between stars—on stars where no human race is.

There was still more to it: the tag line that he couldn't remember.

Finally he had to stop. The suit was heating up too much from his exertion. He took a marker-beacon from the backpack and planted it on the broken ground. The moon's soil, churned by meteors and whipped into a frozen froth, had an unfinished look about it, as though somebody had been blacktopping the place but stopped before he could apply the final smoothing touches.

From a pouch on his belt Kinsman took a small spool of wire. Plugging one end into the radio outlet on his helmet, he held the spool at arm's length and released the catch. He couldn't see it in the dim light, but he felt the spring fire the wire antenna a hundred yards or so upward and out into the crater.

"Father Lemoyne," he called as the antenna drifted in the moon's easy gravity. "Father Lemoyne, can you hear me? This is Kinsman."

No answer.

Okay. Down another flight.

After two more stops and nearly an hour of sweaty descent, Kinsman got his answer.

"Here . . . I'm here . . ."

"Where?" Kinsman snapped. "Do something. Make a light."

" . . . can't . . ." The voice faded out.

Kinsman reeled in the antenna and fired it out again. "Where the hell are you?"

A cough, with pain behind it. "Shouldn't have done it. Disobeyed. And no water, nothing . . ."

Great! Kinsman frowned. *He's either hysterical or delirious. Or both.*

After firing the spool antenna again, Kinsman flicked on the lamp atop his helmet and looked at the radio direction-finder dial on his forearm. The priest had his suit radio open and the carrier beam was coming through even though he was not talking. The gauges alongside the radio-finder reminded Kinsman that he was about halfway down on his oxygen, and more than an hour had elapsed since he had spoken to Bok.

"I'm trying to zero in on you," Kinsman said. "Are you hurt? Can you—"

"Don't, don't, don't. I disobeyed and now I've got to pay for it. Don't trap yourself too." The heavy, reproachful voice lapsed into a mumble that Kinsman couldn't understand.

Trapped. Kinsman could picture it. The priest was using a canister-suit: a one-man walking cabin, a big, plexidomed rigid can with flexible arms and legs sticking out of it. You could live in it for days at a time—but it was too clumsy for climbing. Which is why the crater was off limits.

He must've fallen and now he's stuck.

"The sin of pride," he heard the priest babbling. "God forgive us our pride. I wanted to find water; the greatest discovery a man can make on the moon . . . Pride, nothing but pride . . ."

Kinsman walked slowly, shifting his eyes from the direction-finder to the roiled, pocked ground underfoot. He jumped across an eight-foot drop between terraces.

The finder's needle snapped to zero.

"Your radio still on?"

"No use . . . go back . . ."

The needle stayed fixed. *Either I busted it or I'm right on top of him.*

He turned full circle, scanning the rough ground as far as his light could reach. No sign of the canister. Kinsman stepped to the terrace-edge. Kneeling with deliberate care, so that his backpack wouldn't unbalance and send him sprawling down the tumbled rocks, he peered over.

In a zigzag fissure a few yards below him was the priest, a giant, armored insect gleaming white in the glare of the lamp, feebly waving its one free arm.

"Can you get up?" Kinsman saw that all the weight of the cumbersome suit was on the pinned arm. *Banged up his backpack, too.*

The priest was mumbling again. It sounded like Latin.

"Can you get up?" Kinsman repeated.

"Trying to find the secrets of natural creation . . . storming heaven with rockets. We say we're seeking knowledge, but we're really after is our own glory . . ."

Kinsman frowned. He couldn't see the older man's face, behind the canister's heavily tinted window.

"I'll have to get the jumper down here."

The priest rambled on, coughing spasmodically. Kinsman started back across the terrace.

"Pride leads to death," he heard in his earphones. "You know that, Kinsman. It's pride that makes us murderers."

The shock boggled Kinsman's knees. He turned, trembling. "What . . . did you say?"

"It's hidden. The water is here, hidden . . . frozen in fissures. Strike the rock and bring forth water, like Moses. Not even God himself was going to hide this secret from me . . ."

"What did you say," Kinsman whispered, completely cold inside, "about murder?"

"I know you, Kinsman . . . anger and pride. Destroy not my soul with men of blood . . . whose right hands are . . . are . . ."

Kinsman ran away. He fought back toward the crater's rim, storming the terraces blindly, scrabbling up the inclines with four-yard-high jumps. Twice he had to turn up the air blower in his helmet to clear the sweaty fog from his faceplate. He didn't dare stop. He raced on, breath racking his lungs, heart pounding until he could hear nothing else.

But in his mind he still saw those savage few minutes in orbit, when he had been with the Air Force, when he had become a killer. He had won a medal for that secret mission; a medal and a conscience that never slept.

Finally he reached the crest. Collapsing on the deck of the jumper, he forced himself to breathe normally again, forced himself to sound normal as he called Bok.

The astronomer said guardedly, "It sounds as though he's dying."

"I think his regenerator's shot. His air must be pretty foul by now."

"No sense going back for him, I guess."

Kinsman hesitated. "Maybe I can get the jumper down close to him." *He found out about me.*

"You'll never get him back in time. And you're not supposed to take the jumper near the crater, let alone inside of it. It's too dangerous."

"You want to just let him die?" *He's hysterical. If he babbles about me where Bok can hear it . . .*

"Listen," the astronomer said, his voice rising, "you can't leave me stuck here with both of you gone! I know the regulations, Kinsman. You're not allowed to risk yourself or the third man on the team in an effort to help a man in trouble."

"I know. I know." *But it wouldn't look right for me to start minding regulations now. Even Bok doesn't expect me to.*

"You don't have enough oxygen in your suit to get down there and back again," Bok insisted.

"I can tap some from the jumper's propellant tank."

"But that's crazy! You'll get yourself stranded!"

"Maybe." *It's an Air Force secret. No discharge: just transferred to the space agency. If they find out about it now, I'll be finished. Everybody'll know. No place to hide . . . newspapers, TV, everybody!*

"You're going to kill yourself over that priest. And you'll be killing me, too!"

"He's probably dead by now," Kinsman said. "I'll just put a marker beacon there, so another crew can get him when the time comes. I won't be long."

"But the regulations . . ."

"They were written Earthside. The brass never planned on something like this. I've got to go back, just to make sure."

He flew the jumper back down the crater's inner slope, leaning over the platform railing to see his marker-beacons as well as listening to their tinny radio beeping. In a few minutes, he was easing the spraddle-legged platform down on the last terrace before the helpless priest.

"Father Lemoyne."

Kinsman stepped off the jumper and made it to the edge of the fissure in four lunar strides. The white shell was inert, the lone arm unmoving.

"Father Lemoyne!"

Kinsman held his breath and listened. Nothing . . . wait:

the faintest, faintest breathing. More like gasping. Quick, shallow, desperate.

"You're dead," Kinsman heard himself mutter. "Give it up, you're finished. Even if I got you out of here, you'd be dead before I could get you back to the base."

The priest's faceplate was opaque to him; he only saw the reflected spot of his own helmet lamp. But his mind filled with the shocked face he once saw in another visor, a face that had just realized it was dead.

He looked away, out to the too-close horizon and the uncompromising stars beyond. Then he remembered the rest of it:

They cannot scare me with their empty spaces
Between stars—on stars where no human race is.
I have it in me so much nearer home
To scare myself with my own desert places.

Like an automaton, Kinsman turned back to the jumper. His mind was blank now. Without thought, without even feeling, he rigged a line from the jumper's tiny winch to the metal lugs in the canister-suit's chest. Then he took apart the platform railing and wedged three rejoined sections into the fissure above the fallen man, to form a hoisting angle. Looping the line over the projecting arm, he started the winch.

He climbed down into the fissure and set himself as solidly as he could on the bare, scoured-smooth rock. He grabbed the priest's armored shoulders, and guided the oversized canister up from the crevice, while the winch strained silently.

The railing arm gave way when the priest was only partway up, and Kinsman felt the full weight of the monstrous suit crush down on him. He sank to his knees, gritting his teeth to keep from crying out.

Then the winch took up the slack. Grunting, fumbling, pushing, he scrabbled up the rocky slope with his arms wrapped halfway round the big canister's middle. He let the winch drag them to the jumper's edge, then reached out and shut the motor.

With only a hard breath's pause, Kinsman snapped down the suit's supporting legs, so the priest could stay upright even though unconscious. Then he clambered onto the platform and took the oxygen line from the rocket tankage. Kneeling at the bulbous suit's shoulders, he plugged the line into its emergency air tank.

The older man coughed once. That was all.

Kinsman leaned back on his heels. His faceplate was fogging over again, or was it fatigue blurring his sight?

The regenerator was hopelessly smashed, he saw. *The old bird must've been breathing his own juices.*

When the emergency tank registered full, he disconnected the oxygen line and plugged it into a special fitting below the regenerator.

"If you're dead, this is probably going to kill me, too," Kinsman said. He purged the entire suit, forcing the contaminating fumes out and replacing them with the oxygen that the jumper's rocket needed to get them back to the base.

He was close enough now to see through the canister's tinted visor. The priest's face was grizzled, eyes closed. Its usual smile was gone; the mouth hung open limply.

Kinsman hauled him up onto the railess platform and strapped him down on the deck. Then he went to the controls and inched the throttle forward just enough to give them the barest minimum of lift.

The jumper almost made it to the crest before its rocket died and bumped them gently on one of the terraces. There was a small emergency tank of oxygen that could have carried them a little farther, Kinsman knew. But he and the priest would need it for breathing.

"Wonder how many Jesuits have been carried home on their shields?" he asked himself as he unbolted the section of decking that the priest was lying on. By threading the winch line through the bolt holes, he made a sort of sled, which he carefully lowered to the ground. Then he took down the emergency oxygen tank and strapped it to the deck section, too.

Kinsman wrapped the line around his fists and leaned against the burden. Even in the moon's light gravity, it was like trying to haul a truck.

"Down to less than one horsepower," he grunted, straining forward.

For once he was glad that the scoured rocks had been smoothed clean by micrometeors. He would climb a few steps, wedge himself as firmly as he could, and drag the sled up to him. It took a painful half hour to reach the ringwall crest.

He could see the base again, tiny and remote as a dream. "All downhill from here," he mumbled.

He thought he heard a groan.

"That's it," he said, pushing the sled over the crest, down the gentle outward slope. "That's it. Stay with it. Don't you die on me. Don't put me through this for nothing!"

"Kinsman!" Bok's voice. "Are you all right?"

The sled skidded against a yard-high rock. Scrambling after it, Kinsman answered, "I'm bringing him in. Just shut up and leave us alone. I think he's alive. Now stop wasting my breath."

Pull it free. Push to get it started downhill again. Strain to hold it back . . . don't let it get away from you. Haul it out of craterlets. Watch your step, don't fall.

"Too damned much uphill in this downhill."

Once he sprawled flat and knocked his helmet against the edge of the improvised sled. He must have blacked out for a moment. Weakly, he dragged himself up to the oxygen tank and refilled his suit's supply. Then he checked the priest's suit and topped off his tank.

"Can't do that again," he said to the silent priest. "Don't know if we'll make it. Maybe we can. If neither one of us has sprung a leak. Maybe . . . maybe . . ."

Time slid away from him. The past and future dissolved into an endless now, a forever of pain and struggle, with the heat of his toil welling up in Kinsman drenchingly.

"Why don't you say something?" Kinsman panted at the priest. "You can't die. Understand me? You can't die! I've got to explain it to you. I didn't mean to kill her. I didn't even know she was a girl. You can't tell, can't even see a face until you're too close. She must've been just as scared as I was. She tried to kill me. I was inspecting their satellite . . . how'd I know their cosmonaut was a scared kid. I could've pushed her off, didn't have to kill her. But the first thing I knew I was ripping her air lines open. I didn't know she was a girl, not until it was too late. It doesn't make any difference, but I didn't know it, I didn't know . . ."

They reached the foot of the ringwall and Kinsman dropped to his knees. "Couple more miles now . . . straightaway . . . only a couple more . . . miles." His vision was blurred, and something in his head was buzzing angrily.

Staggering to his feet, he lifted the line over his shoulder and slogged ahead. He could just make out the lighted tip of the base's radio mast.

"Leave him, Chet," Bok's voice pleaded from somewhere. "You can't make it unless you leave him!"

"Shut . . . up."

One step after another. Don't think, don't count. Blank your mind. Be a mindless plow horse. Plod along, one step at a time. Steer for the radio mast . . . Just a few . . . more miles.

"Don't die on me. Don't you . . . die on me. You're my ticket back. Don't die on me, priest . . . don't die . . .

It all went dark. First in spots, then totally. Kinsman caught a glimpse of the barren landscape tilting weirdly, then the grave stars slid across his view, then darkness.

"I tried," he heard himself say in a far, far distant voice. "I tried." For a moment or two he felt himself falling, dropping effortlessly into blackness. Then even that sensation died and he felt nothing at all.

A faint vibration buzzed at him. The darkness started to shift, turn gray at the edges. Kinsman opened his eyes and saw the low, curved ceiling of the underground base. The noise was the electrical machinery that lit and warmed and brought good air to the tight little shelter.

"You okay?" Bok leaned over him. His chubby face was frowning worriedly.

Kinsman weakly nodded.

"Father Lemoyne's going to pull through," Bok said, stepping out of the cramped space between the two bunks. The priest was awake but unmoving, his eyes staring blankly upward. His canister suit had been removed and one arm was covered with a plastic cast.

Bok explained. "I've been getting instructions from the Earthside medics. They're sending a team up; should be here in another thirty hours. He's in shock, and his arm's broken. Otherwise he seems pretty good . . . exhausted, but no permanent damage."

Kinsman pushed himself up to a sitting position on the bunk and leaned his back against the curving metal wall. His helmet and boots were off, but he was still wearing the rest of his pressure suit.

"You went out and got us," he realized.

Bok nodded. "You were only about a mile away. I could hear you on the radio. Then you stopped talking. I had to go out."

"You saved my life."

"And you saved the priest's."

Kinsman stopped a moment, remembering. "I did a lot of raving out there, didn't I?"

Bok wormed his shoulders uncomfortably.

"Any of it intelligible?"

"Sort of. It's, uh . . . it's all on the automatic recorder, you know. All conversations. Nothing I can do about that."

That's it. Now everybody knows.

"You haven't heard the best of it, though," Bok said. He went to the shelf at the end of the priest's bunk and took a little plastic container. "Look at this."

Kinsman took the container. Inside was a tiny fragment of ice, half melted into water.

"It was stuck in the cleats of his boots. It's really water! Tests out okay, and I even snuck a taste of it. It's water all right."

"He found it after all," Kinsman said. "He'll get into the history books now." *And he'll have to watch his pride even more.*

Bok sat on the shelter's only chair. "Chet, about what you were saying out there . . ."

Kinsman expected tension, but instead he felt only numb. "I know. They'll hear the tapes Earthside."

"There've been rumors about an Air Force guy killing a cosmonaut during a military mission, but I never thought . . . I mean . . ."

"The priest figured it out," Kinsman said. "Or at least he guessed it."

"It must've been rough on you," Bok said.

"Not as rough as what happened to her."

"What'll they do about you?"

Kinsman shrugged. "I don't know. It might get out to the news media. Probably I'll be grounded. Unstable. It could be nasty."

"I'm . . . sorry." Bok's voice trailed off helplessly.

"It doesn't matter."

Surprised, Kinsman realized that he meant it. He sat straight upright. "It doesn't matter anymore. They can do whatever they want to. I can handle it. Even if they ground me and throw me to the media . . . I think I can take it. I did it, and it's over with, and I can take what I have to take."

Father Lemoyne's free arm moved slightly. "It's all right," he whispered hoarsely. "It's all right. I thought we were in hell, but it was only purgatory."

The priest turned his face toward Kinsman. His gaze moved from the astronaut's eyes to the plastic container, still in Kinsman's hands.

"It's all right," he repeated, smiling. Then he closed his eyes and his face relaxed into sleep. But the smile remained, strangely gentle in that bearded, haggard face; ready to meet the world or eternity.

A SLIGHT MISCALCULATION

It is not often that a writer has the pleasure of seeing one of his short stories dramatized. "A Slight Miscalculation" was so honored by the Penn State Readers' Theater as one of the highlights of Paracon VI, the 1983 convention of the Penn State science fiction fans. It was great fun to see the characters of the story come to life, and even though most of the audience already knew the story, the final punch line achieved the desired gasp of surprise and laughter.

This story originated over a bowl of Mulligatawny soup in an Indian restaurant in mid-town Manhattan. Judy-Lynn Benjamin (she had not yet married Lester Del Rey), was then the managing editor of Galaxy *magazine. She and I threw a few ideas back and forth and came up with "the ultimate California earthquake story." Unfortunately, the top editor at* Galaxy, *whose tenure was brief but not brief enough, failed to see the humor in the piece and asked me what scientific foundation I had for the story's premise. I sent the manuscript to Ed Ferman at* The Magazine of Fantasy and Science Fiction. *He bought it with no questions asked, proving that he has not only a delicately-tuned sense of humor but a high standard of literary values, as well. Or so it seems to me.*

NATHAN FRENCH was a pure mathematician. He worked for a

research laboratory perched on a California hill that overlooked the Pacific surf, but his office had no windows. When his laboratory earned its income by doing research on nuclear bombs, Nathan doodled out equations for placing men on the moon with a minimum expenditure of rocket fuel. When his lab landed a fat contract for developing a lunar flight profile, Nathan began worrying about air pollution.

Nathan didn't look much like a mathematician. He was tall and gangly, liked to play handball, spoke with a slight lisp when he got excited and had a face that definitely reminded you of a horse. Which helped him to remain pure in things other than mathematics. The only possible clue to his work was that, lately, he had started to squint a lot. But he didn't look the slightest bit nervous or highstrung, and he still often smiled his great big toothy, horsey smile.

When the lab landed its first contract (from the State of California), to study air pollution, Nathan's pure thoughts turned—naturally— elsewhere.

"I think it might be possible to work out a method of predicting earthquakes," Nathan told the laboratory chief, kindly old Dr. Moneygrinder.

Moneygrinder peered at Nathan over his half-lensed bifocals. "Okay, Nathan my boy," he said heartily. "Go ahead and try it. You know I'm always interested in furthering man's understanding of his universe."

When Nathan left the chief's sumptuous office, Moneygrinder hauled his paunchy little body out of its plush desk chair and went to the window. *His* office had windows on two walls: one set overlooked the beautiful Pacific; the other looked down on the parking lot, so the chief could check on who got to work at what time.

And behind that parking lot, which was half-filled with aging cars (business had been deteriorating for several years), back among the eucalyptus trees and paint-freshened grass, was a remarkably straight little ridge of ground, no more than four feet high. It ran like an elongated step behind the whole length of the Laboratory and out past the abandoned pink stucco church on the crest of the hill. A little ridge of grass-covered earth that was called the San Andreas Fault.

Moneygrinder often stared at the Fault from his window, rehearsing in his mind exactly what to do when the ground started to tremble. He wasn't afraid, merely careful. Once a tremor had hit in the middle of a staff meeting. Moneygrinder was out the window, across the parking lot, and on the far side of the Fault (the eastern, or "safe" side) before men half his age had gotten out of their chairs. The staff talked for months about the astonishing agility of the fat little waddler.

A year, almost to the day, later the parking lot was slightly fuller and a few of the cars were new. The pollution business was starting to pick up, since the disastrous smog in San Clemente. And the laboratory had also managed to land a few quiet little Air Force contracts—for six times the amount of money it got from the pollution work.

Moneygrinder was leaning back in the plush desk chair, trying to look both interested and noncommittal at the same time, which was difficult to do, because he never could follow Nathan when the mathematician was trying to explain his work.

"Then it's a thimple matter of transposing the progression," Nathan was lisping, talking too fast because he was excited as he scribbled equations on the fuchsia-colored chalkboard with nerve-ripping squeaks of the yellow chalk.

"You thee?" Nathan said at last, standing beside the chalkboard. It was totally covered with his barely legible numbers and symbols. A pall of yellow chalk dust hovered about him.

"Um . . ." said Moneygrinder. "Your conclusion, then . . . ?"

"It's perfectly clear," Nathan said. "If you have any reasonable data base at all, you can not only predict when an earthquake will hit and where, but you can altho predict its intensity."

Moneygrinder's eyes narrowed. "You're sure?"

"I've gone over it with the CalTech geophysicists. They agree with the theory."

"Hmm." Moneygrinder tapped his desktop with his pudgy fingers. "I know this is a little outside your area of interest, Nathan, but . . . ah, can you really predict actual earthquakes? Or is this all theoretical?"

"Sure you can predict earthquakes," Nathan said, grinning like Francis, the movie star. "Like next Thursday's."

"Next Thursday's?"

"Yeth. There's going to be a major earthquake next Thursday."

"Where?"

"Right here. Along the Fault."

Nathan tossed his stubby piece of chalk into the air nonchalantly, but missed the catch and it fell to the carpeted floor.

Moneygrinder, slightly paler than the chalk, asked, "A major quake, you say?"

"Uh-huh."

"Did . . . did the CalTech people make this prediction?"

"No, I did. They don't agree. They claim I've got an inverted gamma factor in the fourteenth set of equations. I've got the computer checking it right now."

Some of the color returned to Moneygrinder's flabby cheeks. "Oh . . . oh, I see. Well, let me know what the computer says."

"Sure."

The next morning, as Moneygrinder stood behind the gauzy drapes of his office window, watching the cars pull in, his phone rang. His secretary had put in a long night, he knew, and she wasn't in yet. Pouting, Moneygrinder went over to the desk and answered the phone himself.

It was Nathan. "The computer still agrees with the CalTech boys. But I think the programming's slightly off. Can't really trust computers, they're only as good as the people who feed them, you know."

"I see," Moneygrinder answered. "Well, keep checking on it."

He chuckled as he hung up. "Good old Nathan. Great at theory, but hopeless in the real world."

Still, when his secretary finally showed up and brought him his morning coffee and pill and nibble on the ear, he said thoughtfully:

"Maybe I ought to talk with those bankers in New York, after all."

"But you said that you wouldn't need their money now that business is picking up," she purred.

He nodded, bulbously. "Yes, but still . . . arrange a meeting with them for next Thursday. I'll leave Wednesday afternoon. Stay the weekend in New York."

She stared at him. "But you said we'd . . ."

"Now, now . . . business comes first. You take the Friday night jet and meet me at the hotel."

Smiling, she answered, "Yes, Cuddles."

Matt Climber had just come back from a Pentagon lunch when Nathan's phone call reached him.

Climber had worked for Nathan several years ago. He had started as a computer programmer, assistant to Nathan. In two years he had become a section head, and Nathan's direct supervisor. (On paper only. Nobody bossed Nathan, he worked independently.) When it became obvious to Moneygrinder that Climber was heading his way, the lab chief helped his young assistant to a government job in Washington. Good experience for an up-and-coming executive.

"Hiya Nathan, how's the pencil-pushing game?" Climber shouted into the phone as he glanced at his calendar-appointment pad. There were three interagency conferences and two staff meetings going this afternoon.

"Hold it now, slow down," Climber said, sounding friendly but looking grim. "You know people can't understand you when you talk too fast."

Thirty minutes later, Climber was leaning back in his chair, feet on the desk, tie loosened, shirt collar open, and the first two meetings on his afternoon's list crossed off.

"Now let me get this straight, Nathan," he said into the phone. "You're predicting a major quake along the San Andreas Fault next Thursday afternoon at two-thirty Pacific Standard Time. But the CalTech people and your own computer don't agree with you."

Another ten minutes later, Climber said, "Okay, okay sure, I remember how we'd screw up the programming once in a while. But you made mistakes too. Okay, look—tell you what, Nathan. Keep checking. If you find out definitely that the computer's wrong and you're right, call me right away. I'll get the President himself, if we have to. Okay? Fine. Keep in touch."

He slammed the phone back onto its cradle and his feet on the floor, all in one weary motion.

Old Nathan's really gone 'round the bend, Climber told himself. *Next Thursday, Hah! Next Thursday. Hmmm.*

He leafed through the calendar pages. Sure enough, he had a meeting with the Boeing people in Seattle next Thursday.

If there is a major 'quake, the whole damned West Coast might slide into the Pacific. Naw . . . don't be silly. Nathan's cracking up, that's all. Still . . . how far north does the Fault go?

He leaned across the desk and tapped the intercom button.

"Yes, Mr. Climber?" came his secretary's voice.

"That conference with Boeing on the hypersonic ramjet transport next Thursday," Climber began, then hesitated a moment. But, with absolute finality, he snapped, "Cancel it."

Nathan French was not a drinking man, but by Tuesday of the following week he went straight from the laboratory to a friendly little bar that hung from a rocky ledge over the surging ocean.

It was a strangely quiet Tuesday afternoon, so Nathan had the undivided attention of both the worried-looking bartender and the freshly-painted whore, who worked the early shift in a low-cut, black cocktail dress and overpowering perfume.

"Cheez, 1 never seen business so lousy as yesterday and today," the bartender mumbled. He was sort of fidgeting around behind the bar, with nothing to do. The only dirty glass in the place was Nathan's, and he was holding on to it because he liked to chew the ice cubes.

"Yeah," said the hooker. "At this rate, I'll be a virgin again by the end of the week."

Nathan didn't reply. His mouth was full of ice cubes, which he crunched in absent-minded cacophony. He was still trying to figure out why he and the computer didn't agree about the fourteenth set of equations. Everything else checked out perfectly: time, place, force level on the Richter scale. But the vector, the directional value— somebody was still misreading his programming instructions. That was the only possible answer.

"The stock market's dropped through the floor," the bartender said darkly. "My broker says Boeing's gonna lay off half their people. That ramjet transport they was gonna build is getting scratched. And the lab up the hill is getting bought out by some East Coast banks." He shook his head.

The prostitute, sitting beside Nathan with her elbows on the bar and her Styrofoam bra sharply profiled, smiled at him and said, "Hey, how about it, big guy? Just so I don't forget how to, huh?"

With a final crunch on the last ice cube, Nathan said, "Uh, excuse me. I've got to check that computer program."

By Thursday morning, Nathan was truly upset. Not only was the computer still insisting that he was wrong about equation fourteen, but none of the programmers had shown up for work. Obviously, one of them—maybe all of them— had sabotaged his program. But why?

He stalked up and down the hallways of the lab searching for a programmer, somebody, anybody—but the lab was virtually empty. Only a handful of people had come in, and after an hour or so of wide-eyed whispering among themselves in the cafeteria over coffee, they started to sidle out to the parking lot and get into their cars and drive away.

Nathan happened to be walking down a corridor when one of the research physicists—a new man, from a department Nathan never dealt with—bumped into him.

"Oh, excuse me," the physicist said hastily, and started to head for the door down at the end of the hall.

"Wait a minute," Nathan said, grabbing him by the arm. "Can you program the computer?"

"Uh, no, I can't."

"Where is everybody today?" Nathan wondered aloud, still holding the man's arm. "Is it a national holiday?"

"Man, haven't you heard?" the physicist asked, goggle-eyed. "There's going to be an earthquake this afternoon. The whole damned state of California is going to slide into the sea!"

"Oh, that."

Pulling his arm free, the physicist scuttled down the hall. As he got to the door he shouted over his shoulder, "Get out while you can! East of the Fault! The roads are jamming up fast!"

Nathan frowned. "There's still an hour or so," he said to himself. "And I still think the computer's wrong. I wonder what the tidal effects on the Pacific Ocean would be if the whole state collapsed into the ocean?"

Nathan didn't really notice that he was talking to himself. There was no one else to talk to.

Except the computer.

He was sitting in the computer room, still poring over the stubborn equations, when the rumbling started. At first it was barely audible, like very distant thunder. Then the room began to shake and the rumbling grew louder.

Nathan glanced at his wristwatch: two-thirty-two.

"I knew it!" he said gleefully to the computer. "You see? And I'll bet all the rest of it is right, too. Including equation fourteen."

Going down the hallway was like walking through the passageway of a storm-tossed ship. The floor and walls were swaying violently.

Nathan kept his feet, despite some awkward lurches here and there.

It didn't occur to him that he might die until he got outside. The sky was dark, the ground heaving, the roaring deafened him. A violent gale was blowing dust everywhere, adding its shrieking fury to the earth's tortured groaning.

Nathan couldn't see five feet ahead of him. With the wind tearing at him and the dust stinging his eyes, he couldn't tell which way o go. He knew the other side of the Fault meant safety, but where was it?

Then there was a biblical crack of lightning and the ultimate grinding, screaming, ear-shattering roar. A tremendous shock wave knocked Nathan to the ground and he blacked out. His last thought was, "I was right and the computer was wrong."

When he woke up, the sun was shining feebly through a gray overcast. The wind had died away. Everything was strangely quiet.

Nathan climbed stiffly to his feet and looked around. The lab building was still there. He was standing in the middle of the parking lot; the only car in sight was his own, caked with dust.

Beyond the parking lot, where the eucalyptus trees used to be, was the edge of a cliff, where still-steaming rocks and raw earth tumbled down to a foaming sea.

Nathan staggered to the cliff's edge and looked out across the water, eastward. Somehow he knew that the nearest land was Europe.

"Son of a bitch," he said with unaccustomed vehemence. "The computer was right after all."